To Kim,

Autumn's Magical Pact

I hope you'll enjoy
the first in my
new series.

Best Wishes!

Leigh Ann Edwards

Autumn's Magical Pact

Maidens of the Mystical Stones:
Book 1

Leigh Ann Edwards

TULE
PUBLISHING

DEDICATION

For Daniella Joan.

I was already planning to dedicate each book in my Maidens of the Mystical Stones series to one of my four grandchildren. Originally, I thought I'd do the dedications in the most logical or fair way and follow birth order. But when I found out *Autumn's Magical Pact* was being released on Daniella, my only granddaughter's birthday, I soon changed my mind.

To my beautiful, intelligent, kind, witty, amusing, helpful, strong, resilient, amazing medal-winning archer, Daniella—this one's for you my sweet girlio. I'm incredibly proud of you. I love you more than I could put into words even if I used a gazillion dictionaries and thesauruses. Wishing you much happiness now and always!

CHAPTER ONE

Medieval Wessex

THE TORTUROUS ACHE in Rhianwyn's heart was nearly unbearable. It even hurt to breathe. She watched the wooden coffin lowered into the ground and began to softly sob. Knowing she'd never see her mother's lovely face or hear her voice again was unimaginable. Her father draped a comforting arm around her shoulder. He was suffering his own misery—his compounded with discernable guilt for Rhianwyn's mother, Mererid, died in childbed.

Rhianwyn no longer listened to the priest. Instead she watched a red squirrel scamper up a nearby tree. She smiled inwardly at the unruly tufts of hair by its ears. Her gaze then followed a flock of starlings creating their unique formations in the sky. Rhianwyn longed to soar like those birds or at least feel as carefree as she had only days ago. She didn't want to hear of souls, heaven, or hell. She only wanted her mother. Mererid had been strong, healthy, and vivacious, but she'd been cursed with the cruel fate so many women met.

As a healer, Mererid often assisted with midwifery. Rhianwyn sometimes accompanied her. Far too often they'd seen women die in childbed or soon after. Yet always bright and optimistic, Mererid hadn't feared that. She said death was merely part of life; that a person lived as long as they were meant to and people should rejoice in all the days they were given and not dwell on the duration. Mererid also believed life here was only part of a soul's eternal journey. Rhianwyn yearned to possess more of her mother's faith and positivity.

Although she adored children, Rhianwyn had already decided she'd never want babies. In fact, she swore she'd never lie with a man if she might meet the dismal fate of dying in childbed. She'd voiced that to her mother only weeks ago. Mererid encouraged her to speak to her and never judged Rhianwyn's thoughts or feelings. She only assured her that she'd change her mind. When she was of an age to fall in love or experience physical longings, she *would* desire to lie with a man for it was perfectly natural to want that. She said besides the intrinsic pleasure, it brought joy and comfort. But now, Rhianwyn's mind was firm—she most certainly *would not* share intimacies in a man's bed.

"Time to go, daughter." Her father's voice pulled her from her musings.

Rhianwyn nodded. The grave attendants began to shovel dirt on the coffin. The other people here walked away. Rhianwyn glanced across the cemetery to see the priest had gone to the next burial—Elspeth Jory's mother. Elspeth wasn't exactly Rhianwyn's friend. In truth, they were at odds more than they agreed, but she was an acquaintance near her age and Rhianwyn enjoyed their lively conversations.

Elspeth, her parents, and siblings were castle servants as

their parents had been and theirs—for generations. Elspeth's father was a groundskeeper. Elspeth and her mother, Nora, cleaned the king's and his family's chambers. Nora, had recently died of childbed fever. Elspeth's newborn brother was living with her eldest brother and his wife. Her father worked long hours and men were seldom responsible for an infant's care.

"I'd like to stay a while longer, Father," Rhianwyn said.

He looked like he didn't fully approve, but he didn't protest. William Albray was kind-hearted and soft-spoken. Although he loved her without question, he'd find it difficult parenting his strong-willed daughter without her mother.

"Don't be long, Rhianwyn. You shouldn't be out after dark and there'll be people coming by to pay their respects."

"I'll be home before sunset, Father. I promise."

She affectionately touched his cheek. He smiled, but it didn't mask his grief. He'd deeply loved his *Welshland beauty* as he often referred to Rhianwyn's black-haired, blue-eyed mother.

The grave now filled, the grave diggers went to stand by the crowd near Elspeth's family, waiting to complete the grim task there, too. Elspeth had four older brothers, all married. She had three younger brothers, several nephews, and now her new baby brother. She'd undoubtedly miss her mother even though Elspeth hadn't been close with Nora—not like Rhianwyn and Mererid. But her father wouldn't be her only family.

Finally alone, Rhianwyn lowered herself to the ground

and wept unrestrainedly.

"Oh Mam, how am I to live without you?" Rhianwyn whispered half expecting to hear her mother reply with her unfaltering gentle wisdom. Instead she only heard the monotone voice of the priest saying the same words he'd said at her mother's grave.

Rhianwyn looked beyond this churchyard to another — the cemetery for paupers or outcasts. She espied Selena, the girl most mothers wouldn't have permitted their daughters to befriend. However, Rhianwyn's beautiful mother hadn't been like most. Mererid accepted everyone and inspired Rhianwyn to do the same. Therefore, Rhianwyn *had* befriended Selena when they were small girls. Though she didn't see her often, she was Rhianwyn's best friend.

Only a handful of women stood with Selena while her mother, Beatrice, was buried. No priest spoke or prayed for her. In the church's opinion Selena's mother's soul was already damned. There was no great crowd of mourners as her mother, Mererid, the respected healer had drawn or Elspeth's mother with many castle servants in attendance. There was only the other harlots, as Selena's mother had been. Beatrice hadn't died in childbed, but at the hands of one of the men who paid her for what was done within a bed.

Mererid hadn't hidden those truths from Rhianwyn even though her father hadn't agreed and he seldom voiced his disapproval of anything her mother did. William hoped to shelter Rhianwyn. Mererid reasoned since their daughter, now fourteen, had recently experienced her first womanly bleeding, she'd benefit more from her being straightforward even regarding matters such as physical relations in order to prepare her for life. Unfortunately, she hadn't prepared Rhianwyn for living without her.

Selena morosely sobbed, too. Previously, she'd been comforted by the other women, but they'd left her. Elspeth also stood alone at her mother's grave now. Elspeth was thirteen, Selena only twelve—all young to be motherless. Rhianwyn went to Elspeth, only a stone's throw away.

"I'm sorry for the loss of your mother," Rhianwyn said as Elspeth quickly wiped away her tears. She was a strong girl in appearance and countenance. Tall and sturdily built with somewhat sharp features, her blonde hair pulled back from her face and neatly plaited; she took pride in appearing stoic. This sometimes made her seem abrupt, unlikable—almost cold-hearted. But intuitively gifted, like Mererid, Rhianwyn was able to see what others couldn't. Elspeth wasn't as cantankerous as her gruff demeanor suggested. She simply seldom allowed her tender, vulnerable side to be seen.

"And I yours," Elspeth finally replied.

"Thank you." Rhianwyn tucked her light-brown hair behind her ear. "I'm going to comfort Selena now."

"You *can't* be seen with *her*." Elspeth scowled. "She's the daughter of a sordid woman."

"I don't need your approval to do what I like, Elspeth Jory. When my own mother first came to Wessex, she was treated unkindly simply because she was from Cymru."

"She didn't choose to be from Welshland," Elspeth retorted, like that, too, was not something anyone would want to be.

"Do you actually believe Selena's mother chose to do what she did? It was surely out of necessity."

"I'd be a beggar before I'd ever be a whore," Elspeth haughtily replied.

"A whore sleeps in a warm bed and is fed regularly—two meals a day from what I've heard," Rhianwyn said, even knowing it would antagonize the other girl.

"Carnal heat of the flesh within that *warm bed* got Selena's mother killed," Elspeth said.

Elspeth knew more on the topic of coupling than most girls her age for she lived in the castle's servants' quarters. Loads of scandalous happenings occurred there as well as the usual amount of gossip regarding those events.

"Was it not similar heat within a warm bed that saw our own mothers dead?" Rhianwyn dared to say.

"With a man to whom they were wed." Elspeth crossed her arms.

"That doesn't change the sad truth they all lie in a grave now." Rhianwyn said.

"You're contemptible, Rhianwyn Albray. Our mothers will be in heaven. Hers will not!"

"If you wish to believe that, so be it. My hope is that they're all somewhere better with no sorrow, pain, or fear. Whether it's truly heaven... I doubt even the priests know, and clearly not all priests will find out with their sometimes reprehensible behavior. Now, I *am* going to Selena for she didn't choose her mother or how she lived or died any more than you or I."

Rhianwyn lifted her mud-caked skirts and made her way across the uneven soggy ground. Although often rainy here, today the steady drizzle added to her heavy heart and the solemn dreariness in the graveyard. She climbed the fence at the edge of the cemetery, snagging her best kirtle and cussed under her breath thinking a grieving daughter probably shouldn't cuss.

This bleak cemetery had only remedial wooden crosses tied together with rope or twine. Few names were carved for most low-born couldn't read or write. Some graves bore small unmarked stones, unlike the graveyard where Mererid and Nora now rested with stone crosses and markers painstakingly etched. If families were illiterate, they honored their loved ones, often even sold their possessions to pay someone to immortalize their names upon the headstones.

Selena, the gentlest person Rhianwyn knew, wept even harder in seeing Rhianwyn. She went to Selena and held her close. Mererid always said if you were embracing someone—make it worthwhile. Hold them tightly whether in joy or sorrow—either way you'd both benefit. Selena's sobs wracked her slight frame. Rhianwyn wept with her and brushed a red curl from her thin, pallid face. When Elspeth joined them, her closely guarded tears escaped... her hard exterior shattered in seeing Selena's deep grief.

"My condolences in the loss of your mother," Elspeth managed.

"Thank you," Selena sniffled. "My heart aches for both of you, too." She still trembled, clinging to Rhianwyn.

"Where will you stay now?" Rhianwyn asked, concerned.

"I must remain at the house on the edge of the village—where I was born and I've always lived. The women there are all I have now."

"But won't you be expected to…you know…do what women do in that house of ill repute?" Elspeth asked.

"Elspeth!" Rhianwyn scolded.

"It's all right, Rhianwyn," Selena said. "Everyone knows that's what will eventually become of me. Though likely not for a while. Thankfully, Shandy doesn't permit children to be used by men."

"Perhaps you could come live with Father and me," Rhianwyn suggested.

"Your father wouldn't agree. Your cottage is small and I'd be another mouth to feed when times are hard. Besides, men want my kind for only one thing."

"Father's not like that," Rhianwyn disagreed.

"Most men are like that," Elspeth said. "Now your father's alone, he'll probably be sneaking down the back lane to *that* disorderly house like many others."

Rhianwyn threw a pointed stare at Elspeth, but mournful weeping effectively disrupted their conversation. It came from the treed cemetery up the hill near the castle. It was the churchyard reserved for nobles—lords and ladies, kings and queens, and their families. The girls looked at each other, then walked up the hill and peered through the trees.

"It's the princess," Selena whispered.

"Her mother, the queen's, died, too," Elspeth added.

"I heard that even though she was heavy with child herself, your mother was called to attend the queen when her physicians and her midwife couldn't assist her," Selena said to Rhianwyn.

Rhianwyn nodded. "That's true. Sadly, the queen and her babe were already lost by the time Mam got there."

"It's just as well." Elspeth looked serious. "Or she might've been flogged for not saving them. The king's physician was lashed and thrown in the dungeon. The midwife's forever banished or so it's been said."

"Castle gossip's not always reliable." Rhianwyn shook her head.

"There's usually some truth to every rumor," Elspeth said.

"I don't believe that," Rhianwyn replied. "Does the cook spit in the broth when he's in a particularly foul mood?"

Elspeth actually laughed at that. Selena and Rhianwyn smiled, too. It felt good to smile. She hadn't in the days since her mother died, though it brought guilt, too.

"I've never seen it, but it might be true," Elspeth replied. "I certainly don't eat the broth, just to be safe."

"Why's the princess unattended?" Selena asked. "I thought she wasn't permitted to be alone or do anything on her own…even wipe her own backside."

"It *is* odd she's without her lady attendant." Elspeth nodded. "The king's probably already off finding another wife to provide him with a male heir."

"What are you doing?" Elspeth asked as Rhianwyn pushed away the thick branches intending to climb the iron fence.

"Going to offer condolences for the princess's loss, too."

"You cannot!" Elspeth said.

Elspeth's bossiness irritated Rhianwyn, especially today when her emotions were already raw.

"Why do you presume you can tell me what I can do? You should know that only spurs me on," Rhianwyn replied.

When Rhianwyn did climb the fence and walked toward the princess, she saw three knights by the gate. They all stared but one. Sir Severin was a friend of her father's. Therefore, he nodded to Rhianwyn as she approached the princess.

This cemetery had elaborately fashioned gravestones, tall crosses, huge ornate monuments—some nearly as large as the immense sunstones on the open plain near their village.

Princess Lilliana looked up. Through her fine veil, Rhianwyn saw her dark-brown eyes were red and swollen. She was attired in rich black robes and cloak. Usually she was seen in stunning golds, reds, or purples. Her pitch-black hair was fashioned in a knotted braid wrapped elaborately about her head.

"I doubt you know who I am…" Rhianwyn began.

"I know you," Princess Lilliana said, lifting the veil. "Your father sometimes advises mine and your lovely mother was a renowned healer. I'm sorry to hear she was taken to the Lord in the same manner as mine and that both babies were lost. I did so long for a sibling. Being an only child is very lonely."

"I feel that, too. I'm sorry for the loss of your mother, our queen. She was kind to me whenever I saw her when with my mother."

"She truly liked your mother, Rhianwyn," Princess Lilliana said. "I believe she considered her a friend. She requested her presence much earlier during her lengthy womanly ordeal, yet Father wouldn't have her fetched. Instead he listened to his inept physician, the old male healer, and the midwife. If he'd permitted your mother to see mine earlier...perhaps..." She stoically raised her pointed chin and sniffled.

Elspeth and Selena approached now, too. Selena curtsied to the princess. Elspeth only nodded.

"We've all lost our mothers—all laid to rest this day," Rhianwyn said. "In my mind that forever binds us."

Rhianwyn noticed the displeased expression on Elspeth's face. She resented the king and his family. Most in Elspeth's family were honored in a life of servitude, but not Elspeth. She was ashamed of her position and loathed her duties.

"It's a grievous pain that cannot be remedied," Princess Lilliana finally replied. "I was sorely saddened to hear of your losses, also."

"I didn't think you'd know *anything* about us or that our mothers died," Elspeth said.

"I insist that Agnes, my lady attendant, tell me all the news about the kingdom."

Rhianwyn saw the knights looking their way. They'd soon be made to part. The princess wasn't allowed friends—certainly not common-born.

"We should meet again for we'll understand each other's pain," Rhianwyn said. "No matter our positions or circumstances, our mothers will be greatly missed and we'll surely crave female companionship. None of us have sisters either."

"I doubt that'll happen," Elspeth argued. "*She* wouldn't dare risk being seen with the likes of us." Elspeth motioned to the princess.

"You wouldn't ordinarily be seen with the likes of me." Selena looked somewhat accusingly at Elspeth. "You'd never have come to speak with me if Rhianwyn hadn't, nor would either of us approached the princess if not for Rhianwyn."

"Call me Lilliana," the princess whispered so the knights wouldn't hear.

"That'd see us taken to the dungeon straightaway," Elspeth scoffed.

"When alone we'll be equals and I hope one day…close friends." Lilliana ignored Elspeth's comment. "You needn't address me by my title. We'll all simply be grieving daughters. Although it's difficult for me to get away from the castle, I'll persuade Agnes to let me walk here to the cemetery—perhaps on this date each moon."

"I'd like that," Rhianwyn said. "I hope we can arrange it."

"The gossipmongers would surely find out," Elspeth replied.

"How can they begrudge us time in the graveyard honoring our beloved mothers?" Rhianwyn said.

"They can't." Selena shook her head.

"Then let's swear to it." Rhianwyn held out her hand.

"Swear to being friends with a princess?" Elspeth dubiously asked.

"She's willing to be friends with someone who'll one day surely be a harlot," Selena said.

"I have no friends other than my lady attendant," Lilliana sadly admitted. "Please agree to this."

Elspeth shrugged and stared hard at the princess.

"We all need friends," Rhianwyn said.

"We do." Eagerly, Selena placed her hand atop Rhianwyn's. Lilliana didn't hesitate but added hers, too. Elspeth still looked uncertain, but finally put her hand on the princess's hand.

"We're forever bound," Rhianwyn whispered.

"We're forever bound," the others repeated as the knights approached.

"Time to go back to the castle, Princess," Sir Severin said and the four girls nodded, each returning to their homes.

CHAPTER TWO

Five years later

S ELENA, ELSPETH, AND Rhianwyn browsed the noisy, bustling village market. The mingled aromas here ranged from the enticing scents of savory and sweet pies and roasted wild game sold by the vendors, to the earthy smell of horses and sheep. On the breeze was the fragrance of phlox from the nearby meadow.

A juggler, attired in colorful garments, skillfully tossed about several apples, entertaining the crowd. Lively music was being played. One man recited poetry; two others comically danced while those watching laughed. A pantomime was presently delighting the village children. The sun was shining, the sky was bright blue with puffy white clouds, and Rhianwyn breathed deeply enjoying the typical contagious merriment of the market.

The women observed items offered by the locals…vegetables, delicious baked wares, fresh cream, and honey. There were also merchants who'd traveled a distance or from far-off shores. They sold cups and dishes, pots, furs, and ready-made garments, but also various weapons, gold and precious jewels, spices, luxury textiles—sometimes even expensive silk or exotic animals.

Elspeth's voice disrupted Rhianwyn's present enjoyment by going back to their contentious conversation.

"You can't simply decide you'll never be married, Rhianwyn... no matter how bloody stubborn you are," Elspeth said.

"Me, stubborn!" Rhianwyn exclaimed, staring at her headstrong friend. "If Father continues to request I remain living with him to cook and care for him, I pray it'll prevent me from a forced marriage. Besides, why would I even want to be married?"

"You should let someone take care of you for a change," Selena said. "You're beautiful, Rhianwyn and desired by many men."

Rhianwyn only shook her head as the three friends continued browsing. Occasionally they picked up items to appease the glares of the vendors for they seldom bought anything.

Selena had no coin; everything she required was provided by Shandy and Fleta, the women who owned the brothel where Selena remained living. Elspeth was paid a monthly pittance for being in the king's employ. Elspeth lived with her father and younger brothers in the castle's servants' quarters. Servants wore matching attire and ate most meals at the castle—both provided by the king.

Rhianwyn's ample garden at the cottage ensured she didn't need to buy vegetables. She bartered for other items required in her healing. The meager coin she occasionally earned was used to purchase herbs and spices, not found here, to create more remedies. Being able to assist the ailing or wounded was exceedingly important and it was what gave her purpose.

"Your father's fallen out of favor with the king since his magical spells haven't ensured the king has produced a male heir, so it's doubtful he'll grant him further requests," Elspeth said. "If I'm being truthful, your father's become more peculiar. His mind isn't as it should be."

"Father *is* a gifted mage. True, he's a bit eccentric and forgetful, but I won't be forced to wed simply because men of power decide I'm of an age to marry and carry children," Rhianwyn argued.

"King Thaddeus wants his kingdom to expand and flourish," Selena said.

"Because women continue to birth numerous children doesn't indicate the kingdom is flourishing—not when many go hungry." Rhianwyn shook her head.

"I'd give anything to be wed and have many children," Selena admitted.

"Your mother didn't die in childbed, therefore that mightn't deter you as it does Rhianwyn and me," Elspeth said.

"I'd rather she had," Selena declared with uncommon determination, then lowered her voice. "At least your mothers weren't murdered and *you* won't be forced to become a harlot."

"I've told you, Selena, that doesn't have to be your fate," Rhianwyn countered.

"I'm deeply indebted to Shandy and Fleta. They've given me a place to stay and food these years since my mother died. Soon, they expect me to begin paying them back."

"By spending years flat on your back," came Elspeth's sardonic reply.

Rhianwyn threw her a look of reproach.

"Perhaps I could call in debts beholden to me for my healing and pay Shandy what she feels is owed to her," Rhianwyn suggested. "If not, maybe you and I can go far away from this village."

"You daren't cross Shandy, Rhianwyn. She's ruthless and frightens me to the core," Selena said, her voice trembling. "Those who oppose her often come to harm—sometimes even disappear."

Rhianwyn stared at Selena worriedly. She'd heard those disturbing rumors, but hoped those women longed to abandon the disreputable life and simply left the brothel.

"The drafty loft where you sleep and the measly amount of food you eat surely didn't put Shandy out much," Elspeth said. "Maybe you can find a man to wed you, Selena…someone who'd pay Shandy what she deems you owe her," Elspeth suggested. "You're virginal. That's what men often want when searching for a wife."

"Most wouldn't believe that even though it's what Shandy hopes to use to draw the highest bidder for my first time with a man," Selena whispered. "I'm a daughter of a harlot. I'd never attract someone with means to pay what Shandy'd ask to release me of my debt. Besides, highborn men wouldn't even be permitted to marry me."

"I *will* think of something," Rhianwyn said, though she'd already wracked her mind trying to discover a way to assist lovely, gentle Selena. Rhianwyn's heart despaired in considering how it would change her if Selena was used by lustful or perverse men.

"You have your own worries, Rhianwyn," Elspeth said.

"The king's advisors surely aren't aware you've reached nineteen years—well past marrying age—or they'd be insisting you are wed. Women are obliged by law to marry and produce children. I'm to wed in weeks. You know I don't relish that thought—especially to that obnoxious brute, the sheriff's son, Godric. Sheriff Percival requested it and my father agreed."

"Godric's a despicable boor." Rhianwyn tensed even thinking about him. "If I could find a way to see you avoid that, too, I would, Elspeth."

"I'd like to drag a knife across his throat. That would prevent the wedding."

"You mustn't speak those threats aloud," Rhianwyn warned. "Should anyone hear, you'd be held accountable. Women are expected to be meek and submissive."

"Elspeth, if not Godric, they'd only find someone else probably equally displeasing," Selena said. "At least he'll have means to provide a home and sustenance. Plus, you'll only have to share *one* man's bed and he's not old, ugly, or fat."

"Godric doesn't have to be old or physically unattractive to be vile," Elspeth replied. "He's mean-spirited, perhaps dangerous. His first wife *was* found dead on the abbey steps, her neck broken." Elspeth frowned. "Some believe she was hoping to seek sanctuary with the monks. If Godric wasn't the sheriff's son that would've been considered most suspicious. Do you suppose she really fell?"

They all shared a knowing look, agreeing it was doubtful.

They meandered through the village market where the

three met each Saturday afternoon. Lilliana joined them less often—still only monthly in the cemetery. Since the princess had recently reached seventeen, apparently an adequate age for the king's daughter to wed, she was even more heavily guarded to ensure she remained innocent or no one questioned that she was chaste. The four young women enjoyed their times together and had stayed friends since that day in the graveyard despite being very different in stations and personalities.

Selena was tender, kind-hearted, excitable, and filled with wonder, but easily influenced, highly emotional, and the most timid of the four women. Rhianwyn tried to be vigilant in protecting her. She thought of Selena as a younger sister in need of guidance and shelter. Therefore the situation at the brothel with Selena soon expected to become a harlot was ever on Rhianwyn's mind.

Elspeth was very comical. She joked and kept the others amused, ensured they laughed together a lot. However, Elspeth was cynical, spoke her mind to a fault offering her unwanted opinion often. She had an immense chip on her shoulder regarding being a servant. She and Rhianwyn had many healthy debates over the years but staunch disagreements, too. Elspeth couldn't see anything favorable in her situation. She wasn't close with her family and mostly avoided them. Her father was perplexed dealing with his only daughter which was probably why he'd agreed to Elspeth marrying Godric.

Lilliana was the most reserved and refined of the friends, as one might expect of a princess. Yet she also spoke and laughed freely with them when they were together. Lilliana was incredibly lonely in her privileged noble life. Other than her lady servant, Agnes, who was only five years older, Lilliana saw few people. Rhianwyn wished they could spend more time with her—that she could join them at the market. But she couldn't be seen with common-born.

When they met at the cemetery beneath the gnarled ancient oak tree, they often talked for a lengthy time. Agnes stood guard to make sure no one found out. The princess could easily manage Agnes—had her wrapped around her finger. Lilliana could cleverly manipulate nearly everyone to her way of thinking.

Rhianwyn enjoyed the greatest freedom of the four friends, had the most contact with people, but reveled in her solitude, too. She was proud to offer remedies to others. She liked being needed and took her healing seriously. Elspeth sometimes accused her of being too serious about it.

"Elspeth, at least you don't have to move to *Welshland* when you marry, as I've recently heard poor Lilliana must," Selena said, then looked at Rhianwyn sheepishly. "Sorry, I remember your mother was Welsh."

"Cymru is beautiful," Rhianwyn used the Welsh word. "I journeyed there with my parents when I was a child. I'd gladly visit again or maybe even live there."

"If I was *poor* Lilliana, I'd be marrying a prince, still living a life of opulence, being waited on hand and foot by others which would be a damn welcome change," Elspeth said.

"I'd wholly dislike that life," Rhianwyn replied. "I

couldn't imagine having someone assist me with bathing, dressing, and more private matters. I like living in the woods surrounded by nature and solitude. When my healing isn't required, I can go exploring and searching for my herbs. I'd even prefer to be like Radella."

"Surely you're jesting," Elspeth said. "That crotchety old woman lives alone in a bloody cave. Who'd want that lonely, destitute life?"

"She's not ruled by a man. She never carried children therefore never risked dying in childbed. If I was like her, husbandless for life, I could provide healing without someone dictating my every move. I like my independence."

"Rhianwyn, *you* haven't spent every day since you were a girl toiling in drudgery… always serving others." Elspeth's always strong voice became louder.

"But Elspeth, you've heard some of the offensive things Rhianwyn must do and see as a healer," Selena said. "They include blood, vomit, pus, and the like."

Selena, notably squeamish, actually gagged and Elspeth smirked. She was a little mean-spirited herself. Perhaps as his wife, Elspeth would put Godric in his place.

"Who empties the damn chamber pots of the king and princess?" Elspeth continued. "Who strips her bloody sheets monthly and shows them to the marriage advisor and priest so they know the princess remains virginal?"

"That's completely absurd and would prove nothing other than she isn't with child," Rhianwyn said. "It doesn't indicate she hasn't lost her innocence."

"Do you suppose she has?" Selena asked, her green eyes

wide now.

"I doubt it," Elspeth replied. "She's mostly confined to the castle gardens or her chambers and always accompanied by Agnes. There are knights posted outside the princess's door day and night. She certainly hasn't told us if she's had intimate experiences."

"She might not," Rhianwyn said. "Not everyone's as open about such topics as you, Elspeth."

Elspeth slyly smiled again. She'd had several sexual partners and sometimes shared detailed accounts of her intimate encounters that her friends didn't want to hear. Rhianwyn wasn't certain if Elspeth honestly had so much experience or if she exaggerated in hope of astonishing or impressing them. She boasted her carnal knowledge and involvement, though for a woman, that was considered shameful—even unlawful if men of influence learned of it. Women were commonly placed in the dungeon for adultery, fornication, or even rumors of tempting men.

Selena's cheeks flushed in earnest. She was much contrary to Elspeth. For someone who'd spent her whole life in a brothel, Selena was largely sheltered—almost unbelievably naïve. Perhaps that was Shandy's intent to keep her entirely uninformed. Still, how she hadn't learned some of the happenings at the brothel, Rhianwyn didn't understand.

Elspeth had enlightened Selena by relating her own sexual encounters. Selena hadn't been aware what *actually* happened between a woman and man during coupling. Her eyes had grown wide as shields when Elspeth told her. She was mortified to learn the act was what left a child in a woman's belly…that everyone who'd ever carried a child had done *that* or had it forced upon them.

When Rhianwyn was attending to her healing, Elspeth further educated Selena. She'd escorted her to the meadow to watch horses mating, which deeply disturbed Selena. Rhianwyn had even gone to the castle later to admonish Elspeth.

"If you felt compelled to show her, you could've taken her to watch sheep mating. It wouldn't have left her so dismayed," Rhianwyn had said.

"Don't worry. I told her men weren't hung like horses…well not many," Elspeth incredulously replied. "Watching cats mating would've been worse. If she'd heard the brutal screeching she'd be terrified to be with a man. Or dogs—if she saw them stuck together she'd surely fear that happens with people, too."

"She's already terrified and I doubt she actually needed to *see* it done."

"She'll be more than seeing it soon enough. We should at least prepare her!" Elspeth reasoned.

Rhianwyn wasn't sure how you'd prepare a timid, modest woman to become a harlot and subject to men's lustfulness. Rhianwyn had answered Selena's curious questions when Elspeth told her of the sexual act and after watching the horses. She'd also consoled her when she began her womanly bleeding for she was horrified—certain she was dying. Rhianwyn regretted not mentioning that before it occurred but presumed the women at the brothel would've at least informed Selena of that.

"Anything you'd like to share with us on the subject of

sarding, Rhianwyn?" Elspeth grinned at her.

Rhianwyn sighed and shook her head. She certainly wouldn't share such information. Although Elspeth and Selena were her friends, she preferred keeping personal matters to herself.

"Oh look!" Selena excitedly widened her eyes. "There's the impressive-looking lord who's recently gained hold of Brockwell Manor." She pointed to a notably handsome man on a horse on the road outside the markets.

"Word has it he's after finding a wife," Elspeth added. "He's a grand-looking man."

"He certainly not fat, old, or repulsive. He's uncommonly attractive—so tall and muscular," Selena added.

Rhianwyn could see that despite being timid, Selena was becoming interested in appraising men—surely by Elspeth's influence.

"*You* should go talk to him, Rhianwyn," Selena said. "Men find you enchantingly beautiful even without you trying to attract them. Charm him and I'll wager he'd gladly marry you. The king's advisors have been recommending changing the law so highborn men aren't limited to marry only women of their station."

"Likely because most unmarried noble *ladies* here haven't matured to childbearing age," Elspeth said, "or they're all sniveling bores or malicious bitches. But Selena, the man's *Irish*!"

"What's wrong with the Irish?" Rhianwyn asked. "Do you think only Saxon men are worthy of considering for a husband?"

"So you would like to wed Lord Brockwell?" Selena

looked serious.

"Of course I don't want to wed *him*. I don't even know him. I told you I don't want to marry anyone. Besides, he's a noble lord. I doubt he'd marry a common-born even if the king should change that law. He's sure to be arrogant and demanding. He likely only wants a woman to give him a dozen sons…which I wouldn't. I told you, I'm not ever being wed."

"You probably won't have a choice," Selena said.

"You would've wed three years ago," Elspeth dared to say.

Rhianwyn cleared her throat and looked away, fighting tears even after all this time.

"That was unkind, Elspeth," Selena reprimanded.

"We're really never to mention Anslem Brockwell because he was killed?" Elspeth shrugged. "You cared for him, Rhianwyn."

"And now he's gone," Rhianwyn said, nonchalantly picking up an onion, examining it like it was the most interesting item in the market, trying to push away thoughts of Anslem.

"You needn't pretend you don't still mourn him," empathetic Selena said.

"But you should consider taking a husband before one's picked for you," Elspeth added. "You could marry Sir Everard, that strikingly good-looking knight tomorrow, if you'd give him the time of day."

"I should've listened to my head and not my heart and never agreed to wed Anslem. But because of that I've learned a brutally hard lesson. I'll *never* agree to marry a knight—not again! I will not lose someone while betrothed or become a widow soon after we're wed," Rhianwyn firmly stated.

"You could marry Everard's even more appealing older brother, Sir Cassian." Elspeth apparently ignored Rhianwyn. "He gazes at you with interest. I know he's also a knight but a most worthy catch! He has a tall, appealing sturdy form—probably a fine, sturdy spindle, too." She raised her eyebrows and smiled. "He undoubtedly knows how to pleasure a woman."

Rhianwyn shook her head disapprovingly but felt her cheeks go warm and likely red. "Is that *all* you ever think about?"

"Don't tell me you never think of it, Rhianwyn." Elspeth smirked.

"Elspeth, I thought you'd decided you didn't like men," Selena whispered, sounding confused.

"I like men quite a lot—just not as well as women," Elspeth readily admitted. "Besides, lying with women doesn't cause concern of becoming with child."

A sudden loud commotion from the far end of the market abruptly interrupted their discussion. The Irishman's large black steed whinnied, reared, and fiercely leapt about. Rhianwyn couldn't see the man now, though he'd be hard to miss. He was as tall as the tallest of the king's knights and built just as powerfully. That hadn't gone unnoticed in the few times she'd caught sight of him though she'd never admit to looking close enough to assess his appearance.

His horse was tied by the nearby elms away from the

market. Several children stood not far from where the temperamental horse was tethered.

"Here, hold this." Rhianwyn passed her basket to Selena, lifted her skirts and hurried off toward the calamity.

CHAPTER THREE

R HIANWYN PUSHED THROUGH the patrons and vendor stalls in the crowded market. Most of the children had backed away from the agitated horse, but one small girl appeared too frightened to move. Apparently no one wanted to approach the crazed animal to help her. He was a beautiful beast but obviously something startled him. Where was the damn owner? How careless to leave a horse unattended if it had such wildness. The horse continued to fiercely buck and snort.

"Walk toward me, Maisie," Rhianwyn calmly said. Evidently the girl was too afraid.

"Rhianwyn, there's a snake," the child finally whispered, pointing.

Rhianwyn espied it near the tree where the horse was bound. She stepped between the child and the horse, speaking soothingly to the animal as she picked up a stone and tossed it at the black snake, stunning it. Then she threw her knife and nearly sliced off its head. The snake's tail twitched, then it was still.

"Calm down boy. I won't harm you; I adore horses," Rhianwyn said. "But you must stop jumping about. You're going to hurt yourself."

Rhianwyn touched Maisie's shoulders. She finally ran

toward the other children.

"For the love of Christ, woman, what's goin' on?" the Irishman said when he drew near. "Are you completely mad or simply witless? Clearly you must be or you'd not be approachin' a riled animal you're unfamiliar with! You're bound to get yourself killed! Step away from my horse, immediately! What'd you do to make him so bloody unruly?"

"I assure you, *I* did nothing!" She kept her head bowed, inhaling deeply attempting to stem her own mounting temper at his outburst. "Only an irresponsible person would leave an easily unsettled horse unattended near children!"

"He wasn't anywhere near children." The man sounded irritable. "I tied him away from the market and he wasn't unsettled then. I only left him long enough to get him some carrots."

"Your land has several plentiful apple trees. They're often a favorite of horses and there's numerous gardens surely rife with new carrots."

"The gardens lie barren. Lord Giles Brockwell dismissed most servants before spring planting. But how do you know of the orchards?" he asked.

She finally looked up at the imprudent man. When he gazed at her, he appeared genuinely taken aback. He stared hard as though he should recognize her, although they'd never met. She'd previously only seen him from a distance. But she couldn't deny the instant attraction—one she certainly didn't welcome.

"My family's cottage is on the edge of Brockwell land,"

Rhianwyn managed, which was true but not why she knew much about the Brockwell holdings.

He continued to stare at her, gazed at her hair and looked deeply into her eyes. He seemed speechless. She finally turned from his intense gaze for his own deep blue eyes were mesmerizing. Her body grew warm with primal attraction. She'd been trying to ignore those natural urges, but seeing this very masculine man—his undeniably handsome face and praiseworthy body, fueled them most assuredly.

"You must step away from my horse before he hurts you." He finally spoke again. "I wouldn't wish harm upon the one person that Giles Brockwell requests visitation. He rambles on incessantly about a woman with unusual pale-blue eyes he must soon speak to in hope of receivin' forgiveness before he dies."

Rhianwyn's throat tightened. "There are other blue-eyed women," she replied.

"You're not the young woman Giles speaks of then?"

"Possibly," Rhianwyn replied.

"I thought so," the man said.

"I've no desire to speak with him. I've had enough unpleasant dealings with him."

"As to the matter at hand; my horse is temperamental and doesn't tolerate anyone other than me near him which is precisely why I didn't take him through the market." He drew so close she could smell his manly scent along with the enticing smell of his dark-brown leather overcoat. She moved away stepping closer to the horse.

"By God's bones, woman, do you heed nothin' at all?

There's a fine line between feisty and bloody foolish. If you're tryin' to prove you can ingratiate yourself with my horse as ably as you have the ill-tempered Giles Brockwell, you're sure to be lyin' dead at my feet, and your uncommonly pretty face will be left not noticeably so."

She turned and glared again. His eyes brazenly fell to her body even though her thread-worn cloak mostly concealed her womanly form. She ignored him and talked to the impressive beast.

"No wonder you're so damn capricious and kicking up such a fuss. I'd be doing the same if I had *him* for a master!"

Approaching closer to her, Lord Brockwell grinned at that. His broad smile was as beguiling as his eyes which only annoyed her more and worse still… it frightened her. Being attracted to men had brought disharmony before.

"Well… are you going to give him the carrots you needed so *very* badly or would you like me to do it?" Rhianwyn stared at him.

"Now you're just bein' outright reckless." Still, he handed her the carrots.

"Hoping to see me trampled to death, then?" she asked sarcastically.

"I think he might've done so already if he was of a mind to."

Rhianwyn showed the carrots to the horse. Not only did the large animal take them, but he nudged her hand like a gentle mare and she tossed the man a smug smile.

"He actually seems to… *like* you." The man sounded dumbfounded.

"Is that so entirely unbelievable?" she joked. "Animals tend to be fond of me. They know I love and respect them."

"So I see." He nodded as she stroked the horse's neck.

"It was a snake," Rhianwyn said.

"What?" the man asked, evidently further bewildered by his horse's acceptance of her.

"A snake…you know…those long slithering beasts with no legs. I've heard Ireland doesn't have any but surely you know what a snake is?" she taunted.

He now wore a slightly perturbed expression that somehow only made him more appealing. She fought a smile.

"I've journeyed to many countries with an abundance of snakes. Because I'm Irish doesn't mean I haven't left Irish shores."

"Apparently not; we *are* in Wessex," she said.

"You've an unusually mordant tongue for a woman."

"So I've been told," Rhianwyn said. "A snake startled your steed—a black adder. They're venomous."

She pointed to the dead reptile. The man looked impressed.

"You killed it?" he asked.

"I couldn't risk it biting your horse or the children."

"You're not fainthearted then?"

"As women surely must be?"

"Most are." He perhaps enjoyed perturbing her, too.

"Many men don't have a penchant for snakes either," she said.

Selena and Elspeth watched from the crowd of onlookers. Elspeth waggled her eyebrows teasingly and Selena smiled, both clearly encouraging her to continue conversing with the ruggedly attractive man.

"I must join my friends," Rhianwyn said.

"Thank you for calming my horse and seeing the child safe. Is she your daughter?"

"Absolutely not. I've no children nor do I ever intend to."

"That's an odd proclamation from a woman."

"Because our sole purpose is to produce children?" Her hackles rose.

"It is why you were blessed with a womb." There was a trace of arrogance in his tone again.

"Women buried in churchyards who died in childbed probably wouldn't consider it such a blessing!"

"Surely there're many others who think their children to be their greatest blessings," he argued. "Does your mother not believe you're a gift from God?"

Rhianwyn stepped away, not wishing to converse any longer much less of her mother or this objectionable subject.

"Goodbye, handsome one," she said to the horse.

"Goodbye lovely lady," the man bowed and grinned.

"I certainly wasn't speaking to *you*," she said.

"Because you don't find me so or because you wouldn't admit it if you did?" he asked with another smirk.

"Clearly there's no vanity in your family for you have it all," she replied.

He only smiled broader. "My horse's name's Dubh. It's Gaelic for black."

"Nearly the same in Welsh," she said.

"You know that language?"

"Only a little. My mother was from Cymru."

"Was your beauty and spiritedness inherited from her?"

"Some say I look like her, but she had the shiniest black hair and bluer eyes."

"And your spiritedness?"

"Mam had a lovely serene temperament." Rhianwyn wasn't certain why she spoke freely to him.

"It's your father who has a fiery spirit then?"

"No, Father's gentle and unpretentious."

Rhianwyn went to Selena, reclaiming the basket. She removed her blade from the snake, wiped the blood on the grass, put the knife in her pocket, picked up the dead reptile and placed it in the basket. Selena shuddered and the man watched her every move.

"Why do you take the snake?"

"The meat's edible. The fangs can be employed as piercing tools; the skin is used in remedies and the venom for potions."

"Do you have someone in mind you wish to poison?" he jested.

"I said *potions*, but it's true the venom could create a potent poison."

"You're knowledgeable regarding snakes," he said.

She only nodded. "Farewell, Dubh; stay clear of adders and we'll all be better off." Rhianwyn petted the horse's silky neck again, inhaling the much-loved scent, remembering the times Anslem had taken her riding.

"You won't give me your name or ask me mine?"

His deep voice and charming Irish lilt jarred her back to the present. Born with a keen sense of smell, Rhianwyn inhaled his masculine scent again. Not unpleasant like men who didn't wash or bathe regularly—but musky and enticing. It created visceral arousal. Her breasts reacted and she was thankful her cloak concealed her peaked nipples. A distinct tingling sensation of womanly need pulsed between her thighs. Her skin grew hot and she inhaled.

"Lord Brockwell didn't mention my name when he spoke of me?" she finally asked.

"He simply said he'd request only one at his bedside before he dies—a woman with unusual pale-blue eyes."

"I won't meet with the objectionable man even on his deathbed, and since I don't expect to converse with *you* again, the exchange of names isn't necessary."

"Are you always difficult and unfriendly or just with me?"

"She's a bit difficult with everyone," Elspeth answered.

Rhianwyn found that ironic coming from her.

"But she's also the best, most loyal friend anyone could ever hope for," Selena added.

"Will one of you lovely ladies tell me your beautiful blue-eyed friend's name since she seems disinclined?"

The man flashed a charming grin. Selena returned the smile, even fluttered her eyelashes. Elspeth openly appraised him from head to boots and wore a seductive expression. Rhianwyn cast a look of warning to her friends discouraging them from telling him.

"I s'pose we'd better not," Elspeth said.

"Being mysterious makes you more intriguing and ensures I'll want to get to know you better, *Suile Gorma*." He smirked at Rhianwyn.

"That's definitely not my intention." Rhianwyn looked at him closer despite her resolve not to. It was difficult not to. He was an indisputable sight of glorious masculine grandeur. Impressively tall and brawny and undeniably dashing in his fine leather overcoat, long light tunic, tight fitted breeches, and tall black boots. His jaw was chiseled, his nose straight, his lips broad and tempting. His wavy medium-brown hair was tied back. He didn't claim a beard, but neither was he clean-shaven which made him more sensually attractive. On his belt he carried a hefty sword in a gilded scabbard. Both scabbard and hilt bore a Celtic design. Seeing his alluring eyes, her heart raced and her body tingled, wholly unsettling her.

Several other women now stared at him, too.

"My name's Broccan Mulryan." He offered his hand.

The way he said his name with his appealing Irish accent further captivated her. Rhianwyn was reasonably certain he recognized he'd unsettled her and it pleased him. The attraction was obviously mutual as he continued to appraise her—unabashedly staring at the swell of her breasts beneath her cloak.

She briefly accepted his outstretched hand but soon pulled away. It was warm, strong, large, and lightly calloused. It didn't seem the hand of a lord who'd lived a privileged life. There was even the recognizable ridge that came from consistent use of a sword, not typical of lords—more like a knight.

Rhianwyn shrugged, trying to seem uninterested.

"You're not and never shall be anything to me but the new lord of Brockwell Manor."

Attempting to conceal a scowl at her continued coolness, he untied the horse's reins.

"Good day, ladies." He nodded, looking again at Rhianwyn, then Elspeth and Selena before he smoothly mounted the large horse. It was evident the man had much experience with horses.

"If you want to learn her name, she's the village's most gifted healer. You could ask anyone," Selena called after him.

He turned with a grateful smile at Selena and a mischievous grin at Rhianwyn. He even boldly winked. The horse trotted off, hooves clomping on the cobblestones till they were out of sight.

"Well… he's clearly the epitome of arrogance and ostentation!" Rhianwyn sneered.

"She actually likes him or she wouldn't give him a second thought." Elspeth nudged Selena and laughed. "I'd wager he has her thinking of carnal pleasures."

"I do not *like* him, Elspeth Jory, not by any measure and would you stop presuming everyone's as inclined to coupling as you? And Selena Lovelace—it's a damn good thing you're my friend or I mightn't speak to you again," Rhianwyn said huffing aloud. "I don't want that presumptuous, smug, puffed-up, cocky *man* to know anything about me."

"He might be all those, but he's also the most sensual man I've seen in an age, and you were being rather a bitch," Elspeth said.

"I was only being aloof. I don't want his or any man's notice; you're both well aware of that."

"Rhianwyn, you'd have to place a sack over your head not to be noticed," Selena said.

"Better enshroud your body as well not to turn men's and some women's heads, too." Elspeth grinned.

"What's *suile gorma*?" Selena struggled to repeat what Lord Brockwell had called Rhianwyn.

"It's Irish. I believe it means blue eyes," Rhianwyn said.

"Fortunes, fortunes. Who'd like to learn their future?" a woman called from the markets, ending their present conversation.

Elspeth, Selena, and Rhianwyn turned to see a bent old woman in a hooded cloak, though they'd never seen her here before.

"I'd like to know my future?" Selena eagerly walked toward her.

"Not me." Elspeth made a face. "Even if I had coin, I wouldn't waste it on that. I know what my future holds. I'll be married to someone I despise, work in the castle serving others till the day I die."

"That sounds very pessimistic, Elspeth," Rhianwyn said. "Mam used to tell me to always find something positive. It won't change your situation, but with an optimistic attitude, it lessens the difficulty."

Elspeth only rolled her eyes unfavorably at Rhianwyn.

"Would you three pretty young maidens like me to tell you what your future holds?" The woman gestured to them.

"We've no coin." Selena sighed, clearly disappointed.

"I prefer not to know," Rhianwyn said.

"You sound no more optimistic than me," Elspeth chided.

"Perhaps we could trade services." The woman eyed them. "I smell herbs. Is one of you a healer?"

"Rhianwyn is," Selena exclaimed.

"I need something to assist with sleep. Prophetic visions rob my sleep at night," the old woman admitted.

"I do have a potion for that." Rhianwyn nodded. "If you want your future told, Selena, I'll pay with a potion."

"Well, if *you're* paying, I suppose I might as well have my fortune told, too." Elspeth stepped forward, now eager.

Rhianwyn went to reach for her satchel and then shook her head for she'd left it at home today. "I don't have the potion with me."

"You'll pay me next time then," the woman suggested.

Rhianwyn noticed she kept the hood up, aptly concealing her face. Perhaps she was scarred or disfigured.

"What do we do?" Selena sounded excited and her eyes sparkled.

"Give me your hands—all of you?"

Selena and Elspeth held their hands before them.

"You, too, healer."

"Come on Rhianwyn; don't be such a stick-in-the-mud!" Elspeth said.

Rhianwyn gingerly held her hand out, and the woman touched them each in turn.

"You three are deeply connected."

"That's true," Selena said, smiling.

"Obviously you can see that for we're here walking and

talking together." Elspeth skeptically rolled her eyes.

"Your fourth friend is also an intricate part of your circle though that's mostly kept concealed," the woman continued.

"She couldn't have known that," Selena whispered to the others.

"How is this telling our futures?" Elspeth scowled at the fortune teller.

"I sense there is friendship and affection for one another but also some jealousy and resentment. There is comparison and rivalry, too."

"Those traits are common in almost all people," Rhianwyn said and the woman spoke on.

"Your futures are entwined in a very unusual way. Fate will see the four of you grow much closer...closer than anyone might imagine. You'll be magically connected."

"Pfftt!" Elspeth huffed.

"I like the sound of that," Selena said.

"It won't always be as you'd hope," the woman replied.

"Is that all?" Rhianwyn just wanted to leave for she'd been overtaken with an uneasy sensation. Shivers ran up her spine.

"You'll each find romantic love. Three have already met their future loves—one only recently. The other has yet to meet the one you'll be paired with but you'll each become close to all of them as well."

"If you think I'll ever love Godric, you've entirely no gift of second sight," Elspeth said. "I despise the notion of being *close* to him."

"I want to find love," Selena dreamily added.

"Looks like *you* could find love even now, Rhianwyn." Elspeth gestured to three of the king's knights headed toward them.

Rhianwyn turned to look, then glanced back at where the strange woman had been to find she was simply gone. Rhianwyn didn't have long to consider it for the knights approached.

CHAPTER FOUR

THE GROUP CONSISTED of Sir Severin, the Grand Cross, head of the knights' order; Sir Everard, the man who'd asked for Rhianwyn's hand on several occasions; and his older brother, Sir Cassian, who'd asked only once. Cassian had been Sir Anslem, Rhianwyn's betrothed's, valued friend. He was with him when Anslem was tragically killed in France.

"Maiden Albray," Sir Everard addressed her, stepping so close, she backed up.

"There's been an incident with one of the knights the king recently enlisted. We need a healer," Sir Severin said.

Elspeth rolled her eyes. She resented how often Rhianwyn was called away during their times at the market.

"Where's the physician, Dorsett?" Rhianwyn asked. "He's the king's choice to attend to his knights."

"Passed out in his chambers," Sir Everard said.

"It's barely midafternoon." Rhianwyn scowled. "And his nephew, his budding apprentice?"

"I'd not trust Hadley with a sick dog." Sir Severin shook his head.

"Nor would I. He's also often indecent with women, but he's soon to be second physician," Rhianwyn said. "What of the healer, Marlow?"

"He can barely see the nose on his face," Everard said.

"You could find Radella," Rhianwyn suggested.

Radella was once a revered healer. She taught Rhianwyn much about healing after Mererid died. Oddly, a few moons ago, she'd severed connections with Rhianwyn. She didn't know why for Radella refused to see or speak to her.

"Radella's old and ailing—likely wouldn't make it up the keep's steep steps even if she was agreeable to attending to knights," Everard said.

"If the knights hadn't been mostly naked and disorderly the one time she agreed to go to there, she would've been more liable to return," Rhianwyn scolded.

"They *were* drunk and full of piss and vinegar that night." Sir Severin nodded.

"We want to introduce you to those who've recently joined our order while we're present, so they'll be made aware they're to respect you." Sir Cassian finally spoke.

Rhianwyn wondered if it was obvious she avoided making eye contact with him.

"I don't even have my satchel with my remedies and other necessary items," she argued.

"That's peculiar. You almost always have it with you." Selena looked surprised.

"I was only to be visiting with my friends since Elspeth claims I never take time away from healing," Rhianwyn said.

"You've always been ready and willing to help others whether humble or noble born, Maiden Albray," Sir Severin replied. "Anyone who understands anything of healing knows you're the best healer probably in all of Wessex."

"Now you're shamelessly hoping to influence me with flattery," Rhianwyn said.

"Would I do that?" Sir Severin jested, scratching his graying beard.

"I have your satchel," Sir Cassian admitted removing it from his shoulder where it had been concealed by his sword.

"You went inside Father's cottage?"

"William told me I was always welcome." Sir Cassian's amber eyes now gazed intently. "How *is* your father?"

"He's well enough… as ever," Rhianwyn coolly said.

Her father often suggested she wed Cassian but she staunchly disagreed, resolute she'd never marry a knight.

"Could we come meet the new knights, too?" Selena put her hands together, pleading. "I've heard much about the knights' keep."

"I doubt you'd want to go *there*." Elspeth discouraged Selena. "It's notoriously raucous. The din can often be heard from the castle's courtyard."

"It's not a place for women," Sir Severin agreed.

"What am I, Sir Severin?" Rhianwyn asked, taking the healer's satchel from Cassian with a look of disapproval for going into her cottage. She placed it over her head and across her chest.

"You're a woman, sure enough, but also a skilled healer. Because you were Anslem's betrothed, you're forever respected by my knights and off-limits for anything dishonorable."

"Marriage is certainly honorable." Sir Everard smiled at Rhianwyn.

"Rhianwyn's firmly avowed she'll *never* marry a knight," Selena said, staring at Everard.

"I won't stop hoping to wear Maiden Albray down so she'll eventually give in." Everard grinned.

"No knight will be permitted to wed her," Sir Severin declared.

Both men accompanying him looked displeased.

"That's not up to you, Sir Severin." Rhianwyn bristled. "It's distressing enough the king, his priest, and advisors can determine who and when a woman marries."

"Are you saying you've changed your mind and do want to marry a knight?" Sir Severin looked serious.

"I definitely *do not*. Still, I don't want others deciding my future."

"I thought there was a man needing healing?" Elspeth said. "Clearly his injuries aren't severe if you stand here gabbing."

"The wound requires mending, and an elixir for pain and to prevent festering," Sir Everard said.

"Here." Rhianwyn passed Everard her satchel. "Since you apparently know what must be done, I won't be needed after all. I'll continue visiting with my friends."

"No." Everard put his hands up. "I'm only guessing. I'm no healer. Tyree wouldn't want my hands on him."

"You're suggesting he'd want Maiden Albray's hands on him?" Sir Cassian asked, his body tensing.

"He's a man," Sir Severin said. "Of course he'd like her hands on him, but we'll be there to ensure there's no liberties taken."

"If he attempted anything untoward, I'd see to it he'd be needing further healing," Rhianwyn declared and Cassian smiled.

"I'll see you next market day." Rhianwyn looked at Selena and Elspeth.

Elspeth frowned. Selena only nodded and waved. Rhianwyn didn't miss how Selena stared at both Cassian and Everard. Selena *was* expected to remain virginal. Shandy, the brothel owner, had ambitious intentions of having Selena's first time with a man prove most worthwhile. Apparently many who regularly frequented the house, as well as several other men in the village and countryside, were vying for the right to be the first with Selena and willing to pay a handsome price.

Thankfully that's what had kept Selena from already being with men for coin. She was becoming more beautiful. Her petite, slender, late-to-mature body, had recently blossomed. Combined with her lovely curly auburn hair, fair skin, and pretty green eyes, she'd begun to turn heads.

Rhianwyn intended to meet with Shandy and Fleta, her more genial sister, on Selena's behalf. Selena was easily frightened and believed she had no other option but to become a harlot. She was mostly kept in the brothel, but with strict expectations to keep clear of men. Rhianwyn wondered why Shandy permitted her to attend the markets, but Aldrich, Shandy's hired enforcer often followed Selena. Shandy might purposely want Selena seen about the village to be viewed by men. She always wore a form-fitted gown and had her hair fashioned prettily.

Although inexperienced, Selena had begun to notice men lately. Elspeth claimed after the initial coupling, Selena likely wouldn't be opposed. She said it was probably in Selena's blood to want to lie with many men...like her mother. Rhianwyn believed it was only innate urges found in all people.

Mererid had certainly been correct about that. No matter how much Rhianwyn feared carrying a child...the fact remained, those primal surging physical desires were very real. Sometimes heated lust coursed through her in a way the church and the priests would much oppose. Even men weren't to openly admit to desires of the flesh. However men's base needs *were* accepted. There was even the absurd belief if a man didn't release his seed regularly he might become gravely ill—perhaps die. Therefore priests ignored it when men—even married men, lay with harlots, defiled young women, or committed adultery.

Women always bore the blame of men's misdeeds. Wives were criticized for not seeing adequately to their husband's needs. Harlots were unfairly shunned and not the married men who frequented the brothels. Rhianwyn deeply resented the inequitable injustices toward women in regard to physical need.

She fully recognized her own persistent needs and the restlessness that accompanied those longings. Cassian glanced at her now and her cheeks colored. She turned away—too quickly.

"I haven't seen William recently," Cassian said.

Rhianwyn only shrugged. Cassian obviously wanted to speak further but not with others there. She didn't trust herself to be alone with him for she was very much attract-ed to him. She also wouldn't tell Cassian or even her friends that her father hadn't been home for weeks. It wasn't uncommon for William to go off perhaps on one of his magical quests...but he'd never been away this long. She feared something untoward might've happened. Therefore she must pretend he remained at their cottage or she'd definitely be forced to marry. Women weren't permitted to live alone. Even elderly widows were forced to remarry. If no one wanted to wed them they were heartless-ly turned out of their homes to become beggars.

Loud singing interrupted her disparaging thoughts and Rhianwyn smiled. She hadn't seen the carefree minstrel, Keyon, for some time. He was noted for entertaining with his gems-horn, lute, and fine singing voice, but Rhianwyn also adored listening to tales of the various places he'd traveled. She envied his freedom to wander.

"Good afternoon, Keyon," she said on spotting him.

He grinned as he approached closer than most would dare considering she was accompanied by three large, fierce-looking knights. If they hadn't been there he would've affectionately embraced her.

"Maiden Albray, I've missed your lovely face. I see you have your own order of knights, including the Grand Cross and his Knight Commander," Keyon bowed to Severin and Cassian in turn.

"Where have your journeys and adventures taken you this time, Keyon?" Rhianwyn asked excitedly.

"Only East Wessex. What've you been up to these weeks, Maiden Albray? Tell me you haven't wed."

"I haven't…nor do I plan to," she steadfastly replied.

"You're determined you won't wed a knight, have turned down the smith's son, even the hound handler and the head groom when you're notably fond of dogs and horses; perhaps you might marry a minstrel? I promise I'd sing to you milady and take you on my many journeys."

"That's tempting, Keyon." She looked at the man's long unkempt red hair, shaggy beard, ragged garments, and peculiar perpetually darting eyes. "But I admit I'm not fond of beards and prefer to have a home no matter how delightful it would be to see other locations."

"I'd shave my beard today—my head, too, if I thought there'd be a chance you'd be mine." He grinned.

They were only friends but by their conversation, the others wouldn't know.

"I'm perfectly content being a healer and daughter, Keyon. But thank you for your offer. I hope to hear you sing while you're in the village."

"I'll sing now if it pleases you." Keyon tapped his lute. "I even wrote a song for you."

"By Christ's cross, he's as smitten as most others," Sir Severin said.

"Maiden Albray's on her way to attend an injured knight," Everard explained. "She hasn't time for flighty singing."

"I'm not opposed to you singing while we walk," Rhianwyn replied and Everard cast her an unappreciative look.

The minstrel, slight of body and not of noticeable height especially standing near the brawny knights with their chain mail garments and immense knightly arming swords, smirked. He tossed his worn pack over his back, strummed his lute and began to sing.

> *"Pretty Rhianwyn, lovelier than any I've seen.*
> *Her beauty unrivaled by peasant or queen.*
> *Her soft light-brown tresses boast ribbons of gold.*
> *Eyes more enchanting than tales of old…*
> *Pale blue and breathtaking, 'tis hard to turn away*
> *And her skin is fairer than other young maids.*
> *Desired by men poor and noble, both far and near,*
> *Sadly this rare woman won't be endeared.*
> *The form of an angel, lips cherry red,*
> *Rhianwyn's sweet kiss would leave me happy should day's*
> *   end find me dead."*

"That's bloody awful." Cassian shook his head.

"That was lovely, Keyon." Rhianwyn scowled at Cassian. "Perhaps you might alter the ending for it was rather grim."

"That's not nearly the end. There's several more—"

"That's all I'll hear," Sir Cassian interrupted.

Keyon smirked at Rhianwyn.

As they walked on, the three knights' expressions and demeanors changed for they approached several men-in-arms, the sheriff's men. There was a long-standing feud between them. The knights were more deeply respected. Although the sheriff and his men were appointed to keep the village safe, the two groups were often at odds. The lines were blurred as to who protected what area.

The sheriff's men were to uphold laws, patrol the village and the county land. The knights protected the king, his daughter and the people of the kingdom and sometimes went off fighting in faraway lands and distant battles. The rivalry created unpleasant, dangerous encounters.

Because the knights frequently called on Rhianwyn to assist with injuries caused during training, she was often a target of ridicule by the men-at-arms. However, she'd caught the sheriff's nephew, Winston's eye. She didn't want his attention although he was far less offensive than his cousin, Godric, the sheriff's son who took pleasure in using his position of power over others. Godric had his consorts, Rupert and Fenwick carry out his unsavory wishes. All three were disrespectful with women.

Rhianwyn didn't want to consider how Cassian or even Everard and Severin would react if they found out Godric had once attacked her. He'd had Rupert and Fenwick hold her down while he lay atop her, speaking crudely. Though she'd struggled, they were strong and he was rough. He'd rubbed his scratchy beard against her face and inappropriately touched her—might have raped her if Maxim, the castle's huntsman hadn't come along. He'd thrown Godric off her and thoroughly beaten all three men.

Unfortunately, Maxim paid dearly when a large group of the sheriff's men jumped him. Maxim killed two in the skirmish but the lot of them assailed him so violently, he'd nearly died. Rhianwyn attended to his injuries; it took weeks for him to recover. Maxim insisted she never speak of what led to it maintaining her honor and reputation would be irreparably soiled. He was correct. Still, it infuriated her Godric had gotten away with his misdeed. Now

Maxim mostly avoided the village and Rhianwyn felt responsible.

"Taking your harlot to the knight's keep in the light of day?" Godric called and Cassian tensed.

"If you don't react, it'll disempower him, Sir Cassian." Rhianwyn noted his vexed expression.

"He cannot be permitted to speak of you like that," Cassian said.

"We want no trouble today, Godric," Sir Severin warned. "Maiden Albray's a healer to my men…nothing more."

"You let on that's why she's taken to your training field and your keep so regularly, but I presume differently," Godric replied. "I'd like to know if you all share her or if she only permits her favorites to have her?"

The two younger knights' hands went to their swords and Rhianwyn shook her head.

"Sometimes it takes a bigger man to walk away," she whispered. "I know his slanderous insults aren't true."

"He could make others believe there's truth to it," Everard said.

"Troublemakers will always spread lies and horse shit." Rhianwyn spoke a little louder this time, glaring at Godric.

"Leave her alone!" Winston said to Godric.

"I forgot, cousin, the pretty healer has you and your spindle in a constant rigid state. But she'll not look your way. You're not a knight, a huntsman or an Irishman. By accounts from the market today, she'll soon be giving her honey to the new Lord Brockwell. Apparently she's once again set her sights on becoming lady of Brockwell Manor.

She thinks herself above her station, a commoner born to a mad mage and a Welshland bitch!"

"At least Mam didn't *choose* to leave like your poor mother who couldn't face the despicable vulgarian she brought into the world," Rhianwyn hissed and the stockily built man with the short black hair and beard stepped forward.

"Don't speak of my mother!" He unsheathed his sword. "Or I'll cut out your bitter bleating tongue."

"You started it by insulting *my* mother." Rhianwyn knew she should simply ignore him as she'd advised the knights.

All three knights unsheathed their swords, too.

"If any harm should come to Maiden Albray by you, any of the sheriff's men, or your two damn henchmen, Godric Percival, you'll meet my sword or that of another of the king's knights." Sir Severin's weathered face was stern.

"You wouldn't be able to prove it was me who harmed her. It could be that deranged huntsman or the strapping, tall Irishman. Some say he has a less than commendable past."

"That would be like the wolf calling the lamb guilty," Rhianwyn said.

"Sheath your sword, Godric," Winston urged.

"It *is* a little too public here," Godric flagrantly replied returning his sword to its scabbard. Fenwick and Rupert followed, though clearly begrudgingly. The knights finally did so, too.

When a young man stepped from behind the group of sheriff's men, Cassian frowned.

"What are you doing with *them*?" he chastised his brother, Lucian.

"If you actually hope to be a knight one day, it'd be wise to stay clear of them," Sir Severin added.

"Are you listening, Short Stuff?" Everard taunted. "Use your head for once, *little* brother."

"Everard, that's unkind," Rhianwyn said, aware the youngest brother bemoaned his short stature, small frame, and the nickname Everard gave him.

"I don't need the daughter of the mad mage defending *me*," Lucian snarled.

"You'll need someone to defend you from me, brother," Cassian said. "If you don't show the lady some respect."

"She's not highborn so not a lady *yet*, Cassian." Lucian snapped. "Though she'll probably go to the Irishman's bed straightaway if it ensures her that title and a place in Brockwell Manor instead of the pitiful wee hovel she lives now. Maybe it wasn't Anslem she wanted but the hope of living in that immense manor house."

"Shut the hell up, Lucian," Cassian seethed.

"Better close your mouth, Short Stuff!" Everard said.

"Going to make me, Everard? Or maybe it'll be our eldest brother since he pines for her... his dead friend's betrothed. How honorable is that?"

"You'll never become a knight with that attitude," Cassian replied. "Nor if you hang about with that unconscionable lot." He gestured to the sheriff's men. "But if that's what you wish to aspire to, I'm sure Father would be proud of you for striving that high, little brother!"

Cassian used sarcasm which was uncommon.

Lucian was a squire, but didn't take his training seriously. A fever years earlier left him pale, often sickly, not nearly as powerful as other men in his family. Perhaps he knew he'd always be compared to his famous fallen father, Sir Roderick and his brothers who'd attained stellar reputations as knights. Maybe resentment caused his unpleasant attitude. Lucian scowled at his brothers and Rhianwyn.

"Go ahead, let the mad mage's daughter lead you around by your cocks." Lucian wore a mocking smile.

"Your father would be most displeased with you, young Lucian," Sir Severin said. "Someone who's always longed to be a knight shouldn't speak with little regard to a woman or his elder brothers. You could lose your position as squire and all hopes of achieving knighthood if I deem it so."

Lucian only sneered, spat on the ground disrespectfully, and walked away. Sir Severin's eyes darkened. He'd undoubtedly dismiss Lucian for that belligerence.

"We're nearly to the keep." Rhianwyn hoped to ease the tension. Everard and Cassian looked like they'd like to teach Lucian a lesson right then.

"I suppose this is as far as I'll be permitted," Keyon said.

Rhianwyn didn't favor leaving Keyon when the untrustworthy sheriff's men remained. They were given to bullying.

"Come in with us." Rhianwyn touched his arm.

"To the infamous knights' keep?" Keyon excitedly stared up at the foreboding stone tower ahead.

"You can't invite others to *our* keep," Everard said.

Rhianwyn frowned. Stopping on the uneven cobble-stones, she passed her satchel to Everard again.

"Then I won't be entering *your* keep, *Sir* Everard. This was Mam's satchel, therefore it's my most valued posses-sion. I request it returned to me later. I'll go back to the market. Come along, Keyon. I'm sure Elspeth and Selena will be glad to hear you sing, too." She stepped away from the knights and placed her arm through Keyon's.

"You'll not set off with that riled lot near." Sir Cassian looked at Godric and his men.

"We've no time for foolishness, lass. There's a man waiting for your healing," Sir Severin scolded.

"Am I being ordered to the knights' keep, where typi-cally no women other than harlots are permitted?" Rhianwyn stared up at him.

"As a healer you're sworn to assist." Sir Severin's jaw tightened.

"I'm not recognized as a healer by the king or his physi-cian."

"You are by the knights and the people," Sir Cassian said.

She sighed loudly but nodded.

"Was it nonsense then, what was said of you and the Irishman?" Everard asked as they walked on.

"I heard you had a lengthy encounter with the new Lord Brockwell today," Keyon said.

"With Broccan Mulryan?" Cassian looked more intent-ly at her.

"However did you hear that?" Rhianwyn asked the minstrel.

"Word travels quickly on market days," Keyon said.

"What kind of encounter?" Cassian pressed.

"It was nothing. His horse was agitated. I calmed him so he didn't injure a child. Lord Brockwell rudely demanded I keep away from his steed."

"So your first impression of him wasn't positive?" Cassian sounded pleased.

"He's obviously full of himself."

"It's said he has his sights set on you now," Keyon said.

"There's not a damn word of truth to that," Rhianwyn argued as they approached the castle's keep. "We've only just met."

"I'd like to know what you heard, minstrel." Cassian nudged Keyon.

"Since I can't invite Keyon to the keep, he couldn't possibly continue speaking," Rhianwyn said.

"Come up with us then," Cassian agreed.

CHAPTER FIVE

IN THE LARGE open tower chamber, two new knights stared at Rhianwyn. Another blatantly looked her up and down and whistled.

"Is this woman to be our night's pleasure? She's a beauty, but doesn't look like a harlot," he said.

"This is Maiden Albray, an accomplished healer," Everard explained.

"Don't gawk at her like that!" Cassian ordered. "She's as fine a healer as anyone would wish to have attend to them."

"Fine...very fine, indeed." One knight gazed at her.

"I'd be happy to have her *attend* to me," another said and Cassian bristled.

"I'd not vex her," Sir Severin warned. "If you wish for her to see to your injuries in the future, you'll want to be on her good side. The castle physician's a drunkard, his apprentice an imbecile. The healer Marlow's nearly blind, and the ancient woman healer wouldn't touch a man with a jousting pole. Therefore, don't infuriate Maiden Albray. She also knows how to wound someone as aptly as heal them."

Rhianwyn respected Sir Severin. He was stern with pages and squires, expected perfection from his knights. He permitted no disobedience or discourtesy. Knights were to be honorable. He abided harlots being brought to the knights' keep insisting none meet rough treatment and ensured the knights rewarded them well for their services. Severin reasoned it was better than the knights easing their frustrations with drink, being disorderly in the village, possibly fighting or ending up at the house of harlots sating their base needs anyway.

"Who's injured?" Rhianwyn asked.

A stocky man shakily raised his hand, then belched, reeking of ale.

"Who gave him drink?" Rhianwyn accused.

"He helped himself," Ulf, a Norsemen, once a Viking raider but now a respected knight, said.

"Tell me your name?" She nodded to the wounded man.

"I'm Tyree," he replied weakly.

"You're from Cornouia," she said, intrigued.

"How did you know?" Tyree asked.

"Because you sound like you're from another bloody world," Everard joked.

"Those from Celtic lands have a similar way of speaking. My mother was from Cymru," Rhianwyn said.

"Now that *is* another world." Another knight laughed.

"Where's the wound?" Rhianwyn asked.

Tyree turned. She felt her eyes widen on seeing the small battle-ax lodged near his shoulder.

"You might've told me how serious this was!" She looked disapprovingly at the men who'd fetched her.

"Did you think we'd seek you out if it wasn't urgent?"

Sir Cassian questioned.

"Since when do you train with axes?" She'd spent time watching the knights train but never with axes.

"That was my suggestion," Ulf sheepishly said, but smiled at Rhianwyn for they'd been friends since she healed him from a sword's wound.

"No wonder you wanted drink." Rhianwyn nodded to Tyree. "It was wise you left the weapon where it is. But now… Tyree must be placed on a table in a lighted area."

Several men carried a table to the window.

"His garments must be cut away," Rhianwyn said.

Cassian sliced the chain mail garment and tunic and three men helped Tyree lie face-down on the table.

"I'll need rags to stop the bleeding once the weapon's removed. Here, drink this. Ingesting it will make you sleep for some time when combined with ale, but if you don't, the pain will be torturous."

He only nodded. She passed the vial of remedy and he drank. Rhianwyn removed her worn cloak and draped it over a chair. Her threadbare light-brown kirtle, was thrice patched. The close-fitting bodice emphasized her full breasts though she diligently attempted to dissuade men's attention. She always tied her hair loosely and tucked it inside her tunic instead of attractively fashioning it. Men were typically drawn to a woman's hair and breasts.

Some new knights whistled again. This time Cassian angrily removed his sword.

"Perhaps the lot of you barbarians didn't hear. Maiden Albray's to be shown as much respect as your mothers. Once promised to the bravest and best of our fallen brothers, she'll be treated perhaps as a younger sister—protected and…"

"If I looked at my sister like you look at her, my father'd have my damn ballocks," Sir Hamish, a Scot, interrupted.

Cassian's body tensed. If he didn't calm down, she'd be dealing with another wound. He was slow to anger, but when infuriated, Cassian was dangerous. She glanced at Sir Severin. He knowingly nodded.

"There's no need for us all to remain here. We'll permit our healer to do what she must. Ulf and Aleric stay behind; hold Tyree down if required. The rest of you go eat your supper."

"It's a bit early." Everard looked out the arched window at the sun's position.

"Then go have ale…just get the hell out of here and let Healer Albray work," Severin said in a terse tone seldom required. "We'll have the minstrel come entertain us."

Keyon smiled widely at that.

"Do you need anything else?" Cassian clearly didn't want to leave her.

"Only something to better tie back my hair," Rhianwyn said.

Cassian passed her a leather strand taken from his own dark-blond plait. She nodded appreciatively and he and the others left.

IT TOOK SOME time to remove the weapon, stop the

bleeding, and mend the wound. Rhianwyn placed a remedy and bandages upon it and Tyree slept restfully.

The sun had begun to set. She must go to her cottage without delay. At one time, she hadn't feared walking alone in the woods even after dark. But she'd seen the way far too many men looked at her…and after what occurred with Godric, she was more cautious.

"Come eat with us." Ulf touched her arm. "You've earned your supper, Maiden Albray."

"I'm probably not permitted in the knight's dining hall."

"Who'd stop you?" Ulf replied.

"Those new to the order might. Knights like to behave unmannerly when in their keep, not as Sir Severin expects when I'm in their presence. Besides, if there are harlots here, I'd rather not witness what might be occurring…no matter how open some are with sarding in the presence of others."

Ulf smirked at her using the crude term for sexual relations. "It's nearly dark. You can't walk unattended."

"Keyon could walk with me although by the sound of it he's busy entertaining the knights."

"How would the minstrel protect you," Sir Cassian asked approaching them, "hit an offender with his lute?"

"Perhaps." She was unable to prevent a smile.

"You should eat something. You look weary and pale," Cassian said.

"I've been trying to convince her to sup with us, but she believes she'd not be accepted in the hall," Ulf explained.

"I wouldn't recommend that when a good many men have partaken in too much drink. I'll fetch food and sit with you while you eat in the courtyard," Sir Cassian suggested, looking hopeful she'd agree.

"I have broth at home," she replied.

"There's very little food there," Cassian argued.

"You went into my home—not only took my satchel but snooped about to see if I have food? I disapprove of that. I've a garden with ample vegetables. I fish and the huntsman leaves me rabbits when he's near."

"You shouldn't be in contact with him, Maiden Albray," Ulf said. "He's believed to be dangersome. Unusually tall and powerful, he could easily harm you if he took a notion."

"He's gentle with those who don't threaten or rile him," Rhianwyn said. "He even gave me my knife."

Cassian shook his head disapprovingly. "You'll one day trust the wrong person, Rhianwyn. You're also well aware women aren't to carry weapons."

"I need a knife for cutting vegetables and herbs... and during my healing," she argued. "Do you propose I bite the thread with my teeth when mending a wound?"

Cassian looked at her more desirously even with Ulf there. She thought he might reach out to touch her face or hair. Ulf and Cassian were good friends. Cassian might've confided his feelings for Rhianwyn...or told him *more*.

"I need to see you." Cassian stepped closer.

She looked up into his light-brown eyes and shook her head.

"I must be leaving, though I'll need to borrow a lantern. I didn't intend to be away this long. Let me know if Tyree requires further attention. I've left a remedy to be given tomorrow in two lots."

"You can't walk home alone." Cassian grasped her hand.

"You should find a woman," she whispered. "Maybe you wouldn't be so concerned about *my* well-being."

"Anslem was my best friend and you're his betrothed. I'll *always* look out for you."

"I *was* his betrothed. He's been gone three long years. You don't need to watch out for me any longer."

"Until you're wed, it remains my duty. Anslem asked that I see you protected."

Sir Severin interrupted their conversation when he approached carrying a delicious-smelling pheasant's breast.

"Here Maiden Albray, take this for your services. I'll walk you home on the way to my cottage."

"That's out of your way. I'm sure Mabel would like you to return straightaway since you've so little time together."

"We've had twenty years together. Most days she'd likely be pleased if I stayed in the keep with the unmarried knights."

Rhianwyn smiled knowing Sir Severin and his wife, Mabel were happily wed.

"I could walk Rhianwyn home," Keyon said, now joining them.

"I'll do it, lad." Severin shook his head.

"I'd see no harm come to her," Keyon argued.

Ulf smiled. "At least *you're* mostly harmless."

"Any man with a spindle isn't completely harmless to a

woman's honor or reputation." Sir Severin's bushy eyebrows knitted.

"Are you not a man then, Sir Severin?" Keyon dared to ask.

"I am, but sworn to one woman. I take my marriage oath as seriously as that of my knighthood. To be honest, I'd rather cross any man no matter his skill or fierceness than my lady should I do anything dishonorable with another woman."

Rhianwyn smiled. She respected Sir Severin's commitment to his marriage.

"Thank you for your healing services." Sir Cassian nodded respectfully to Rhianwyn. "And stay away from that Irishman."

Rhianwyn looked curiously at Cassian in seeing his seriousness.

"Good night," Ulf added as the two younger knights started toward the hall, although Cassian glanced back several times.

"Would you like to walk with us, minstrel?" Sir Severin pointed to him.

"Indeed I would," Keyon happily replied.

"Where will you sleep?" Rhianwyn asked.

"I'll find a stable or barn," Keyon replied good-naturedly as they descended the winding stone stairs and stepped out into the open courtyard.

Thankfully there was no sign of Godric and the others. The sun was sinking low—the sky splashed with crimson and purple. They walked down the narrow cobblestone streets Rhianwyn adored. She'd memorized every stone for she'd lived here her whole life. They went through the village square, empty now with the market closed. Only a few people were about.

Rhianwyn glanced up at the towering wood-framed shops, most with living quarters above them that jutted out well above the road. The street was so narrow in many places only a horse and small cart could pass. Larger wagons had become lodged trying to get through.

They passed small stone-and-wood cottages, all with thatched roofs. Smoke curled from chimneys and the smell of wood smoke appealed to Rhianwyn.

"I'll leave you then." Keyon headed toward an open stable. "Thanks for permitting me to entertain your knights, Sir Severin. It was nice to see you, Maiden Albray. I hope we'll meet again before I move on. Unless the king should call for me to entertain him, then I'll linger."

"Good night, Keyon," Rhianwyn said. "One day you'll catch the king's attention and he'll recognize your talent. If you'd like rabbit stew, stop by Father's cottage. You could sing and play for me again."

"Tomorrow?" His eyes lit up.

"The day after. I expect the huntsman to deliver a rabbit or two by then."

"I'd like that." Keyon merrily skipped toward the stables, whistling.

Sir Severin looked at her with disapproval. He carried an enclosed candle as they strode in silence for some time through the forest that darkened as they walked deeper into the woods.

"What is it? Speak plainly, Sir Severin."

"Though I've never had a daughter to worry of or offer guidance, I feel I must speak."

"I'd like that."

"I think you'll not like what I have to say." He frowned.

"Tell me what's on your mind."

"Apparently you don't know the powerful effect you have on men, Rhianwyn." He'd never used her given name; she straightened on hearing it.

"Your beauty's rare, that's true enough. But there's something more about you beyond your lovely face and fine womanly form. Your mother was like that; men were drawn to her, too. I'm not too old to recognize when a man hungers for a woman, and you've many who want you. Some mightn't ever act upon those desires…others would be less honorable. The sheriff's son isn't to be trusted in that regard. Others closer to me are driven nearly to madness with need for you."

"I don't encourage men," Rhianwyn argued.

"You've just invited the young minstrel to your cottage. You apparently engaged in a lengthy conversation with Broccan Mulryan today. Women readily fall for his good looks and Irish charm. You permit the huntsman to deliver his game. Some say he's not sound after that beating. He's a physically powerful man. Though you believe him to be trustworthy, how would you defend yourself if he proved otherwise? That knife you possess would barely faze him. He's as big and strong as a damn ox."

"Keyon's a dear friend. The conversation with Lord Brockwell wasn't lengthy. I'll not be falling for his charm regardless of his appearance... and Maxim's a principled man, protective of women. He's so shy he'll barely look at me. In truth, he suffered that beating defending *me*... but he's completely sound and I don't permit men inside the cottage."

"Cassian hasn't entered your cottage when you were present?"

"Not without Father there."

"But he did," Severin cleared his throat uneasily, "have his way with you without your objection?"

Rhianwyn felt her face flame. She was dumbstruck he was aware of it.

"I wasn't born yesterday, lass. I notice the looks you two exchange and see he burns for you though he's riddled with guilt because of it. You must agree to be with him in an honorable wedded union... or end what the two of you've been up to. Tell him you'll never share more than friendship."

"I *have* told him that. I...we... I haven't been alone with him in m-months," she stammered.

"Unless you marry another, he'll never stop hoping you'll change your mind, though guilt haunts him in having his dearest friend's woman."

"Anslem's dead. I'm no longer his!"

"Yet you won't agree to be Cassian's woman either— not in a decent manner, only as illicit lovers."

"I told you that hasn't happened in months. How did you know about it?" she whispered.

"He can't keep his eyes off you and recently you'll barely look at him. Do you love him?"

"I care for Cassian but it's not love. I admit I yearned for him as a woman does for a man. Think of me what you will for confessing that."

"I don't judge you, lass. Women have longings, too. But you must sever ties with Cassian. His mind's not where it should be. It never will be as long as he hopes you might wed him or return to sharing intimacies. It's a dangerous thing for a knight to be so distracted."

Rhianwyn inhaled deeply. "I'd never wish to put Cassian at risk but I don't want to marry...especially not a knight. He knows that."

"When the king's priest or advisors realize you're living alone you *will* be ordered to marry."

"I'm not alone. I..."

"Don't try to pull the wool over my eyes, lass. Your father comes and goes as he pleases and mightn't be a typical protective father, but he visits me on occasion to share ale and conversation. I haven't seen him for weeks. How long has he been gone this time?"

"Past two moons," she reluctantly admitted.

"Christ, lass. It's a perilous thing to be living alone deep in the woods with no man to protect you."

"Do you believe my gentle, often eccentric father could protect me? In truth, lately he's gone even when he's here."

"Still... knowing a man's at home does deter those with less than virtuous intentions."

"I bolt the door," she insisted.

"How long would a bolt or shuttered windows last if a powerful, determined man was intent on getting to you? This cottage, put together with only straw, sticks, and mud, was never sturdy; now it's sorely dilapidated. A strong man could break through without difficulty. It'd be tinder in no time should someone light it afire to force you out."

"Surely no one would stoop that low," Rhianwyn whispered. "I don't require a husband and won't be forced to wed simply because I'm alone."

"It is the king's law." Sir Severin sounded stern.

"No one knows I'm alone, so the king shan't ever learn of it."

"And when he summons your father?"

"I'll tell the king he's off on another of his quests…and pray Father will soon return."

"Should you be attacked and obscenely violated, even if you're not gravely injured, you'd lose suitable prospects for a husband. Pick a man. You could have any number. Cassian would give much to wed you. As would Everard, though that'd cause a division between the brothers you'd not want to create."

"If I were a man, I could remain unmarried all my life if I chose."

"It'd be a lonely life."

"Worse than spending my life with someone I didn't love?"

"I'll afford you one moon. If your father hasn't returned and you've not accepted a proposal, I'll have no choice but to inform the king's advisors."

"That's not fair," Rhianwyn said. "I told you in confidence of my father's absence."

"If my most valued knight should lose his nerve or his head along with his heart that would aggrieve me more. I already lost my other best knight…"

"Because of me," she whispered. "Go ahead, say it."

"In truth, Anslem Brockwell never would've become a knight if not for you. He'd have been Lord Brockwell, lived a noble life he inwardly loathed. Giles Brockwell would never agree to the daughter of a mage, mad or not, marrying his only son. Still, Anslem couldn't forgive his father for denying him that."

"I couldn't see Anslem forever parted from his father, his home, and his birthright. I wouldn't go away with him as he wanted and leave my father alone…often in a muddled state. Yet, Anslem refused to return to Brockwell Manor after his father spoke so cruelly to me. He became a knight instead… perhaps to spite Giles."

The discord of that time still brought pain though it was over three years ago. When Rhianwyn wouldn't run off with him, Anslem trained to be a knight and quickly excelled. Once knighted, he again asked her to wed him. Still, she declined, believing he'd one day resent her.

"If Anslem could've simply lived with your refusal, he wouldn't have requested to go off and fight in another land."

Rhianwyn began to weep. Sir Severin took her in his arms in a fatherly embrace.

"By the time I told Anslem I *would* marry him, he'd already committed to fight in France."

"It grieved him to leave you."

"As it grieved me to see him go," she whispered with a sob.

"Find a man to share your life. You're too special to be

alone."

"I'd rather be alone than risk being hurt again. That's why I've vowed I'll never marry a knight; they seldom live a long life."

"Life is full of risks. I suspect you fear carrying a child and dying as your mother did?"

"Not just my mother—many women," Rhianwyn said.

"My wife would've given anything to bear a child. We weren't so blessed."

"Sir Severin, if your Mabel *had* carried your babe but died bringing that child into the world, what would that've done to you and perhaps the other children she might've previously bore who'd be left motherless?"

He cleared his throat and released her from his comforting embrace.

"As much as it wounds her never experiencing motherhood, I thank the Lord she's still with me."

Rhianwyn nodded.

"You risked such a fate when you lay with Anslem and Cassian?" Sir Severin said.

She shook her head. "I never shared physical intimacies with Anslem. I admit I went to him with such intentions before he left. He not only refused, he seemed sorely vexed for we hadn't even shared a kiss. He told me he wouldn't be with me—hastily sent me away with a torment in his eyes and a coldness that still saddens and perplexes me. Then he left without a farewell."

"I'm sorry that's your last memory of Anslem," Severin replied, "but you did risk carrying Cassian's child."

She frowned, looked away but spoke the truth.

"I was with him… perhaps a dozen times. Eventually I *did* conceive. As soon as I knew I carried a child, I drank a potent elixir causing me to miscarry, then I ended it with Cassian. He doesn't know."

"That truth would gut him." Sir Severin shook his head worriedly. "I believe he loves you—that he had his heart set on you even before you fell for Anslem. You think so little of Cassian you'd easily rid yourself of his child?"

"That's not true. It wasn't easy. It grieved me much. But I don't love him. I wouldn't have married him, then risked my life giving birth when he leads such a dangerous life, it might well have left the child orphaned. I've heard of too many wee ones left to fend for themselves, parentless children abused or sold by slavers like livestock… often to meet a crueler fate than slaughter."

"I don't mean to sound unfeeling, lass."

"Go home, Sir Severin." She sniffled.

"One moon, lass—pick a husband for you'll surely be forced to wed someone."

"If this *husband* doesn't permit me to continue with my healing as most would not…who will you turn to tend to your knights' injuries?"

"I wish to Christ I knew. Best you find a man who holds knights in high esteem…someone like a knight."

"I'll not have my heart broken, twice, Sir Severin."

"Bolt that door," he said as he left.

CHAPTER SIX

B ROCCAN INHALED THE fresh morning air. The sun hadn't risen but he'd slept poorly and needed to walk to clear his thoughts. He couldn't take his mind off the spirited young healer he'd met yesterday. He'd known she was lovely. He'd heard more than one person speak of that. Still, he hadn't expected her to be astonishingly beautiful and her unusual blue eyes—he'd never seen anyone with eyes like that. He'd found himself unable to look away. Surely she was accustomed to men staring.

She was also uncommonly feisty. She'd probably be notably passionate in a bed, too. He dare not permit himself to linger on that thought for his bed had been too long empty.

"I told you she was beautiful!"

The voice startled Broccan and he jumped. He turned to look at the spirit of his friend, Anslem, who'd been coming to him for months now. He'd given him no peace until he agreed to journey to Wessex to seek out the woman he'd loved and to meet his father.

"You can't keep appearin' to me like that with no warnin', Anslem!"

"Clearly I can," the spirit declared. "I see you're already smitten with her."

"I'm not smitten," Broccan replied.

"So she hasn't been on your mind since you met her?"

"A wee bit, yes," Broccan admitted. "It'd be easier if you'd finally tell me what happened between you that left you so tortured. It must've been devastating to leave her behind when you went to fight in France, but I sense there's more to it."

"You'll learn the truth eventually." For the first time Anslem's spirit looked downtrodden. "Spend time with her. You're sure to lose your heart and want to take her as your wife and to your bed."

"Christ, how can you speak so casually about that when you loved her?"

"She's lonely. She needs a husband and lover. It must be you," the spirit said.

"I'm not certain I ever want to marry and I won't commit to living in Wessex forever," Broccan said.

"You'd prefer to go back to your previous life…avoiding your father, drinking, fighting, being paid to track down cutthroats and murderers and killing them?"

"I was a champion fighter who attained much glory in besting others before I began earning substantial coin in finding murderous outlaws. I was damn good at it."

"That's what made you such a valuable knight. When Severin saw your skill with a sword and bow, he eagerly commissioned you," Anslem said.

"There's much I regret about that," Broccan replied. "But I did appreciate getting to know you and striking up our friendship."

"As did I, but now will you do what I ask, my friend?"

the spirit asked.

"Your father's a difficult man. Spending time with him is a challenge."

"You don't have to tell me. I regret you need to do that." Anslem nodded. "But Rhianwyn must be cared for. Once you get to know her, you'll fall in love with her. I'd wager much."

"By God's nails, love isn't something I wish for."

"Maybe not, but mark my words, you will. However, you'll have to make a better impression on Rhianwyn than you did yesterday," Anslem chided, walking companionably with Broccan as though he were flesh and bone and not a vaporous spirit.

"If you honestly expect me to charm her and perhaps... more, you'd best not hang about or that'd throw me off completely," Broccan said. "How could I take her to my bed if I knew you were nearby?"

"I won't be present when you begin to fall for one another; that I promise," the spirit replied, vanishing even now.

Broccan was accustomed to this nearly unbelievable happening of speaking with Anslem's spirit. However, the first time he came to him he believed he'd overdrank or was losing his mind.

Broccan's thoughts went back to the young healer. He *hadn't* made a good impression but hoped to remedy that. He had to see her again not only to persuade her to speak with Giles Brockwell as the ornery old man constantly insisted; not only to fulfill a promise to a dying friend, but also because Anslem was correct, Broccan couldn't stop thinking about her. She probably had that effect on most men, but he fully admitted he hadn't been attracted to woman like this in some time. Knowing she'd been Anslem's betrothed didn't even squelch that.

Broccan walked at a fast past. He hadn't taken the dogs. They'd be rambunctious early morning—likely bark at rabbits or deer. They were well-trained, but he certainly didn't want to disturb young Maiden Albray from her sleep and further disenchant her. How would he conceal his attraction to her?

"*Rhianwyn*," he said the name aloud. It had a beautiful sound to it and matched her uncommon beauty.

She said her cottage was on the edge of Brockwell land. He'd taken Dubh for a long ride yesterday, looked at the stone cottages along the boundary of the estate. Some homes had women working outside or a family present; others had children's garments hanging on lines. The only area he hadn't covered was the forest. She and her father must live there.

Broccan trudged through the dark woods. He found himself hoping she didn't live here. She had such a brilliance to her. She shone brighter than anyone he'd ever met and shouldn't be found in a dreary forest. He espied a very small cottage, a hut really, in obvious disrepair. The thatched roof was nearly bare in places. No smoke rose from the chimney. By the state of the derelict structure there mightn't be a usable hearth within.

He looked at the area outside where fires were created. A small battered kettle hung on an iron hook and a larger one sat upon the ground. Perhaps this wasn't where she lived. Maybe it was an old man living in such squalor. Yet there was a well-attended garden with vegetables and herbs, even flowers. Broccan walked closer. He was nearly to the home when the door opened. He leapt behind a tree attempting to conceal himself.

It *was* the lovely Rhianwyn who stepped from within. The rising sun shone through the trees, lighting the small clearing. It fell upon her and he was mesmerized by her beauty. Her hair was unbound and cascaded to her waist— lovely light-brown tresses with strands of gold further highlighted by the sun's rays.

She was garbed only in a sheer shift. She shivered in the early morning freshness, stretched, and smiled up at the sun. Stepping to the side of the cottage, she tugged up the bottom of her garment and squatted giving him a clear view of her lovely arse. He noted a red mark. He wasn't close enough to determine, but it didn't seem like a birthmark—almost appeared as though it was a purposed-placed image like Vikings tended to bear.

Broccan stood stock still, trying to remain unnoticed especially since he'd gazed at her for a time, but his footing wasn't sound; a twig snapped beneath his boot. Her head shot up and he saw certain fear in her eyes. When she spotted him, she looked slightly perturbed, but there was also notable relief in seeing it was him.

RHIANWYN HAD BEEN distracted, her mind unsettled. She'd barely slept thinking of all her many concerns and worrying of her father. The peculiar fortune teller from the market and what she'd said, also plagued her thoughts, though she knew not why. Rhianwyn didn't even look around to see if anyone was about. Instead she was absent-mindedly relieving herself when she heard something. She prayed it was only a squirrel or deer. Her heart raced for it could be anyone…even Godric. She looked up to see Lord Brockwell. She felt her cheeks color but inwardly was soothed. Although she didn't know him, had even heard rumors of his colorful past, she didn't believe he'd harm her.

"You might at least turn around," she rebuked.

He cleared his throat uncomfortably but looked away.

"I was out walking. You said your cottage was on Brockwell land; I decided to see where you might reside," he explained.

She finished what she was doing, wiped herself with moss, then straightened her shift.

"Well, now you've found our cottage, what is it you want?" she asked.

She reached inside the cottage door and procured her woolen crossover shawl then tied it at the back. She located an iron strike-a-light, walked to the charred circle, struck the object against the flint to start the fire, then added wood from the dwindling pile.

"You don't have a hearth inside?" he asked.

"It's not been used in a long while."

She saw him look at her meager cottage, the size and the state of it. He surely pitied her.

"Your father's still sleeping?" Broccan asked.

"He…left just moments ago," she replied, lying through her teeth.

"Your wood supply isn't large. Would you let me chop some for you?"

"I'm usually capable but I wrenched my elbow. The ax is large and heavy. My father's been wholly occupied lately, but he'll surely replenish the supply when he returns tonight. Besides, I'm certain you have important *lordly* things to do," she said.

He laughed at that and she grinned, liking the sound of his laugh.

"And what might those be?" he asked.

"I'm not even a noble lady much less a lord. I'm sure I don't know the duties of a lord. Perhaps consuming great quantities of abundant food and drink, counting your worthy coin, calculating your ledgers, sternly ordering your many servants about, riding your extensive lands reveling in all you own, finding a noble lady to marry so she'll warm your bed and provide you with numerous sons."

"You do amuse me, Maiden Albray." He removed his overcoat and tossed it upon the ground.

She stared at his broad chest and shoulders. He picked up the weighty ax and swung it with ease. She found herself wishing he'd remove his tunic, too, for seeing his muscular chest would undoubtedly be most agreeable. That thought fully fascinated her. She looked away, her cheeks warm in seeing his muscularity. He was easily accomplishing what would've taken her an age, reinjured her elbow, and caused several blisters.

"What food will you prepare to break fast?" he asked as

he worked.

"Are you inviting yourself to my table?"

He smiled again that damn beguiling smile; it caused a heat within her as much as watching him at work.

"Not unless you'd be inclined to invite me."

"I drink a concoction in the morning consisting of beneficial herbs placed in boiled water—a medicinal tea of sorts. If you'd like to join me in return for chopping the wood, I wouldn't object if you leave soon after."

"You have plans this morning then?" Broccan asked.

"Becoming attired would be first."

"I don't find it necessary for I'm quite likin' the look of you just now," he jested staring at her bare feet and nearly see-through shift that fell just below her knees.

"You're a very forward man, Lord Brockwell. Does such brash talk make women clamor to your bed?"

"You do seem most interested in my bed. You've twice mentioned it this mornin' and the mornin's barely broken."

Her cheeks flamed. Turning away, Rhianwyn procured the dried herbs and placed them in the kettle over the fire. She entered the cottage again, closed and bolted the door. Leaning against it, she inhaled several times for the man wholly unnerved her. She hurriedly donned her petticoats, longer shift, and rust-colored kirtle, tying it at the sides, placed a shawl over that, then pulled on stockings and boots. The chopping outside stopped and she heard footsteps.

"Maiden Albray, I apologize if I've affronted you," he said through the door. "It was in jocularity. I meant no disrespect."

Opening the door, she gazed up at him standing there looking fine and very tall. His tunic was partially opened, his chest glistening from his recent exertion. His appealing face wore an abashed expression. She lowered her head completely unhinged by her primal attraction to him.

"You didn't affront me. I've come to expect such talk from men."

"I suppose, but it doesn't excuse my behavior. Though in jest, sure it was inappropriate and..."

"Would you like the tea or not?" she asked.

"I would." He sounded stunned she'd still offer him tea.

"It mightn't be to your liking. Not everyone favors it. Elspeth says it's terribly bitter. Selena can barely stomach it. She gags, which is how she reacts to anything she doesn't like."

"You're makin' it sound quite appealin', sure you are," he joked again.

"If you add honey, it's lovely, but I've none...would you like a chair then?"

"I'll sit by the fire." He leaned against a log, looking quite at home.

She touched her hair, felt her eyes grow round and gasped.

"What is it?" he worriedly asked.

"I haven't tied back my hair. I seldom leave it unbound."

"You've the loveliest hair I've ever seen. The way the sunlight dances upon the golden strands..."

"Maybe you should go," she said.

"Because I've spoken of your beautiful tresses?"

"I won't fall for your Irish charm. If you compliment me in hope to besot me so I'll permit you to bed me, you can stop straightaway."

"That wasn't my intent. In future I'll remember you don't react well to praise." He fought a frown as she passed him a cup of steaming liquid.

She knotted her hair, tucked it inside her garments, then sat on the other side of the fire with her tea. She tried not to look at him which was obviously impossible and probably more conspicuous that she was, indeed, enamored by his worthy frame and ruggedly appealing face.

"What do you think of it?" she asked when they'd sat in silence for a time.

"It's not unpleasant though the scent's a bit pungent. It wouldn't fill my empty stomach. Is this truly all you eat each mornin'?"

"I don't require the quantity of food a stalwart man would to sustain me."

"What does your father eat then?" Broccan asked.

"He's slight...not powerfully built like you. He sometimes breaks fast at the village inn," she lied.

"I should likely be going. My dogs will need to be let out. I must feed them and my horses, too."

"You have dogs?" she asked, well interested. "You feed your animals yourself and don't have servants do it?"

"I've two Irish wolfhounds I brought with me when I journeyed here, along with Dubh and a mare. I take pleasure in feedin' and spendin' time with them. You like dogs as well as horses?"

"Very much," she said.

"You should have a dog then."

"I did once."

"If you had a dog you wouldn't need to be fearful on hearing something outside your home," he said.

"Dogs require feeding and…"

"You haven't much food?" he dared to ask.

"No common-born has plentiful food, Lord Brockwell."

"Yet your father spends coin eating at an inn?" he asked.

Damn, that's what she got for telling untruths. "Only occasionally," she said.

"How does your father obtain coin to provide for you?"

"He's a mage," she admitted.

"Truly?" He looked surprised.

She nodded. "He was once well-important to the king, but not lately."

"You go hungry because of that?"

"We have a garden." She pointed to the vegetables. "I fish, too. We don't go hungry and I make some coin from my healing."

"Does your father not hunt?"

"We only own the cottage not this land. My father made an arrangement with Giles Brockwell before I was born. We live here but special permission would need to be granted to hunt. My father must speak with Lord Brockwell annually to renew the agreement to remain living here."

"I'd gladly sign over this bit of land to him. It's not as though it's fit for planting. Your father can hunt on Brockwell land as he wishes. I'll come speak with him of those matters this very day."

"He'll probably be home late. Besides, the huntsman brings rabbits—even a stag on occasion. We had hens but a fox got them this spring."

"I can bring you game if you wish, maybe make a fox-proof coop for hens."

His concern was touching but Rhianwyn didn't want his pity or charity, much less have any more contact with him than necessary...not when her heart quickened and skin grew heated when he was near. She certainly didn't want to fall for him or into his bed.

"Thank you for your concern, but we'll manage. Now... I should soon be off. I've several people I'd like to check on this morning. One requires care for a wound, another for a broken bone."

"You take pride in your work as a healer?"

"I do." She smiled and he smiled back magnanimously.

"Thanks for the tea," Broccan said.

"Thank you for chopping wood." She was unable to prevent smiling at him yet again.

He had an unusually charismatic manner and it couldn't only be because he was so physically attractive or because of his charming Irish way of speaking.

"You're honestly opposed to meeting with Giles? It would likely only take a few moments. Then he'd stop houndin' me to ask you. I'd accompany you there and back and stay during the conversation to make certain he wasn't unkind if that's your worry."

"I'm sorry he hounds you so, but I'll not give him the satisfaction of going to him," she replied.

"It does sound important. I believe he may even wish to bequeath you something," Broccan said.

She shook her head. "I very much doubt that. He despises me. But if he does so out of guilt from past unpleasantness, tell him whatever he might bequeath to me can be given to hungry children or people in far greater need."

Broccan sighed. "That won't appease him."

"Perhaps he'll soon die and the hounding will finally be ended."

Broccan stared hard at her.

"You think me coldhearted?" she said.

"I only know a little of the history between you and Giles. It's not for me to judge. I know he can be a difficult man."

"Difficult, cruel, heartless, mean-spirited, quick-tempered, insultingly evil-tongued."

"I'm sorry you saw that side of him. I mostly see a regretful, broken old man, weary of body and soul."

"You should consider yourself fortunate," she said. "Now, I must go."

She took the cups to the cottage, found her healer's satchel and slung it over her shoulder.

"Might I walk you partway, at least through this forest? Do you suppose it's wise to walk alone?"

"I like the forest. You may walk with me if you feel the need to hang about with common-born."

"I don't permit a person's station in life or at birth to dictate that. I spend time with whomever I wish."

"You're not like any other nobles I've known, Lord Brockwell," she said.

"I wish you'd call me Broccan. I don't require a title from anyone bar my servants and that's only because it's expected."

"If I called you by your given name in the presence of other highborn, I could be flogged."

"By God's nails, that seems bloody harsh!"

He gently took her hand but she tensed.

"Have you been flogged? Did Giles have you flogged for your association with his son? Is that why you despise him so?"

"I've never been flogged. But pain and scars inflicted by others don't have to be caused by physical wounds."

"What can I do to take away some of your woes, Maiden Albray?"

"Why would my plight concern you?" she asked. "What do you hope to gain?"

"Must there be somethin' I'd gain?"

She only shrugged. "Again, I appreciate you chopping the wood, Lord Brockwell. Perhaps don't stray far from a privy today for the tea does tend to cleanse a person's constitution."

She smirked when his very blue eyes grew wide.

"You gave me a potion that'll make me shite...er...cause my bowels to liquefy?" he asked in disbelief.

She laughed earnestly at that and he chuckled, too.

"It doesn't *always* have that effect. I'm only warning you it could."

"You're not like any woman I've ever met, Rhianwyn Albray. I'd like you to come meet my dogs and my other horse. Perhaps we could go ridin' one day for I'd very much like to keep your company." He didn't wait for a reply as he started toward Brockwell Manor.

CHAPTER SEVEN

A FTER SPENDING THE entire day seeing several people in need of healing, including the knight, Tyree, Rhianwyn returned to her cottage. She washed and peeled vegetables to make soup. She was kneeling on the ground, procuring herbs to add when she heard someone approach. She started and looked to see Lord Brockwell again.

"Do you wish to give me such a fright you'll stop my heart?"

"I'd rather the sight of me made your heart beat fast," he said.

She shook her head, even rolled her eyes at his audacity. "You're the boldest man I've ever met and clearly vain if you think the sight of you affects me or my heart in any way."

"The sight of you gladdens my heart," he replied.

"You've a silky tongue that's surely gotten you into vexation before." Still she smiled, then inwardly chided herself.

"Perhaps a wee bit," he admitted crouching beside her and smiling, too. "What are you doin' now?"

"Collecting herbs to flavor the broth."

"Speakin' of which, I brought some items for you."

He reached inside a sack and pulled out a jar of honey.

She was about to argue but by his determined expression, she didn't. "Thank you," she said. "But I've no way to pay you."

"I did some lordly things today…counted my coin to discover I'm not in need of payment." He chuckled and she smiled, yet again.

"You have the loveliest smile," he said. "I'd bring you honey every day if it would make you happy and sure the honey couldn't be as sweet as you, *Go Leor Suile Gorma.*"

She cleared her throat, uncomfortable now and brushed the soil from her skirts.

"If you wish for me to understand you might speak in English."

"I think you know what I said."

"Pretty blue eyes?" she asked and he nodded.

"Your eyes are a much deeper shade of blue," she said and their eyes locked. The attraction was undeniable.

"You find them pretty?"

"You're a bit of a jester, Lord Brockwell."

"I suppose so. But at any rate, I also had a hog butchered recently. Here's some meat for your broth and more for another meal. I'll bring those supplies tomorrow to fix the pen, then get hens so you'll have eggs, too."

"You'd think I appear to be starving by how charitable you're being. I assure you there are others far worse off than me…with no home, no garden."

"Tell me who they are; I'll see what can be done to better their lot, too. I'm still in need of more servants. Perhaps I could employ some of those you mentioned. Giles frightened most servants away. Now people are wary to work at Brockwell Manor."

She stared at him for a long while searching his eyes.

"You must expect something in return?" she finally said.

"Only your friendship and perhaps your company on occasion. Let me take you riding. Come share a meal with me at my manor house. You fascinate me, Maiden Albray. You're on my mind constantly and have been since we met."

"The kingdom's law states nobles can't marry common-born and I'll not share your bed... so this won't go beyond friendship."

"I believe that rule will soon be changed. Besides, I don't know that the law includes an Irishman, noble or not for many consider them lower than Saxon men of Wessex."

"You're saying your eventual intent is to wed me then?"

"Well now... bein' that we only met yesterday, it may be a bit premature to contact a priest, find a church, and invite others to our weddin'."

She laughed and his eyes smiled along with his appealing lips. She had the greatest desire to lean closer so he might kiss her. Instead, she spoke again.

"You're not of a mind to woo me so we might share physical intimacies?"

"If you want the plain truth, I won't deny that's crossed my mind as I'm certain it does with most men. You're a beautiful, enticin' woman. But don't you believe a man and woman can share only friendship?"

She shrugged. "My friend Elspeth thinks it's not possible, but I have several male friends."

"Yet you believe you and I can't be *only* friends?"

Her heart beat faster. "You think you already know me so well to be able to determine what I believe?"

"I think I'd like to get to know you much better." He moved closer. She hastily stood with the fresh cut herbs, walked to the fire, lifted the kettle's lid, and placed them inside.

"Will you accept the pork?" he asked.

"Will you expect to share my soup, too?"

"Would your father be joinin' us then?" Broccan asked.

"He often works very late…"

"Do you even have a father?"

"Of course I do," she replied.

"Your wood pile didn't suggest that's so…neither does the state of your home. The roof's in need of rethatchin'. Your cottage looks like a brisk wind would blow it over. Your father wasn't here early mornin' nor is he now though the sun will soon set. If I'd a daughter of your age and beauty, I wouldn't leave you unaccompanied so frequently. Men of lesser moral fiber would surely take advantage if they knew."

"Then I'm relieved you have such high morals and would appreciate you not mention to others the long days my father's away."

"I won't say a word, but I'll bring some men by tomorrow to redo the roof and perhaps see if the hearth could be altered so you can have a fire inside. It must be bone-chillingly cold in the winter without a workin' hearth."

She shook her head. "I don't want that."

"It isn't cold in the winter?" he asked.

"It is… but I have a cloak, my shawl, warm blankets,

and some furs, too. I don't require charity nor wish to be obliged to you in any way. What do you want in return? No one does so much for someone they scarcely know without wanting something."

He stared at her. "Just agree to come see Giles for a few moments."

Her body bristled, her temper flaring.

"I knew it," she said with her hands on her hips. "Take your pork and your honey and go back to your damn manor house. I don't need your assistance or beneficence. As I said, there are others who need it far more."

She scowled when he unwrapped and dropped a whole ham in the broth then set the bundled pork and jar of honey by her door.

"If you should arrive here tomorrow or send someone to repair the roof or the hearth, I'll turn everyone away," she declared.

"You'd cut off your nose to spite your face, Maiden Albray? So be it. I'll not beg you to permit me to assist you. Tell me of the others who require help and I'll see what I can do to aid their plights. You needn't be distressed, I won't be botherin' you or darkenin' your doorstep again."

She crossed her arms defiantly, but didn't reply.

"I got the impression you were open-minded, Maiden Albray, but you constantly presume I must have an ulterior motive to being neighborly. True, I'd like you to see Giles for his days are numbered, but clearly you have your reasons. If you can live with knowin' you denied a dyin' man his atonement, you might be conscious of healin' bodies, but clearly people's mind or souls aren't worthy of your empathy. An experienced healer would know they should be given as much credence as bodily despair."

She glowered, but bit her tongue rather than continue bickering. "Those who require alms or employment are often found in the village square," she finally said. "Now…I'd like you to leave."

"Believe me. I'm goin'." By his intense expression he was notably displeased.

She watched him walk away and her heart ached, though why he or his opinion should matter, she didn't want to consider.

NEARLY A MOON passed without seeing Broccan and with no word from Sir Severin. Rhianwyn hoped he hadn't followed through on his threat to tell the king about her father being absent. She prayed he wouldn't. Yet her father still hadn't returned. Rhianwyn feared the worst and worried for him terribly.

Today was Saturday and Rhianwyn perused the market with Elspeth and Selena. She was trying to forget her woes and enjoy her time with her friends when they noticed a woman dressed in fine garments and elaborately fashioned blonde hair. She was accompanied by a man who appeared much more affable.

"Sarding hell, I might have to leave for a time," Elspeth said. "If I must contend with that snooty bitch, Corliss Barlow, I'd be liable to punch her in her always-scowling face. She's the haughtiest woman I've ever met."

Elspeth glared at Corliss and headed toward the gate.

"Do you suppose she's really that unlikeable?" Selena asked.

"Thankfully I haven't had much to do with her, but I've heard she does think herself above everyone," Rhianwyn replied.

As the woman walked closer she arrogantly sneered at Selena and Rhianwyn, a disapproving scowl on her pinched face. "There should be a separate market for highborn so we don't have to put up with the likes of them!" Corliss stared at Selena and clearly assessed Rhianwyn's patched kirtle.

"That would be very boring," the man with her said.

"But Oliver, dear brother—servants, whores, and the daughter of the mad mage, surely we shouldn't need to be made to be anywhere near *their* kind."

"Just get what you've come for and we'll leave if you're so opposed," Oliver said.

Corliss lifted her head high and when walking by, purposely bumped Selena. Rhianwyn steadied her and Selena blanched at her unkindness.

"If you truly wanted to avoid us perhaps you shouldn't be so eager to draw near." Rhianwyn felt her temper flare.

"Were you speaking to *me*?" Corliss said, her nostrils flaring.

"It was *you* who so rudely pushed my friend."

"Your friend, the whore?" Corliss sneered. "I suppose only someone with an inherited madness would be seen with such a woman."

"Corliss, there's no need to be mean-spirited," Oliver,

said. "The maidens aren't bothering anyone but you."

"They should be burned as heretics, one for her sordid sins, the other for madness," Corliss said.

"If someone honestly believed I was mad do you suppose they'd be wise to rile me?" Rhianwyn asked.

"What could you do to harm me?" The woman looked somewhat unsure.

Rhianwyn opened her satchel. "This is potent poison from snake venom. It causes paralysis of the lungs." Rhianwyn pointed. "This is foxglove which aptly stops the heart. Belladonna and monkshood are also both fatal if ingested. Need I go on?"

"Are you threatening me?" Corliss looked appalled and Oliver actually smirked.

"I don't intend to be near enough to you to be able to harm you, but I'd advise you to stay away from me and my friends especially if you intend to continue with your unkind insults. If I bumped into *you*, perhaps inadvertently spilled one of these potions upon you, who's to say what might happen."

"You are mad!" Corliss spat.

Rhianwyn widened her eyes, purposely stepped closer and the woman backed away so fast she nearly lost her balance, stepping into a fresh pile of pungent horse shit. The horrified look on her face was undeniably rewarding. Selena put her hand over her mouth but couldn't stop giggling. Oliver laughed as well. Corliss glared before she marched off leaving a trail of dung behind.

"Not many dare to lock horns with my sister," Oliver said. "I admire your feistiness, Maiden Albray."

"How do you know who I am?" she asked.

"I've inquired of your name before. There are none so beautiful as you here in this kingdom...or likely anywhere for that matter," Oliver said.

"You don't fear my madness?" Rhianwyn asked, ignoring his comments.

"I've lived with my sister for too long to fear much," he said. "But I suppose I should find her before she wreaks havoc about the market. It was lovely to see you, both of you." Oliver wore an interested look as he bowed and left them.

"He might be more dangerous than his sister," Rhianwyn said as Elspeth rejoined them.

"What did you say to Corliss?" Elspeth asked Rhianwyn.

"She showed her the poisons in her healer's satchel." Selena giggled again.

"Too bad I missed it, but I saw the horse shit on her fancy boots. Wish she'd fallen face first in it."

"You should've seen how her brother looked at Rhianwyn," Selena said.

"He looked at you as well, Selena," Rhianwyn replied.

"Other than the Brockwells, the Barlows are probably the wealthiest nobles," Elspeth said. "I wouldn't mind spending time with Oliver, if I didn't have to be in the company of his vicious sister. She's despicable to the servants when she attends the king's feasts with her family. She thinks herself a sarding queen. I'd like to take her down a peg or two just to see that appalled look on her face again."

"The knights must need your healing again, Rhianwyn." Selena gestured as several knights approached. Cassian's stern expression appeared ominous.

"Maybe not," Elspeth said. "This must be for another matter."

Cassian looked at Rhianwyn. "It's with regret I must inform you by the king's order, if you don't accept an offer of marriage this week, you and other unmarried women without a father who've recently spoken against it, shall be declared marriageable. Your name shall be given to all men in search of a wife. Their offers will be made known to the king's advisors," he said.

Rhianwyn's breath hitched and her heart fell.

"My offer stands," Sir Cassian whispered, his eyes serious.

"And mine," Sir Everard declared, glaring at his brother.

"I'll not be married against my wishes," Rhianwyn replied firmly.

"But you *will* be wed, Rhianwyn," Sir Cassian said. "For unfortunately, your cottage will be handed over to others. You'll have nowhere to live."

"I'll stay deep in the forest or in a damn cave like Radella rather than be ordered to be married," she fervently argued.

"Marry one of us or someone of your choice." Sir Cassian's gaze was set upon her face.

"I'd marry either of you." Selena cast an interested look at Cassian and Everard.

"Sorry, Selena, you know we're not permitted to marry…your kind," Everard said.

"Selena's lovely, gentle and *pure*." Rhianwyn's temper piqued. "Any one of you would be fortunate to take Selena as a wife."

"We can't go against the king's laws," Everard explained.

Those of noble birth or high standing were typically disallowed from marrying a woman even with a rumored soiled reputation regardless of whether it was proven true. Because Selena lived with harlots and her mother had been one, she was evidently labeled a fallen woman unsuitable for marriage to any man of supposed good standing.

Rhianwyn was sorrowful for Selena, for Elspeth and for herself. Even Princess Lilliana—for sadly none of them had a say in their own future.

"Are you well, Rhianwyn?" Sir Cassian asked, concerned.

She knew he fought the urge to take her in his arms. She longed to be comforted but only looked away.

"How in the hell could she be well, you lot of heartless boors?" Elspeth stoutly said. "You're telling her you're soon giving away her family home and she'll be forced to be wed. She's evidently lost her father and now this. Do you suppose she feels like dancing just now? Christ, I'd like to blacken all your eyes!"

"I *am* very sorry," Cassian repeated.

Everard nodded. "As am I."

"We all are, Maiden Albray," Sir Tideswell, another knight said, "but there's naught to be done about it. Choose someone to marry or the king's advisors will. They might send you to the spinster market if you're difficult about it."

"I'd as soon go to the axman's block," Rhianwyn hissed.

Twice a year unmarried women ages fifteen and upward, whether widowed, orphaned, or unbidden for by the king's invitation for proposals, were taken to the village square like sheep or cattle. It wasn't much different than the slaver's market though that was considered clandestine.

"If you're obstinate, Maiden Albray, that isn't unthinkable," Sir Tideswell said.

"It would be over my dead body Rhianwyn ever meet such a bleak fate." Sir Cassian stepped closer.

"You shouldn't refer to her by her given name, Cassian. You'll have others thinking you've shared more than fondness," Sir Severin warned in a low voice, avoiding Rhianwyn's glares. Apparently he'd been true to his word and told the king or his advisors of her situation.

Cassian looked away, his jaw tightening.

"Being wed to someone I don't wish to marry would be bleak. It's not my intent to insult either of you," she said to Cassian and Everard.

"It's no different than an arranged wedding, Rhianwyn." Elspeth crossed her arms. "I've no choice but to marry bloody Godric who's probably dipped his *spindle* in every willing female in the village and beyond...as well as some likely unwilling."

"Soon, I'll have no choice but to permit any man who pays Shandy to... *have* me," Selena woefully said.

"Having no say in my fate...in any woman having no

say in our fate, is bloody unfair." Rhianwyn's voice trembled in her fury regarding the inequitable treatment females suffered.

"No one's debating that, Rhianwyn," Cassian said, receiving another warning scowl from Severin, "but I'd rather you marry my brother or someone who'll treat you well than take your chances at the spinster market. Anyone with coin could pay to marry you."

"It could be a scrimpy price if you're too willful," Everard added.

"You could end up married to a smelly old curmudgeon with no teeth who bathes but once a year or a mean-spirited drinking man," Sir Severin suggested. "By law you'd have no choice in sharing his bed."

"I should be permitted to stay in my cottage…to provide for myself with my garden and my healing," Rhianwyn emphatically stated. "I don't need a bloody husband!"

"After propositions are tallied and reviewed, the king will have final say in who you'll wed. Marry one of us for the king favors his knights," Cassian said.

"Rhianwyn, it might be the best to hope for," Elspeth agreed.

"I must go to my cottage…while it's still mine to go to," Rhianwyn lamented knowing she'd soon give way to tears.

"You're young and beautiful. I suspect a lot of men have their eye upon you," Cassian said and Rhianwyn left without even a word to her friends.

CHAPTER EIGHT

"You MUST GO to Rhianwyn. She needs guidance and cheering this day." Anslem's spirit startled Broccan by materializing while he was out riding.

"She doesn't want to see me and to be truthful, she's a damn difficult woman. She's exasperatin' and too proud for her own good."

"She'll be worth whatever difficulties she might present. She requires someone to discourage her from what she's about to do."

"What is she about to do?" Broccan curiously asked.

"Go find out for yourself." Anslem grinned before he disappeared.

"You're a bit exasperatin' yourself," Broccan said but he headed his horse toward Rhianwyn's cottage.

"Looks like somethin's troublin' you," Broccan said.

Rhianwyn glanced at him from the corner of her eye as she took the last garment off the line, folded it, and placed it in a satchel. She tried not to be affected by his presence but admitted her heart fluttered on seeing him.

"What are you doing here?" Rhianwyn asked.

"I know… I told you I wouldn't come by again. I was in a bit of a temper that day. I apologize. I shouldn't have tried to force you to see Giles."

"Does he still live?" Rhianwyn asked.

"I believe the miserable old codger's so stubborn, he won't die until he speaks with you."

"Then he'll live forever," she said.

"I'd hoped to perhaps see you at the market again, but I haven't attended as I'd like. I've been busy managing the estate; Giles has left it in a rather unorganized state. But Dubh was in need of a good ride and eager to see you again, isn't that right, boy?" He smiled and the horse whinnied.

Rhianwyn fought a smile but turned away.

"You're still sore at me and truly leavin' without another word?" Broccan asked.

"I'm getting Dubh a carrot."

She pulled two, brushed them off, and walked to where Broccan sat upon his horse, both of them looking grand.

"Since you've said you don't have carrots, you may have what you'd like from my garden until others take possession of this cottage," she said.

"You're movin' to another home or village then?" He sounded disappointed as he looked at her stuffed satchel.

"Another village, yes." She nodded though her plan was far from well thought out. She didn't want to wait to see who might put in a request to wed her. If Cassian or Everard did she'd be forced to wed a knight after all her insistence she wouldn't.

If she refused or was willful she could be sent to the

spinster's market. She would *not* be paraded about, surveyed, and graded by having her hips deemed able to deliver babies, a body that would be pleasing to a man...or a meek temperament. Sold to the highest bidder. But neither would she marry a knight and soon be a widow.

"You don't seem entirely at peace with this decision," Broccan said distracting her.

"If I don't leave I'll be forced to marry someone not of my choosing. Anyone could make a bid to the king...therefore I intend to run off to escape this undesirable fate."

"Is this common?" The horse crunched on the carrots and she stroked his powerful neck.

"Marriage bids are another means for the kingdom to earn coin other than through citizens giving a large portion of their crops and livestock to the king. Women don't even require dowries. The king wants his subjects to produce children for the population has declined in neighboring areas. My father's been gone a while now and by the king's law women aren't permitted to live alone."

"Surely there've been men ask for your hand before?"

"A few. Now my name's been placed on the list of women available to all men wishing to marry. There may be offers, but I'll not be forced to marry a knight nor will I be taken to the spinster market if I refuse to wed who the king chooses."

"The spinster market?"

"Where desperate men or aged widowers search for a wife—someone to warm their beds and care for their children. It infuriates me women have no say. I won't be paired with any man—to serve him in or out of his bed or be a damn brood mare. I'll go to another village and speak falsehoods of my age."

"You'd not pass for a wee lass," Broccan said. "Your age is apparent by your well-blossomed form. You're bound to have many offers of marriage. You're an uncommonly pleasing woman to look at."

"You're really very bold with your glances and opinions. If you believe a woman's only value is her appearance, then you're as ignorant and shallow as most men."

He dismounted.

"I hope I'm neither," he said looking deep in thought. "You're gifted with horses and it's plain you like them. Perhaps you could come work in my stables. If you had employment and a place to stay so you're not alone, would that let you off the hook for marriage...at least for the time being? And no...it's not charity I offer...nor expectations of sharing my bed."

"I won't stay at Brockwell Manor, not while Lord Giles still draws breath. Besides, I'm a worthy healer. But most husbands won't abide their wife's time occupied with tending to the ailing or injured."

"I'm sorry for this unappealing situation you're in, Maiden Albray."

"It's not only me. Many others face adversity. Elspeth must marry that damn brute, Godric, the sheriff's son and Selena's fate is...most undesirable."

He looked deeply concerned. She thought he might even attempt to hold her in comfort.

"Thank you for your concern, Lord Brockwell, but I'll

find a solution on my own." She petted the horse's neck.

"Giles continues to request your audience. If you don't agree to come soon…it'll be too late."

"I told you, I owe him nothing," she replied.

"Have you ever lived anywhere but this small village?" Broccan asked.

She shook her head.

"There are many dangers out there, Maiden Albray, even for a man, but more for a woman traveling unattended. Though I don't approve of the law forcin' all single women to be wed, there's some reasonability to it. Many dishonorable sorts abuse women in unimaginable ways. How would you cope if one dangerous man much less a gang of unconscionable louts should happen upon you with lecherous intentions?"

She sighed. How *would* she cope? Meeting unscrupulous men could see her dead in a ditch and suffering much afore that gruesome end. Selena needed her and Rhianwyn wouldn't want her friends to always wonder what had become of her. If her father returned to find her gone, that would devastate him.

"My plight's not your concern, Lord Brockwell."

She said no more but simply went inside her cottage.

RHIANWYN CONCLUDED BROCCAN was correct, she couldn't risk being harmed and couldn't leave Selena alone to face her unwelcome fate. Rhianwyn went about her usual activities hoping to take her mind off her worries.

She took pain elixir to the blacksmith's apprentice for he'd burned his hand. Examining the wound and applying an herbal concoction, she was satisfied it was healing. She went to the knight's training field to check on Tyree's wound. It was much improved. Next, she visited two women soon to give birth. There was an experienced midwife in the village, but she was much in demand—often needed by more than one woman. Therefore Rhianwyn assisted, though she feared midwifery more than any healing duties, even brutal injuries, festering wounds, or disease.

Leaving the second woman's cottage, she saw the usual group of children playing in the street. Ranging from ages two to nine with matted hair, barefoot, and clad in rags, her heart ached for them. They were all motherless. Their fathers worked in the castle, mill or stables. Children ten and older were put to work in the fields, shops, or manor houses. Perhaps they knew no different or because they were children, they easily found joy, but she'd never heard these youngsters complain.

She assisted the poor waifs when she could with food, sometimes other necessities. She'd heard Broccan offered alms to several children and to homeless people. He'd also provided jobs for a dozen people. She commended that and should thank him. Could he really be just a good man or was he trying to impress her so she'd agree to meet with Giles Brockwell?

The children smiled upon seeing Rhianwyn and ran to her. She greeted them with embraces and reached into her pocket producing crisp fresh carrots mindful to give wee

Henry, Hattie, Thomas, and Gertrude the thinly cut carrots. She'd seen children choke in their hungry eagerness.

The morning was dreary—cloud cover blocked the sun. She stood listening to their exuberant chatter, when she felt the spatter of rain. The pure elation on the children's faces was much contrary to the adults who looked upward with disapproving scowls scurrying for cover so their clothing wouldn't be dampened. But the children squealed in delight as the sprinkling turned to a worthy shower.

Maisie took her hand. Rhianwyn set her cloak under a tree, unlaced her worn boots and happily romped in the rain with the children. The glee on their faces at her playing with them, gladdened her heart. She lifted her face to the sky...soft refreshing rain wetting her hair and face. They twirled and danced till the sun peeked through the clouds and the rain stopped.

"Now, stay in the sun and let your garments dry," Rhianwyn said. "Mind the slippery cobblestones when near the horses and carts... and look out for each other. Stay together. Next time I hope to have apples for you."

They smiled again, nodded and called their farewells as they raced off down the cobblestones, their small feet toughened from constantly walking on the uneven stones. With autumn nearly here, days would soon grow colder. She hoped to barter with the shoemaker for shoes for the children. Would any husband permit her to offer her time, food, or coin to help out these less-fortunate little ones? She sighed and heard a familiar strum on a lute.

"Fair lady, Rhianwyn, what's turned your smile down?

Tell me what I might do to take away that fretful frown," Keyon melodically sang.

She did smile then. Keyon often cheered her.

"Hello, Keyon. You're back so soon."

"I regret I didn't share your promised meal last time and left without farewell. I heard of a neighboring lord needing a minstrel for his feast. Is it your thoroughly drenched garments that have you looking sorrowful?"

"No. I'm worried for the children. The days grow cool and none have shoes."

"Many adults go barefoot, too. Your shoes and mine are nothing to boast about." Keyon looked down at his boots with several holes.

"I want better for the children," she said.

She pulled on her stockings and boots as they conversed.

"Has the huntsman delivered a rabbit recently for I've a powerful hankering for rabbit stew?" Keyon asked.

"Perhaps later today. Stop by my cottage tonight, I'll cook supper and invite Selena and Elspeth, too."

"It's to be a grand feast then... a party if you like." Keyon smiled broadly.

"Hardly a feast, but it'd be good to break bread with friends even if there'll be no bread."

"You could ask Lord Brockwell to have his cooks bake bread and invite him, too," Keyon suggested.

"Why would I do that?"

"Because he's watching you as we speak. Even when you were dancing about in the rain, he stared at you as though he'd never seen a woman before."

Keyon looked down the street; Rhianwyn followed his gaze. Sure enough Broccan was watching and she met his eyes. He waved and smiled. She only nodded. She finished lacing her boot and retrieved her cloak.

"I almost forgot, I have the salt you requested from Epsom." Keyon produced a pouch of salt from his pack.

"I'm much indebted to you, Keyon. You do know I've only remedies to repay you and supper this night."

"I don't require payment, Rhianwyn. If you're not opposed to me calling you by name? Although Lord Brockwell might disapprove by the way he continues to stare. I believe you've entranced him along with every other hot-blooded male in the kingdom."

"I don't want to *entrance* anyone." She stuffed the salt in her satchel and cast a scowl at Broccan. He smiled again then turned away.

His gaze unsettled her. As always it left her skin warm and her heart beating faster. The attraction was powerful and growing each time she saw him.

"Stop by early evening, Keyon. I'll perhaps catch trout in the lake."

"I look forward to it. May I bring something?"

"Only your voice…but perhaps…"

"What is it? Speak plain, Rhianwyn."

"Perhaps you might bathe," she hesitantly replied.

"I suppose I should." He sniffed his underarm. "It's been some time."

"It's not something everyone believes necessary, but for those with a keen sense of smell, bathing more frequently is welcomed," Rhianwyn admitted.

"You always smell delightfully sweet." He dared to smell her hair.

"I bathe often and use potions to wash my hair. I didn't intend to offend you, Keyon. Since you sleep in stables, bathing's surely not a luxury you regularly partake in."

"The waters in Bath are delightful. You'd like it there," he said.

"I've heard it's marvelous. I'd like to go one day. I'd gladly journey many places," she replied wistfully. "If you happen to see Selena or Elspeth, please invite them for supper."

"I'll do that. I might procure ale or mead." Keyon's brown eyes darted back and forth.

They smiled in parting.

NEAR HER COTTAGE Rhianwyn heard a familiar barking. Looking through the trees she saw the immense brindle canine hurtling toward her. She braced herself but still he toppled her to the muddy ground and she fell laughing. The old dog appeared like a puppy playfully licking her face and effectually pinning her down.

"Champion, move this instant," a deep voice commanded.

The dog obeyed without question wagging his tail as three other dogs and the man approached. He was unusually tall—taller than the knights, taller than Broccan or anyone Rhianwyn knew. His appearance was foreboding, his jaw fiercely set, his eyes piercing but Rhianwyn knew of his inner gentleness. One eye remained partly closed from the beating he'd endured in protecting her. He offered his hand and Rhianwyn took it.

"Hello Maxim. It's good to see you, and of course, all of you, too." She petted the other three dogs, then Champion who rallied most for her attention.

"And you, Lady Rhianwyn," Maxim said, though he wouldn't meet her eyes.

He was unusually shy, especially with women. Once the king's best archer and huntsman, he still provided stags and rabbits for the castle kitchen. The incident with the sheriff's men left him warier of people and gave Maxim a jeopardous reputation. Few dared go near him.

"Has that unmannerly hound hurt you?"

"No, I'm well enough." Rhianwyn looked at the mud on her backside. "I'm glad to see he's still full of zest."

"He has a strong will," Maxim said.

He certainly did. Champion was once shot by an arrow. Rhianwyn hadn't believed he'd survive. He'd been Anslem's beloved dog. He wanted her to keep him. When Giles learned she was in possession of his son's dog, in his fury, he shot him in her presence rather than permit her to have him.

She'd forgiven Lord Brockwell for disallowing them to be married. She hadn't even been agreeable of Anslem going to his father with her by his side to request permission to marry her. She still hadn't forgotten the man's hurtful insults but would never forgive him for harming Anslem's dog.

She'd nursed the immense mastiff back to health thinking he'd never walk again. The arrow was through his chest, into his leg—barely missing his heart. After Champion recovered she'd given him to Maxim for he cherished his dogs.

"You could take Champion back now," Maxim said. "I've heard that cruel old miser's soon to be dead."

"He'd miss you and the other dogs." Rhianwyn shook her head.

"He adores you, Lady Rhianwyn. Besides, he's growing slower and holds us back sometimes. If he stayed with you, that'd ease my mind for he'd protect you."

"He would." She petted the dog again, then crouched so she could place her arms around his thick neck.

"Would you be content with me, sweet old boy?"

He wagged his tail and licked her face again.

"But I don't even know where I'll be by this time next moon."

"Where you'll be?" Maxim sounded confused.

"I'll soon be forced to wed. I don't know where I'll live and mightn't remain near the village."

He stared at her as though he wanted to speak, but he'd already said more today than she'd ever heard from Maxim Robertson.

"If I had a home...or a way to see you provided for...I..."

"That's kind of you, Maxim."

His face turned ruddy.

"You'd not consider marrying me because I'm twice your age or because you fear what's said about me is true?" He dubiously glanced at her.

"Age has no relevance and I know you're sound of mind, not dangerous."

He nodded but wouldn't meet her eyes. She inwardly cussed. Maybe Elspeth was correct, men couldn't be friends with a woman without eventually wanting more. She recognized the need in Maxim's serious brown eyes. He was a man after all. He even glanced at her breasts, then turned away.

"I've brought the rabbits." He broke the uncomfortable silence.

He pulled two skinned rabbits from a sack. Although it was often only nobles who enjoyed the luxury of meat, Rhianwyn believed it was necessary to a well-rounded diet. Meat also staved the hunger longer.

"Thank you, my friend. I have the elixir I promised you. How's your shoulder?" she asked as they walked to the cottage.

"In much need of your remedies. It aches unmercifully by nightfall and it's near petrifiable each morning."

"Unfortunately, with constant repetition of shooting the long bow, it does often strain an archer's shoulder. The aching and stiffness may continue to worsen with cold weather and longevity."

He smiled and Maxim seldom smiled except at his dogs.

"Did you just in a kindly manner tell me I'm old, Lady Rhianwyn?"

"You aren't old. But living a hard life and sleeping upon the ground year round does cause a body to protest."

"My dogs keep me warm." He looked adoringly at the

one greyhound and the other two mastiffs, like Champion.

They reached the cottage. She retrieved a vial and a small bottle, passing them to him.

"This one's to ingest, the other's an ointment to rub upon your shoulder."

He bowed appreciatively and she placed her kettle on the hook over the low fire and added wood.

"Do you wish me to chop these into smaller pieces?" He motioned to the rabbits.

She nodded. He pulled a small hatchet from his pack, placed first one, then the other on the iron stand near the wood pile. Four blows saw the job done. She placed them in the kettle.

"I'll get the water for you." He took a bucket.

"You must stay for supper...the minstrel Keyon and I'm hoping Elspeth and Selena will be here, too."

"Maiden Selena." His eyes lighted at that.

Maxim had met Selena when Rhianwyn was tending to his injuries. Her quiet gentleness appealed to Maxim's own shyness.

"Yes, I'll return to the village to invite Selena and Elspeth."

"I doubt they'd wish to have me there," he said.

She'd never heard Maxim sound lonely. He usually welcomed the solitude being alone in the forest.

"Selena's kind. Keyon's accepting of everyone and Elspeth...well...she's opinionated, but not as harsh as she'd have others believe."

"Like me," the large man said.

"You're not harsh, Maxim...only a little misunderstood."

"If I summon the nerve, I'll return later to sup with you and your friends, Lady Rhianwyn."

"I'd like that," she replied as he left, three dogs following him and Champion looking unsure.

"Go with them, sweet boy and come back later for rabbit stew."

The dog wagged his tail happily following Maxim who smiled back at Rhianwyn.

CHAPTER NINE

RHIANWYN WALKED TO the hot spring where she always bathed. It was surrounded by trees making it private. She removed her muddy garments and left them on a nearby rock. She'd wash them later. She dipped her toe in the hot water, but hearing footsteps, she was fully aware whoever stood there had a clear view of her from behind. She turned her head, recognized the intense blue eyes staring at her.

"If you're following me trying to be inconspicuous, you've failed. And if you're following me with such boldness as to watch my every move, you still leave me wondering why."

Broccan stepped from the thicket and grinned, though his usual collected manner might be somewhat shaken on finding her unclothed.

"You're not going to shriek and hide? You're in a rather vulnerable position just now."

She glanced at him again. "I suspect you've seen a good many women's backsides." She waded into the very warm water, keeping her back to him until she was fully immersed, then turning toward him.

"Why do you say that?" he asked, sitting on a rock, obviously amused.

"You're tall, strong, not difficult to look at, and a wealthy noble. I presume you could have nearly any woman you desired and have done so with regularity."

"You're very bold yourself, Maiden Albray."

"For speaking my mind or not hastily covering myself when I saw you skulking about?"

"I wasn't skulking at least not well." He laughed. "How's the water? I thought I might join you."

"That *would* be bold," she said, her heart beating faster. "But it wouldn't be to your liking."

"Why's that?" he asked. "Sure bathin' with you would be much to my likin'." His eyebrow rose suggestively.

"Men typically can't withstand the extreme temperatures of this water. It's very hot here but icy cold where the waterfall cascades from the rocks."

"Women can bear such temperatures?"

"We've no *jewels* to protest." She smirked.

"I see." He was obviously amused. "You're correct, sure I'd rather not boil or freeze my ballocks. Do you come here often?"

"At least every other day."

"I might risk the temperatures." He gazed at her as the steam rose from the water. "I favor how lovely and pink your skin's become."

She patted her face moving closer to the waterfall then dove beneath. The change in temperature was invigorating. When she resurfaced, he was standing on the rocks above the waterfall looking down at her.

"I'll leave you to bathe uninterrupted."

She nodded.

"Unless you'd be acceptin' of me watchin' you leave that water," he suggested. "I *would* be eager to see that."

"And then?" she asked.

He looked unsure.

"Would you expect me to permit you to have me?"

"By God, no. Because I admit to wanting to see *all* of you after seein' your lovely round arse and beautiful flawless skin and because I admitted havin' such thoughts, doesn't indicate I'd believe you'd offer yourself to me so freely."

"Sure that isn't what you're suggesting?" He raised his eyebrow seductively.

"Go home, Lord Brockwell. Find a woman of your station to marry or a harlot to sard. I recognize that desirous look."

"What man alive wouldn't wear such a look after seein' you without garments?"

"As a healer I understand the powerful desires of men."

"I doubt even a healer *fully* understands, Maiden Albray." He sensually gazed at her before he left.

After donning clean garments and washing the others, Rhianwyn brushed out her long hair and tied it back. She pulled carrots, onions, and parsnips from the garden, washed them in the stream, chopped them, placed them in the rabbit stew, thickening it with a bit of barley, adding salt and several herbs for flavoring. It smelled divine as it bubbled. She added wood to the fire again, covering the pot intending to go speak with Elspeth and Selena but was pleasantly surprised to see them enter the clearing.

"Hello," she happily called and they waved.

"Keyon invited us to your feast," Selena said.

"Hardly a feast, but I'm very glad to see you both."

"I brought cheese from the dairy shed." Elspeth held up a worthy slab.

"I have mead. I took a little from the supply at the house," Selena admitted.

"I'll get chairs," Rhianwyn said, excited to have her friends here.

"We can sit here on this perfectly good log." Elspeth grinned.

"Keyon said he'd be here soon. He was rather mysterious," Selena said.

"Do you have tankards?" Elspeth asked.

"I have six. Even if Maxim shows up, that'll be enough." Rhianwyn thought aloud.

"Maxim?" Selena asked.

"*He's* going to be here?" Elspeth said.

"Maybe," Rhianwyn replied.

Elspeth rolled her eyes like she didn't approve.

"Maxim provided the rabbits, therefore I invited him. He's a good friend."

"He's a nice man, Elspeth," Selena confirmed.

"Would your father approve of you entertaining men?" Elspeth asked.

"Well it's not as though I'd be alone with them in the cottage."

"You're surely aware sarding doesn't only occur inside cottages." Elspeth was likely trying to make her uncomfortable.

When a branch rustled nearby, all three women's eyes followed the sound. Four dogs raced out of the woods. Again Champion leapt toward Rhianwyn stopping short of knocking her over. Selena tensed, looking terrified. Bitten by a dog when she was a child, she'd feared them ever since. Elspeth stared at them with distaste. Living in the castle's servant's quarters, no dogs were permitted; she had no fondness for them.

"I didn't know we'd be dining with hounds." Elspeth made a disapproving face as the dogs wagged their tails.

Selena trembled and closed her eyes.

"I know if you fear something, me telling you there's no need, won't be beneficial, but I promise you those dogs won't harm you, Selena," Rhianwyn said.

"I'd not permit it," Maxim said whistling. The dogs returned to sit obediently by his side.

Selena and Elspeth stared at Maxim's immense height and size. He was actually a nice-looking man, albeit fierce-looking especially with his scarred eye. Still, Selena smiled at Maxim and Elspeth attempted to hide her infamous glower.

"Come sit with us, Maxim. I suspect Keyon will be here directly," Rhianwyn said.

He nodded, purposely sitting a good distance from the women, though Rhianwyn didn't miss how often he glanced at Selena. Cheerful whistling was heard and Keyon came into the clearing though he was largely unrecognizable. His beard was completely shaven. It was obvious he'd bathed and had his hair shorn to collar length.

"Keyon, you look much changed!" Rhianwyn said.

"Is it a change for the better, Maiden Albray?" he asked turning around so they could see the whole effect.

"You look very comely," she replied, noting he appeared quite handsome.

The other two women agreed.

"How did you afford the bath, shave, and haircut?" Rhianwyn asked.

"I sang for the bath and a razor."

"This is Maxim." Rhianwyn gestured to him.

Keyon appeared intimated by the immense man. When Maxim stood he was a good head taller. "Maxim, meet Keyon."

"Hello." Keyon gingerly approached Maxim, offering his hand. He nodded, shook Keyon's hand though didn't speak. Keyon rubbed his hand afterward. Maxim likely didn't know his own strength.

"I'll get the tankards," Rhianwyn said.

"I brought ale," Keyon said.

"Did you sing for the ale wife?" Elspeth smirked.

"I sold my gems-horn," Keyon admitted.

"Keyon, you didn't!" Rhianwyn said.

"It was heavy to cart about and I have my lute." He patted the lute slung over his shoulder.

"I said I'd like you to sing but didn't want to make you feel you must bring ale."

"I wanted the ale and I'm of a mind to share it with my friends." Keyon smiled.

Rhianwyn went for the tankards, then stepped from the cottage to see Broccan approaching. She stared for he came bearing a large cloth sack. By the delicious scent, it was freshly baked bread. Her eyes questioned him.

"I ran into your minstrel friend earlier. He said you were in need of bread to go along with your supper. I wasn't certain how many might be attendin' your gatherin' so I brought six loaves. If that's not sufficient…"

"That's plenty. Thank you," Rhianwyn said.

"There's butter, too," he added, producing a smaller bag.

"That's very generous." She nodded to him.

The dogs wagged their tails staring at Broccan. Rhianwyn stood holding the tankards and he the bread, both still looking at each other.

"This is Lord Brockwell, although I suppose you've all met him except for Maxim. Maxim's the castle's huntsman."

Maxim stood again. Broccan shook his hand heartily though Maxim seemed less sure.

"Perhaps we might bring the table from your cottage?" Keyon suggested.

"I'll get it." Maxim started for the cottage.

That seemed to be the signal for the dogs to bound toward Broccan.

"They probably smell my dogs on me." Broccan smiled. "Wait till I disperse of the food, then I'll gladly pet you."

"You have dogs?" Maxim asked.

"Two wolfhounds I brought with me from Ireland."

Rhianwyn passed the tankards to Elspeth and Selena, then opened the door for Maxim. After he easily carried out the table, Broccan set the bread and butter on the table, then crouched and petted the four dogs. Maxim's face softened in seeing that.

Rhianwyn went back in for bowls. How many should she get? It would be inhospitable not to ask Broccan to eat with them when he'd brought food. She sighed. The more time she spent with him, the more attracted she was to him.

"What's taking so long?" Selena stepped in the cottage.

"I'm getting bowls and spoons," Rhianwyn replied as Selena's eyes skirted the tiny unadorned home.

"Is that your bed?" she asked.

"That's Father's. Mine's there." She pointed toward the blanketed division.

"It's small like mine." Selena peeked at it.

"It is," Rhianwyn said. She'd twice seen the cold, dark space where Selena slept. She and Elspeth climbed a tree and crawled through the brothel's attic window to visit Selena, luckily without Shandy discovering.

"Are you hoping Lord Brockwell will be gone when you go back outside?" Selena asked. "He's spending time with the dogs, although I'd wager much he's lingering so he can see *you*, Rhianwyn. By the way he looks at you he's clearly besotted."

"He isn't, Selena."

"If you say so." She smiled mischievously. "I can take those bowls out if you intend to hide here."

"I'm not hiding," Rhianwyn said.

Selena smirked. "Elspeth thinks you're being rude."

Rhianwyn grinned. "She's probably correct."

"Want me to take your hand?" Selena tittered.

"You're amusing, my friend."

They walked out together and Broccan glanced up from where he sat on the ground surrounded by the dogs. He might be sometimes arrogant and brazen, but if he helped feed the children, provided jobs for the needy... and dogs and horses liked him, he must be a good man. Even if she didn't want to dwell on his endearing traits.

"I suppose I should be goin'. I'll leave you to your supper," Broccan said.

All eyes went to Rhianwyn.

"Stay and sup with us," she finally said.

He broke into a wide grin that caused an unusual flutter in her chest.

"It won't be what you're accustomed to. I can cook a medicinal elixir far better than food, but..."

"I'd very much like to stay, Maiden Albray," Broccan replied.

"Apparently the dogs would like you to stay," Elspeth commented as they remained near him.

Rhianwyn set the bowls and spoons on the table, then removed the warm bread from the sack. It smelled so good, her mouth watered. She unwrapped the butter and went back for butter knives. When she returned Broccan was cutting hearty portions of bread with his knife.

Elspeth set out the cheese and sliced it. Keyon topped up everyone's ale and mead. Maxim removed the kettle's lid and Rhianwyn passed him the ladle. It was almost like having family working together. She couldn't remember when she'd previously eaten with her father. The last time she'd felt like she was part of a family was when her mother still lived. She tried to fight the brimming tears, cleared her throat, but hastily returned to the cottage where they fell earnestly.

"Why are you hiding now?" Elspeth brusquely said coming inside.

Rhianwyn sniffled, keeping her back to her. Elspeth turned her to look at her worriedly.

"What is it Rhianwyn?" She sounded tender—even embraced her. "I haven't seen you weep since the day your mother was buried."

"I miss Mam and Father so...miss having a family," Rhianwyn whispered.

"You could have most of mine," Elspeth joked, lightly wiping the tears from Rhianwyn's cheeks. "There's something more."

"Father might never return. When I'm sent from this cottage, memories of Mam and Father will be gone."

"They won't, Rhianwyn. As long as you're alive, you'll keep them in your heart."

"Why are you being so sweet?" Rhianwyn asked.

"I see how this grieves you no matter how strong you always seem. I don't want you to be unhappy, my friend. If you'd give the Irishman a chance, I wager he'd take away your sadness." She glanced toward the bed and widened her eyes suggestively. "At the very least you'd make some *memorable* memories together."

"Elspeth Jory!" she scolded but smiled, feeling better after her cry and her friend's affection.

"Do you ladies need a hand?" Broccan called from outside the open door.

"We'll be there straightaway," Elspeth said. "Unless you'd *like* to come in."

Rhianwyn shook her head and actually swatted Elspeth's arm. She chuckled.

"Did you need something?" Broccan looked in.

"I can't reach that pitcher." Rhianwyn struggled for something to say.

Broccan had to duck to step inside, then easily reached up and passed it to her. He was so close she could feel his warmth and smell his enticing scent. She closed her eyes wanting to be lost in it for a time.

"Thank you." She took the pitcher and hastened outside.

RHIANWYN WAS GLAD she'd made a good amount of stew. These men possessed hearty appetites. Although Maxim hadn't spoken much, he seemed to enjoy the camaraderie. The men drank their share of ale, and she and the women had nearly finished the mead. Rhianwyn was feeling lighthearted for the first time since her father left and she'd learned she'd lose her cottage.

Keyon sang and played. He and Broccan told stories of some of the places they'd journeyed. There'd been laughter and conversation aplenty. The sun had nearly set. Rhianwyn retrieved an enclosed candle and two torches. Maxim pushed them into the ground and lit them. Broccan added wood to the fire and then chopped more. She tried not to stare when he took off his overcoat and his muscles bulged through his tunic, although Elspeth and Selena apparently weren't bothered about being conspicuous. In her increasingly inebriated state, Rhianwyn couldn't stop dwelling on how she'd felt when he stood near her and imagining what it would be like for him to pull her close, hold her, kiss her and...

The dogs jumped up. They stood looking toward the woods, then barked. Rhianwyn was relieved to see, Isolde, another castle servant. She glanced at Rhianwyn uncertainly.

"I invited her," Elspeth said.

"You're welcome, Isolde, of course. Have you eaten? There's food and drink," Rhianwyn warmly greeted her.

"Thank you. That'd be appreciated," Isolde said.

Rhianwyn located another bowl and spoon. Thankfully there was still stew left. Isolde sat near Elspeth and by the looks they shared, she was Elspeth's latest lover.

When full darkness fell, the two women danced to Keyon's music.

"Come on everyone, dance!" Elspeth insisted.

Selena grasped Rhianwyn's hand and pulled her to merrily dance as well. Rhianwyn sat down afterward, feeling breathless.

Rhianwyn saw Broccan eyeing her like he might ask her, but Selena, emboldened by the drink, asked him instead. He nodded and Rhianwyn smiled at Selena's joy as she and Broccan danced. She thought Maxim would like to dance with Selena but with his timidness toward women, he wouldn't. When the dance was ended, Selena asked Maxim. Even by the firelight, Rhianwyn could see he was mortified.

"Dance with me, Maxim," Selena insisted, laughing in her obvious intoxication.

"Sorry, Maiden Selena, I've never danced."

"I'm not a good dancer, but I'll try to teach you," Selena said.

He nervously cleared his throat but finally stood. Selena was petite and he towered over her, but she took his hand and they managed to stumble through a song. Selena giggled happily and Maxim smiled. Rhianwyn had been busy watching them and didn't notice Broccan approach. It might be that drunkenness was overtaking her, too.

"Will you honor me with a dance, Maiden Albray," Broccan asked.

She inhaled his masculine scent thinking it was dangerous to get any closer.

"I don't really dance," she said, her tongue feeling thick.

"I beg to differ. I saw you dancin' twice this very day."

"Dancing with Selena or in the rain with children isn't the same," she further argued.

"Then pretend I'm a child and rain's fallin' down upon us even now."

"That's absurd," she said, staring up for he was tall, brawny, and so gloriously handsome.

Undeterred, he clasped her hand and lifted her to her

feet. He took her in his arms and pulled her closer than she expected.

"I'd like you to be as at ease as you were with those children...to feel entirely uninhibited with me one day," he whispered in her ear and his lips near her skin made her tingle from scalp to toes.

"I wouldn't hold my breath," she said coolly. "I don't expect to get that close to any man."

"You've obviously never known an Irishman's tenacity."

"This dance is a bit friendlier than I might like."

"You don't like bein' friendly then?" He stared down at her.

By the firelight his eyes were mesmerizing, his presence magnetic.

"Is this how you dance in Ireland?"

"It is when a man wishes to kiss a woman but doubts she'll permit it and dancin' is second to what he really wants to do...or perhaps third," he said boldly, and she pulled away. He came after her.

"I apologize. I've had a bit too much to drink. I spoke without thinkin' it through. Don't be riled at me, Maiden Albray."

"You should find a lady, Lord Brockwell...someone of your kind. You needn't mingle with common-born. I'm certain there's a good many women of your standing who'll marry you, dance with you...or more. I thank you for the food and..."

"Rhianwyn." He dared to call her by her given name. The way he said it only made her tingle more. "I don't want to hang about with lords and ladies. I much prefer this type of gatherin' and if I'm bein' truthful, you're the most captivatin' woman I've ever met. Dance with me. You have my word I won't speak of kissin' you."

Though they wouldn't be able to hear what was said, Elspeth and Selena watched closely. Maxim looked like if she gave the word, he'd see Broccan Mulryan sorry if he didn't step away. She smiled, reassuring the others. Keyon continued to sing. Not wanting to cause a stir, Rhianwyn took Broccan's hand again. This time he kept an acceptable distance between them and bowed graciously when the dance was over.

"Thank you," he said. "Now if our minstrel would like a turn dancin', I could perhaps play for a bit. If you'd lend me your lute, Keyon."

"You play?" Keyon sounded impressed.

"Not with your skill, but I play and sing a little," Broccan replied.

"I've heard the Irish are often musically gifted." Keyon nodded.

"Well... I'd not go so far as sayin' I'm gifted."

Keyon gladly passed Broccan the lute and excitedly glanced at the women.

"I intend to dance with each one of you ladies. Do you know how rare it is that I'm able to dance? I'm always the one making music."

Selena went to him and they were soon dancing gleefully. Though Rhianwyn thought Broccan Mulryan was sometimes given to arrogance, he was apparently modest of his musical talent. He could play well. His voice was deep and pleasing.

Keyon danced with Elspeth and then Isolde, too, and was dancing the second time with Rhianwyn when the dogs barked loudly again. Rhianwyn wondered who would be here for the hour was late. She prayed it wasn't Godric with his unwelcome bunch of men possibly intent on ruining the previously pleasant night.

CHAPTER TEN

WHEN SOMEONE IN a hooded cloak accompanied by two others, stepped into the torch light and lowered the hood, Rhianwyn was surprised to see it was Lilianna. Cassian and Ulf were with her.

"I heard there was a gathering I wasn't invited to," Lilliana said with a friendly laugh.

"I would've invited you if I'd thought you'd be able to attend," Rhianwyn replied.

"She fairly insisted on coming here." Ulf glanced about at all in attendance.

Cassian looked like he wasn't in favor of it. When he espied Broccan she noticed the disapproval on his face. Broccan appeared equally disgruntled. Had they met before to have such a disagreeable reaction?

"We brought undiluted ale and wine, too," Lilianna said. "But you must introduce me to your friends."

Rhianwyn didn't miss the way Lilliana closely observed Broccan.

"We've a minstrel I've never seen before," Lilliana said.

"Not a minstrel, the new Lord Brockwell," Elspeth replied.

That clearly got Lilliana's attention. Rhianwyn introduced her to the others. She nodded to each.

"This is Princess Lilliana," Rhianwyn added.

Broccan looked surprised.

"When with my friends, I'm only Lilliana," she urged.

Still, the men stood and bowed to her.

"If I wanted people to behave this way, I could've stayed in the castle," she scolded. "I don't long for your reverence but your friendship."

She went to sit near Rhianwyn.

"I've no other tankards," Rhianwyn said.

"Then we'll share." Lilliana smiled taking Rhianwyn's cup and drinking a very long drink. "I might share with all of you."

She proceeded to go to each of the others and took a hearty drink from everyone. When she sat beside Broccan, very close, Rhianwyn noted, Broccan looked at her with interest. Lilliana *was* stunningly beautiful. Her jet-black hair and exotic almond-shaped, large dark-brown eyes were undeniably striking.

"You shouldn't be drinking so much," Cassian warned. Lilliana sneered.

"Return to the castle, Cassian… if you're going to be like an old woman nagging me."

"What do you suppose might occur if anything should happen to you while you're on our watch?" Cassian asked.

"Nothing will happen. Relax! Have a damn drink, Cassian. By your gloomy expression, you look like you could use one."

Cassian glanced at Broccan again and then at Rhianwyn. She could see Cassian was uncomfortable.

"I'll give you back your lute, Keyon," Broccan said. "I

should be leavin' anyway."

"Don't go," Lilliana pleaded. "We've only just arrived. I did wonder when I'd finally get to meet the new lord of Brockwell Manor."

"I thought Giles hadn't officially given him that title." Cassian's tone was unusually caustic.

"Is that any of your concern?" Broccan replied, equally abrasive.

"Cassian, I swear if you can't be more carefree, I'd prefer you leave straightaway," Lilliana admonished. "Ulf can accompany me home or perhaps Lord Brockwell." She smiled at Broccan flirtatiously.

"As I said, I should be off." Broccan respectfully dipped his head. "It's been a delightful evening. Thank you for the delicious stew, Maiden Albray and the dance… and for the company of all of you."

Broccan smiled at the others, but stared longest at Rhianwyn. Cassian glowered at him.

"Would you deny a princess a dance?" Lilliana asked.

"I thought you were only Lilliana?" Broccan grinned.

That brought a quick smile to Lilliana's pretty face.

"True, but I would very much like to dance with you, Lord Brockwell. It's a rarity I'm permitted to dance."

Broccan finally obliged her and Lilliana drew him near, even lay her head upon his chest. Cassian scowled at that, too. Rhianwyn felt an unexpected twinge of jealousy. Cassian looked at Rhianwyn as though he might ask her to dance. How could she turn him down without looking conspicuous? Thankfully, he didn't.

When the dance was ended, Lillian even pulled Broccan's head to her and brushed her lips against his. He quickly stepped away.

"Now, I *will* take my leave," he said.

"Thank you for the bread and butter. Take what's left," Rhianwyn suggested.

Broccan came to stand by her and smiled winsomely. "No, keep it or perhaps offer some to the others." Broccan gestured to Cassian, Ulf, and Lilliana. "Or take it to the children in the village. Good night. I do hope to see you again soon."

Broccan lingeringly gazed at Rhianwyn. She saw Cassian stand taller, his hand hovering near his sword. Broccan looked almost pleased about that. After Broccan was gone, Rhianwyn was left wondering why the men seemed to bear such animosity toward each other.

Lilliana insisted on dancing with the two knights though Cassian seemed uncomfortable when she kissed him, as well. Ulf danced with Selena and Rhianwyn, too. It was nearly dawn when the knights finally convinced a drunken Lilliana it was time to return to the castle before she was found out, and they'd be in more trouble than she might imagine. Elspeth and Isolde left earlier. The steamy looks they'd shared indicated they had something besides drinking or dancing in mind though Rhianwyn thought Ulf looked at Elspeth with affectionate propensity.

"Maxim and I'll walk you home, Selena," Keyon offered.

Although Selena had begun to sober up, she was still a bit unsteady.

"Won't Shandy be angry you're out so late?" Rhianwyn

asked.

"She's away in London. Besides, I'll just sneak in the upper window," Selena replied.

"I'll assist so she's unharmed," Maxim assured Rhianwyn.

"The dogs can stay with me till you return," Rhianwyn said.

Maxim nodded and they set off. Rhianwyn placed the large kettle on the ground, letting the dogs share what was left of the stew. She wrapped up the two loaves of bread and the butter. She'd take them to the children tomorrow. Her thoughts returned to being held in Broccan's arms... his admittance to wanting to kiss her and more. She dwelled on that possibility, imagining it with clarity. Her cheeks became hot for the thought appealed to her more than she'd like.

She picked up the bowls and tankards and set them inside, realizing she'd forgotten to have the men carry the table in. It was solid; even if she dragged it, she'd struggle. When Maxim returned for the dogs, she'd ask him to do it.

"I'll take the table in if you wish."

She turned quickly for the dogs hadn't barked.

"It can wait," she said as Broccan walked nearer.

"No one stayed to help you clear up?"

"They were a little drunk." She shrugged. "I don't mind."

"Let me carry the table in," he insisted.

She finally nodded. He picked it up with nearly as much ease as Maxim had. She motioned to where it should be placed and he set it down.

"Is there anythin' else you'd like me to do?" His eyes briefly went to the bed.

"Thanks for your assistance, but I'll be going to bed soon."

He grinned as though to say that's what he'd been suggesting but he only went out the door, then peeked back in.

"Come see my dogs and my other horse sometime. I could take you out ridin' if you like. While you're there maybe you could see Giles for a wee bit. He wants to speak with you in a fierce way and his time grows short. It would bring peace to a dyin' man for it's clear he wishes to make amends."

"Ask me when I'm not filled with drink."

He smiled again. "I liked our dance very much, Rhianwyn."

"You're uncommonly audacious, Lord Brockwell...both in using my given name and in speaking so forwardly."

"With a straight face tell me you disapprove entirely. With no blush in those lovely cheeks." He dared to step inside again, reached out, brushed a strand of hair from her face and her entire body hummed with need. He gently lifted her chin and lowered his head to hers but she stepped away. She yearned to have his lips on hers but if that happened she had no doubt it wouldn't end there, but with him in her bed. She wasn't sure if she was glad or disappointed that Maxim would be back for the dogs soon. But it was enough of a deterrent for her to discourage Broccan's advances.

"Leave straightaway!"

"Before I weaken your resolve and you permit me to kiss you?"

"You're incorrigible!" Still, she smirked.

"Would you be more inclined to agree to a kiss if I promise to leave straight after?"

"Now!" She pointed to the door.

This time Champion went to Rhianwyn's side, obviously sensing her impatience.

"I'd never hurt her, old boy." Broccan dared to pet his head and again moved so close he could've kissed her. "Good night, Rhianwyn."

"Good night," she said.

He left and she closed the door after all four dogs came inside.

Damn that man for making her want the kiss…and more.

"WHEN WERE YOU planning to tell me?" Sir Cassian cornered Rhianwyn near the castle courtyard the following day.

"Tell you? Tell you what?" Rhianwyn was completely uncertain.

Cassian grasped her hand and pulled her behind the stone wall. Looking down at her with desperation, he tried to kiss her. She turned away.

"No," she said. "I told you long ago…we can't—kisses always lead to… other things."

"By God, Rhianwyn. I burn for you. Marry me, not

that bloody Irishman. Is it his wealth you long for? I wouldn't have thought you the kind of woman who'd yearn for plenitude. I thought you relished the simple life. I hoped you'd agree knights are noble even if they're not rewarded with prominent wealth but only good standing with the king and the people. And you know nothing about Broccan Mulryan—not how he's earned his coin or if Brockwell estate's been justly left to him by Giles."

"What are you talking about, Cassian?"

He touched her hair and pulled her closer. Again, she pushed him away.

"I'm referring to you becoming so close to that damn Irishman that he gazes at you with blatant desire. I had a run-in with him earlier. He intends to ask permission to marry you. He was apparently granted audience with the king this morning. If King Thaddeus agrees, you won't be free to marry me any longer."

"Cassian…listen to me *once and for all.* I'll not wed you or any knight and I've heard nothing of Lord Brockwell's intentions."

"You didn't tell *Lord Brockwell* you needed a husband?"

"I told him I'd be forced to be wed and that I'd lose the cottage, but I certainly didn't suggest *he* request to marry me."

"Tell me you don't feel something for me, Rhianwyn? You were unquestionably passionate when we were together."

"I care for you but I don't love you, Cassian. I never meant to hurt you and shouldn't have let it go so far. You comforted me when we were both grieving Anselm's loss."

"It went far beyond comforting, Rhianwyn. You didn't stop me when it became more than kisses and it wasn't always me who came to you."

"I'm not denying that, Cassian, although if anyone knew you'd be commended while I'd be shamed."

"Not all would think it commendable to bed my best friend's betrothed. I love you despite always feeling guilty for *having* his woman."

"It wasn't while I was his betrothed. He was already gone when we were together. But do you think I feel no guilt on that count? He left to fight because of all that happened with his father and me. He's dead and I've been intimate with his best friend."

"Make our actions honorable then," Cassian pleaded. "Marry me. The Irishman likely only wishes for a wife to produce heirs. Tell him you can't marry him for you don't intend to carry children."

"He knows," she said.

"You've discussed that personal subject with him?" Cassian seemed hurt.

"I told him I don't wish to bear children, but we didn't discuss *him* marrying me."

"Marry me, Rhianwyn," Cassian said again, once more holding her close.

"You think you'll change my mind if we sard again?" She stiffened in his arms.

"Don't cheapen what we shared," he replied. "You're a healthy woman with desires."

"I don't think of that," she admitted.

"Because you know you'd eventually give in to your

desires. As you would with the Irishman. I've seen how you and other women look at him and know of his reputation of beguiling women. Tell him you won't marry him so he'll withdraw his proposal. Your stubbornness in not marrying me or even my brother may be my undoing. I'd go bloody mad to know he'd have you in his bed."

"Why are you opposed to me marrying Lord Brockwell, yet you'd accept me marrying Everard? Do you think Everard wouldn't request me in his bed or that he'd share me with you?"

"That's cruel, Rhianwyn. I just want you safe. The Irishman has a less than virtuous past."

"Why do you dislike him so much?"

A group of people walking by forced Cassian to step away. She recognized his torment in wanting her. She didn't deny the few times they'd been intimate had been thrilling. It temporarily eased her sorrow…despite the guilt. But she hadn't counted on Cassian falling in love with her.

"It's likely only you can stop him from marrying you, Rhianwyn, but still, I intend to find Lord Brockwell and tell him to stay the hell away from you." Cassian briskly walked away giving her no time to argue.

RHIANWYN LIE AWAKE tossing and turning. Not only was she bewildered as to why Cassian and Broccan seemed to dislike one another even before Broccan told him he'd ask to wed her. Not only was she fighting the powerful natural womanly desires that often afflicted her at night, but she also couldn't forget the sensation of Broccan's arms around her—his lips near hers when he'd nearly kissed her. She'd imagined what it would be like to lie unclothed in his arms, to share physical intimacies. Those erotic thoughts caused her body to respond with dampness between her thighs and increasingly unsettling need. She inhaled deeply...for the briefest time even considered going to find Cassian to ease her primal urges. She shook her head at that notion. She wouldn't use or hurt him.

To think Broccan had gone to the king and requested her hand without mentioning it to her, greatly displeased her. What was Cassian referring to in Broccan's past and about Brockwell Manor? She finally arose deciding to bathe in the hot pool in attempt to ease her fretfulness and her growing womanly desires.

BROCCAN RECOGNIZED CASSIAN'S aggravated voice at the door, heard Matty, the woman who had raised him from an infant, telling Cassian, Lord Brockwell wasn't taking visitors. He'd already had two heated run-ins with him earlier in the village and been tempted to draw his sword. He certainly didn't want to see Cassian again. But apparently the man wouldn't listen and came in without permission.

Their eyes met when Broccan glanced up. Filled with drink, Broccan likely wouldn't fare favorably in a sword-fight even if he had usually won the sparring matches they'd once taken part in. That was years ago when they were friends. Now, they were anything but. Matty looked concerned as Cassian strode into the hall with a grim expression.

"Don't fret, Matty. I'm certain Sir Cassian won't take up much of my time."

Matty nodded but wore a strained expression as she left the men.

"How dare you barge into my home uninvited and unwelcome?" Broccan snarled.

He saw the furious gaze on Cassian's face though in Broccan's opinion, he was the one who should hold deep resentment toward the other man.

"Stay away from her!" Cassian blared.

"From her? Who...Matty?" Broccan sarcastically asked.

"You know bloody well who I'm talking about. Stay away from Maiden Albray."

"Because you want her for yourself?" Broccan asked. "Her friends tell me she's avowed to never wed a knight and you're sworn to the knighthood for all your years."

"I'll endeavor to convince her to marry me. You're not worthy of her," Cassian said, his body tense, his eyes furious.

"Because you and I share a disparagin' history doesn't make me less worthy to be her husband. I'd see Rhianwyn provided for. She'd live here...where Anslem wished her to be...where she deserves to be."

"She loathes Giles. She doesn't even like this manor house or the estate. If you actually knew her you'd be aware she'd never want to live as a lady."

"You believe she should remain in her dilapidated cottage, cold and hungry a lot of the time…or perhaps you'll take her to live in the knights' keep?"

"I'd provide a home for us…if she'd agree to wed me."

"Until you're called off to fight and likely killed in battle, like Anslem…leaving her your widow."

"If you stay away from her, she might come round to my way of thinking." Cassian ignored Broccan's last comment.

"She's meant to be here," Broccan argued.

"Why?" Cassian asked.

"There are many truths I've recently discovered. If Rhianwyn marries me, we'd inherit this…all of this." Broccan looked around the grand manor house.

"Does she know the truth? Have you told her you knew Anslem…that you were there when he was killed?"

"I'll tell her when I gain her trust. I doubt she knows much of what actually happened in France. Sure you wouldn't have told her for you'd have had to admit to your wrongdoings, Cassian…some I'll never forgive."

"I told you what happened that day. But apparently there's no reasoning with you for you're as bloody stubborn as ever and you're pissing drunk, Broccan."

"You're right; you'll never convince me you were justified in your actions and besides, it's my home…my ale. Why shouldn't I drink?"

"You'd not be able to defend yourself in such a state." Cassian's tone was droll.

"I doubt you'd be capable of killin' me even when I'm filled with drink. It always infuriated you I was more skilled with a sword than you…that Thaddeus and Severin commended my abilities and Severin asked me to help train the men with you, his valued Knight Commander. Me…an Irish warrior and champion fighter but a man who hadn't worked my way up the ranks of the knighthood when I was named your equal."

"You'd like to challenge me then in your drunken state?" Cassian said. "You could be killed before you're actually named Lord Brockwell."

"You still feel you're the one wronged even after all you did there in France?"

"I know much about your past so don't pretend you're innocent, Broccan," Cassian said.

"You should go now before I show you my skills haven't faded in these years since we last saw each another on that battlefield. You certainly didn't expect to see me again."

Cassian glared but finally left clearly enraged.

CHAPTER ELEVEN

R HIANWYN HAD NEVER been to the hot pool in darkness, but the moon was nearly full lighting her way.
She wasn't fearful coming here although it was avoided by
most for it was said the devil heated the pool with the fires
of hell. Rhianwyn shook her head at the absurdity. People
could be so easily frightened and superstitions ran rampant.

Rhianwyn looked through the silver birches across the
grasslands to the towering sunstones. The moon shone
upon them casting an ethereal glow and making it appear
the stones themselves were luminous. She remembered her
mother mentioning that. Mererid claimed when the stones
gleamed, something life changing would soon occur to the
person who witnessed it. She said the stones glowed the
night Rhianwyn was born. They'd also radiated light the
night before Mererid died. Rhianwyn wasn't certain she
wanted to witness it even though they looked phenomenal-
ly beautiful.

She soaked in the heated water which only made her
more aware of her building womanly needs. Standing with
the waterfall's cool water cascading down upon her was
exhilarating, but it left her no less unsettled.

The longer she dwelled on Broccan Mulryan, the more
she wanted to have it out with him regarding his proposal,

before she lost her nerve.

RHIANWYN MADE HER way through the thick forest, the moon offering enough light to see. When she arrived at Brockwell Manor, the huge sprawling estate was mostly in darkness. A candle burned in only one window. If she knocked now, who'd answer? Would she waken Giles Brockwell?

She no longer cared for she'd worked herself into a state and needed to speak with Broccan. She pounded loudly on the door even as she glanced down at her bare feet and thin shift with only a shawl covering her, not even a kirtle or petticoats. She wondered if anyone would answer, but she pounded again till she finally heard footsteps, not heavy boot-falls—surely not Broccan.

The door opened. A slight older woman with long un-bound gray hair and a perturbed expression peered out. She was in a nightdress, wrapped in a shawl, and carried a candle.

"I wish to speak with Lord Brockwell," Rhianwyn said.

"It's a bit late," the woman reprimanded in an Irish accent. "The older Lord Brockwell's asleep. I wouldn't think of wakin' him. The younger's had other visitors this night who've already riled him. He'll not want to be disturbed again."

She started to close the door, but Rhianwyn pushed past her.

"I don't give a damn what he wants; I need to speak

with him."

"You'd be wise not to, lass… for he's been at the drink and he's in an uncommonly foul mood."

"That makes two of us. I *will* see him!" Rhianwyn demanded.

"Would you be Maiden Albray?" the woman asked.

"I am, but how did you know?"

"Ah, well I do see what all the fuss is about for you've a good amount of beauty to ye. You're clearly spirited, too, but it's a bit unmannerly payin' a visit in the dead of night."

"I suppose so, but I won't be dissuaded."

"Sure you've never seen young Broccan in such rancor for he even snapped at me."

"May I ask who you are?"

"I'm Matty. I helped raise the lad from a babe."

"I must see him… please," Rhianwyn added.

"I'll take you to him, but mind you've been warned."

Matty motioned for her to follow. The old woman carried the candle shielding the flame with her cupped hand through the dark corridor of the stately manor house Rhianwyn had been in only once before. They came to the great hall with a lengthy wood table, an immense hearth, a few crossed swords and shields and several sets of animal horns and heads mounted upon the walls.

Broccan leaned forward, elbows on the table, a brooding look upon his face with two large wolfhounds at his side, both fully alert and staring at Rhianwyn.

"You've another visitor," Matty said.

"I've no patience for seein' anyone else this night."

Broccan didn't look up from the jug of ale he clutched.

Rhianwyn could smell the pungent odor of ale.

"Just send them away, Matty…and come to it, who in their right mind would come visitin' at this hour?"

"Someone presently not in their right mind," Rhianwyn said.

His head snapped up on hearing her which caused the dogs to stand more alert. He narrowed his eyes that looked well affected by drink.

"You'd be wise to leave now, Maiden Albray," he said.

"I've been warned you're in a temper." She lifted her chin defiantly.

"I didn't say he was in a temper. I said he was in a foul mood," Matty said.

"You're both right." Broccan drunkenly nodded. "So come back in the mornin' if you're so inclined. Hopefully I'll be in better temperament and not filled with drink."

"I'm here now and I aim to speak with you. I don't care of your mood or your drunkenness. Apparently we've much to discuss."

He looked her up and down unabashedly.

"You don't appear suitably dressed for a social call."

"I don't bloody well care how I'm attired!"

She glowered, boldly walked in and sat at the table, a few chairs away from him. Matty obviously waited to see who'd win the standoff.

"Go back to bed, Matty. I'd wager Maiden Albray won't stay long."

"Don't be unkind, either of you," Matty said before she left.

The dogs came to sniff her and Rhianwyn petted them. Broccan looked surprised.

"Most wouldn't be given such warm reception by my loyal guard dogs especially when they've spoken in such a dour tone to their master." Broccan took a long swig from the jug he held. "This is Fionn and Oisin."

"They're father and son?" she asked.

"You know Irish legends?" Broccan again sounded surprised.

"My mother was a great storyteller and knew much of the legends of all Celtic lands."

He looked only somewhat less perturbed as she continued to stroke the dogs' backs and they both leaned against her.

"There's no denyin' you have a way with animals."

"You aren't going to offer me any drink? It would seem you've had your share and then some."

"It's unusually strong ale and mightn't be to your likin'," he replied.

"Let me be the judge of that."

He nodded to the sideboard. "Help yourself. There's mead or ale. Tankards and goblets as well. Might as well familiarize yourself with the place since you *will* be livin' here soon. I presume that's what you're here to discuss. That's what *everyone's* been here to discuss tonight," he said under his breath.

Rhianwyn stood and took a bottle, uncorked it and sniffed. It was mead. She didn't bother with a goblet, but returned to the table with the bottle. He stared at her again.

"What have you done?" she asked.

"Done?" he replied.

"Why have you spoken to the king and requested to marry me?"

"I'm only protectin' you. You're sure to have many offers of marriage by the king's invitation, but mine would see you always cared for lavishly. Should you not have other suitable offers, I'm only protectin' you from the despicable spinster's block. I inquired of it and heard men sometimes buy women pretendin' they'll marry them, then take them to be sold to brothels or on slave ships to other countries. With your beauty... those long beautiful light-brown tresses with the streaks of gold, your unusually captivating pale-blue eyes, and a body surely envied by all women and desired by all men...you'd fetch a pretty price but not have a pretty future."

"Just go to the king. Tell him you've reconsidered, that you don't want to marry the daughter of a Welsh woman and a mad mage."

"I have no quarrel with the Welsh and you already told me he was a mage," Broccan said.

"Many fear magic, others believe Father's mad which could be an inherited trait."

"Magic is much revered in Ireland."

"And the possibility of madness?"

"We're all a little mad at times," Broccan replied.

She stood with the bottle, took several swigs, then paced staring at the man. Even drunk he was undeniably sensual.

"There are many reasons you wouldn't wish to marry me."

"Such as?" he asked.

"Firstly...I'm not virginal?"

"I'm not myself," the stubborn man said.

"Men aren't expected to be," she sneered.

She sighed, sat down again at the absurdly long table. She stared at the hearth. The flames had died down. The glowing logs crackled lightly.

"Most men want a chaste bride. It truly doesn't matter to you that I'm not virginal?"

"Why would it? I probably couldn't bring to mind the number of women I sarded, much less their faces or names. In truth, I probably didn't know their names—certainly not the whores."

He brushed his wavy brown hair from his face for it wasn't tied back tonight. It appealingly fell to his shoulders. "You'll be marrying a man who once sought out and killed men for coin."

"Killed men?"

"Outlaws, fiends, and murderers, but yes, I've killed more men that I could count. Plus, I occasionally drink in excess and spend time with whores. Therefore you previously having other men's cocks within you isn't objectionable...as long as mine...as your husband, will be the last."

She stared at him. His hair unkempt, his face not cleanly shaven but covered in sensual stubble. There was a jeopardous pull to him.

"I won't marry you!"

"You'd have to take that up with the king," Broccan said. "He'll decide who you marry. Here have a stronger drink. You look like you could use one."

He pushed the jug toward her, but she shook her head. Therefore he filled a goblet and set it before her. She stared, finally took a long gulp, then coughed for it was very potent.

"As your future husband, I also insist you stay away from *Sir Cassian*. He and I do not see eye-to-eye on the subject of this marriage. We had several unpleasant encounters, just today. I see he wants you. Was it Anselm you lay with? I've heard you were his betrothed, so it'd be natural you'd want to be with him."

It sounded like Broccan was fishing, wondering who she'd been with. She said nothing.

"You'll not reveal the man or men you've lain with then?"

"I never lay with Anslem," she whispered.

She thought Broccan seemed relieved. Although why that would matter, she couldn't discern.

"Cassian came here and told you not to marry me?" she asked.

"Sir Severin arrived first…insisting I marry you straightaway. He claims you're a dangerous distraction to his knights. Cassian came soon after, rather insistent I withdraw my offer of marriage. Our discussion nearly saw us come to blows. If I'd not been filled with drink, I would've accepted his challenge. I presume he wants you for himself."

"I won't marry a knight. He well knows that. But tell me why you want to marry me."

"I need a wife," Broccan replied.

"I'm common-born," she argued.

"I don't care about titles and the king recently revoked that rule. You're exceptionally pretty with a fine form and you're most fascinatin' when you're not bein' so damn bullheaded and difficult."

"I wouldn't make a good wife. I told you I mix potions far better than I can cook."

"I employ several cooks. Having a wife that's a healer might be more beneficial, and you're unassuming, Maiden Albray, for your rabbit stew was the best I've ever tasted."

"I've never lived as a noble. I prefer being out in the sanctity of the forest procuring herbs. I'd feel stifled living here... unable to walk free in nature. I wouldn't even understand what's expected of me. I don't know how to plan feasts or host noble lords and ladies. I wouldn't know what to say, how to behave, or what to wear. You and I would be entirely mismatched."

"My family *is* high born, but as you've just learned I didn't always live that life. I don't intend to host elaborate feasts. You won't need to learn how to be a noble. You can remain just as you are. That's what intrigued me...how comfortable you are with who you are."

"I don't want to be your wife. I don't want to be anyone's wife," she rephrased.

"I need a woman and require a wife...and I do very much want *you*."

"Marry another who'll gladly give you children. Take me as your personal harlot or mistress if appeasing your base needs is the true reason you'd wish to marry me."

His eyes narrowed. "That's a very brash statement."

"I promise...you could have me whenever you wish, but let me remain living in my cottage and performing my duties as a healer."

"Why would you suggest such a clandestine arrangement?" He looked astonished.

"I told you. I like my life as it is. I admit, I do recognize the attraction between us but I don't want children, not ever."

"If you freely offer yourself to me whenever I desire, you'd surely become with child."

"If we aren't wed, I won't be expected to bear your children. I can drink elixirs to hopefully ensure no children are conceived. If they are, I can take another potion to expel them before they grow. As a last resort I'd find a woman learned in such matters who'd see them rooted from my womb."

By his stern expression he found that objectionable. He sat down not far from her and poured her another drink. She drank readily as he reached for another jug.

"What would become of you if the priests heard such unholy admissions?"

"I suspect I could be burned as a heretic for not going forth and multiplying, perhaps banished from the village, sent to a slaver, or maybe to a house of harlots."

"You'd risk all that rather than carry a child?"

She didn't deny it.

"Still...I fail to see how this would end your conundrum when the king's law states all women must be wed."

"Tell the king you wish to wed a noble lady but that

you'll keep me as your private harlot. They're exempt from his law of marriage."

"You're honestly so opposed to marriage and children, it wouldn't bother you your good name is befouled by being a whore or my mistress?"

"I don't expect a man to understand having his life dictated with no say in his future."

"Sure it's easy for you to offer to be with me in such a manner when there's no way to prove you'd follow through. If I did marry an undoubtedly drudgingly boring noble woman who'd perhaps willingly carry my children without threatening to dispose of them, you could simply renege on your libertine proposition. How would I hold you to it?"

She stared into his very blue eyes, a little glassy with drink. Her own eyes were somewhat unfocused from the combination of mead and ale. She didn't often drink, definitely not this much or this fast. She stared at the man. He *was* most appealing and the thought of coupling with him had been on her mind even before she'd drunk too much.

His tunic was partly unlaced revealing some of his muscular chest. His dark breeches were tight and showed his well-formed thighs. She longed to run her fingers through his wavy hair. She stared at his tempting lips and he looked back at her with discernable hunger.

"You wish for me to prove I'll be with you? Would that ensure you'll speak with the king and rescind your proposal?"

He didn't reply but stared at her body. She stood a little shakily. If he agreed to this bargain, she *would* follow through and be his mistress.

CHAPTER TWELVE

RHIANWYN STARED AT Broccan. "I swear I'll stay true to my word. I'll be yours till you tire of me and no longer wish for me to be your mistress—until your eyes rove to another or you fall in love with your wife."

Broccan's chair was pushed back. She leaned against the table to stand just in front of him glancing toward the door hoping Matty or no other servants would appear. Rhianwyn gazed into his eyes and he drank more. She removed her shawl then her hands went to her shift's ties.

"If yer hopin' I'll prove myself honorable by stoppin' you, sure you'll be disappointed."

She didn't reply, but slowly, sensually unlaced her shift. He didn't blink, probably presumed she wouldn't go much further. She opened the garment to reveal her cleavage. He only stared harder. Ordinarily she'd have a kirtle to remove, too. She untied her hair and shook it so it fell to her waist, then slid her shift down one shoulder.

"You *should* leave. I'm too filled with drink and too long without a woman to show restraint." His voice was already husky with arousal.

Their eyes met.

"This isn't a game, Maiden Albray. You mightn't be innocent but it's doubtful you know how deep a man's desires run or you wouldn't toy with me. You also don't know what effect an unattired woman has on a man or... perhaps you know all too well and like havin' that power over a man."

She didn't reply, but instead sensually pulled her shift down so her breasts were uncovered but her nipples remained concealed by her long hair. He blew out his breath.

Again, she looked toward the door. Hopefully everyone was asleep. He didn't touch her as she'd expected, instead he glanced around the hall as though looking for someone, too, though they were alone. Only attired in the shift covering her from below her breasts to above her knees, she looked into his eyes then tossed her hair so her breasts were uncovered. His gaze rested upon them and he swallowed hard.

"By the saints! Your skin is flawless. You're exquisite," he whispered.

When he still didn't make a move, she gathered the fabric of her shift and seductively pulled it up. She slightly parted her thighs and looked at the front of his breeches. His erect manhood was unmissable and like the rest of him, large and commendable. She'd definitely aroused him, yet still he didn't touch her.

She leaned back pressing her backside against the table then placed her bare foot on his chair as she slowly raised her shift higher. Again, he only stared. She was beginning to lose her nerve when he didn't respond to her seduction. Their eyes met and his exuded a smoldering quality.

"Do you wish for me to disrobe you?" she asked.

His eyebrow arched but he didn't reply, therefore she lifted his tunic's hem. He raised his arms enabling her to pull it over his head. She stared at his gloriously powerful chest, muscular shoulders and arms, his rippled stomach. He had several scars on his chest and a larger scar on his belly. She lightly caressed his broad chest and he groaned.

"You have beautiful hair." He leaned closer and placed his face to her hair, inhaling deeply. "With a sweet fragrance." His voice was now huskier.

Her skin tingled with the sensation of him so close and she ached to have him touch her, considered placing his hand to her breast.

"This is the last time I'll warn you," Broccan said. "If we go beyond this point, I won't be dissuaded even if you should suddenly change your mind. So if you're only tauntin' me, I…"

"I'm not," she assured, raising her shift so high her womanhood was nearly visible.

He caressed her foot then grazed her ankle and she jumped at the sensation, for it wholly aroused her.

"You really should go," he whispered again even as he moved closer.

"Are you asking me to leave?"

"If you don't this *will* lead to something you might not actually want."

"Why do you presume I don't want it? Because I'm a woman and proper unwed women aren't supposed to want this? Women have needs, too. You've admitted you've had more than your share of women. With how attractive you are, I'd wager you ensured they wanted it."

"You think I'm attractive…just not enough to marry."
He touched her calf and slowly slid his large, warm hand
up the length of her thigh, beneath her shift to her backside
and then her waist. He did the same on the other side then
suddenly lifted her onto the table. She gasped as he stood
before her ensuring his erect manhood was between her
thighs pressing against her sex straining through the fabric
of his breeches.

"You play a dangerous game, Rhianwyn."

He pushed a wisp of hair from her face, then seductively caressed her lips with his thumb which drove her mad
with desire.

"By God, I want you." He finally lowered his lips to
hers.

She met them in a far-from-tender kiss. His tongue was
in her mouth and she liked the sensation as he ardently
kissed her and she moaned.

"Though it's true, I'm not innocent, neither am I as
experienced as you might wish a mistress to be," she
admitted.

"Christ, you excite me, Rhianwyn," he whispered pulling her closer.

His fingers trailed from her face to her throat, then
down to her breast. She writhed her hips and moved
against him wanting him to take her straightaway. He
ended the kiss and his lips went to her breast. She arched
her back pressing against his mouth. He took her nipple in
his mouth and teased it with his tongue. It peaked so
abruptly she moaned even louder.

When he moved his hand, she presumed he was reaching to unbutton his breeches, but instead he pulled a knife from his pocket. She felt her eyes grow wide for she didn't actually know what he intended. He said he'd killed before—surely not women.

However, she'd seen how perverse men could be. She'd occasionally been called to the brothel to tend to bites and wounds inflicted by demented men. Broccan grasped her shift cutting straight through the garment leaving her uncovered. He drew in his breath then tossed the knife on the table, kissed and suckled one breast, then the other before gently lying her upon the table. The coolness of the table beneath her back was startling, but when his mouth moved from kissing her breasts… to her belly… to the tuft of hair above her womanhood, then lower… she cried out, now wild with arousal. She'd never experienced this form of intimacy. Not wanting to completely lose control, she tried to wriggle free. He held tight and continued pleasuring her till she gasped and cried out as she intensely climaxed, her entire body quivering.

She sat up and took the knife herself. He stared but permitted her to place the weapon to his groin. She cut away the four gold buttons on the side of his breeches each falling to the stone floor with a distinctive *ping*. His entrancing blue eyes were consumed in lust now. She pulled back his breeches, releasing his large, erect manhood, then slid them over his hips. He made a guttural sound as she fondled him up and down the length of his firmness, then eagerly caressed the tip till he moaned loudly.

He looked into her eyes as she guided him to her sex. He hesitated, perhaps waiting for her to finally stop him.

"I want you…inside me," she whispered and he exuberantly thrust forward.

He moaned as he filled her to the hilt and she gasped at the thorough penetration. He still seemed disbelieving that she'd permit this. She held his muscular shoulders as they moved together more frantically and she experienced another dizzying release.

"I want to continue this in my bed," he throatily said.

"I won't go to your bed, Lord Brockwell."

"But you'll allow me to have you on my table," he perplexingly replied moving faster and with more purposeful thrusts, then suckled her breast so hard, she cried out.

"And anywhere else you might desire," she rasped, "but never in your bed where you'd have a wife."

He was breathing raggedly but moved away, pulled off his breeches and closed the sliding doors to this hall. Lifting her into his arms he placed her upon the rug before the fire and lay beside her. They passionately kissed and were joined again without delay. The heated passion continued till he moaned and gave way to his long denied release.

"Broccan, are you in there?" Matty called from outside the door.

He opened his eyes—shook his fuzzy head. He'd had a good deal to drink and not much sleep to speak of.

"I am," he groggily replied.

"You spent the night there when there's a dozen beds in this manor?"

"This was more convenient." He glanced at the beautiful woman asleep in his arms. One dog lie behind him, the other beside Rhianwyn.

She sighed contently before her unusual pale-blue eyes opened to stare up at him. She muttered something indiscernible. It was Welsh, probably a cuss word, but she wore a hint of a smile, too. If she remembered half of what they'd shared, they both had good reason to smile. It was like nothing he'd ever experienced before with *any* woman.

"Will Maiden Albray be stayin' to break fast, then?" Matty asked. "I didn't hear her leave so I presume she's there with you."

Rhianwyn's face became delightfully rosy.

"Please bring food enough for two, Matty. I think the lady and I have a bit of talkin' to do."

"Talkin'? Sure that's what you'll be doin' Broccan. You'd think I was born yesterday." Matty's voice trailed off as her steps receded.

"You permit her to wait on you at her age," Rhianwyn said.

"Matty delights in doin' things for me. It's why she insisted on comin' with me from Ireland."

Rhianwyn moved from his arms with no attempt to cover herself and petted the dog near her before she stood. She located her shredded shift, held it up, frowned and shook her head.

"You could at least turn away," she said.

"It's a bit late to become modest, Rhianwyn. I think after last night we're well past that. Besides why would I turn away? You're exceptionally beautiful."

He saw her glance his way, observing him, too.

"You're rather exceptional yourself."

That mere glance made him hard again.

"I'm not sure how much you remember of what occurred last night," he said.

"Never doubt I recall *everything*."

"With fondness or regret?" he asked.

"I'm not regretful."

He smiled at that. "You're in considerably better form this morning," she said.

"Why wouldn't I be? That was a night unlike any other."

She blushed again.

"You're even lovelier with your face flushed." He enjoyed looking at her perfect body. Her youthful breasts were full but firm and high, her waist was small. Her legs were shapely—her skin flawless but for the purposely placed mark upon her lovely round arse. He'd viewed that closely. He wondered who'd placed the red dragon, the symbol often associated with Cymru. Usually only Vikings had such marks upon their bodies.

She reached for her shawl, wrapping it around her.

"Clearly your shift's no longer suitable for coverin' you—sliced apart as it is. It was threadbare anyway."

"That's the reason you cut it, then?" she asked.

"I cut it because I couldn't wait to see all of you," he admitted.

He leaned on his elbow, unclothed and well aroused. She located his breeches and tossed them at him and he grinned. She smiled a sensuous smile that made his heart soar.

"I can't believe you permitted me to place a weapon near your spindle!" She smirked.

"By the wanton look in your eyes then, I didn't think you'd be after doin' it any damage. You trusted me with the knife. I only returned the trust."

"I didn't believe you'd hurt me either," she replied.

"I'd quite like to repeat everything we shared...even now. You did say I could have you whenever I wanted."

"Here in the light of day when Matty will surely return any moment? Besides, I must go home to attend to weakening your seed which should've been done straight after."

"Straight after...which time then?" he asked.

"I shouldn't have fallen asleep."

"Well the joinin' did go on for some time and we were rather exuberant." He waggled his eyebrows.

Again her cheeks colored in him speaking of it.

"I liked holdin' you while you slept...nearly as much as what we did before we slept."

She blew out her breath so her fringe fluttered on her forehead. She'd done that last night when they'd finally separated after coupling repeatedly. They'd been breathless and exhausted. A knock now stopped her halfway across the chamber with the shawl not even covering her lovely arse.

"May I bring your tray in?" Matty asked.

"Yes, I'm famished," Broccan replied.

"Certainly, tell her to come straight in," Rhianwyn sarcastically whispered.

"Good morning, Lord Brockwell, Maiden Albray."

Matty showed no trace of surprise in seeing her mostly unclothed.

"It is a fine mornin' to be sure." Broccan grinned widely.

"You're a bit of a scoundrel, Broccan, but you don't tend to have your female friends stay the night," Matty said.

"Are you tryin' to get me in shite with this lovely lady, Matty? I've never even had a woman visit Brockwell Manor much less spend the night."

"I didn't intend to stay… I fell asleep," Rhianwyn said.

"I shouldn't wonder. You must be shattered. By the sounds comin' from this chamber till the wee hours of the mornin' and the garments strewn about the hall there's no doubt what's occurred. But why's your garment slashed and those buttons cut away?"

"We were perhaps a bit eager, Matty."

"I must go." Rhianwyn cast an uncertain look at Broccan.

"Sure you're not going to permit the lass to walk about the manor like that?" Matty asked.

"I must leave," Rhianwyn said.

"You'll give the servant boys a bit of a start if they see you like that." Matty looked at Rhianwyn. "With your arse not even covered."

"You'd give them more than a start. They'd be walkin' about with rigid coc…" Broccan didn't finish for both women glowered.

"Stay, Rhianwyn," Broccan urged. "I'll find you something to wear."

"There's no need," she said. "I'll borrow this."

His leather overcoat was draped over a chair. She placed it around her shoulders. It fell to her knees. Even that made her look sensual.

"Are you sure you won't eat?" he asked.

"I must go," she said again.

"Don't leave yet," he pleaded.

He stood, also not bothering to cover himself.

"Lord help us!" Matty shook her head and looked away.

"Have you no modesty at all?" Rhianwyn asked.

"Matty changed my wraps as a babe. There's no need for modesty."

"You would've changed just a bit since then!" Rhianwyn stared at his erect manhood. She was bolder than most women and he could tell she'd be agreeable to more intimate time together. He hoped to convince her to stay.

"Have some damn decency, Broccan! Cover yourself!" Matty ordered. "Lord, you've had a bit of the devil in ye since you were a babe and had woman following ye around before you were barely old enough to know why. But now, Maiden Albray, you should eat and if you like I could have a bath filled for you."

"You have a tub for bathing?" She sounded tempted.

"Large enough for two." Broccan waggled his eyebrows again. "It's in my chambers, but it could be taken to another bedchamber since you're opposed to going to mine."

"Why?" Matty asked. "Clearly you're not opposed to sharing quite a lot with him."

"Lord Brockwell's aware I'll not behave as his wife nor

do anything he'd expect of a wife."

"You don't think he'd want his wife to do what the two of you were doin' then?" Matty curiously asked.

"Maiden Albray seems to believe wives and mistresses are to be treated entirely different."

"Not that he hasn't had a good many women, but never a wife or mistress."

"Just sit and break fast with me," Broccan insisted.

She stared at the table and blushed again probably remembering their passionate encounter there.

"I won't dine at your table as a wife would."

"Sure men and their mistresses do take meals together," he replied.

"I must go," Rhianwyn repeated, yet again.

"I'd appreciate it if you'd speak with Giles before you leave," Broccan dared to mention. Her expression changed.

"Perhaps I should take audience with Giles just as I am." She gestured to herself wrapped in his overcoat. "I'd surely prove I'm the low-born whore he labeled me when Anslem tried to convince him I was worthy of marrying him."

She ended the sentence in a whisper and Broccan regretted speaking of Giles.

"He's a crude, thoughtless man at times." Broccan nodded.

"He wishes to ask your forgiveness, lass," Matty tenderly said.

"So he can die without a guilty conscience?" Rhianwyn replied. "Tell him I forgive him for not permitting us to marry. Most nobles wouldn't want their son to marry a common-born. I even forgive the spiteful insults…but I'll never forgive him shooting Anslem's beloved dog just so I wouldn't have him."

"He shot a dog?" Broccan asked in disbelief.

"With an arrow. It took weeks for me to bring him back to health."

"By Christ's cross, he must've been a fiend!" Broccan stated.

"I heard he was once a cruel man," Matty agreed. "Now, he's simply old, grieving, and broken. Hasn't even the strength to walk. If he received forgiveness from you, Maiden Albray, it'd comfort him on his journey after he passes."

Broccan could see it tore at her kind healer's heart to know the man was ailing despite the fact she obviously despised him, but she shook her head.

"Even if his journey is made less trying, I doubt where he'll end up will be peaceful."

"I'd very much like you to stay, Rhianwyn, but if you won't, take some food with you," Broccan encouraged, changing the subject.

She looked at the platter Matty carried, but shook her head still holding the shredded shift.

"I could try to mend that for you, though it looks perhaps beyond repair," Matty said.

"That's kind of you, but if I can't mend it then I'll use it to make bandages."

Matty set the tray on the table and Rhianwyn left the hall.

"Rhianwyn, please don't go. We must speak," Broccan

called down the corridor, feeling increasingly distressed with her leaving.

She'd affected him far more than he wanted. By the time he pulled on his buttonless breeches and made it outside, she was gone.

"You may've finally met your match, Broccan," Matty said when she saw him staring toward the forest. "Best not let her get away."

"I fear it'll be a challenge to hold on to her," he replied.

CHAPTER THIRTEEN

"R HIANWYN," BROCCAN CALLED outside her cottage, but heard no reply.

He could think of scarcely anything bar her since they'd been together two nights previous. His mind was consumed with memories of their intimacy and his body ached to be with her again. He'd not come by yesterday though he barely resisted. He decided to give her time—not make her aware how truly besotted he was.

Thankfully Anslem's spirit hadn't appeared to him for that would've been undeniably awkward. He'd surely know they'd lain together.

"Why are you standing at my door?" Rhianwyn asked and he jumped. "If you've come for your overcoat, I intended to return it today."

"I needed to see you," he admitted.

"What do you want?" Her voice wasn't cool, but not noticeably friendly either.

"I think you know." He stepped closer.

"Have you spoken to the king of changing your mind about wanting to be married?"

"I haven't. He isn't easy to request audience with."

"Yet you saw him earlier this week with apparently no wait."

"You truly don't want to be married?" Broccan asked.

"Why would I?" Rhianwyn replied.

"Because what we shared was remarkable! Tell me you didn't like it every bit as much as me...that you didn't experience pleasure."

"Obviously there'd be no point in denying that." She walked past him and entered the cottage.

"Then why wouldn't you want us to be married so we can continue such pleasures every night?"

"I've already explained; I don't want to be anyone's wife. We can still share pleasurable relations when I'm your mistress."

"By Christ, Rhianwyn... I want you even now." He followed her inside, nearly striking his head on the door in his hurry, then pulled her into his arms and kissed her.

She returned the kiss without hesitation but then pushed him away. "Tell me you'll speak with the king; that was the bargain."

"What should I tell him?" He breathed heavily, just wanting to have her straightaway.

"Tell him you've decided you can't risk siring a child who might inherit my father's madness."

"Even if I did speak such absurdity, that wouldn't prevent you from bein' wed to another. I tell you plain, I don't want another man to have you as a wife or a lover."

"I'll continue to be with you if you inform the king you won't wed me. Tell him you want me to remain only your lover."

"That would irreparably soil your reputation, Rhianwyn. I don't want that. I want you for my wife."

"I suppose as a noble you're accustomed to getting whatever you want?" she said. "When the passion dies you can take another woman, but if we're wed it would complicate this. God forbid, I grew to care for you, I doubt I'd approve of you having a mistress."

"Why would the passion die?"

"Doesn't it always? By the number of men who seek other women and harlots, I'd suggest it does."

"I've been with a lot of women but never shared anythin' like I did with you. I want that always."

"I refuse to bear your children!"

"Sure you'd change your mind when we grow to love one another," he said.

"I won't!" she fervently proclaimed. "You see, you *would* expect it of me. I swear, I'll be with you whenever you desire if you speak with the king...but not as your wife...and no babies!"

"You're a damn stubborn woman!" He stared down at her, wanting her so badly he was mad with desire.

"Simply another reason why we shouldn't marry." She shook her head.

"I'm sorry your parents shared such a dismal life together," Broccan said.

"They didn't." She seemed taken aback. "They loved each other very much."

"Then you should want that, too," he said.

"I don't deny that you and I share powerful attraction, and the heated passion *was* extraordinary, but I refuse to fall in love with you."

"We can't choose when we fall in love. It happens when

it happens. Didn't Anslem love you very much and you him?" Broccan dared to say.

Her eyes changed; they filled with pain.

"I won't risk the torture again—loving someone and losing them. Nor will I experience the deep grief my father and I felt when we lost Mam."

"I didn't take you for a coward, Rhianwyn," Broccan said. "But if you won't risk love because you fear you'll lose it, then you're not permitting yourself to know joy or to truly live. Sure your mother and Anslem would both be very disappointed in you."

She glared, reached up, and slapped him hard across the face. "Leave now!" she ordered, her hands now on her hips.

"You told me I could have you whenever I chose." He held his face that stung like fire.

"I said only if you spoke to the king and told him…"

He roughly pulled her to him and kissed her. She responded with wild, matched passion as they frantically tore at each other's garments and were soon disrobed. He lifted her in his arms and neared the bed, but she shook her head.

"Not Father's bed. I won't dishonor my parents' memory. Here." She pointed beyond a hanging threadbare blanket.

He carried her to the other bed. "I doubt we'll both fit on that narrow bed," he grumbled, "and it's bloody cold in here, Rhianwyn."

"Then warm me now," she insisted.

They fell upon the bed and were joined without delay, both loudly moaning. They moved together, soon breathless with their ardor. She gripped her thighs against his hips and stared into his eyes.

"I swear you *are* the devil," she gasped into his chest in reaching her pinnacle

Besides her moans and cries of pleasure, he'd begun to recognize how she responded during her crest. She tightly squeezed him, digging her thumbnail into his back, chest, shoulder, or palm as she achieved her release. Not enough to break the skin, but it left a mark afterward that pleased him in remembering their passion.

She'd only just met her second acme before he reached his own. She wouldn't permit him to affectionately hold her afterward but moved straightaway, stood, and took a potion from the shelf.

"Leave now so I can attempt to render your seed impotent," she ordered.

His breathing was still labored from their heated encounter. He shook his head disapprovingly at her casual way of admitting her intentions. When he didn't move, she pulled her shift on over her head, took the potion, and stood beyond the blanket that divided the cottage into two areas.

This would be complicated. Broccan wasn't certain how to ease that. Soon after, she pulled the blanket aside and stood looking at him. The scent upon her had a distinct acridity from the remedy she'd used. He remained in her bed, covered only with inadequate blankets.

"Come lie with me," he coaxed.

She looked at him in disbelief. "Again?"

"You think I couldn't? Your beauty arouses me, I assure you. But I did mean come lie beside me. Let me hold you and keep you warm."

She looked reluctant, but surprised him by appeasing him.

Only for a little while. It's market day and Elopeth and Selena will expect me."

"I'll take whatever time you'll afford me," he admitted, pulling her close and covering them both.

"There's to be no tenderness or affection between us… only lust and primal need."

"I think you know nothing about being a mistress, Rhianwyn." He caressed her soft shoulders.

She looked up at him with hunger in her eyes again, then kissed him so passionately, he was hard again without question.

THE NEXT FORTNIGHT was a flurry of secret encounters and unprecedentedly wild uninhibited passion. Broccan and Rhianwyn met in the woods or her cottage. She refused to come back to the manor. Sometimes they barely greeted one another before they feverishly kissed, disrobed, and enjoyed heated carnal desires. Other times in their eagerness, they didn't make it to her cottage. He lifted her skirts while she unfastened his breeches, and they were joined without their garments removed. Once he took her against a massive yew tree and far from gently. Sometimes he thought he might be coming on too strong, but she gave it back to him with equal torridity. She craved their time together as much as he did, and he reveled in that. Occasionally she permitted him to hold or gently caress her afterward, but usually she left to attend to ensuring she didn't conceive

"I don't want to go to your bed today," Broccan said when they met near her cottage.

"You already tire of our times together?"

He saw the uncertainty in her eyes.

"By Christ, I'd never tire of that, *Go Leor Suile Gorma*." He gazed at her tenderly. "I have another place in mind for us."

He took her hand and led her to a small stone cottage near Brockwell Manor. Smoke rose from the chimney invitingly.

"This is for you," Broccan said.

"I told you…"

"Don't fight me on this, Rhianwyn," he interrupted placing his fingers to her lovely full, rosy lips. "I insist on providing a warm, comfortable place for us to be together. I'll see to it you keep your own home for it seems important to you. But stay here. This cottage has a hearth to cook inside and a larger bed."

He opened the door and led her in. She glanced around at the simple cottage—a table and two chairs, a meager cupboard, and a midsized bed took up the space. But the hearth was blazing welcomingly.

"You could create your potions and remedies here, too… in warmth and comfort."

Her eyes filled with tears and she shook her head. "Would your wife approve of having your *mistress* staying so close to the manor?"

"Rhianwyn." His patience was waning.

She pulled away. He shook his head in frustration and sat at the table.

"Have you decided what lady you might offer a marriage proposal?" she asked.

"If you must know, I met with Maiden Barlow last evening. I was invited to a meal with their family."

That clearly stunned Rhianwyn. He didn't miss her frown as she tucked her hair behind her ear.

"And last Sunday I walked in Elwin Manor gardens with Maiden Elwin for a time."

"That's...good," Rhianwyn whispered but she wouldn't meet his eyes. "Have you a preference to whom you might wish to marry?"

"You don't seem to approve of either...though you constantly push me to take a wife."

"Corliss Barlow is spiteful. She humiliates their servants and the castle workers when she attends the king's feasts with her parents. She's malicious and hateful. Maybe kindness toward common-born isn't important to you."

"I don't approve of people belittling anyone. Flora Elwin does appear to bear a more gracious countenance and lovely full lips. Kissing her wouldn't be objectionable."

"If you're trying to provoke my jealousy, you won't..."

He stood, lifted her into his arms and stared into her captivating eyes. "I'll not think of another woman, much less takin' one for a wife when all I can think about is takin' you to bed, Rhianwyn. He carried her there without delay.

BROCCAN IMPATIENTLY KNOCKED on the door and Rhianwyn finally opened it.

"Why haven't you been to our cottage in three days? I came here looking for you, too," Broccan said.

"I was probably busy with my healing and collecting herbs. I can't be with you just now."

"Rhianwyn, I'm crazed in needin' you. With sharing intimacies so frequently, I've greatly missed bein' with you these days."

Her cheeks colored. "In three more days, I'll meet with you again…but for now…"

"Rhianwyn?" he interrupted but she wouldn't meet his eyes. "Are you unwell?"

"No. It's only…it's…my monthly *womanly* time," she whispered sounding uncharacteristically embarrassed.

He sighed in relief. "Christ! Is that all? I thought you'd changed your mind on being with me or you'd something gravely wrong with you by your dour expression."

"Most men know little of the occurrence and are often offended by it."

"When will you learn, I'm not most men?" Broccan asked.

She meekly smiled and began closing the door.

"I want to spend time with you," he said.

"I just told you, we can't…"

"We *can* do other things with our time alone. I'll saddle the horses. Let's go for a ride. We'll take my dogs and spend an afternoon together. Beddin' you isn't the only thing I wish to do with you…though by how regularly it's happened recently I suppose you'd not know that."

"We shouldn't spend so much time together anyway."

He exhaled. "Then perhaps I really should be spendin' my time with noble ladies. Or maybe since the king's recently approved weddings of nobles and commoners, and you're so cursedly opposed to marriage, I should take Selena or Elspeth as my wife."

She stared, looking a little crestfallen, but eventually nodded.

"That *would* save Selena from a life that would undoubtedly crush her gentle spirit. I'm sure you'd treat her kindly and she does want children. You'd likely have to pay Shandy a fair coin, but... surely you could manage it."

"Perhaps I'd prefer Elspeth?" Broccan baited Rhianwyn. "By her unhidden gazes, Elspeth appears to show some interest in me, although I thought she had a preference to women."

"She likes both men and women," Rhianwyn said. "Elspeth is sometimes fractious but not as difficult as she lets on. If you married her it would save her from an unappealing fate marrying Godric. You might make an enemy of him and his father, the sheriff. He and Elspeth's father made the arrangement but there's no love between Elspeth and Godric. Elspeth does have a fondness for frequent physical relations so you two would be compatible in that regard."

Broccan stared at her again and shook his head.

"Lovely Rhianwyn, still you don't know when I jest. Wait here and I'll fetch the horses."

"YOU SEE, WE can have a lovely time together without couplin'—lively conversation, a nice walk, a ride through the meadow," Broccan said.

He smiled as they threw the sticks for Fionn and Oisin who happily raced into the lake to fetch them.

"I didn't know being a *mistress* involved such activities," Rhianwyn said.

He'd grown to dislike that word. He wanted her for so much more than physical joining, but when he pushed, she distanced herself except for sexual relations.

"I'm to meet with Maiden Hazel Ripley this day," Broccan said. "Her father's apparently eager to find her a husband."

"Have you seen Hazel Ripley?" Rhianwyn asked.

"I have not," he replied.

"She's a tall, sturdily built woman, but you're a fine tall man so she'll not tower over you, which is off-putting to most men."

"Maybe *she'll* carry *me* to our bed then," he jested.

She only smiled, sat against a tree, and closed her eyes, her long dark lashes resting on her fair skin. He sat beside her, laced his fingers through hers, then gently pulled her hair from within her garments, undoing the clasp to let it fall down her back.

"What are you doing?"

"I love your hair unbound." He softly touched his lips to hers.

"No tender affection." She hastily stood.

"I'll get the horses." He tried not to sound perturbed.

CHAPTER FOURTEEN

"WHY DO YOU insist on staying here, Rhianwyn?" Broccan held her in her small bed after sharing heated intimacies.

"The cottage you chose is lovely. But when you marry, even if I should remain your mistress, I wouldn't share your bed in a location where your wife could easily discover us and be hurt and humiliated."

"If it was Hazel, she'd be liable to give me a worthy black eye with her rather formidable height and strong arms."

She prettily smiled up at him and he held her closer.

"Have you been courting Corliss and Flora as well?"

"I've been rather busy of late with you, lovely Rhianwyn," he said, caressing her breast and kissing her.

"I'm meeting my friends at the market so we can't linger today."

He glanced toward the fireless hearth.

"You must be dreadfully cold midwinter and cooking outdoors year-round must be difficult."

"Many common-born do. I dress warmly and..."

"Come stay with me, Rhianwyn. If not the cottage, there's the guesthouse. All chambers there have large hearths. You don't have to stay in the manor house if

184

you're opposed. Christ, the stables would be warmer than this."

"This cottage holds memories no other location has."

"We'll make our own memories, my sweet Rhianwyn."

She stiffened at him calling her his. He was well aware it wasn't just lust he felt. He was losing his heart to her just as Anslem told him he would. She glanced toward her father's bed.

"You miss him much?" Broccan said.

"I miss them both. Though we drifted apart after Mam died, Father was my family. Do you have family back in Ireland?"

"My father lives but he's a miserable old codger who thinks wealth and title more important than anything."

"He sounds like Giles." She cuddled closer on hearing he wasn't on favorable terms with his father. "You told me you've never been wed, but have you been in love before?"

"Once...nearly, I suppose."

"Nearly in love...or nearly married?"

"I was probably in love with her. She was a feisty warrior woman, learned with a sword and she had an infectious laugh."

"Why didn't you marry?" Rhianwyn asked.

"Something came between us," he replied.

"Where is she now?"

"I'm not certain. We parted on unpleasant terms." He cleared his throat, feeling the familiar fury when he thought of Doirean.

"Yet you don't fear becoming close to another?" Rhianwyn asked.

"People aren't meant to be alone, Rhianwyn," Broccan said.

"I find purpose in my healing."

"But you're beautiful, young, and healthy; you deserve more than simply serving others."

"I admit I feel restless when the lustful urges happen…which is partly why I've agreed to be…"

"My mistress…so you've said numerous times," he replied, increasingly irked at her insistence of only agreeing to a sexual relationship. "Who would you recommend I marry since you seem set on that and don't approve of the ladies I've previously spoken of?"

She tensed. As much as she claimed she wanted him to marry another, he was beginning to wonder.

"I'm seldom in the company of anyone who'd be the best match for a wealthy lord. Elspeth sometimes serves during large feasts. You might ask her. The king's advisors could find a suitable match. You could even request the king's advisal when you *finally* speak to him of wanting to revoke your request to marry me."

"You have a fiery temper to match your passion, Rhianwyn. I see the stormy look in your eyes, the way you set your head and purse your lips when you're displeased."

"You think you know me so well?"

He kissed her. "I want to *know* you again." He stroked her breast and the nipple hardened instantly.

She reached beneath the covers and fondled his manhood. He closed his eyes reveling at the pleasure her touch evoked. She startled him when she pushed him back and straddled him guiding his firmness inside her as she mounted him, then rode exuberantly above him. He grasped her breasts as her long, lustrous light-brown locks caressed his chest. How could he not want to hold on to her and *this*...forever?

They lay together again after the feverish encounter. For all her pushing him away in regard to marriage, she delighted in the coupling. They were silent for some time. She rested her head on his chest and he watched her as she looked like she might drift off to sleep. Lately, she didn't seem as insistent on hurrying away to contend with the potion. He gently caressed her cheek.

"You're so delightfully warm and big," she said.

"Big am I?" he jested, his eyebrow rising.

"I don't suppose you need me to tell you you're well endowed, Broccan Mulryan."

"You know so much of the size of men's cocks?" he taunted, kissing her shoulders.

"I've seen more than I'd like when tending to maladies. Drunken knights or aged men with festering carbuncles on their backsides." There was humor in her lovely voice.

"That sounds fascinatin'!" he laughed. "Tell me again why you wish to remain a healer."

"It's in my blood. My mother was a healer. It gives me purpose and brings me satisfaction easing people's pain or discomfort even in small ways."

"Would you ease my discomfort, Maiden Albray?" He touched her breast.

"By God, you're virile!"

"Let me have you again," he said, "then maybe go ridin' with me, although you did a bloody fine effort of ridin' earlier."

Her lovely blush made his heart gladden.

"I must soon meet my friends. It's the only day we spend together. Shandy permits Selena to leave for half a day and Elspeth has Saturday afternoons off."

"What of the princess? She's your friend, too?"

"Only a few people know that."

He stroked Rhianwyn's hair and she looked into his eyes.

"What is it about you, Broccan? Why do you make me want you so readily and how can you ensure I meet my release so quickly?"

He didn't reply but thoroughly kissed her and placed his hand between her thighs. She arched her back and moaned as he entered and withdrew his fingers and she gasped.

"I want you again," she whispered. "I think you've placed an enchantment upon me."

"I'm equally enchanted." He kissed her throat.

She turned her back to him sensually writhing her lovely round arse against his erection.

He eagerly entered her placing his hands upon her breasts as she moved with him. Nothing had ever been like this…not even marginally close no matter how many other women he'd had, not even Doirean.

"What's suddenly plagued your mind?" she asked.

"Nothing," he said, but she moved away, turned to him, and stared.

"Bloody hell! You can't stop partway through it," he cried in torment.

"Your mind wasn't on me," she accused. "It was far away, perhaps dwelling on your warrior woman with the laugh you favored or another you took to your bed. I don't ask for fidelity. As a mistress that isn't my place, but when you're here with me and indeed, when you're *inside* me, I insist you be present *only* with me."

She started to rise, but he roughly pulled her to him.

"You're on my mind, Rhianwyn...always!"

He held her more forcefully and entered her again with greater fervor.

"You're like a fire in my soul," he whispered.

"And you mine," she admitted.

They continued moving together, kissing ardently as they reached their crests together. She cried out pressing her thumbnail into his shoulder. He wanted to be lost in this moment with her in his arms, him within her forever. A voice outside interrupted their bliss.

"Rhianwyn?" Elspeth called.

"Rhianwyn? Are you well?" Selena asked. "We worried when you weren't at the market gate. You're always there first."

"Tell me you locked the cottage door," Rhianwyn whispered.

"I did not," Broccan said, grinning.

"Why does that make you smile?" she whispered again.

"I'd not be opposed to them finding us together. Then perhaps I could tell the world I'm sharing the bed of my *Suile Gorma*, the most beautiful woman..."

"Hush!" she warned. "You mustn't tell anyone."

"You told me to inform the king you're my mistress."

"Rhianwyn!" Elspeth called. "Are you dead?"

"If I was dead, it'd doubtful I'd be able to reply." She laughed.

"What the hell ails you, then?" Elspeth asked.

"We're concerned," Selena said.

"I woke with an unsettled stomach and a fuzzy head," Rhianwyn lied.

"Have you been drinking?" Elspeth questioned. "That's also not like you."

"I'm worried about Father and who the advisors might choose for my husband."

"You're a very poor liar, Rhianwyn," Broccan whispered, taking her nipple in his mouth and suckling it till she moaned aloud.

"Have you the morbid cramping caused by the cursed monthlies?" Selena asked.

"Nothing like that," Rhianwyn managed as Broccan touched her womanhood and she writhed to meet his intimate caresses.

"Are you coming or not?" Elspeth impatiently asked.

"That's been goin' on half the mornin' and I believe it'll be happenin' again straightaway," he whispered seductively, pulling the bedcovers over his head. He held tight to her backside placing his mouth on her womanhood. She grasped his hair and pulled. He groaned.

"What was that?" Selena asked.

"It's nothing," Rhianwyn said.

"We're coming inside," Elspeth replied.

"Stay where you are!" Rhianwyn warned.

"Is what you have contagious?" Selena sounded worried.

"No, I'll meet you soon." Rhianwyn's breath was now raspy.

"I'm coming in straightaway to see what's bloody well ailing you," Elspeth said, "for you don't sound entirely yourself."

Rhianwyn climaxed intensely muffling her moans in her pillow. Broccan finally released her and moved from beneath the bedcovers. He roguishly smiled pulling his hand through his tousled hair. She blushed, made a face, shook her fist at him, then located her shift and hurriedly pulled it over her head before stepping beyond the hanging blanket.

"Hello," she greeted Selena and Elspeth who'd let themselves in.

"Are you sure you're well?" Selena said. "You seem breathless."

"And you're flushed," Elspeth added looking around suspiciously.

"I told you, I've been suffering an ailment today."

"Rhianwyn Albray have you a man here?" Elspeth glanced at the blanket.

"Have you ever known me to entertain a man here or anywhere, Elspeth?"

"No, but you're of an age to start wanting that. You shared a close dance with Lord Brockwell that night. He seemed to have his sights on you."

"He looks at all women. He's a damn philander. He's apparently been seen in the company of at least three noble ladies recently."

"Yes, I heard he's begun searching for a wife," Elspeth said. "He's even met with Corliss Barlow. Maybe the man has entirely no taste."

"I'd like him to look my way before he weds," Selena said. "He's mightily handsome. If I must become a harlot, perhaps he could be my first. He's bound to have the coin to make Shandy consider it."

"I wouldn't mind having a go at him myself," Elspeth said. "I bet he knows how to make a woman quiver. Being so large and tall I'd wager he has an impressive spindle."

Rhianwyn grinned, even giggled.

"You're behaving very peculiarly," Elspeth said.

"She's not wrong," Selena added. "You're not even dressed. You're usually up early...out collecting herbs or creating remedies. I've never seen your hair unbound and looking quite so... *messy.*"

Elspeth nodded. "Not that she spends loads of time with her hair. She ties it and tucks it in her shift. She's the prettiest woman I know though she does nothing to enhance her beauty."

"She doesn't need to, Elspeth. Rhianwyn's naturally lovely."

"When you're done assessing my appearance, would you like me to finish dressing, or are you going to the market without me?"

"If you don't hasten we might as well forget the market. It's already late afternoon," Elspeth grumbled.

"Is it?" Rhianwyn said.

"Are you sure you're well?" Selena asked.

"You sound bloody daft. Did you take a potion that's

addled your mind?" Elspeth added.

"You're simply full of compliments. You two go on; I'll meet you next market day."

"Rhianwyn, it wouldn't be the same without you." Selena sounded sorrowful. "I wish Lilliana could join us, too. The four of us have been such good friends for so long. I fear it'll all be changed soon. Our times together are numbered. You two must be married. Lilliana will move away and I'll be sentenced to a life I'd never choose." She sighed heavily.

"Let's not think of that today," Elspeth said. "We'll wait outside so hurry up; make yourself presentable, Rhianwyn."

"I will," Rhianwyn agreed.

BROCCAN HEARD THE door close and the bolt drawn. Rhianwyn poked her head behind the blanket curtain. She wagged her finger, pretending a scowl, then startled him when she lie beside him.

"You, Lord Brockwell, are a damn lustful fiend! Making me experience release with them right there. I'll pay you back one day," she whispered.

"I'd be agreeable to you paying me back even now." He chuckled.

She widened her eyes, then stunned him entirely by taking him in her mouth and running her tongue up and down his cock until he wanted to die he was so gloriously aroused. Then she moved away, smirking mischievously.

"By Christ's cross, you can't leave me in such a state," he whispered hoarsely.

"I must go." She reached for her kirtle, stockings, and boots. "If I should see you when in the presence of others you must behave accordingly. Close the door tightly behind you." She tossed him a sassy grin.

"If you leave me now in this unenviable state, I *will* see you sorry, my beautiful Rhianwyn. My heart is full when I'm with you. I admit I never want to be parted. My life's begun to revolve around you."

"I suppose mistresses have that effect on men," she replied coolly, taking her healer's satchel as she left.

BROCCAN DRESSED AND stepped outside, his mind filled with erotic memories of what they'd shared. Rhianwyn had even permitted him to spend the night. Christ, he longed to spend every night with her. Again, he was relieved Anslem's spirit hadn't come to him since he'd begun bedding Rhianwyn.

Broccan closed the door and turned to see Cassian standing there looking angry, hurt, and not a little drunk.

"You shouldn't think yourself special because she permits you to have her," Cassian said. "She allowed me that for a time, too. But should you lose your heart to her and she realizes that truth, she'll end it with you as quickly as she did with me, *Lord Brockwell.*"

"You're drunk, Cassian. Stay out of my way. Are you following me or spying on Rhianwyn?"

He didn't reply but further antagonized Broccan. "You don't believe me...that I had her, that she once sought pleasure in my arms?"

"You'd be wise to shut the hell up, Cassian," Broccan said, now enraged learning Rhianwyn *had* been with him.

He'd suspected that might be true when Cassian was opposed to Broccan wanting to marry her, yet hearing him speak of it infuriated him. It wouldn't be the first time they'd argued over a woman or even the first time they'd been with the same woman, although he didn't like to dwell on that.

"You and I are seldom wise, Broccan."

"Go sleep it off before Severin finds out you're not behavin' like he expects his knights," Broccan said.

"If she knows you care," Cassian repeated, "you'll lose her. But if you marry her, she'll never be happy."

"I suppose you think *you* could make her happy?" Broccan replied, though he'd been resolute he wouldn't speak of this to Cassian.

"I'm not sure she'd be happy as any man's wife. She's too fearful of being controlled by a man."

"I'd never attempt to control her, but it's important she become my wife. You were there when Anslem asked me to marry her. I have no doubt that's why you did what you did in France, then rushed back here trying to make her your own."

"She *was* mine for a time and I assure you she *liked* it," he drunkenly slurred.

"If you speak of this any further, I'll see you pay, drunk or not. A decent man wouldn't mention such truths if he truly cared for the woman," Broccan warned.

"I don't just care for her, I'm sarding in love with her and she knows it! That frightened her away as it will with you should she learn you care," Cassian said. "But loving her *will* destroy you, as it has me… as it did Anslem. It drove him to madness and caused his death. You know that as well as I."

"You don't know what you're talkin' about. Just *shut your damn mouth*, Cassian before I close it permanently!"

Cassian staggered and sneered. "Maybe that wouldn't be so bad…not nearly as torturous as living without her and knowing you're sarding her."

Broccan put his hand to his sword but forced himself to walk away.

CHAPTER FIFTEEN

R HIANWYN'S MIND WASN'T on the wares at the market or her friends who chatted together companionably. She paid little attention. Her thoughts were on Broccan; he filled her senses. Her womanhood was tender from the many times they'd been joined, yet she wanted him still. He was the finest man she'd ever looked upon, a generous, capable lover, too…and he was becoming much more.

Her heart pounded, her stomach fluttered, and her womanly parts tingled just thinking about him. They'd been coupling sometimes several times daily. Neither seemed to be able to get their fill of the other. She'd even let him stay last night. He'd been ready to leave when he'd kissed her neck. She'd caressed his chest, tugged down his breeches, and he'd roughly taken her there against the door. Then she led him to her bed. Being held in his powerful arms as she slept—his large warm body next to her made her want that…always! She was beginning to care deeply—feared she was falling in love with him. He'd nearly admitted that same sentiment today.

"Why do you suddenly wear such a long face?" Elspeth asked. "Are you unwell again?"

"You've been very quiet, Rhianwyn," Selena said.

"Again, I'm dwelling on who might be selected for my

husband."

Rhianwyn certainly hadn't always been straightforward with her friends. They didn't know she wasn't chaste—knew nothing of her time with Cassian...and now Broccan. Elspeth would undoubtedly be surprised but she'd understand. Selena would likely be stunned to learn of it, as would Lilliana. Rhianwyn sometimes wondered what her mother would think. For someone who'd vowed she'd never lie with a man...she'd markedly changed.

"You might just as well go back home, Rhianwyn. You can't keep up a conversation."

"You're unkind sometimes, Elspeth," Selena said. "We should be comforting our friend. Rhianwyn, please tell us why you're behaving so peculiarly today."

"Good afternoon, ladies." The deep voice behind them saved Rhianwyn from replying but made her skin tingle and her heart race.

"Good afternoon," Selena timidly said as Broccan approached them.

"Lord Brockwell," Elspeth addressed him, blatantly eyeing him.

"Hello," Rhianwyn said, feeling unusually shy especially considering all they'd shared.

He managed to appear friendly but not too friendly looking at all of them.

"May I walk with you?" he asked.

"Please do." Selena smiled sweetly.

"If you like." A look of interest gleamed in Elspeth's eyes.

"Have you no opinion, Maiden Albray?"

"I'm not opposed. But where's your horse?" she asked, knowing full well he must've come straight from her cottage and hadn't had Dubh with him.

"I don't bring him to markets any longer. A woman once scolded me for having an unruly animal near children," he said with that damn magnetic smile.

"She must've been off-putting to be so opinionated?" Rhianwyn smirked.

"She was actually quite intriguing."

"Are you two flirting?" Elspeth asked.

"I presume Lord Brockwell flirts with all women," Rhianwyn said.

"Tell me, since the three of you seem to be regular attendees of the market, what should someone look for to buy?" Broccan changed the subject.

"Some of the best wares would've already sold. We *were* late to arrive today." Elspeth looked accusingly at Rhianwyn.

"Most of what's here we couldn't afford anyway." Selena gazed at Broccan.

"If you could buy whatever you'd wish, what would it be?" Broccan glanced at Rhianwyn. She looked away. "Each of you, what would you like?"

"I'd buy jewels," Elspeth said.

"What occasion would you have for wearing jewels?" Selena questioned Elspeth.

"None, but…one day, I'd like jewels and fancy gowns."

"And you?" Broccan asked Selena.

"I'd like rich desserts and sweet cakes. Shandy insists we stay away from such foods should we become plump and unattractive."

Broccan looked at Selena intently.

"Does she actually know what men want in a woman?"

"She should. She's been selling them to men for long enough," Rhianwyn said.

"I doubt men want a woman with no meat on their bones, nothing to hang on to when they're sarding." Elspeth winked seductively at Broccan.

"A healthy soft woman is preferred over one who looks like she's been half-starved," Broccan said.

Selena glanced down at her body. She was slight but had recently developed.

"Would you like a sweet cake?" Broccan asked Selena.

"Desperately," Selena admitted.

"Select one then and I'll buy it for you," Broccan said.

"Truly?" Selena sounded excited. She hurried toward the vendors with baked wares displayed.

"And you Maidens Jory and Albray, if you'd like food, a gown, even a jewel, I'll buy them—only one of each, mind you."

"What do you want in return?" Elspeth narrowed her eye.

"Nothin' but to make three lovely ladies smile."

Elspeth looked doubtful. Still, she left them to survey the tables with jewelry and garments.

"What would you like, sweet Rhianwyn?" He dared to lightly graze her hand.

Her body tingled. She felt the heat from her sex to her breasts to her face.

"I don't need anything."

"I beg to differ. You need a new shift. I did capably destroy yours and have yet to replace it, though if I had my way, you'd be naked in my bed every moment...even now."

"My God, you're appealing," she whispered.

"And you." His voice deeper with recognizable arousal.

"Did you offer to buy my friends gifts so we'd be alone?"

"I have coin to spare...and see none of you are showered with possessions. I like to make women happy." His eyebrow rose and his lips curved in a sultry smile.

"Broccan Mulryan, you may be my undoing."

"And you mine. By Christ, I want to kiss you. You left me in a torturous state earlier. I'd like those lovely lips upon my..."

She shook her head, widening her eyes in warning as Selena joined them.

"I've narrowed it down to the apple tart or the spiced ginger cake." Selena sounded delighted.

"Get them both and a kirtle, too, if you like," Broccan replied.

Selena stared at him clearly gauging if he were serious.

"If I eat too many sweets, I'll need a new kirtle. Shandy would pitch a fit if she knew I was eating these."

"I won't tell." Broccan winked.

Selena's lovely green eyes shone. "Are you certain?"

"I told you... I have coin to spare...probably more than I could spend in a lifetime even if I had a wife and several mistresses. It would please me if you find something you like."

Selena looked up at him like she might cry and swallowed hard.

"How I wish I could be included in that lot," she admitted before hastening off again.

"Selena's smitten with you and Elspeth's quite taken, too," Rhianwyn said.

"I'm smitten with only you, my sweet, Rhianwyn," he whispered. "Do you suppose they'll be preoccupied long enough that I might accompany you down a secluded lane, lift you against a stone wall, raise your skirts, and take you with vigor?"

Her cheeks grew warm and he smiled.

"They won't be long and they're already suspicious. If we disappeared together they'd know something's up."

"Oh somethin's most definitely up." He looked at her with lustfulness that made her skin warm. He boldly dared to stand close enough she could feel his arousal against her body which fueled her desire most assuredly.

"You're irredeemable, Broccan." She saw the hunger in his eyes.

"Select a kirtle or jewels, anything, Suile Gorma, or they might suspect something."

"Material items aren't something I value. I'd be more apt to buy items for healing or maybe something for needy children."

"You have a kind heart." He reached out, brushing her hair from her forehead. She jumped for the attraction was so visceral, she nearly conceded and went to that lane he spoke of. He cleared his throat and stepped closer.

"Do you have any notion how much I want you?" he

asked. "You control my thoughts, both wakin' and sleepin'. All I can think of is your sweet face, your mesmerizing eyes...your soft flawless skin...your beautiful..."

"You two look serious," Elspeth said on approaching. "If you're trying to talk her into buying something for herself, it's unlikely. She only thinks of others which makes the rest of us seem selfish."

"Did you find something?" Rhianwyn asked Elspeth instead of replying to her comment.

"I'd feel uneasy having someone buy a garment or jewels," Elspeth admitted.

"Truly, I want to," Broccan assured her. "Unless it's something unusually expensive, I have the coin."

"Aren't you afraid of being set upon by thieves?" Elspeth asked.

"I don't carry coin aplenty. As a lord I'm allowed credit at markets and shops," he said.

"I can't imagine living like that." Elspeth sounded in awe.

"Find something you like," Broccan repeated.

Elspeth stared for a moment, then went to look again. Rhianwyn turned away walking fast, but Broccan followed.

"What's unsettled you?" he asked.

"We're of such different worlds, Lord Brockwell. Find a wife or a mistress of your own station."

"I'm not bloody well obsessed with differences of social class. It's you who dwells on it constantly." He sounded notably impatient.

She walked away again. This time he didn't follow. She inhaled deeply wishing she'd never permitted herself to get close to him.

"Something heavy on your mind, Maiden Albray?" a cheerful voice asked.

"Keyon, it's nice to see you again. I thought you'd left."

"I did. I've been to a few neighboring villages but this feels most like home for I have friends here."

"You do," Rhianwyn said.

He took her arm as they walked.

"What's caused the sadness in those beautiful eyes?" Keyon asked.

"I'm not sad, Keyon."

He didn't seem convinced but only compassionately touched her shoulder. He walked with her as they passed a vendor selling spices. She spotted ginger which wasn't native to Wessex but wondrously beneficial to stomach maladies.

"How much?" she asked the shrewd-looking man with olive skin and black hair.

He listed his price. She only nodded and walked away.

"I'll buy the ginger root for the lady," Rhianwyn heard Broccan say. "How many do you require, Maiden Albray?" he asked.

"One or two," she replied.

He returned with half a dozen and passed them to her. She placed them in her satchel.

"I'm grateful. Thank you." She nodded.

"Hello Keyon," Broccan greeted.

"Lord Brockwell," Keyon congenially said.

"Call me Broccan, please. Maybe you could convince Maiden Albray to find something for herself, too."

"Rhianwyn...if Broccan's willing to cater to you, permit it. You offer much consolation to many. If I had the coin, I'd indulge you, too."

Broccan put his hand in his breeches' pocket. Pulling out several coins he passed them to Keyon. "Here, maybe she'd take these from you, since she's put off with me just now."

Rhianwyn scowled.

"I've found a kirtle if you're truly willing to buy one for me," Selena enthusiastically interrupted. "Elspeth's located one, too, but come see if it's what you'd be willing to spend. I've never had a ready-made garment before, always only those handed down."

Broccan nodded. Selena took his arm and stared up at him adoringly. Rhianwyn sighed.

"So that's what has you maudlin? You and Broccan have had a lovers' quarrel?" Keyon asked.

Rhianwyn stared and shook her head.

"I'm only joking," Keyon replied. "However, I see there's an attraction between you."

She only shrugged.

"So what're you going to purchase with his coin?" Keyon asked.

"Buy something for yourself," Rhianwyn said.

"I won't. Not when it's to be for you." Keyon shook his head.

"May I have the coin then?"

He passed it to her without pause. She went to a nearby vendor. Selecting a thick gray, woolen cloak, she shook it out, placing it near Keyon to measure the fit.

"How much?" she asked.

The woman replied. Rhianwyn paid her then passed the cloak to Keyon. "You'll be warmer on your travels with winter soon upon us."

"You're a stubborn woman," Keyon said. "You could use a new cloak, too."

"You need it more," she insisted.

Rhianwyn glanced at the coins left and made her way to the shoemaker's stall. On market day he sold more shoes here than in his shop. "How much would be required to buy eight pairs of children's shoes?" she asked.

"Even with more remedy for my mother's cough and the other for my wife's uneasy stomach, you'd still need fair coin."

"This much?" She held out her hand.

"Since you're being so generous, I'll donate the rest. Do you know the sizes?"

She smiled, glancing at the shoes. She'd seen the children's wee feet enough to guess. She pointed to several pair and the shoemaker placed them in a sack. She gave him the two vials of elixir, then passed him another.

"What's this one for?" he asked.

"For the raw spot on your hands from continually sewing through leather," she said.

"You're a good woman, Maiden Albray. Here, I'll include some stockings for the children, too."

"Thank you," Rhianwyn said, tears of gratitude welling.

"You *are* a good woman, Rhianwyn," Keyon said. "Broccan would be lucky to have you. I believe he knows that. You're the one limiting yourself. You could have knights, lords, or nearly anyone, but I see Broccan *has* caught your eye. Don't sell yourself short."

"You're a good friend, Keyon. Now, I'll find the children and give them their shoes."

She glanced back to see Selena and Elspeth well engrossed speaking with Broccan, both women laughing at something he'd said. She started toward the market entrance where she'd likely find the children.

"Should I let everyone know where you've gone?" Keyon asked.

"Thank you. Tell them I'll join them later."

BROCCAN SAW RHIANWYN parting company with the minstrel and starting for the gates. He wanted to rush after her, but he wouldn't. At present, her friends seemed far more eager for his company. Selena held his arm and clung to his every word. Elspeth wore a look he recognized. He'd seen it in enough woman. She'd share his bed without pause if he showed interest.

"What do you suppose Rhianwyn would like if she'd permit me to buy her something?" Broccan asked.

"She needs garments," Selena said. "She has fewer than either of us though never admits to wanting more."

"She could use hair clips," Elspeth added.

"Would you help me find items for Rhianwyn?"

"She mightn't accept them," Elspeth said. "She's as proud and stubborn as anyone I've ever known."

"Surely she wouldn't turn down simple items if they're

already purchased," Broccan mused.

"She might, but let's select some and see." Again Selena appeared excited.

THE SMILES ON the children's faces made Rhianwyn's heart glow. The stockings were warm and the shoes fit even better than she'd hoped. She'd thank Broccan for the coin later. He did say she could spend it on whatever she desired. She was starting back to the market when she espied Halsey Winthrop, her belly growing with child and presently hobbling.

"Halsey, what's happened?" Rhianwyn called out.

"It's nothing, Rhianwyn. I stepped on something a while back."

"Let me look," Rhianwyn said.

"I'm in a hurry. I lingered longer than I should've at the market. My husband'll be unhappy if his supper's late."

By her tone Rhianwyn knew Halsey feared her husband. Rhianwyn had suspicions about him. A time or two Halsey had bruises she explained away, but not convincingly.

"It won't take long," Rhianwyn assured her. "Come sit on this stump."

The woman complied. When she lifted her bare foot, Rhianwyn was stunned. A wound oozed septicity. She'd not seen many this purulent that didn't end in death or severing the limb.

"This needs attention straightaway," Rhianwyn said.

"But my husband's supper," Halsey shakily said.

"He'll not be getting his supper if you're completely lame or lying in a graveyard," Rhianwyn warned.

The woman began to weep.

"Forgive me. I shouldn't have been so blunt, but you need to know how serious this is."

"I stepped on a shard of broken pottery. It wasn't anything Adam did to me."

"He didn't break the pottery?" Rhianwyn asked. Halsey lowered her head.

"And it's not that he hasn't done hurtful things to you before."

"He has a temper…like his father and grandfather."

"I'll rinse this with a solution then place a poultice upon it to draw out the poison. If it enters your blood it'll take your life and consequently your unborn child."

"Do what you must," Halsey whimpered.

"This will sting," Rhianwyn said.

She poured the stringent liquid and Halsey cried out clutching tight to the stump.

With the wound clean it was easy to see there was still something in her foot.

"How long have you been walking on this?" Rhianwyn mused.

"Better than a week," Halsey replied.

Rhianwyn used her grasping tool to pull out the shard, then poured more pungent remedy upon the wound.

"You won't require a poultice, only a remedy to help this heal and a bandage to cushion it when walking."

"It feels better already," Halsey said after Rhianwyn put

salve upon it and wrapped it.

"Meet me here tomorrow. I'll look at it again."

"I don't know if…"

"I'll come to your home," Rhianwyn suggested.

Halsey nodded. Trying to take a step, she still limped.

"Here." Rhianwyn took off her own worn boots and passed them to Halsey.

"But then you'll go without, Rhianwyn."

"I don't have a surly impatient husband expecting me to make meals."

"Bless you, Rhianwyn. You're an angel, you are."

The woman's grateful tears touched her. Rhianwyn smiled. Halsey shivered for she hadn't even a shawl.

"Here, take this, too."

Halsey looked uncertain but Rhianwyn passed her the cloak.

"I'd like you to have it. You must stay healthy for that babe." Rhianwyn touched Halsey's swollen belly.

"My husband isn't a bad man, Rhianwyn. He works dawn till dusk in the sheriff's stables earning little. He's worried is all. We've barely enough to make rent and buy food. Knowing there's a little one coming has increased his concern."

"That baby didn't get in your belly without his help," Rhianwyn said. "And nothing excuses him taking his frustration out on you."

"He does care for me," Halsey said before walking away with a much less noticeable limp.

Rhianwyn wondered if Broccan could offer Halsey's husband a position in his stables for better wage. She'd discuss it with him sometime soon.

CHAPTER SIXTEEN

RHIANWYN RETURNED TO the market. Elspeth and Selena were with Keyon and Broccan. Filled with merriment, they each held bundles. They all had a juicy leg of chicken. Even Elspeth, typically less cheerful, was beaming until she saw Rhianwyn.

"Where are your boots and your shawl?" she curtly asked.

"Given to someone who needs them more," Rhianwyn explained.

"That was generous, Rhianwyn," Selena said.

"You were asked to select new garments, instead you buy for others and give yours away," Elspeth rebuked. "This goes beyond generosity and borders on martyrdom. I sometimes think you do so to draw attention to how saintly you are."

Rhianwyn stared at Elspeth, feeling the sting of her unkind words. "Think what you like, Elspeth. It's odd you're comfortable being lavished with gifts by someone you'd usually ridicule for having affluence…and coin surely provided indirectly by Giles Brockwell, whom none of us favor."

"Ladies, no bickering please," Broccan said. "I assure you this coin is mine alone, earned from previous employment and my estate in Ireland, not even indirectly from Giles."

"We're having a nice day, Rhianwyn. Please don't spoil it," Selena whispered.

"I won't," Rhianwyn said, "I'll go home now to take the ginger and boil it to create a remedy."

"Must it be done immediately?" Broccan asked. "Stay with us; have something to eat. If our healer doesn't care for herself, she'll be of no use to those in need of healing."

"These chicken legs are delicious, Rhianwyn. Stay," Selena pled.

"I'd like that, too," Keyon said.

"Broccan's bought you a beautiful kirtle, some petticoats, two shifts, and a lovely fancy bodice," Selena said.

Rhianwyn stared, not wanting to accept the gifts.

"It appears you need some shoes now, too," Broccan said. "I was told you bought several pairs today...but nothing for yourself."

"There are others in greater need. Because I derive contentment assisting others doesn't make me a martyr," she defended. "It's best I return to my cottage for I'd only dampen your joyful moods with my saintliness. See you next week, Selena and you Elspeth, if you can bear to be in the company of someone so self-sacrificing only hoping to achieve notice."

"Rhianwyn, that isn't what I meant," Elspeth said, but Rhianwyn was well in a temper.

"You must look at the gifts Broccan bought you," Selena encouraged. Rhianwyn noted she called him by his given name and was probably already falling for him. She hoped Selena wouldn't be hurt. Maybe if Rhianwyn broke off relations with Broccan, he *would* marry Selena. He had the king's ear and could perhaps convince him if they knew Selena was chaste.

"You keep the purchases, Selena." Rhianwyn started off without looking back.

"She's the most damnable stubborn woman I know!" Elspeth blared. "When she gets her back up, there's no bloody reasoning with her."

"I hoped you'd come to the sunstones with us," Broccan called after Rhianwyn. "I've not yet seen them. Your friends offered to show me and said you know much of their history and the legends of the location."

Rhianwyn wanted to be with him, there was no denying that, but maybe she'd also like to prove Elspeth wrong—that she wasn't always unreasonable even when in a temper. She turned around and met Broccan's eyes. Damn that man—he could melt her heart in a single gaze.

"You honestly haven't been to the sunstones?" Rhianwyn thought it unlikely. He'd been here for some time and the stones were an extraordinary sight.

"Never," Broccan said.

"Well then, you must," she replied.

"Should we take ale?" Keyon asked, obviously relieved Rhianwyn seemed less riled.

"That'd be grand," Broccan said. "And food."

"You intend on spending some time there then?" Rhianwyn asked.

"I can't be home too late or Shandy will…"

"Will what?" Broccan asked. "Does she harm you?"

"She doesn't beat me but she's intimidating. She'll interrogate me on where I've been, who I've been with and what I've been doing. She might even…"

"Might what?" Broccan encouraged but Selena's cheeks were now bright pink.

"Might have her examined to make certain she remains virginal," Rhianwyn said.

"She'd do that?" Broccan asked with obvious disgust.

"I didn't know that could be determined by an examination." Keyon's cheeks were ruddy, too.

"It's demeaning and not even accurate," Rhianwyn declared. "There are other ways to pierce a maidenhead besides sarding. Girls who've climbed a fence and fallen have…"

"By Christ, she's a healer nonstop," Elspeth interrupted, rolling her eyes.

Rhianwyn ignored her and continued, "There are also methods to make people believe a woman's virginal. I doubt even Shandy knows that."

Broccan looked at her uncertainly.

"It involves sheep's intestines and… I won't elaborate," Rhianwyn said.

Selena looked like she might lose the contents of her stomach.

"I might like to speak with you on that for my upcoming wedding night, Rhianwyn," Elspeth said.

"Godric doesn't deserve a virgin. He doesn't deserve anyone. We must come up with a way to ensure you don't have to wed that bastard," Rhianwyn said.

"You're well fired up today, Rhianwyn," Elspeth replied. "What has you so impassioned?"

She glanced at Broccan then looked away.

"Before we leave the market, we should find more food. You've eaten nothing, Maiden Albray," Broccan said.

"These chicken legs are delightful and the sweets I ate earlier were heavenly." Selena looked radiantly happy.

"I'll try one of each if that'll appease everyone," Rhianwyn said sassily, and Broccan grinned.

"One of each sweet pie and cake in the entire market?" Broccan jested.

"One chicken leg and one sweet, probably a pudding or custard, maybe a marzipan cake. What I'd really like is a Bara Brith. They're a Welsh tea bread that Mam used to make. I've not had one since she's been gone." She stared off remembering.

"Does anyone here make them?" Broccan asked.

"Not that I've seen," Rhianwyn replied.

"Perhaps I should take you to Welshland for a Bara Brith. It's only a long day's ride, two if you break it up."

"You've been to Cymru?" she asked, surprised.

"I have." He smiled. "I've been to many places."

Elspeth again looked suspicious at them staring at one another.

"I'll settle for a custard pudding, but a chicken leg first," Rhianwyn said.

"Come with me, we'll fetch them." Broccan held out his hand.

Would it appear more obvious if she didn't accept? She finally took his outstretched hand and he squeezed it.

"A chicken leg for the lady," Broccan said to the vendor.

He passed her the drumstick. She inhaled the delicious scent before she tasted it.

"She smells everything before she eats it," Elspeth chided.

"It's prevented me from eating rancid food but that's also part of the enjoyment of partaking, using all senses."

"I agree," Broccan said.

His sexual implication was clear to Rhianwyn.

"This really is delicious." Rhianwyn tried to eat in a ladylike manner. "Mmmm."

"I've never seen you eat anything that fast." Selena watched her closely.

"I haven't eaten anything today," she replied.

"Nothing?" Broccan said.

She wanted to strike him for he was clearly referring to her having his manhood in her mouth.

"Nothing worthy of mention," she replied.

He turned away but she noticed he grinned.

"Are you two sharing a bed?" Elspeth asked.

"What?" Rhianwyn questioned, hoping she seemed offended or stunned.

"You're clearly flirting," Elspeth replied.

"You think I share a bed with everyone I flirt with?" Broccan said. "I'd be shattered."

"Have you shared his bed, Elspeth?" Rhianwyn asked.

"Of course not. Well… not yet," she added.

"And you Selena?"

"You're well aware I haven't shared *any* man's bed," Selena stated, cheeks rosy again.

"Has Lord Brockwell not been flirting with the two of you?" Rhianwyn asked.

Both women nodded.

"If I shared a bed with every woman I flirted with, I'd never need to sleep in stables." Keyon laughed his distinctive laugh.

"Are you ready for custard pudding, Maiden Albray?" Broccan asked.

"I am," she said.

"I might like one, too?" Selena eyed them as they stood by the vendor still with baked wares displayed even though the day was late.

"We'll take a dozen," Broccan said. "Actually, I'll take them all."

The woman smiled happily but then gave a brash grin to Broccan obviously eyeing him closely though she was old enough to be his mother.

"Where's the best place to get ale?" Broccan asked.

"Straight from the ale wife's the best price," Elspeth said. "Though not likely something you'd have to consider."

"Does it taste best?" Broccan asked.

"I think so." Keyon nodded. "The monks make a great ale and beer, too. Who usually purchases your ale for you?"

"My servants, but I admit shopping with locals is more fun."

Broccan passed Rhianwyn a custard pudding from the sack, then one to each of the others. They ate as they walked.

"They're delicious, Rhianwyn. What a good choice!"

Selena said.

"Keyon, if I gave you coin, would you take these two ladies to purchase ale, while I take the other to get shoes before the market closes?" Broccan asked.

"I'd be glad to. I have a little coin of my own to contribute."

"Your contribution will be your voice and your music. You can use your coin to sleep in an inn. Come to it you could stay in my guesthouse."

"On your estate?" Keyon sounded disbelieving.

"It's not as though I sleep there," Broccan replied. "You might as well make use of it."

"I must be dreaming," Keyon excitedly said.

"This entire day has been a dream," Selena added, clutching her package. "You must look at the kirtles Elspeth and I selected, Rhianwyn."

"And the garments he purchased for you, although we did help him choose," Elspeth said.

"Except the blue kirtle—he alone selected. He said it'd match your eyes perfectly," Selena added.

"What of the sumptuary law?" Rhianwyn mentioned. "Common-born aren't permitted to wear extravagant or brightly colored clothes. We can't appear we're dressing above our means or competing with nobles."

"We won't wear them where anyone would question it," Elspeth impatiently said.

Rhianwyn only nodded.

Broccan reached inside his overcoat to pull out a small pouch that jingled with coin. "Use whatever's needed, Keyon. We'll meet you later at the sunstones."

"How much ale should we buy?" Keyon asked.

"Six jugs, enough for us to have a fine evenin' togeth-er," Broccan suggested. "Before anyone protests, I'll walk you ladies home and explain where you've been."

Keyon grinned. Selena looked ecstatic. Even Elspeth appeared nearly gleeful as they parted.

Broccan insisted on buying Rhianwyn new boots of higher quality than she'd ever owned. When he assisted with tying them, he grazed her leg and she quivered.

"You could use new stockings, too."

"Broccan you can't overindulge me with gifts."

"Aren't men noted for lavishing their women with many gifts?" he whispered.

She only smiled as they started across the flat plain leading to the sunstones. They'd only gone a short distance when Broccan leaned nearer and kissed her.

"You mustn't do that in plain sight," Rhianwyn scolded looking around to observe who might've seen.

"I was just getting the bit of custard off you lip." He happily grinned.

"We've nearly been found out a few times today."

"Would that be so terrible?" he asked. "I'd like to shout *I'm sharin' the bed of the loveliest woman.*" Then he did shout it and she stared, her mouth agape.

"Mistresses are supposed to be secretive," she scolded.

"Other than openly telling the king," he sarcastically replied.

Apparently undeterred, he took her hand. She didn't want to argue. What she actually wanted to do with him didn't include only holding his hand.

"I can't believe you've never been to this stone circle," she said.

"I've heard much about it. There are several similar formations in Ireland. None quite so large as those." He pointed in awe at the sunstones.

"Some people fear them. Others revere them," Rhianwyn said. "It's believed this circle was once used for sacrifice or burial, probably built by the Druids, and used by them for certain. It's said they still meet here in secret, though I've never seen. How these massive stones were brought here is a mystery. Some reason it was done by magic. The stones draw many people during the solstices. There are other circles near here, too, Avesbury and the wooden circles, but this one seems the most mystical. Some say there's even an Irish connection. Something to do with a magical old woman and Old Scrat."

"Old Scrat?" Broccan asked.

"The devil," Rhianwyn replied. "He supposedly tricked her and gained possession of these stones that once were located in Ireland."

"Do you suppose I should claim them back for Ireland then?" he joked.

"Unless you could get the devil to assist you it might be a feat to return them." She grinned.

As they neared the immense formation, Rhianwyn reveled at the sheer magnitude of these stones no matter that she visited them regularly. When she glanced at him, she saw he only stared at her.

"You're more sensational than these stones, Rhianwyn," he said.

"Oh be gone with you and your male desires that make you speak such absurd untruths."

"You really don't know how to accept adulation, do you?"

"You're telling me you're not aroused now which influences your compliments?"

"Of course I'm bloody well aroused. You left me in a state, pleasured me with your mouth till I was near my release, then just left. I've been aroused all damn day as I am whenever I'm near you. I want to have you here and now!" he admitted.

"Here in this circle of stones?" She glanced around uncertainly but with some intrigue as well.

"You wouldn't permit it?" He stepped closer.

"The others could be here any time," she whispered but didn't protest when he pulled her into his arms for a lingering kiss.

"You have a magic of your own, Broccan Mulryan." She peered beyond the stones to the flat plain to see no one.

"We'd have to be quick about it, then." She stared up into his ruggedly handsome face.

"We can't disrobe in our limited time," he murmured, even as he pulled her kirtle and shift down, baring her breasts.

His calloused hands upon them made her immediately ready and she hastily untied his breeches.

"Here behind this stone so we won't be seen even if they approach," she said and he eagerly agreed.

He sat leaning against the stone and she pulled open his breeches enough that his manhood was released. She raised her skirts and sat upon his firmness till he filled her. He moaned deeply as she moved above him. His mouth on her breast, she gasped, then he whispered in her ear.

"You're the only woman I want, Rhianwyn. All I'll ever want…agree to be my wife. Make me a happy man." He squeezed her backside tightly.

She emitted a series of gasps. As soon as her release came and his soon after, she swiftly moved from him, righting her garments. She wouldn't look at him and finally turned away. He came to her still buttoning his breeches.

"Rhianwyn? Jesus, what riles you now?"

"You ruin the specialness of what we share by speaking of marriage. If you can't abide by our bargain, I'll not be with you in any way…not even a mistress. My mind's firm on this and…"

"By Christ's cross, Rhianwyn. I don't want to wed another and I don't sardin' want another man to have you." He firmly grasped her shoulders. "I don't want you only as a sordid secret. I want us to be together always."

Footsteps and voices alerted them to others approaching. She straightened her hair. He looked tormented when she finally met his eyes.

"Rhianwyn…I'm falling desperately in l…"

"Don't you dare speak those words, Broccan," she whispered.

"Hello," Selena called. "Are you here, Rhianwyn, Broccan?"

Rhianwyn tried to stem the tears threatening to fall and inhaled deeply, hoping to compose herself before she replied to Selena, even though she would've preferred to simply run away and not have to face anyone.

CHAPTER SEVENTEEN

S TILL TRYING TO tame her raw emotions, Rhianwyn inhaled. "We're just here, Selena," she called.

"There's someone in need of a healer," Keyon said.

Rhianwyn cleared her throat. "Certainly. I'll do what I can."

"I doubt you'll want to know what for." Selena sounded shaky.

"Rhianwyn wouldn't turn anyone away," Elspeth declared.

They stood near the circle but the elderly man with them stared at the sunstones.

"I'm not going in there!" he heavily slurred.

"What is it you require, Ackley?" Rhianwyn asked the ragged old drunkard who often came to her for healing.

"I've an infernal carbuncle upon my sarding arse. I can't sit—can't move without grievous pain."

"They are most unpleasant." Rhianwyn was actually grateful for the distraction.

"What's to be done, Maiden Albray?" Ackley asked.

"It'll likely need to be lanced."

"Do it then, girl. I'd give you the damn shirt off my back if you take away this wretched discomfort."

"I don't require your shirt." Rhianwyn walked toward

him.

Ackley was already dropping his breeches and baring his ass as Selena, Elspeth, and Keyon entered the stone circle.

"By Christ." Elspeth shook her head. "Why you permit people to come to you at all hours requesting any number of unsavory tasks, I'll never understand."

"I don't expect you to understand, Elspeth."

"Will it hurt fiercely, girl?" Ackley asked.

"Only briefly; then you should experience relief." Rhianwyn opened her healer's pouch, took out a vial, pulled up his tunic, and poured some remedy over the old man's backside. She located her knife and observed the very large bump upon his posterior.

"Should I bite on something?" he slurred again.

"Just take a deep breath." She touched the tip of the knife to the protrusion, then jumped back for the pressure behind the pustule was great.

The old man roared and leapt about more than she would've thought possible for he was somewhat crippled.

"Now hold still. I'll need to apply steady pressure to expel the remainder of the foulness and place healing remedy on it, then you can go back home."

She did so, then poured more on his backside, the knife, and her hands. The powerful remedy had an acrid odor. She dabbed the wound with a rag and he smiled.

"Ahhh, that's loads better, girl. Your mam would be proud of you. She delivered all three of my children...sadly all dead now...like my Cora."

She knew the old man suffered deep loneliness like

many elderly people.

"Do you have ale for the night, Ackley?"

"Not so much."

"I'll get you more." Rhianwyn entered the circle of sunstones to see everyone standing. "Go ahead, sit and drink...you needn't wait for me."

"I was waiting to see if I might spew," Selena said, clearly fighting a gag.

"I wasn't sure I wouldn't as well," Elspeth admitted.

"Now I need a drink," Keyon said.

Broccan only looked distressed, perturbed, or both.

"May I give some ale to Ackley?" she asked Broccan.

"If you like." He shrugged indifferently.

She could see he was displeased—not about her giving away his ale, but because she hadn't permitted him to profess his feelings.

"Why would you give the pathetic old man more ale?" Elspeth unkindly said. "You're abetting his drunkenness."

"Is it putting you out in any way if I give it to him?" Rhianwyn asked.

Elspeth shook her head. "Has he a way to pay for your services?"

"What do you think?" Rhianwyn whispered, taking a small jug of ale. "Ackley can have my share."

Elspeth muttered something under her breath.

"I don't expect you to comprehend doing anything for someone that isn't required or rewarded with coin," Rhianwyn said. "I'll walk Ackley back to the village. Good night Keyon and Selena. Thank you for the food, Lord Brockwell. It was generous of you to share your wealth with common-born."

Broccan's eyes flashed with his own annoyance but he nodded.

"I wish you'd stay!" Selena sounded aggrieved at the division between her two closest friends.

"You're not addressing me with a fond farewell?" Elspeth crossed her arms.

"Good night, Elspeth. Enjoy *your* share of Lord Brockwell's ale."

Rhianwyn took Ackley's arm for the old man stumbled.

"I'll see you to your cottage," she said. He smiled revealing a nearly toothless mouth.

When they got to his abode, Rhianwyn helped him inside holding her breath at the stench. He'd lived alone for years in this small shack that made her cottage look like a castle. She knew he lived in squalor, but the filth of the place was deplorable. Perhaps she'd return tomorrow to attempt to clean.

"Good night, Ackley," she called as she left, and he'd already settled on his bed with his jug of ale.

She considered going back to the sunstones and apologizing, but to who?

"I'm sorry." She jumped on hearing Elspeth.

"For what?" Rhianwyn asked. "For being you? Then I'd have to apologize for being me. We both know we're often at odds…but that doesn't mean we can't be friends. I only wish you'd realize how important my healing is to me."

"I do, Rhianwyn," Elspeth admitted but wouldn't meet her eyes. "I only wish I had something that mattered so much to me. But now, Selena's in tears; Keyon's upset, and

Broccan's not looking cheerful. Come back. Have a drink so the others don't think my abrasive attitude forced you to leave."

"If that were true I'd never go near you, Elspeth Jory," Rhianwyn said. "But my unpleasant demeanor this night isn't only because you and I squabbled. I have much on my mind."

"Then come drink to relieve your worries." Elspeth placed her arm through Rhianwyn's.

Though she thought it unwise to be anywhere near Broccan tonight, Rhianwyn conceded. Elspeth never apologized and didn't ask much of her, so she'd comply.

"YOU'RE BACK!" KEYON stopped strumming his lute; it had been a noticeably melancholy tune.

"I'm so glad you've returned." Selena embraced Rhianwyn with tears in her voice.

Broccan nodded. He sat drinking from a jug of alc. By his intense eyes, he hadn't let go of his quarrel with her.

"The ale's there." He pointed to it but didn't make a move to get if for her as she knew he would have if they hadn't had the disagreement earlier.

"I'll get it." Selena found two small jugs and passed them to Rhianwyn and Elspeth.

"Any requests?" Keyon asked.

"Play something cheerful," Elspeth said sitting next to Selena.

Rhianwyn remained standing, not certain how long

she'd stay, for the stones had begun to glow as she'd seen the night she'd first been intimate with Broccan. Something life changing, she thought to herself.

"You're not sitting, Maiden Albray?" Broccan's coolness was unmistakable.

"I'm a bit chilled," she said.

"Well if you hadn't given away your shawl and boots." Elspeth rolled her eyes.

"I have new boots," she said, pointing. "I forgot to thank you for these, too."

"Consider them a gift to a healer who gives much to others," Broccan replied.

"What of the other garments you bought for Rhianwyn and the pretty hair clasp you chose for her?" Selena asked.

"I'm not sure she'd accept them. Maybe she could find someone else in need," Broccan said.

"If you two would like the garments…"

"They wouldn't fit us, Rhianwyn," Selena interrupted. "You've a far more shapely form than me and they'd be too short for Elspeth."

"Perhaps they could be returned then…"

"By Christ, woman! You're so bloody stubborn sometimes I want to shake you," Broccan said.

"I'd like to see you try!" Elspeth glared at Broccan, her hackles visibly rising, fists curled.

"It was only a figure of speech," Broccan said. "I wouldn't actually shake her. I'd have to be a good deal more riled than I am now."

"Sit down, Rhianwyn." Keyon gestured to where the others were sitting. "You're making me a wee bit nervous standing there like you aim to run away."

"Because it's likely she *will* if she hears somethin' she doesn't like or disagrees with somethin' said," Broccan suggested.

Elspeth stared at him but nodded.

"Sounds like you're having a party we weren't asked to attend," a male voice called from beyond the stones.

Rhianwyn turned to see Godric, his two contentious companions, Rupert and Fenwick, plus Winston and two others of the sheriff's men.

Broccan bristled when Godric approached Rhianwyn.

"What are you doing here?" Godric asked Elspeth. "I don't want the woman I'm to marry hanging about with other men. I'd really rather you sever ties with the little whore and the mad healer, too. I'll make damn certain of that once we're wed."

"Sard off," Elspeth said and Godric glared.

"I'll not put up with that disrespect once we're married!" Godric looked at Elspeth like he loathed her as much as she did him.

"Well we aren't married yet and if I had my way, I'd wed damn Ackley Coutts before I'd marry you. I'd rather put up with stench and festering carbuncles than arrogant, mean-spirited temper."

"You have a sharp tongue that *will* soon be dulled," Godric threatened.

"You should leave before I need to teach you something on how to treat ladies," Broccan warned.

"I've heard how lords treat women, Irishman—charm them, sard them, and toss them away."

"You know so much of lords, do you?" Broccan rose to his full height which was considerably taller than the other men. He placed his hand to his sword's hilt.

Godric barked a harsh laugh. "What does a lord know of a sword? As sheriff's men we're extensively trained, therefore I'd not advise you to cross any one of us much less all of us." He looked at the men with him.

"We don't want any trouble," Winston said. "Let's leave, Godric."

"You're such a sarding coward. I can't believe you're my blood." Godric eyed Winston with disgust but stepped closer to Rhianwyn.

"I think you and me should take a little stroll." Godric leered.

"Why would I do that?" Rhianwyn was repulsed by the way he looked at her.

"I thought we might get to know one other a little better. Soon I'll be a married man without the freedom I have now. The one time I tried to get friendly with you that damn huntsmen happened along," he whispered.

"I wouldn't go anywhere with you. You appall me." Rhianwyn glowered.

"The daughter of the mad mage and the Welsh bitch thinks she's above me," Godric said.

"Can you think of no new insults?" Rhianwyn said.

"Whore to knights and highborn," he added.

"You're a worthless, unconscionable sack of dung. You should've been drown when the midwife first laid eyes upon you," she hissed, pulling out her knife.

"You dare threaten me? Do you know what would become of you if I take this matter to the king or my father? A woman isn't to have a weapon."

Rupert and Fenwick, who always did Godric's dirty work stepped closer to Rhianwyn. Broccan unsheathed his sword with speed and proficiency seldom seen.

"Leave Maiden Albray alone or I *will* show you what I know of a sword."

"Why do you defend her? Is it because you're sarding her?"

"Step outside of the circle, away from the women. They don't need to see me spill your blood," Broccan threatened.

"Are you denying you had the healer earlier? I'd like some of that, too. Can you disclaim if we spread her thighs, we'd find your seed still warm within her?"

"Leave now!" Broccan's voice was lower yet more fearsome.

"He's not worth it." Rhianwyn tried to make eye contact, but Broccan's eyes were fully on Godric and the other men.

"Even if you know anything of a sword, you can't take on all of us?" Godric warned.

"I'll not be part of this," Winston said.

"You two escort the healer to our usual place." Godric jerked his head to the sheriff's two men. "Fenwick, Rupert, and I will deal with Lord Brockwell. Mind we won't kill him, for he does seem to have the king's favor."

"Don't touch her!" Broccan warned, stepping closer and glaring at the two sheriff's men who'd drawn nearer to Rhianwyn.

Godric lunged forward and Broccan easily knocked his

sword from his hand.

The other two men stepped forward swords raised and Broccan stabbed one in the shoulder, the other in the thigh so rapidly, Rhianwyn was in disbelief.

Winston stepped forward to help Broccan, but Fenwick hit him, then grabbed Rhianwyn. She slashed his arm with her knife. Keyon jumped up, using his lute to hit Godric over the head when Godric tried to retrieve his sword. Elspeth jumped on Rupert's back and he quickly threw her off. Fenwick slapped Rhianwyn across the face as Rupert grabbed for her, too. Broccan raised his sword above his head in a skillful way and thrashed it around in a circle in a manner Rhianwyn well recognized for she'd often watched knights train.

"You're not a hired killer, you're a damn knight," she whispered in disbelief as he deftly beheaded the two henchmen.

Selena screamed hysterically. Godric roughly grabbed Rhianwyn. Broccan hit him over the head with his sword's hilt just as Godric pushed her. She fell against one of the immense stones, striking her head.

CHAPTER EIGHTEEN

"RHIANWYN." SHE HEARD voices but they echoed. Her head throbbed relentlessly. She smelled blood and felt a warm trickle by her eye. She wanted to sleep. Someone shook her but she only moaned.

"Thank God; she's alive," Elspeth said.

Rhianwyn heard Selena weeping. She felt herself being lifted into Broccan's strong arms—could tell by his familiar scent and the ease with which he carried her.

"Put their heads in that sack," he said.

"I don't think I can do that, Broccan," Keyon admitted, sounding stricken.

"Oh for Christ's sake. I'll do it," Elspeth said. "Do you suppose they'd notice if I killed one more?"

"I wouldn't advise killing the sheriff's son when those other men are alive to witness it, though it's much on my mind to bloody well kill them all," Broccan said.

Rhianwyn moaned again.

"Who provides healing?" Broccan asked, carrying her trying to cradle her head but the jarring movement hurt as he walked.

"There's the physician and his apprentice; neither are worth a tinker's damn," Elspeth said.

"Marlow, the old healer's nearly blind," Selena added,

still sobbing.

"Radella," Rhianwyn whispered.

"Who's Radella?" Broccan asked holding Rhianwyn closer. She was comforted by his heartbeat beneath her ear.

"She's nearly ancient, but she was once a skilled healer," Elspeth explained. "She taught Rhianwyn much."

"I'll show you the way," Winston offered, accompanying them and not staying back with Godric and the other sheriff's men.

Rhianwyn tried to lift her head.

"Be still, lass," Broccan said. "You've a goose egg and a gash on your forehead."

"You're a damn knight," she whispered again.

"I was a knight once… a long time ago."

"Well you've not lost a knight's aptitude with a sword."

"Some things are never lost," he replied.

"SHE LIVES IN a cave?" Broccan sounded in disbelief.

"She's peculiar, but other than Maiden Albray, she's the best we have here," Winston said.

"Why do you assist us when your cousin and the others have no qualms in hurting women?" Broccan questioned.

"Because I care for Maiden Albray. I once asked her to be my wife. Sadly, she declined."

"Who dares disturb my solitude?" a croaky voice called. Rhianwyn felt relief in hearing it.

"I'm Lord Brockwell. There's someone here in need of a healer."

"I don't care who you are or who needs healing."

"She requested you," Broccan insisted.

Rhianwyn opened her eyes to see the old woman come to the cave entrance.

"Oh girl, what's happened to you?" the woman asked, now clearly concerned.

"She took a nasty knock to the head. The wound's bleedin' badly."

"The head always bleeds badly…well, bring her in then. But only you and her. The others wait here!" the woman ordered authoritatively.

Broccan carried her inside where a lone candle barely lit the chamber.

"Through here. Put her on the bed," Radella directed.

Rhianwyn regretted being released from his protective arms.

"What's happened to her? It's not only the head wound. I see bruises on her arms."

"The sheriff's son grabbed her and pushed her against the stones."

"Which stones?" Radella's voice was strained.

"Those they call the sunstones."

The woman made an odd guttural sound and grasped Rhianwyn's hand.

"Her blood was spilled within the circle of sunstones?"

"Is that a bad omen?" Broccan asked.

"You're Irish. You tell me; is it favorable to spill blood within a sacred place?"

Broccan exhaled and shook his head.

"Go now so I can see to her injuries."

"I don't want to leave her," Broccan admitted.

"I'll be safe here," Rhianwyn weakly managed.

"You're alert and speaking; that's a good sign," Radella said.

"I'll wait just outside then." Broccan squeezed Rhianwyn's hand before he left.

RADELLA GENTLY WASHED the wound.

"Don't fall asleep, lass," she finally said. "Though you'll want to, you must remain awake."

"I won't sleep."

"Drink a little of this. The wound isn't deep enough to require mending. It'll heal well enough, but you're bound to have a wicked aching head. You'll know a knock to the head can be fatal."

She put a cool cloth with herbal remedy on the wound and Rhianwyn winced. Rhianwyn drank the bitter elixir before Radella placed a bandage on her forehead. She wiped the blood from her hair and face. Every part of Rhianwyn's body felt tender. When Radella lifted her skirts and glanced below, Rhianwyn stiffened.

"What are you doing?"

"Seeing if you were violated," the old woman explained.

"I wasn't," Rhianwyn insisted.

"There's bruising on your backside and it appears there's been recent activity…"

"It was consensual."

"Oh girl, you're bound to end up in a heap of trouble for permitting that. If it was consensual, it was damn vigorous."

"It was *passionate*… but why would you care if I end up in trouble? You simply turned your back on me and I never knew why."

The old woman sighed. "You envied my life, dear girl. I don't want you *only* to serve as a healer. I'd be saddened to know you didn't find love or marriage because you chose to selflessly serve others."

"I adore being a healer."

"But it's all-consuming and lonely," the woman rasped. "The older you become the more regrets you'll have. You possess a rare beauty, girl. You're brilliant, youthful, and passionate. I want you to have a full, happy life, but you won't if you always put others before your own needs or if you become with child when unwed. Is that damn lord the man who's had you?" Radella motioned toward the cave entrance. "He seems to care for you."

"Yes, but I won't permit it to be more than physical pleasure. He's a noble and a damn knight and…"

"You must tell me how she is," Broccan's voice interrupted. "I need to meet with the sheriff and the king, but I must know Maiden Albray's well before I leave."

"She'll be well enough but she must be watched closely and cannot fall asleep."

Broccan stepped back in without permission.

"Why not?" Broccan asked.

"Because she mightn't ever wake," Radella said.

"My brain may've been injured," Rhianwyn explained.

"Sometimes that happens with a head injury...someone falls asleep, not to rise again."

"Then sit up and don't you dare sleep," he ordered, sounding distressed.

"Someone must keep her awake...and not doing what you two did earlier."

"What?" Broccan asked.

"You're not to partake in relations with her!" Radella warned. "Not for several days."

Broccan looked at Rhianwyn with an expression of disbelief.

"She didn't tell me, but I've seen the bruises left from the bedding," Radella said.

"You're bruised?" He was obviously distraught.

"It isn't as though you forced me. I was equally desirous," Rhianwyn said.

"There are fingermarks on her backside, much larger than those on her arms probably grasped in passion, not anger," Radella explained.

Broccan stared at her uncertainly, clearly uncomfortable with the turn the conversation had taken.

"You, Lord Broccan, would not be held responsible if you leave a baby in her belly. Rhianwyn would be shamed and you could simply walk away without giving it another thought."

"I wouldn't, I swear!" Broccan said.

"I won't carry a child," Rhianwyn fervently announced, despite the pounding in her head.

"The only way to make that a certainty is if someone slices off his stones or you stop the coupling," Radella admonished them.

"You haven't spoken to me for months. I don't need motherly advice now."

"You came to me, girl."

"I want to marry Rhianwyn; she won't agree to it," Broccan said.

Radella narrowed her eyes on hearing that. "If you have half the intelligence I believe, you'll marry him straightaway."

"And be Lady Brockwell?" she scoffed. "I won't!"

"You deserve to be Lady Brockwell!" Radella replied, but looked away as though she shouldn't have said that. "Take her somewhere safe. Watch over her and give her this." Radella passed a vial to Broccan.

"Can't she stay here?" Broccan asked.

"This cave is damp. She'd catch a chill."

He nodded, taking the vial and putting it in his pocket. "I'll carry her."

"I'm perfectly capable of walking."

"Let the man carry you; don't be so infernally headstrong, girl."

Broccan smiled and lifted Rhianwyn into his arms.

"Don't fall asleep till morning."

"Thank you, Radella. I've missed you."

"And I you, dear girl," she whispered.

BROCCAN TOOK RHIANWYN to his guesthouse, left Keyon with her with promises of singing lively tunes to keep her awake. Then he walked Selena home, thankful he didn't have to deal with the brothel owner. Next he met with the king and the bloody disagreeable sheriff. The entire time his mind was on Rhianwyn and knowing he could've lost her this night.

Then he eagerly returned to her. "You have more color now." Broccan tenderly touched her cheek even though Keyon remained sitting there.

"I'm less dizzy, too," she said. "What happened with the king and the sheriff?"

"I explained what occurred. I'll not be punished for killing those bastards. Winston confirmed my account of the men attacking you—said I was defending you. However, the sheriff isn't convinced his son had any part in it. Winston wouldn't speak against Godric. He likely fears his unscrupulous cousin. I've made a rather bad enemy of the sheriff, but I care not."

Rhianwyn undoubtedly saw the worry on his face as he sat beside her.

"I'm mostly recovered, Broccan. You look worn out. Go to your bed."

"May we have a moment alone?" Broccan asked Keyon.

Keyon nodded and started for the door.

"Thank you for staying with me, my friend," Rhianwyn said.

"There are three other bedchambers in this guesthouse, Keyon. Choose one. Stay as long as you wish," Broccan offered.

"I'm grateful, Broccan. I take it this'll be a lengthy *conversation* then?" Keyon looked directly at him even though he was considerably smaller and less muscular.

Rhianwyn shook her head. "Lord Brockwell will be going to his manor. I'll remain here till morning, then go to my cottage."

Broccan stared at Rhianwyn but didn't speak again till Keyon left.

"I won't leave you," Broccan said.

"You're a damn knight!" she said, yet again.

"You can stop repeatin' that any time," Broccan snapped. "You apparently accepted knowin' I was a hired killer. Why would my being a knight cause such despair? I *was* a knight, but as I've said it was some time ago."

"I'd never have become close to you if I'd known you were a knight."

"I'm weary, Rhianwyn. Let me lie beside you and hold you. It should be safe for you to sleep now. It's nearly dawn."

"I won't."

"You won't what?" He still unbuckled his belt presuming she'd permit him to stay.

"I won't continue our relationship knowing you're a knight."

"Bloody sardin' hell, Rhianwyn. I haven't been a knight in years. I'm not a knight now."

"Once a knight…always a knight."

"I was released from the order by the king and the Grand Cross."

"You're still a knight in your heart and your mind."

"You *would* like to discuss my heart then for you seemed entirely opposed earlier?"

"Please leave me to my sleep."

He stared long and hard, but finally exhaled in exasperation.

"Bloody stubborn woman," he muttered through clenched teeth, leaving without looking back.

CHAPTER NINETEEN

I T HAD BEEN a week since Rhianwyn saw Broccan. He'd stopped by her cottage every day, but she'd determinedly told him to leave without coming out to face him. She could nearly feel his impatience and frustration, but she couldn't handle a confrontation with him just now when her emotions were so conflicted.

Wandering through the orchard Rhianwyn picked up several apples from the ground and placed them in her kirtle's apron. There were enough for each of the children. She smiled at the thought when she heard a voice behind her.

"Are those *your* apples, Maiden Albray?" Sheriff Percival insolently askcd.

She didn't reply.

"Are they yours?" he repeated. "This is Brockwell land."

"They were on the ground and would've gone to waste. I didn't pick them nor do I take them for myself but for children who haven't much to eat."

"Were you given permission?" he asked, his dark eyes and beard so like his objectionable son's it made her cringe.

"Lord Brockwell wouldn't disapprove of me taking apples. He offers alms to the needy."

"Did he give you permission or perhaps you've paid

him with your *services?*"

She stared incredulously.

"The same services you offer the knights. My son's informed me how frequently you're taken to the keep. Perhaps you should be one of Shandy's girls if you eagerly partake in frequent sarding."

"I'll leave the apples if you feel they've been wrongfully obtained," Rhianwyn suggested simply wanting to be distanced from the man.

"You won't get off so easily, Maiden Albray. You'll be taken before the king and his court to address your thievery. You might even meet the executioner's ax." He smiled deviously at that.

"Speak with Lord Brockwell; he *will* tell you he doesn't disapprove of me helping children."

"Lord Giles Brockwell? I doubt he'd grant you mercy when you pursued his only son relentlessly—tormented him till he went to battle and met death rather than deal with the daughter of a mad mage."

"Let me find Broccan Mulryan," she pleaded, trying to ignore the hateful words. "He'll speak in my favor."

"Apparently you have him besotted, too, but since he's not here, you'll come along with me."

The sheriff knocked the apples from her kirtle and roughly grabbed her arm. He bound her hands, tying the rope to his saddle forcing her to walk quickly to keep up with the horse. She stumbled, nearly fell, but caught herself. She'd seen wounds caused when dragged by a horse. She did *not* want to suffer that especially when she was still recovering from her head wound.

As they walked through the village streets, people stared and whispered. Godric and some of the sheriff's men were near the castle. Godric smiled such a smug smile, Rhianwyn longed to slap his face. Lucian, Cassian's younger brother was with Godric. He also jeered.

Nearing the castle, she was relieved to see Sir Severin.

"What's the meaning of this?" he asked. "Why is Maiden Albray bound and nearly dragged by your horse?"

"She's being taken to the king to receive judgment for thievery. It's none of your concern, Severin."

"What's she alleged to have stolen?" Severin asked.

"Apples from Lord Brockwell's trees. I saw it with my own eyes so there's no disputing it."

"I'd wager this is in retribution for the incident when Maiden Albray was manhandled by your men. Your unscrupulous son should be issued punishment...not a young maiden who's surely done nothing wrong."

"You're calling me a liar then? Girl, inform the interfering Grand Cross you took apples that didn't belong to you!" Sheriff Percival ordered.

"Please find Lord Brockwell, Sir Severin," Rhianwyn said.

He nodded and set off without pause.

RHIANWYN WAS TAKEN to the dungeon not straight to the king's court. Thankfully, she wasn't placed with other prisoners for she'd heard men and women were often jailed together. What happened within these dark, filthy chambers was apparently reprehensible.

Recognizing the sturdy boot falls made her heart quicken. A guard scurried ahead and unlocked the door.

"Maiden Albray," Broccan said.

She knew he fought the urge to hold her, but instead he took her hand. "Are you well? Have you been harmed or mistreated?"

She shook her head though the rope burns on her wrists stung fiercely. Her mother's satchel had been taken; she wasn't certain who had her valued possession.

"Come with me," Broccan said. "Rest assured, we'll meet with the king and sort this out straightaway. Sure this was done to avenge Godric's fury. Sir Severin believes that's true as well."

Rhianwyn only nodded. He placed his arm around her to steady her, then lifted her into his arms and effortlessly carried her up the many stone stairs. They saw Elspeth in the corridor and her eyes grew wide.

"What's happened to Rhianwyn?" she whispered.

"A run-in with the bloody sheriff," Broccan replied.

Elspeth worriedly touched Rhianwyn's arm before Broccan carried her directly into the king's meeting room, although Rhianwyn doubted he'd been called yet.

"What's the meaning of this interruption?" King Thaddeus's head advisor asked.

"This young woman was held in your intolerable dungeon merely for taking apples fallen from my trees. She was securing food for needy children. What low vengeful pathetic excuse of a man serves as sheriff to be so petty as to…"

"Broccan Mulryan, I see your passion and your temper have not calmed in these years since last we had occasion to speak at length," King Thaddeus said.

"Do you believe I've no cause for temper, Your Grace?"

"If what you say is true, then you're justified. Someone locate Percival since he's the one who brought the woman here." Two men hurried off. "Can't she stand on her two feet? Has she been injured?"

Broccan gently set her to standing when he spotted her wrists.

"By Christ's cross." He pulled back her sleeves. "How did you obtain these wounds?"

"She was bound and tied behind the sheriff's horse." Sir Severin appeared at the castle's great hall's two large doors, accompanied by several of his knights.

"All the way from the orchard to the castle?" Broccan asked in horrified disbelief.

"Don't make more of this than there is, Lord Brockwell," she whispered. "Simply confirm your permission for me to take the apples and hopefully I'll be released."

"What will you see done to the sheriff for this miscarriage of justice and unnecessary force?" Broccan ignored her warning.

"Why are you so impassioned about this?" the king's priest asked. "She's merely a commoner. What concern is this of yours?"

"An innocent woman has been wrongly accused and manhandled on my estate. Should I not be impassioned regardless of her status? Is it only nobles given fair treatment in this kingdom? That's not what I would've thought of the man I knew those years back." Broccan stared hard at the king.

"We'll both be in the dungeon soon," Rhianwyn again whispered.

"This is Maiden Albray, then?" the king asked. Broccan nodded. "She's the woman who's received the unusually high number of marriage offers in my recent invitation?"

The marriage advisor nodded and the king, his priest and ministers looked at her in question. She stared down at her dirty, torn kirtle and touched her messy hair. After hours in the dungeon, her face was probably smudged and her forehead still bore the not fully healed wound and bruising.

She saw the physician Dorsett and his apprentice Hadley, too. They openly sneered. They deeply disliked her because her services were often preferred to theirs.

"Including your own proposition, Broccan, that boasted a most worthy sum of coin for the favor of her hand in marriage?" King Thaddeus continued, looking at Broccan again.

Rhianwyn stared at him for she was of the understanding he'd withdrawn his request.

"I greatly desire to marry her, yes," Broccan replied.

She glared at him but held her tongue.

"How many offers had she?" the king asked his advisor.

"Twenty-seven," the man read. "Six knights, nine villagers, seven men from the countryside, the sheriff's nephew, the hermit huntsman, a wandering minstrel and two lords, Lord Oliver Barlow and Broccan Mulryan, the Lord of Brockwell Manor."

The king stood. Leaving his throne he descended the steps adjusting his long gold robes as he walked toward them in the center of the great hall. He stared at Rhianwyn as if to discern why so many would wish to take her for a wife.

"Maiden Albray," the king said.

"Yes, Your Grace," she quietly replied, lowering her eyes.

"Why do so many men want you for their bride?"

She shook her head and shrugged her shoulders.

"I have no notion, Your Grace."

"Six knights and two lords," he said. "Do you have a preference as to whom you might wed?"

"I wish to marry no one," she dared to reply.

"That's peculiar. What is it you want then?" the king asked.

"I long to remain a healer which doesn't allow time for a husband or children. As you know the healer Radella was once in demand. I'd ask to be allowed such an honorable life serving others."

The king stared again and Dorsett and Hadley both glowered. They disapproved of her healing methods and resented the knights often requesting her.

"We already have a physician and his apprentice," King Thaddeus said. "I don't believe we're in need of a healer…especially not such a young, pretty woman. No, it's surely your foreordination to marry and have children. That is after all what you were created to do…the purpose of all women."

Rhianwyn dared to raise her eyes—couldn't hide her

scowl but bit her tongue.

"She's spirited I see. Is that what you find most appealing, Broccan?"

"She's kind and caring…intelligent and amusing…and of course beautiful. In truth, there's nothing about her I don't find appealing," Broccan admitted.

"You'd wed her when she seems opposed?"

"I hope to convince her she'd be happy as my wife."

"There are many other men who wish for that as well…as you've heard."

"Have they provided equal coin in their request to marry Maiden Albray?" Broccan asked.

"I'd estimate they have not," the king said staring at the sour-faced man who sat at the ledger book.

He shook his head. "Nothing comparable," the man replied, "not even Lord Barlow."

"You don't wish to marry a lady of noble birth, Broccan?" King Thaddeus asked.

"I've recently kept company of several noble ladies, none so fine or enchanting as Maiden Albray. I want to marry her. You *have* passed the decree stating noble born are free to take any woman as their bride."

"She is a pretty woman. I expect if she didn't wear rags and had her hair fashioned elegantly, she'd be a rare beauty."

King Thaddeus stared at her again…the way many men had stared before.

"Take off your cloak," he ordered.

"Are you plannin' to wed her then, Your Grace?" Broccan asked. "For I think what lies beneath her cloak is no one's concern but a man who'll be her husband."

"You push my continued good countenance in your regard, Broccan. Is she not a subject of the kingdom...a mere woman, therefore a lowly possession to be done with whatever I might desire?"

Broccan stiffened.

"Remove the cloak, woman!" the king ordered.

Rhianwyn saw Godric and his father smile from where they now stood by the door. She was the only woman here among all these men. If Broccan defied the king he could be sent to the dungeon or perhaps the axeman's block.

Rhianwyn stared unblinkingly at the king, unfastened the clasp and let the cloak fall to the floor. He gazed at her breasts—looked her up at down as though he might have intentions of more.

"Should I remove my other garments as well?" Rhianwyn dared to say when the king stared so intently.

"You wouldn't make her suffer such indignity!" Broccan blared and the king looked away. "Tell me the greatest amount of coin ever offered to secure a marriage." Broccan stared at the man who sat by the ledger. "Surely it must be recorded?"

The man looked uncertain but the king nodded. He quoted a figure and Broccan shook his head.

"That's a good deal less than the amount I offered a month ago," Broccan said.

"We've not included this year's bids," the stern man replied.

"Did you pay the Welsh prince a dowry or did he pay for the hand of your daughter?" Broccan boldly asked the king.

"That betrothal was secured with the union of countries and an agreement of peace," King Thaddeus explained.

"And coin… there would've been coin, probably livestock as well," Broccan dared to push. "Whatever was paid, I'll match it, plus what I've already paid."

The king turned to face Broccan again, staring as if trying to determine why he was so adamant he'd have her.

"If she's so valuable, perhaps I should have her made more presentable and shown to the other lords in the kingdom."

"Is my coin not worth the same as others then, Your Grace?" he asked. "Is it because I'm Irish and have only inherited a Wessex manor? Does that deem me unfit to wed a Saxon woman?"

"Maiden Albray's half Welsh," Sir Severin added. "Both lands of the Celts."

"Tell me why you want her so desperately and I might be more inclined to decide in your favor!" the king demanded.

"I told you. She's beautiful, kind and intelligent."

The king looked doubtful.

"You were once the keenest thinker I'd made acquaintance with. Have you lost your mind, Broccan?"

"Not my mind…but maybe my heart," he said and Rhianwyn closed her eyes. "I admit I've fallen in love with her."

"*Love?* That's often the bloody ruination of men," the king declared.

"May I speak with you alone, Your Grace?" Broccan asked.

"Surely whatever you say could be in the presence of my ministers, my priests, and advisors?"

"And the sheriff, his despicable son, half the knights in the order, your priest, your physician, his apprentice and a good many others," Broccan replied.

"It's a private matter you wish to discuss?" King Thaddeus asked.

Broccan glanced at Rhianwyn and she looked away.

"I want no other man to lie with her," he admitted. "I'd gladly behead any man who dares touch her."

"Have you had her or does she remain chaste?" King Thaddeus asked.

"I...we...yes, we've shared a bed," Broccan said, regret in his tone.

"She must've been pleasing if you're prepared to spend endless coin to ensure she continues to do so."

Cassian glowered and the priest looked appalled.

"Do you only say this so her worth will be lessened and other men wouldn't want her?"

"How much coin would be required to make certain she'll be my wife?" Broccan asked again.

"Do you even have such quantity of coin? It's been brought to my attention Brockwell Manor may not be yours after all if you don't wed this woman," the king said.

Broccan sneered at Cassian. Surely he was the only one who knew anything of that.

"Is that true and if so why would Lord Giles Brockwell demand that condition?" the king continued.

"You'd have to speak to Giles of that, it's much more complicated, I assure you."

Rhianwyn stared at Broccan. Would he only inherit Brockwell Manor if he married her? Was that the reason for his interest from the beginning? Had his affections only been pretended? Was Giles Brockwell truly so regretful of his ill treatment of her or did he believe she was owed something because his only son had loved her?

It seemed unlikely but Broccan's interest in her had stemmed from wanting to convince her to speak with Giles. Perhaps that had been his true purpose for pursuing and bedding her. Her temper flared. She tasted blood at continuing to bite her tongue. The king's words pulled her from her disparaging thoughts.

"You're willing to sully the woman's good name— perhaps make her suffer ridicule to marry her. She must be extraordinary. I think I should like her made presentable, then taken to *my* chambers."

Broccan tensed and Rhianwyn felt her heart fall. The notion of having to go to the king's bed wholly repulsed her. He was old enough to be her father…not to mention he was Lilliana's father.

That thought had barely come to Rhianwyn when Lilliana entered the king's court by way of the top balcony. The skirts of her luxurious red gown rustled to alert others to her presence. Rhianwyn stared up at her. Rhianwyn believed Elspeth probably had gone to Lilliana to see what she could do about Rhianwyn's unsettling situation. The princess looked upon them from above.

"You are not to be here, Daughter," King Thaddeus

reprimanded.

"As your daughter and a citizen of your kingdom soon to be departing this country, should I not be permitted to know the workings of your court before I leave? Did my ears deceive me, Father, are you having a young woman ordered to your chambers... a woman close to my own age?"

The king looked away uncomfortably.

"That's none of your concern, Lilliana."

"Perhaps you'll take her for your bride then? Maybe an arrangement could be made that I'll wed Lord Broccan if you'll not grant him permission to wed the young healer. If he pays a hearty sum, that would ensure I'm able to remain in my beloved Wessex which would gladden my heart."

"That could cause a war with Welshland," King Thaddeus argued.

"If you force this woman to your chambers I shall forever be at war with you, Father! Why not grant Lord Broccan permission to wed her?"

"I fear he's deceived me in saying he's shared her bed only in order to make her his wife."

"I wouldn't tarnish Maiden Albray's good name if that weren't true," Broccan said.

"Should she be examined to see if there's validity to the fact she isn't virginal?" Dorsett, the physician, asked, slurring his words, clearly drunk.

"I could assist in that," Hadley said, openly ogling Rhianwyn.

"If either of you touch her, I swear, I'll sever your hands!" Broccan swiftly unsheathed his sword. The chamber filled with the sound of swords being drawn as the sheriff and several of his men did so, as did the knights.

"This matter takes up my time, tries my patience and has caused division between me and my daughter, as well as the sheriff's men and my knights. Now it may be the cause of bloodshed. How can a woman…a mere commoner cause such a stir?"

"What would an examination prove?" Broccan asked. "I told you I've been with her."

"Do you deny that's true?" King Thaddeus asked Rhianwyn.

If she pretended she was virginal she'd likely be taken to the king's chambers. She'd heard he favored virgins. If she admitted she wasn't, she'd be forced to wed Broccan…a knight…a man with secrets who'd deceived her all along. She'd no longer be permitted to be a healer and expected to carry his children, possibly die in childbed…and maybe leave a baby behind. She didn't reply.

"Perhaps the midwife, Josephine could do the examination so the healer doesn't suffer deeper humiliation," Princess Lilliana said. "She's the one who'll do so for me before I'm married."

"Just admit we've been together," Broccan whispered but Rhianwyn wouldn't look at him.

"I can prove I've been with her," Broccan said. "She has a small red dragon symbol on her arse."

The king looked intrigued and Rhianwyn scowled.

"Then show us," King Thaddeus demanded.

Broccan appeared hesitant but sheathed his sword, then took out his knife. All eyes went to him as he grasped

Rhianwyn's skirts and sliced them open so her backside was bared revealing the dragon. He even turned her so the king and his advisors could see more clearly. She pulled away, sneering. The priest gasped. Several men wore lewd expressions. Broccan retrieved her cloak and covered her.

"Well clearly he's seen you unclothed? Is there truth to his other claims?" the king asked.

Rhianwyn remained silent, her fury growing. In her refusal to answer, the king grew impatient.

"Did you place that symbol upon her skin?" the king asked Broccan.

He shook his head. "I don't have skill to do such markings," Broccan admitted.

"It looks like the work of a Viking," Dorsett said.

The king looked at the group of knights.

"Was it the Viking knight who did the deed then?" King Thaddeus asked.

Ulf looked uncertain. When he stared at Rhianwyn, she spoke.

"Ulf did it upon my request. When I attended his injury some time ago, I admired his markings and asked if he'd place one upon my skin."

"Why your ass?" The king appeared interested.

"A woman would be harshly judged for having such a mark in plain view," Rhianwyn explained.

"Do you hold Welshland in such loyalty you wish to bear their mark?" the king asked.

"Or she knows it's a shit country only worthy of ceremony on a backside," Sheriff Percival declared.

"Yet the king sends his only daughter there," Broccan

said.

King Thaddeus threw an unkind stare at the sheriff.

"Did you have the healer, too?" Sheriff Percival asked Ulf.

"Maiden Albray's only a friend," Ulf replied.

"This has taken enough of my time," the king said. "Have the midwife examine the young healer, but Dorsett and Hadley will accompany her while it's done."

"You once told me I could call in a favor," Broccan loudly stated. "Those years ago in France on that battlefield, you told me you owed me whatever I might request. Disallow this examination and permit me to marry Maiden Albray and I'll call it even. Surely the life of a king is worth these two small petitions."

"You're certain this is what you'd request, Broccan, for there'll be no future favors granted?" the king warned.

"I'll request nothing more," Broccan assured him.

"Then you may wed the healer."

"I *would* ask she no longer be permitted to perform the duties of a healer," Dorsett said.

"As a wife and surely soon a mother she'd have no time for healing anyway," King Thaddeus said. "Henceforth you'll not be permitted to serve as a healer in my kingdom, Maiden Albray."

Rhianwyn's heart fell. She lowered her head fearing she might weep.

"I have her satchel," Dorsett said. "I'll see her remedies destroyed. They're certain to be unsafe at any rate."

"Destroy them if you must, but the satchel belonged to my mother and is important to me."

"It shall be returned to her." The king nodded to the physician.

"May we leave now?" Broccan asked.

"Yes, but my priest will wed you in one week's time or this agreement will be nullified," King Thaddeus said.

Broccan bowed respectfully. Rhianwyn managed to curtsey but her legs felt weak.

"Thank you, Your Grace," Broccan said.

Rhianwyn looked up at Lilliana appreciatively. Broccan took Rhianwyn's arm and began to lead her out.

"I want my mother's satchel," she repeated.

"I'll get it," Broccan said.

CHAPTER TWENTY

A S THEY LEFT the castle's courtroom and entered the long corridor, Cassian met Rhianwyn's eyes. He looked displeased. Godric and his father seemed furious with her being set free. The sheriff went to Dorsett.

"I'll see the mad healer's potions destroyed immediately," Sheriff Percival said.

"Maiden Albray requests her satchel returned," Broccan repeated. "And I believe you owe an apology to my future wife for your ill treatment," Broccan demanded.

"I just want to leave," Rhianwyn admitted.

"I was only doing my duty in addressing believed thievery," Sheriff Percival said.

"With far more force than necessary," Broccan replied, looking at Rhianwyn's raw wrists again.

Rhianwyn feared she'd soon weep or collapse. They were barely out of the castle when Godric swooped past them down the steps to the courtyard now in possession of her satchel. He smashed her many remedies on the cobblestones. She wouldn't give him the satisfaction of appearing distressed. However when he used his sword to slash the treasured satchel to ribbons before her eyes, she cried out in dismay. Broccan unsheathed his own sword, knocked Godric's sword to the ground and sliced his tunic just enough to draw blood.

"That's twice you've harmed me. You *will* pay dearly!" Godric snarled, looking down at the faint line of blood forming.

"I look forward to one day dealing with you more unremittingly," Broccan angrily replied.

Rhianwyn retrieved the destroyed satchel, sadly staring at the shredded leather. There'd be no hope of mending it.

"We'll go speak with the king and his advisors of the serious matter of harming and threatening my son," Sheriff Percival said, "since all your favors with the king have apparently been called in." He sneered at Broccan.

"First permit me to accompany Maiden Albray to my guesthouse where she'll remain till we're wed," Broccan requested.

"She'll come with us as witness to your violence toward my son."

"I didn't see it," Rhianwyn lied. "I was looking at my mother's ruined satchel and saw nothing of the altercation."

She glared at Percival and Godric, but glowered at Broccan as well. "Even if I had seen, who'd believe the account of a mad healer?" She seethed.

"You're no longer a healer." Godric grinned, clearly satisfied in that.

"I'll accompany Maiden Albray wherever she wishes," Cassian said, but Broccan grasped her arm.

"We'll walk her to her cottage." Elspeth came up behind them with Selena and Keyon.

Broccan looked at them with gratitude. Rhianwyn

wouldn't meet his eyes and he was swiftly escorted back to the king by the sheriff's men.

"I DIDN'T EXPECT to see you in my court again…certainly not today, Broccan." King Thaddeus shook his head.

"I wholly admit I'd prefer not to be here," Broccan said.

"Is there truth in the sheriff's son's account? Did you draw his blood yet again?"

"I did," Broccan admitted. "I was only protecting my newly betrothed."

"Godric attempted to harm the woman?"

"He unkindly destroyed her mother's possession which is dearly important to my lady's heart."

"Did you destroy the satchel?"

"It was old, worn, and worthless," Godric explained.

"Not to Maiden Albray," Broccan said. "It was promised to be returned to her by your own word, King Thaddeus."

"Is she not in possession of it now?" Godric sneered. "The destruction of an item doesn't warrant spilling my blood."

"It's a mere scratch, Godric, you sarding chicken heart. You expect your father and others to always fight your battles," Broccan said.

"First blood could be grounds for a swordfight." Sir Severin winked at Broccan.

"I doubt you'd want to do battle with Lord Brockwell,"

King Thaddeus said to Godric.

"I wouldn't even want to," Sir Severin professed. "Broccan Mulryan's uncommonly skilled with a sword. Perhaps more than any other."

"He can't be *that* good," Sheriff Percival replied.

"I can't attest to his skills now but when I fought with him, he was better than any knight I've ever known, dead or alive, even Sir Roderick," the king admitted.

"He's simply to be permitted to walk away then with no punishment for harming my son?" Sheriff Percival sounded outraged.

"It wasn't unprovoked but it was a bit harsh...although I suppose he could've disemboweled him," the king said, inhaling and looking to the ceiling. "What's to be done about this?"

"I have a suggestion," Sir Severin offered.

"Speak plainly then," the king replied.

"Reinstate Broccan as a knight. Have him train the new knights and spar with our best. We'd benefit greatly from his knowledge and experience. He was invaluable in training the men in France and as aforementioned valiantly saving your life and many others before nearly dying himself."

Broccan glowered at Severin. Perhaps he was trying to help him out of an unpleasant predicament...perhaps he simply wanted him to return to the knighthood. Either way, Broccan didn't want it...and Rhianwyn would despise it. She was already mightily displeased with him; wouldn't even look at him. She vowed to never marry a knight. This would create greater animosity between them.

"That seems a good solution," King Thaddeus agreed. "You'll remain living at Brockwell Manor…continue with running the estate and yes, marry your young beauty. But you'll train with the knights and instruct them no less than half the days each moon. You'll defend the castle and the kingdom, should it be under attack and if my knights are required elsewhere, you'll journey with them to defend our country."

"If I should refuse these terms?" Broccan asked.

"Sheriff Percival might demand you're sentenced to death for drawing blood of his only son…or I could have you placed in the dungeon indefinitely."

Broccan met the king's eyes in defiance.

"If you continue to push my patience I may display your precious Maiden Albray at the spinster market just to spite you for taking up my time this day."

Broccan curled his fists, wanting to erupt in temper, but knew he'd be issued severe punishment. What would become of Rhianwyn then?

"I'll agree to rejoin the knighthood, but let it be known it's with fervent objection, Your Grace."

"Duly noted, Broccan." The king wryly smiled. "I do look forward to watching you train—beginning tomorrow."

Broccan locked eyes with Sir Severin then bowed to King Thaddeus. "May I take leave?" he asked through gritted teeth.

"Yes, be gone with you. You have a wedding to plan and a sword to sharpen." The king obviously delighted in this turn of events.

As Broccan started down the castle steps, Sir Severin followed.

"It has to be better than being held in the dungeon or perhaps beheaded, *Sir Broccan*," the Grand Cross said.

"I suppose tellin' you to sard off might see me before the king yet again," Broccan replied.

"Just don't say it in the presence of others," Severin said. "I'm your superior but you and I've always been friends, Broccan."

"Was it your intention all along to have me as one of your knights again?" Broccan asked.

"I've never concealed my wishes of wanting you back in our order."

"Sure you're aware Rhianwyn has firmly avowed she'll never marry a knight."

"She has a fiery temper but she'll come round. Better by far than the spinster market or being betrothed to a man who could rot in the dungeon all the good years of his life."

"By her expression earlier, I'm not certain she'd agree. Now, I suppose I best go speak with her."

"As a man married these twenty years, I'd suggest you wait a bit," Sir Severin said.

Broccan nodded as Sir Cassian, Ulf, and Sir Everard joined them. Cassian appeared to be in a foul mood. He glowered at Broccan.

"I wish you *had* died on that battlefield in France!" Cassian blared.

"You did your best to ensure that outcome," Broccan replied caustically.

"Which do you oppose most, Cassian?" Broccan asked.

"That I'll wed Rhianwyn or that I'll be training the other knights with you?"

He didn't reply but Sir Severin shook his head in warning as Cassian's hand went to his sword.

"*You* asked for this, Sir Severin, even knowing our history and you'll surely be made to regret it," Broccan warned as he set off.

RHIANWYN FELT WHOLLY defeated. She'd assured Elspeth, Selena, and Keyon she was well. They'd hesitantly left her alone at her cottage. She welcomed the solitude. She lay on her parents' bed, clutching the shredded satchel and looking at the numerous dried herbs hanging from the ceiling and the remedies on the shelves. She'd hide them. Undoubtedly Dorsett would insist the sheriff have those disposed of, too.

She'd been ordered not to offer healing any longer. How could she comply? She'd be forced to marry Broccan. When she dwelled upon his deception, part of her longed to go to Giles Brockwell and demand explanation... but not today.

Now she'd be expected to carry Broccan's children. Could she truly end a pregnancy with a child they'd created together when she believed she was in love with him?

A memory overtook her though she tried to push it away. She'd hoped that agonizing recollection would one day evade her. But it was clear as the day it happened. Her mother was on this very bed after laboring hard for two days and nights.

Mererid was weak and in grievous pain. She knew her fate...that the child would not be born and she wouldn't live. The midwife had left to attend to another woman. Rhianwyn and Mabel, Sir Severin's wife, were with Mererid when Radella joined them. She'd been in another village. She looked harried as she came to sit with Mererid for they were friends. Rhianwyn was relieved. Now she wouldn't bear responsibility.

"My dear daughter, you've been such a brave young woman. I'm very proud of you my lovely, Rhianwyn, but I'd ask you to leave me now," Mererid said.

"I don't want to go, Mam. I'm a healer; I want to stay."

Mererid clutched her hand tightly and cried out in obvious agony. She'd be courageously keeping quiet through the entire ordeal, but now she screamed and blood thoroughly soaked the blankets. Mererid's face became startlingly pale and Radella gasped.

"My sweet daughter," Mererid whispered. "I've never withheld the truth from you and I won't now."

"Your womb has burst," Rhianwyn guessed.

"My clever, clever girl—such a gifted healer. I'm sorry you had to witness this, that you understand my certain fate and know it will be swift."

Rhianwyn nodded. "I'm proud to be here with you, Mam. I'd choose to be nowhere else."

She leaned over and kissed her mother's cheek and Mererid smiled before her hand grew slack in Rhianwyn's and her head lolled. Her eyes were open but now vacant. Blood gushed disturbingly onto the floor. Radella sadly shook her head. Mabel wept. Rhianwyn heard her father frantically calling from beyond the door demanding to know of Mererid's condition.

Radella hastily sliced open Mererid's belly in hope of saving the child. The boy child was blue, the cord wrapped around his neck, his tiny backside lodged in Mererid's birth canal an impossible position to deliver a baby—a certain death sentence for mother and child…

Rhianwyn hadn't realized she'd begun to weep but the tears fell down her cheeks as she heard a rap upon the door disrupting her tragic memories.

"Rhianwyn, I must speak with you," Broccan softly said.

"Do I have a choice, Lord Brockwell?" she replied, wiping her tears and moving from the bed.

"I promise I won't stay long."

She opened the door and he bent to get in the low doorway. She wouldn't meet his eyes.

"I regret the indecency I caused by tearing your kirtle…"

"And showing my bare backside to the king, his entire court, the priest, the sheriff, bloody Godric, the physician, his perverse assistant, and half the knight's order."

"I'm sorry. I thought it less disturbing than being taken to the king's chambers or suffering a humiliating examination."

"You believe I suffered no humiliation then in having them stare at my ass?"

"I cannot change that…but I pray you know everything I did was only to prevent a more unappealing fate."

"I'm weary, Lord Brockwell. Leave me now…"

"I long to hold you." He took a step toward her.

She backed against the wall. "Keep your damn distance. I'm no longer your mistress and not yet your wife. I've no say in marrying you and soon I'll have no choice to submit to you in a marriage bed...but know this, you *will not* touch me until after we're wed and never again because I desire it. The passion we once shared will *never* be the same. You've deceived me about many things!"

"Rhianwyn." His voice revealed waning patience.

"You never intended on withdrawing your marriage bid to the king, did you? All those times we were together and shared intimacies, you betrayed me. You also apparently have further deceit regarding Brockwell Manor."

"If you'd not been so infernally stubborn and gone to speak with Giles that could've been clarified long ago."

He stared into her eyes and stepped closer, but she put her hand before her.

"For the next seven days, I won't answer to you nor will I see or speak with you. I'll be free to do whatever I might like."

"You *are* my betrothed, Rhianwyn and will conduct yourself in an acceptable manner. I could take you to Brockwell Manor this very day."

"Then you'd have to do it by force. Perhaps you'd like to bind my wrists and pull me behind your horse."

"By God you're a strong-willed woman! I'm of a mind to throw you over my shoulder and carry you there. Why can't you see what I did today was only to save you from a bleaker fate?"

"How did you manage to escape punishment for harming Godric?"

He closed his eyes and exhaled, then put his hand to his brow, kneading the escalating headache that was obviously forming, but Rhianwyn had no sympathy.

"You won't answer?" she said.

"I'd rather leave that for another day," he admitted.

"How are you not in the dungeon or did you call in further favors of the king? You failed to mention you were in France with the king. That's how you knew Cassian. You must have met Anslem, too, then?" She suddenly realized.

He reluctantly nodded. "I knew him. We were both knights fighting against the French who intended to attack your country and mine."

"Were you with Anslem when he died?" she whispered.

He nodded again. "He died with your name upon his lips."

"Did he request you come here to look out for me as he asked Cassian…or request you to marry me? Did you agree out of obligation?"

"He did request I marry you. But as soon as I lay eyes upon you, I began to fall for you in my own right."

"You think I'd believe anything you say now?" she fumed.

He shrugged but looked increasingly angry himself.

"What of Brockwell Manor? Did Giles agree to give you the estate because you were with Anslem when he died or because of guilt or some misguided loyalty to the woman his son wanted to marry?"

"Rhianwyn, it's much more complicated than obligation or loyalty. I will inherit Brockwell Manor regardless for... I'm the only male of the Brockwell bloodline that remains."

Rhianwyn shook her head not understanding and finally slumped upon the chair. He sat beside her, attempted to take her hand, but she pulled away.

"My great-great-grandmother on my mother's side was a Brockwell," he said. "Born and raised in Brockwell Manor she married an Irishman and moved to Ireland. I was named Broccan in honor of her noble surname. After Anslem died, it left me the only male remaining of that line."

"Where do I fit into this?" Rhianwyn asked.

"That you must hear from Giles."

"Definitely not this day," Rhianwyn said wearily. "Now, you should leave."

"You'll need to be fitted for a gown. You'll not be wearing rags to our wedding. You'll be attired as a proper bride."

"Already issuing orders and demands," she sniped.

He shrugged. "I won't order you about or make unreasonable demands but there will be some conditions I bespeak."

"Why are you not in the dungeon? You've yet to explain that."

"Because I've bloody well been ordered to rejoin the knighthood, to train others, and defend the kingdom as required," he finally blurted sounding as irked as she felt.

"I'll be forced to marry a knight which I've adamantly avowed I'd never do... a man who's a noble lord, a relation to Giles Brockwell, the one man I despise, and to reside at Brockwell Manor as a sarding lady. I'm disallowed from healing others which is my life's purpose and perhaps worst of all I'll be expected to bear your damn children."

"Would being the king's whore or sent to the spinster's block really be so much more appealin' then?" he snarled, his tone confrontational.

She didn't reply.

"I'll be here tomorrow after my bloody day's spent at the sardin' trainin' field. I'll fetch you then to have you fitted for a gown."

She curtsied exaggeratedly and sneered. "Yes, Milord! Whatever you might request, Lord Brockwell."

His eyes narrowed and his jaw tightened.

"If that were true, I'd request you share my bed this night so we can heatedly couple in an attempt to dispel some of this day's damn unpleasantness."

"You'd need to carry me kicking and screaming and force the joining for as I said, I'll never willingly go to your bed…a sarding knight and a bloody lord."

It satisfied her to see that angered him.

"I haven't the fight in me this day. However, I'll fetch you at tomorrow's dusk and you *will* be here waiting!" he ordered. "If you even think about leaving the village or hiding… I'll hire someone to watch you day and night like the princess or damn well lock you in my guesthouse till after we're wed! Now…good day, Maiden Albray. Sleep well!"

He left then closing the door with such force, the dust fell from the thatched roof along with several pieces of straw and insects lodged there. Rhianwyn was livid as she stomped upon the scurrying insects, wishing it was Broccan beneath her boot.

CHAPTER TWENTY-ONE

R HIANWYN PLACED SEVERAL remedies in a hollow tree and others in a hole once occupied by a badger. She was resigned to marrying Broccan even though the more she dwelled upon his deception and his arrogance last night, the more opposed she became.

She'd mended her torn kirtle he'd so deftly sliced yesterday in revealing the mark on her backside. He kept the packages with the new items he'd purchased. They remained unopened. She wouldn't give him the satisfaction of accepting his gifts. She couldn't really refuse him providing a gown for their wedding.

Having to spend a lifetime with a man who deceived and now tried to dominate her would be unbearable. Of course they mightn't have a lifetime… she'd likely die in childbed or him in battle. What was more terrifying…having to live with him or living without him? It wasn't as though he didn't make her swoon and sharing his bed had been wondrously engaging…but no, she *would not* think of that. She longed to remain furious in how he'd wronged her.

Rhianwyn finally went to the stone circle for the first time since she'd been hurt. She sat in the middle, looked up at the towering formation, then closed her eyes trying to find peace in the situation and not recall the torrid passion she and Broccan had shared here.

The breeze ruffled her hair and she attempted to let her woes be lifted. When she finally opened her eyes, the sun was setting. Broccan would be at the cottage soon. She was of half a mind to not be there. Why shouldn't she infuriate him? She longed to be able to discuss this with her mother. She couldn't speak of it with Elspeth or Selena. They felt she should be grateful to be marrying Lord Brockwell. Not that she'd told them about his deception or what had occurred in the king's court. They hadn't seen her shredded kirtle. She'd not informed them the men of the court had seen her bare backside or that Broccan announced to them all that they'd shared a bed. Maybe Elspeth would've heard by now through castle gossip.

As she walked away across the open plain, she was nearly certain she heard a whisper. She turned back to the sunstones, but could see no one. Although unplanned, Rhianwyn found herself at the graveyard, sitting by her mother's stone...wondering if she should have a stone placed for her father.

"Well Mam, I'm in a conundrum. You used to tell me to always see the positivity in any situation. Yet you told me to stand up for myself and be true to my beliefs. I know I'm stubborn and have a quick temper, but I don't want to be domineered by a man. I certainly don't want to have to stop offering healing. There are many who *do* depend on me regardless of what bloody Dorsett and Hadley believe."

"The conversation might be a bit one-sided," a familiar melodic voice said.

"Hello Keyon," she greeted the minstrel.

"I'd like to have met your mother if she was so influential you still seek her counsel after these years she's been gone."

"She was strong and kind, beautiful and wise."

"Her daughter's not unlike her then," Keyon said. Sitting beside Rhianwyn, he took her hand.

"You asked to marry me?"

"I knew I had no chance and little coin but…" He cleared his throat uncomfortably. "I see Broccan does care for you."

"Perhaps, but he's deceived me and weds me mostly out of obligation and a promise to Anslem who was apparently a distant cousin."

Keyon's eyes darted back and forth faster than usual.

"I'm here to fetch you. Broccan's delayed at the knights' keep. The knights went there after training. I'm told he's a bit filled with drink. He sent a messenger asking me to take you to the manor. There was mention of a fitting for a gown."

He cringed a little, looking like he expected her to resist.

"I'm pleased it's you who'll accompany me if I must be fitted for this confounded gown. I hope Broccan drinks himself stupefied and spends the night with half a dozen harlots."

Keyon grinned and stood. Reaching for her hand, he helped her up. She brushed off her skirts.

"I think your mother would be pleased you have such a strong will." Keyon chuckled. "Broccan mightn't share that sentiment just now, but I believe he'd expect nothing less."

"WHAT AN ABOMINABLE time to have a gown fitting!" The cantankerous tailor scowled looking out the window at darkness.

"I'm no more eager to do this than you, so leave straightaway," Rhianwyn suggested.

"No…no, Lord Brockwell's already paid me half for my services. I'll not shirk my responsibilities."

"Then get on with it," Rhianwyn said.

"You'll need to remove your kirtle. Leave on your shift. I'm to make an elegant gown and a new shift for the wedding with less than a week to see it done," the slight, pointy-nosed man said as he clucked his tongue, bitterly grumbling.

"Here in the hall, I'm to disrobe?" Rhianwyn griped.

"By the news from yesterday's court, a good many men saw your uncovered backside. Truly this shouldn't be too despairing."

"I wouldn't think bein' only partly unclothed in this chamber should cause reason for modesty," Matty whispered.

Rhianwyn cheeks grew warm. She glanced at the table and the rug by the fire where she and Broccan first shared fervent passion. She sighed, removed her outer garment wishing she could forget that.

"I'm to inquire what color you wish the gown to be?" the tailor said.

"Whatever you like."

"Lord Broccan insisted *you* decide."

"That was good of him since I have no say in choosing to marry him."

"Gold would be lovely with your hair…or maybe purple," Matty offered.

"You choose, Matty."

The tailor threw them a stern scowl.

"Gold, make the infernal gown gold." Rhianwyn knew she sounded as perturbed as the unlikeable man.

"If you'd hold still, I might not jab you with a pin," he groused.

She sighed again.

"Do you request tight-fitting sleeves or the more fashionable wide bell sleeves?" the man asked.

"Whatever you think," Rhianwyn replied.

"You're being most uncooperative. You must have an opinion. I heard you're a strong-willed woman."

"Honestly, I don't care. If I say tight fitting you'll likely berate me for not being fashionable. If I say wide fitting, you'll complain that it'll take longer when time's short. Therefore, do whatever you bloody well prefer and then just sard off."

The man huffed aloud at that, clearly insulted.

"Barnett, are you rilin' my bride-to-be?" a male voice slurred from just outside the door. "I thought that honor was reserved for me."

Broccan leaned against the doorway and looked in; his smile lopsided, his hair loose and tousled. He wore chain mail armor. With his sword on his belt, he looked valiant, strong, and undeniably appealing. Rhianwyn turned away, certainly not wanting to be attracted to him.

"Your betrothed won't offer her opinion beyond saying the gown should be gold and only because your woman servant suggested it."

Broccan came in, staggered slightly, then sat not far from where the tailor draped linen over her shift to take measurements.

"Should the neckline be high and respectable or lower, revealing cleavage as is sometimes seen in ladies' gowns?"

"I'm certainly after seein' Maiden Albray's cleavage," Broccan slurred again, then chuckled.

"Perhaps the gown could be fashioned so my ass might be exposed as well," she sarcastically replied.

Matty smiled and Broccan laughed heartily.

"I doubt that would be considered fashionable." Barnett exasperatedly sighed.

"Just make the laces easily undone." Broccan threw a seductive look her way.

Rhianwyn put her hands on her hips and scowled; the tailor huffed again.

"Will the wedding take place in the abbey or your manor, Lord Brockwell?" he asked. "She'll need a matching shawl if it's at the abbey."

"The priest says either's acceptable," Broccan said.

"Whatever you wish, Lord Brockwell." Rhianwyn curtsied.

"You do need to stand still," the tailor scolded.

"You need to become a damn gravedigger so you've no contact with the living," she sniped.

"Make a shawl, too." Broccan nodded as the tailor removed the cloth. Rhianwyn stood in her shift, suddenly uncomfortable as Broccan eyed her with unmistakable interest.

"I'll finish the gown and shift in three days and a shawl as well," Barnett assured them. "Perhaps I'll complete two gowns of differing styles and colors so you might then choose which you favor, Maiden Albray?"

"That sounds a grand notion," Broccan agreed, his eyes not leaving her.

"I'll require you for a fitting when the garments are completed," the tailor said.

Rhianwyn nodded. Barnett bowed to Broccan and left them. Rhianwyn turned her back as she donned her worn kirtle.

"I still have the other finer garments I purchased for you," Broccan said. "I could get them for you now."

"I don't want them or anything from you."

"Bloody hell, woman; you're headstrong." He raked his hands through his hair.

"And you, Lord Brockwell or Sir Broccan will be made to deal with me for as long as the fates allow."

"May I get you somethin' to eat, Maiden Albray?" Matty intervened. "Broccan must dine; you could join him."

"Thank you, Matty, but Keyon waits at the guesthouse to walk me to my cottage."

She started to the door but Broccan grasped her arm.

"Could you give us a moment, Matty?"

Matty briefly stared but then complied.

"Have you any notion how much I want you?" Broccan asked. "I ache to be with you."

He stood and tried to take Rhianwyn in his arms but she stiffened.

"Go to the brothel to have those infernal desires sated for I've already told you I'll not willingly share your bed."

"Knowing you're impassioned only fuels my need." He pulled her to him.

She pushed at his broad chest as he kissed her. Now she fought not to respond.

"I need you," he moaned and his hand went to the laces on her gown. "Perhaps here on that table where you first gave yourself to me...enticing me so brazenly I couldn't refuse."

"That was only to seal a bargain which you apparently never intended to keep," she argued.

"I actually never agreed to it." He still held her.

"It was implied when you followed through with sarding me," she fumed.

"Don't let on you didn't want it as much as I did," he said. "Christ you were wild with need."

He pulled down her kirtle and shift exposing her breasts, then hoisted up her skirts and reached for the buttons on his breeches.

"You're a damn lecherous barbarian," she hissed, lifting her leg and kneeing him in the groin, then ducked beneath his arm and raced away.

"By Christ, woman. If you damage my ballocks, that *would* change our marriage bed considerably."

"You think I've no experience fighting off lewd men?"

"I suppose you do." His face contorted in a grimace and his hands held his groin.

"I told you, go find a harlot," she replied haughtily.

"It wouldn't distress you if I followed through on that suggestion?"

"I truly don't care what you do, Lord Brockwell." She adjusted her garments and swiftly left the hall, but he came after her.

"You take me to the brink of madness, Rhianwyn. Tell me you don't miss what we share…that your body doesn't crave my touch."

"Go sleep off your drunkenness," she snapped.

Still he followed, overtook her, and stood blocking the door with his brawny frame.

"And you tell me I'm stubborn," she said.

"Stay here… if you like." His tone was softer. "Come eat with me. I'm crazed with need for you, but I won't mention sharin' a bed. I'll have your belongings sent for. I won't expect you to lie with me till after we're wed. There are many rooms in this manor house including the previous lady's chambers. Stay here till our wedding day."

"I told you, I want nothing from you," she replied.

His eyes flashed but he retorted with sarcasm. "Well, you'll be getting something from me soon enough and often. When we're married and you can no longer deny me!"

"You're no bloody better than Godric," Rhianwyn hissed.

He moved then, his eyes stormy as she pushed past him and slammed the door behind her.

CHAPTER TWENTY-TWO

"MY FATHER DOESN'T see anyone without them requesting an audience well in advance, Rhianwyn," Lilliana said. "Some wait weeks. I *am* regretful; but even I'm disallowed to see him when he sits passing judgments, especially after the other day when I came uninvited to his court."

"I do thank you for that, Lilliana. You prevented me from a humiliating examination."

"I'm glad my father listened to reason and that you weren't expected to go to his chambers or share his bed." Lilliana took Rhianwyn's arm as they walked through the castle's corridor in the oldest, least-frequented part of the ancient castle. "It's only because of Sir Severin and Agnes I was able to come meet you today."

"I understand," Rhianwyn replied. "Is it really true you must soon leave for Cymru to be married?"

"It is," Lilliana heavily sighed, too, and Rhianwyn clutched her hand.

"Both Elspeth and I will be wed also and dear Selena..." Rhianwyn couldn't even say the words.

To know Selena'd be forced into the same life as her mother...the same employ that ended her mother's life grieved Rhianwyn much. She felt guilty bemoaning her fate of marrying Broccan, yet now that he'd recently revealed his controlling nature, she abhorred the notion. It had been an impulsive to come here but at least she'd spoken with Lilliana.

"Would you meet me tonight, not in the cemetery…but at the sunstones?" Lilliana asked.

"Why at the stones?" Rhianwyn replied.

"You once said the stones are supposed to have magical qualities…that wishes can sometimes be granted during a whole moon," Lilliana whispered.

"My father and mother believed that, but if it were true surely they'd have met a better fate."

As they rounded a bend in the dimly lit corridor, they stopped short. Rhianwyn's eyes widened and Lilliana stared. Elspeth was with a young woman…a servant, not Isolde, whom she'd invited to Rhianwyn's cottage that night, but Maryanne, who worked in the castle's dairy shed.

Maryanne's bodice was fully open, her shift pulled down. Elspeth's mouth was on her breast and her hand under her skirts. Maryanne's eyes were closed, but she sighed, then gasped several times. Lilliana glanced at Rhianwyn. She smirked as they stepped back waiting till Elspeth and the woman parted. But when Maryanne knelt before Elspeth, pulled up her skirts and began kissing her thighs and upward, Elspeth loudly moaned.

"Best we go back the other way," Lilliana whispered.

They walked in silence but when Lilianna spoke again, it surprised Rhianwyn.

"Have you done that?"

"Been intimate with a woman?" Rhianwyn asked.

"No, had someone pleasure you with their mouth?"

Rhianwyn didn't reply, but asked the other woman the same query. "Have you?"

Lilliana blushed prettily, but nodded. "It's the best way to achieve pleasure without risking becoming with child. A princess *must* be virginal when they're wed…though it doesn't require me to be innocent."

That astonished Rhianwyn. She hadn't suspected Lilliana had any experience in that regard. What was most surprising was that Selena was actually the only one of the four friends who was truly pure and innocent. Elspeth didn't surprise her for she openly spoke of desiring men and women and boasted about her experience. However, hearing about it and seeing it were entirely different. Of course, until recently no one knew of Rhianwyn's time with Broccan or Cassian.

"I'll meet you at the stones tonight after darkness falls," Lilliana said, disrupting Rhianwyn's thoughts. "I'll ensure Elspeth's there. If you'd let Selena know, I'd like one long visit with my friends before everything changes for all of us."

"Won't it be difficult for you to get away?"

"I'll have Agnes sleep in my bed should anyone look in. Ulf will stay outside my chambers and I'll have Cassian accompany me to the stones."

"Cassian?" Rhianwyn was surprised for Lilliana seemed perturbed with him when they'd been at her cottage.

"He won't refuse," Lilliana confidently said.

Rhianwyn wondered how she was so certain.

"Cassian often stands guard outside my bedchamber. Sometimes I open the door and allow him to watch me undress. Occasionally I invite him to my chambers...and permit him to do other things. He refused at first, but I told him he could pretend it was you for I see how much he wants you. Of course there can be no penetration, but he knows how to please a woman, and I've become astute in pleasing him, also."

"Well...I...certainly never thought...I didn't...I..." Rhianwyn stammered.

"Cassian admitted he's been with you, Rhianwyn, but only after I lied and told him you'd told me."

"Lilliana, I've never even told Selena or Elspeth."

"That was disingenuous of me, but do you know how exceedingly boring it is being confined to this castle day and night?"

"Obviously not *that* boring," Rhianwyn said, still stunned Lilliana had shared intimacies with Cassian. Her next words further startled her.

"I've had pleasurable times with Everard and Ulf, too," Lilliana admitted. "Everard hasn't been with as many women as Cassian or Ulf, but he's always eager."

"Lilianna, if anyone found out, they could be placed in the dungeon indefinitely—flogged, perhaps castrated, maybe even executed. Sir Severin would immediately dismiss them from the knighthood."

"I'm very cautious. Don't worry, it won't happen again. I'll be taken to Cymru soon and wed only days later."

"Doesn't your father wish for you to be married in his kingdom?"

"The prince's mother can't journey. She suffers a morbid stomach traveling by wagon or horse. Because Mother's gone...it matters not to me. I couldn't invite my three dearest friends anyway. But it does cause me anguish that I've never even met the prince. What if he's hideous or unkind?"

"I hope he's not unkind. I'm sure the prince is attractive. Mam once said his father was an appealing man."

"Perhaps." Lilliana pushed her black hair from her eyes, sighing again. "We must all accept our fates. I do hope when I return to visit my father, I'll find a way to meet with you, my friend."

"I hope my *husband* will permit me to freely go out. I've recently seen a controlling side of him I don't want to know."

"He fought arduously for the honor to wed you, Rhianwyn," Lilliana said. "And he could surely have any other women. If he wasn't to be your husband, I'd very much like to spend time with him in my chambers, too. I might even permit *his* spindle inside me."

Rhianwyn eyed her friend with further astonishment. Clearly she didn't know Lilliana so well.

The sound of the loud horn announcing the king's departure from his court meant Lilliana would be required to leave to sup with her father.

"I'll see you later," Lilliana said.

"I shall miss even this." Selena's eyes filled with tears as the three women walked in hooded cloaks toward the circle of standing stones.

"Walking across muddy grasslands, probably tripping in a weasel hole, and falling face first in sheep dung," Elspeth dismissed Selena's emotional statement, probably because she wouldn't permit herself to feel such sentiments.

"Just being with you, my friends," Selena said, her pretty auburn hair curlier from the misty night air.

"I'll miss it, too," Rhianwyn agreed. "But hopefully the three of us will still meet at the markets and the graveyard. It's unlikely Lilliana will return often."

"I'll miss her, too," Selena said.

"I won't miss hauling her chamber pot down the forty-seven stairs, then to the pit behind the castle. Couldn't possibly dump it out the window like common folk. Better to make others think the king and his family don't actually piss and shit," Elspeth said.

"Won't you still be hauling the king's chamber pot?" Rhianwyn asked.

"Unless he dies or moves away, too, that *will* still be my job."

"If you're caught in the corridors enjoying salacious activities you mightn't be in the king's employ any longer. Then you could sit home endlessly cooking and cleaning for your new husband," Rhianwyn said.

"How did you know?" Elspeth asked.

"I was in the castle today and nearly ran into you."

"By God," Elspeth said. "No one goes down that corridor...well not that time of day."

"Not to worry, only the princess was with me."

"She knows, too?" Elspeth asked.

"She would've needed to be blind and deaf not to," Rhianwyn taunted.

"Elspeth, you honestly partake in such activities, there in the castle where anyone could happen upon you?" Selena asked.

"Since our friend, the jabberer, has told you, why would I deny it?"

"I thought you preferred us to share everything?" Rhianwyn jabbed her with her elbow as Elspeth often did with them.

"Not everything or I might've been with *you* in that corridor, Rhianwyn," Elspeth said.

"I'm not inclined toward females," Rhianwyn replied.

"You don't know that until you've tried it. It's like only dining on savory foods, then finally trying sweets to find you prefer it...how can you truly know?" Elspeth smiled almost sensually at Rhianwyn. She only shook her head.

THEY WAITED INSIDE the circle of tall stones. The full moon shone brilliantly for the mist was confined to the ground. It made the place appear truly magical and the swirling mist danced in the light breeze fading and gathering somewhat eerily. The moon alternately came in full view and then was obscured by clouds. The three women sat leaning against neighboring stones and smiled at one another.

"Why didn't we meet here before?" Elspeth asked.

"Didn't want to chance stepping in dung," Rhianwyn said.

Selena giggled. She had the sweetest giggle. Her face was so lovely, her nose slightly turned up.

"She's eyeing you closely, Selena. Maybe she *is* considering taking a woman lover," Elspeth laughed.

"I can admire Selena's beauty and yours for that matter, without wanting to have you as lovers," Rhianwyn said. "Besides, I'm attracted to men."

Elspeth grinned, her thick dark-blonde braid falling down her shoulder.

"What do you suppose is keeping Lilliana?" Rhianwyn wondered.

"I hear voices," Elspeth warned.

"We should hide in case it's not her," Selena said.

"It's me," Lilliana affirmed, stepping through the misty night air, walking with Cassian, her arm through his.

He waved to them, but his eyes rested on Rhianwyn.

"May I speak with you, Maiden Albray?" Cassian asked.

She nodded.

"I brought ale," Lilliana revealed. "Cassian carried it. I wanted ale for us to drink on this last time together."

"It won't be the last," Selena said, but they all knew it *would* be the last like this.

"Don't keep Rhianwyn long, Cassian." Lilliana looked intently at him.

They stepped outside the stone circle and Cassian took her arm.

"The   princess   informed   me   she   told you…about…what…she and I…" he stammered and wouldn't look Rhianwyn in the eye.

"You owe me nothing. Certainly not fidelity. Just be careful. I don't want you ending up in the dungeon or losing your good standing with the king or Severin."

"I only want you," Cassian admitted. "To know you're going to marry that…that…"

"That cousin of Anslem's—that man you fought with in France? You didn't think to inform me? I don't need nor want to hear who shares your bed, but you should've told me you knew Broccan—that you all fought together."

"I didn't think he'd admit it was Anslem who believed he'd be a good match for you."

"Did something happen when you fought together? Is that why you dislike him?"

"Isn't the reason for my dislike of him obvious? You think knowing he'll have you…not just a few secretive encounters but *always*, whenever he desires you. You'll share his bed and his life."

"Unless you can change a king's decision there's nothing to be done about it. Besides, I've told you, I don't love you, therefore I wouldn't marry you anyway. You deserve more."

"Maybe you do want the life he can give you… the manor house and servants…the stables with the many horses."

"What I *want* is to stay in my humble cottage…to work with herbs, make remedies, and heal those in need. That's all I've wanted since Anslem died. But now I can't even continue my healing."

"Run away with me, Rhianwyn."

"You've sworn your life to protecting the king and his family. If you ran away…you'd surely be killed when you were found. I won't marry you when I don't love you."

"But you'll marry him? Do you love him?"

"I'm being forced to wed him…and now he's a bloody knight."

"We're waiting for you, Rhianwyn," Elspeth called, impatiently.

"I have to go," Rhianwyn said. "We'll see Lilliana returned to the castle."

"No, I'll be back for her later." Cassian scowled. "Might as well spend time with a woman who appreciates me."

"Be careful, Cassian," Rhianwyn warned again grasping his hand. "I don't want you hurt."

"It's a bit late for that, and in truth, I'd rather suffer a blade or executioner's ax than this sarding shattered heart," he said.

CHAPTER TWENTY-THREE

"NOW YOU LOOK glum, Rhianwyn. You shouldn't have talked to Cassian if you want to have any fun tonight," Elspeth said.

"I'll have fun," she assured them sitting by Selena who looked at her worriedly.

"Ale?" Lilliana pulled out the cork.

The popping sound echoed in the stillness of the night. They moved closer, huddled together beneath two sunstones with another bridging over the top. Lilliana took a long drink, then passed it to Selena, then she to Elspeth and Elspeth to Rhianwyn. She drank long as well. The fermented ale was palatable. She hoped it might ease her fretfulness on several counts. They drank in silence for some time continuing to pass the jug around.

They then spoke of the happenings of the village and castle, the gossip circulating, the news of the kingdom. They laughed a little trying to appear carefree, and drank even more. As the jug became lighter and the laughter came easier, the ale tasted better. They temporarily avoided what was actually on their minds.

"At least the three of you are only being married," Selena finally said. "You'll share intimacies with just one man."

"One repugnant, conceited, dangerous brute who hurt

Rhianwyn and probably killed his first wife," Elspeth replied. "Plus a servant recently heard Godric admit he and his father only want a woman who'll provide him with sons. My mother had several sons. My brothers only have sons. But if he thinks I'll remain true to *that* marriage bed when I'm being forced into the union, he's wrong."

"That could see you put to death if you're unfaithful to your husband," Lilliana warned.

"Only if I'm caught. Perhaps I'll stick solely to women. Harder to prove we aren't simply spending evenings spinning yarn or sewing," Elspeth laughed.

"It might be easier to only have to please men's needs within a bed," Rhianwyn dared to say, feeling the effects of the ale. "True, some men and some acts might be objectionable... but we wouldn't be expected to produce children and no *one* man would rule us. A man who pays for the deed can take a harlot's body, but can't dictate what's done when he's not with her or who she's permitted to see. I've heard if a harlot becomes popular she can be choosier about who she services and how frequently she's bedded. Not being under a man's thumb or accountable to one man might be worth it. And perhaps a little variety in desires of the flesh wouldn't be disagreeable."

"Rhianwyn, you can't mean that?" Selena sounded dumbstruck.

"But I do. I'm not accustomed to being ruled by a man. Father permitted me to speak my mind and make decisions. By my recent encounters with Lord Brockwell and how I feel about him now, I'd just as soon trade places with you, Selena. Except I've seen his obstinate nature, his lewd assertiveness, and his temper when he's filled with drink and wouldn't wish that on you, my friend."

"You think men who visit a harlot aren't often lewd and mean-spirited, Rhianwyn?" Elspeth asked. "Do you suppose the man who strangled Selena's mother was a kind-hearted saint?"

"Elspeth!" Rhianwyn scolded.

"It's not like I don't know how Mother died," Selena said.

"I think I might take my chances living your life, too, Selena," Lilliana replied. "I must go off to another country. They speak a language I don't know. The man I'm to promise to be faithful to all my days I've never even seen. Surely he only wants an heir. After I give him one, if I don't die giving birth, he's certain to turn his attention to other women or whores. I'll still be lonely and neglected. If I don't provide him with an heir I'm liable to be thrown from a tower or given poison so I can be replaced by someone who might."

"I'm sure it would be a *very* difficult life having servants care for you morning to night," Elspeth said to Lilliana. "Wearing luxurious garments, sleeping in a large comfortable bed in a massive chamber. Eating the best foods, having someone carry away your piss and shit. Absolutely *no one* envies the life of a castle servant... the long days and years toiling for ungrateful nobles or royals. I'd trade places with you straightaway, Lilliana, for you've barely a care in the world."

"Other than my previously stated concerns and probably dying in childbed like my mother," Lilliana said.

"That could be the fate of any of us. Those damn male spindles could be like weapons to all of us," Elspeth said.

"I'd trade places with any of you," Selena said. "I think Lord Brockwell's very appealing. Being a princess would be a dream and I'd carry chamber pails and clean endlessly if it meant I wouldn't have to spread my legs for anyone who pays for the deed. I'm fearful of lying with one man much less many."

"But we're *never* to deny a husband," Rhianwyn said. "That's even the sarding law. Husbands can freely rape us if we refuse them, all in the name of carnal gratification for men. No matter that we could already have a dozen children, one at our breast, another in our belly, and *still* we cannot deny them. Until one day when the odds don't fall in our favor and we eventually die in childbed. Elspeth, your mother produced several children, but still died after birthing the last."

Elspeth nodded solemnly.

"There's no debating that, Rhianwyn, but we have no choice," Lilliana said. "Besides what's shared within a bed can be most pleasing, Selena. Well not that I've actually been with a man in the full sense of the word, but sharing intimacies can be an undeniably pleasurable experience."

Selena and even Elspeth seemed stunned by that bold revelation.

"It certainly can," Elspeth agreed.

Rhianwyn nodded. "It's meant to be pleasing, though the church and the priests wouldn't approve of women experiencing pleasure during coupling."

"Being linked to only one man who's an objectionable

boor isn't what I'd choose," Elspeth said. "Someone tell me one thing I should be grateful for in marrying Godric."

Rhianwyn had to think on it awhile but finally spoke.

"Godric is often away with the sheriff's men, either hunting or drinking, skirting the land for lawbreakers. He's known to frequently keep company of harlots. Maybe he wouldn't even expect to share your bed so often. In truth, you might rarely see him."

"Sounds far better than having to move to Welsh-land—leaving my country, home, father, and friends," Lilliana said. "It's unfortunate we can't find a way to switch places if we're all opposed to what fate befalls us."

"I'd be in agreement," Selena replied.

"The grass is always greener on the far-off hill," Rhianwyn said. "It's not as if we can actually switch places and live each other's lives."

"But I would," Elspeth reiterated.

"And I," Lilliana added.

"And me of course," Selena sighed.

They were silent for a while, likely all wondering what living the other women's lives would actually entail when an eerie sensation came over Rhianwyn. The others must have felt it, too, for they shivered and an odd shadow crossed the moon before it covered it completely.

"That's a bit unsettling," Selena said.

"Maybe we should leave." Elspeth's voice trembled, and Elspeth didn't frighten easily.

"We'd trip and fall in sheep dung for sure if we tried to walk without the moonlight for my lantern's peculiarly gone out," Rhianwyn said.

"Mine, too." Lilliana nodded.

Selena grasped Rhianwyn's hand so tightly it made her even more uneasy.

"Is someone there?" Elspeth called.

"Cassian is that you?" Lilliana looked beyond the standing stones.

"Don't play such an unkind trick, Cassian, no matter how displeased you are with me," Rhianwyn said.

No one replied but there was definitely another presence there.

"Perhaps it's someone who'll see us accountable for bemoaning our lot in life or admitting to sins of the flesh," Lilliana said.

"I've not committed such sins," Selena whispered.

"Not yet," Elspeth said.

"I've not come to see you pay for anythin' you've done or will do," a gravelly voice called through the now even-thicker mist.

"Who's there?" Selena asked.

"Someone Irish," Rhianwyn whispered.

"You've a good ear, girl," the ancient voice said.

When the fog abruptly cleared, standing before them was a bent old woman in a dark ragged cloak, leaning on a crooked walking stick. The crone's white hair was long and her eyes dim as though she couldn't see clearly. Something about her reminded Rhianwyn of the fortune teller from the market, but she was much more bent and the fortune teller hadn't sounded Irish.

"Who are you?" Rhianwyn asked.

"My name matters not." Her voice wavered.

"Are you real?" Elspeth said. "Or have we had too much ale?"

"I'm as real as you."

"Why are you here?" Rhianwyn asked. "Would you like some ale and to share our fire? We haven't any food."

"I don't require food or ale, but a time beside your fire would be welcomed."

"How did you get here?" Selena asked.

"By magic, of course," the crone said.

"Of course," Elspeth sarcastically replied, her feistiness returning as her fear abated.

"You don't have to believe me, girl."

"I believe you," Rhianwyn said.

"William Albray had magic, so you'd be more inclined to believe."

"You knew my father? Had...you think Father's died then?"

"I can't say but I heard your conversation earlier," the woman said. "Did you mean it?"

"Mean what?" Selena asked, her green eyes wide as shields.

"Would you really trade places with your friends...experience their fates as you suggested?" the aged crone asked.

The other women nodded their heads straightaway. Rhianwyn didn't reply.

"It isn't possible so why would we speak on it further?" Lilliana asked.

"But if nothin' was impossible would you exchange your lives for the others?" The old woman looked at each of them in turn.

"*I* would." Elspeth held her hand up with enthusiasm.

"And me," Lilliana said again.

"You know I'd trade with any of you," Selena readily agreed.

"Young healer, you hesitate...yet earlier you did earnestly bemoan your lot in bein' forced to wed Lord Brockwell."

"You were eavesdropping?" Rhianwyn asked.

"You weren't speakin' in whispers. Anyone might've heard though much of what you spoke of could see you shunned—even sent to the dungeon or the axman's block."

"How do you know so much about us even beyond tonight's conversation?" Lilliana asked.

"Again, with magic much is possible...nearly anythin' at all."

Rhianwyn dubiously shook her head.

"Are you rethinkin' it then? Wonderin' if bein' wed to the handsome lord would be so unfavorable after all? Maybe you recognize the bond between you even beyond the spark of passion, young healer, no matter that the last times you spoke weren't favorable."

"I'm no longer permitted to be a healer and I certainly don't want to marry a lord who's now a knight—a man who's deceived me from first we met and now demands obedience and expects submission," Rhianwyn stated.

"If my magic permitted you to live a time in each of your friends' lives you'd be in agreement then?"

"Oh, Rhianwyn, you simply must!" Selena pleaded, grasping Rhianwyn's arm.

"What an unimaginably profound experience that would be!" Lilliana replied.

"I'd gladly concede," Elspeth said.

"Explain how it would work," Rhianwyn urged.

"In the next year, you'd each live one quarter of the time in your own fated life, then in that of each of your friends' lives."

"We'd each have to be a whore?" Elspeth said.

"For three moons, aye." The crone nodded. "And for three moons a princess, three moons a castle servant, and three moons as Lady Brockwell."

"We're all whores to some degree anyway," Elspeth reasoned. "Having to submit to men we don't care for or aren't attracted to simply because we're forced to speak vows we don't mean. In my eyes that makes us a whore as much as the harlots at the house just beyond the village. We'll still have no choice to have undesired spindles in our crannies."

"That's true," Lilliana said. "We're not paid in coin but the expectation is there…we will spread our thighs, permit our husbands to satisfy their desires whenever they request it no matter that becoming impregnated could be a death sentence for us all."

"Then perhaps you should experience this one unique possibility for it'll not be offered again." The peculiar woman still looked intently at them.

"How would it happen," Rhianwyn asked, "this unbelievable magical transformation? Would we take on the appearance of each other?"

"Indeed you would. Only to yourselves and each other

will you occasionally recognize your true form. During full moons your reflections might also reveal your actual identities so best you avoid mirrors or water when in the company of others."

"It would be an unbelievable experience." Lilliana sounded more excited.

"How could we possibly say no?" Elspeth asked.

"I want to do it…without a doubt." Selena exuberantly nodded.

"Won't others know us by our mannerisms, phrases, likes and dislikes?" Rhianwyn asked.

"Only someone who knows you especially well. But be warned, you cannot speak of it to anyone. You mustn't tell the truth or purposely give away your identities."

"What would happen if we did?" Selena asked.

"Perhaps somethin' you wouldn't ever wish to occur," the old woman cryptically warned.

"I don't like it," Rhianwyn admitted, "and I don't trust you."

She stared at the crone.

"What you said earlier was just sarding hogwash, then?" Elspeth accused. "You're actually pleased you'll be Lady Brockwell and unempathetic to our less appealing fates."

"What would happen at the end of that year?" Rhianwyn ignored Elspeth's accusations, thinking she was the only one being practical and not swept up in the elation.

"You'll meet here on the anniversary of this night to decide which life you'll choose. However, it must be unanimous. If you cannot agree, you'll go back to your intended life."

"Couldn't it be a majority vote?" Lilliana looked straight at Rhianwyn.

The crone looked like she was considering it.

"What if we should become with child during that time?" Rhianwyn asked.

"My magic will ensure that doesn't happen no matter how much couplin' might occur. I promise none of you'll carry a child that'll be left should you go on to remain in another life."

"You've often said you don't want to risk childbirth, Rhianwyn," Elspeth said. "It'd be a year guaranteed you won't... and you can share intimacies as often as you like knowing it won't happen. How delightful that would be!"

"That alone might be worth it," Lilliana agreed.

"What order would the lives be lived?" Rhianwyn asked.

"You'd be Lady Brockwell, then a harlot, a servant and a princess."

"And me?" Selena questioned.

"Harlot, lady, princess, servant."

"So I'd be servant, princess, lady and harlot?" Elspeth asked.

"Precisely."

"And me...princess, servant, harlot, lady?" Lilliana said and the old crone nodded.

"When would it begin?" Rhianwyn asked.

"Tonight...though no actual change will occur for three moons. There's a full moon and no coincidence you all met here this night when you haven't before."

"What if we decide partway through we don't want

this?" Rhianwyn asked.

"Stop asking all these confounded questions, Rhianwyn!" Elspeth gruffly scolded. "We'd be witless to turn down such an opportunity."

"I can't believe no one else has concerns or isn't asking questions. I don't want to sound self-important or malign each of your duties, but I've trained to be a healer since I was old enough to talk. There's much to remember. I'm certain it *does* take years to learn precisely how to attend to the king's chambers to his liking. I believe it would take time to know how to conduct yourself as a princess but if an error's made by one of you, it wouldn't have such dire results as mine. That could possibly cost someone their life if they were given the incorrect amount or the wrong remedy or don't know how to prevent bleeding or heal a wound."

"But as you've just said, Rhianwyn, you can't perform healer's duties any longer, therefore that won't be a consideration," Elspeth fervently argued.

"People *will* still request my assistance. How could I turn them down if they're in need?" Rhianwyn asked.

"That could see you punished when my father ordered you to terminate your time as healer," Lilliana warned.

"Some knowledge might be remembered from each of the other women's memories," the old woman stated. "However, I wholly admit I'm uncertain how strong or accurate those memories would be when this involves four of you."

"What if you should actually fall in love with your Welsh prince, Lilliana?" Rhianwyn asked.

"Then I'd go back to that life when the year was over," Lilliana confidently replied.

"Not if the three of us decide against that," Elspeth said. "If I should like being waited on as a princess or being in Lord Brockwell's bed, I wouldn't wish to go back to living with bloody Godric!"

"What if you should fall in love with a Welsh woman, Elspeth?" Rhianwyn asked. "Or Selena falls in love with the Welsh prince or…"

"Or they become enamored with your Lord Brockwell…is that your real concern, young healer, that someone else will fall in love with him?" the woman asked.

"That's not it… but I have many reasonable valid concerns," Rhianwyn replied.

"Then this magical transformation shall not be done for you must all be in agreement," the crone said.

"Rhianwyn Albray, I swear, if you don't agree to this I'll never speak to you again!" Elspeth said.

"Are you really my friend then, Elspeth, if you'd force this upon me?"

"You'd deny all of us this chance because you know you have it best, you and the princess," Elspeth said. "You declare your compassion for Selena and me, but you're actually relieved you don't have such a dismal future."

Selena glanced at Rhianwyn somewhat accusingly, too.

"Perhaps our empathetic friend isn't that understanding after all," Lilliana challenged. "Go then, marry your handsome lord knowing you sentence each of us to an undesired life with no options."

"Can't you see? This will erode our friendships," Rhianwyn said. "Mark my words, there's no way we'll all agree to where we want to stay at the end of this. The hard feelings that will occur won't be worth even the most positive experiences."

"It's doubtful our friendships will continue anyway." Elspeth shook her head. "Lilliana will be a hard day's ride away. I'll clean the castle by day, attend to my husband's house, supper, and his bloody desires at night. And poor, dear Selena will be flat on her back from dusk to dawn, surely a good number of men sarding her every damn night."

"Please Rhianwyn...do this for me," Selena begged. "Permit me to know what it is to live another life...three other lives. You'll get to go to Welshland as you've always wished to do."

"I'll run away with you, Selena. You don't need to become a harlot."

"We'd be caught. Shandy would find me and I'd pay dearly. I want this opportunity, Rhianwyn."

"You *do* know we'll each be made to couple with the others' husbands. That'll be damned awkward and humiliating!" Rhianwyn said.

"As Elspeth said, I'll be made to lie with many men...perhaps several any given night." Selena sounded distraught.

"Can't argue with that," Lilliana said.

The three other women and the peculiar old woman stared at Rhianwyn awaiting her reply.

"We could all steal away...go off to London or another village far from here," Rhianwyn suggested.

"I'd likely be recognized wherever we went," Lilliana argued.

"Even if we did escape… four women alone, we'd eventually still be forced to wed against our wishes," Elspeth said. "We might end up becoming harlots permanently so we aren't begging on the street or sold into slavery."

"Alas, being a whore is truly the only life I shall ever know," Selena said, her lovely green eyes filling with tears that tugged at Rhianwyn's heart.

"By Christ! I'll agree to it then," Rhianwyn shouted, regretting it even as the words crossed her lips.

Selena hugged her tightly—actually jumped up and down in her excitement. Elspeth and Lilliana both looked pleased, perhaps even a little smug.

"You mustn't purposely do anything to cause unhappiness for the other women," the crone said.

"Why would we?" Selena asked. "We're dear friends."

"If you fall in love with Lord Brockwell and wish to remain with him, would you want the servant or the princess to lose their hearts to him, too…or the young healer who's soon to be his wife?" The crone seemed almost entertained playing devil's advocate.

"This will be complicated and unimaginably difficult," Rhianwyn said. "At the end of this, it's doubtful we'll ever wish to see one another much less be friends. I fear we'll come to despise each other."

The other three apparently wouldn't permit themselves to see anything unpleasant about the adventurous experience they were about to embark upon.

"You must also ensure you do no harm to the other

women's bodies, minds, or spirits, no matter how unhappy you might be in your own situation," the old woman said, "or something doubly unfavorable could happen to you."

"How will this be done?" Rhianwyn just wanted to get it over with.

"Place your hands upon mine," the crone said.

She held her gnarled hand out; the moonlight shone upon it eerily. Selena placed her hand on the old woman's first, then Elspeth with Lilliana next. Rhianwyn inhaled deeply, still hesitated, but looking at Selena's excited expression, she finally placed her hand atop Lilliana's. A magical glow radiated from their hands and the stones behind them were encased in an ethereal glimmering light.

> *"By full moonlight at magic's peak,*
> *four women's lives changed—appearances altered*
> *three moons spent in each.*
> *Amid winter's solstice, transformation will begin,*
> *at the end of one year, we meet here again.*
> *Fates will be decided by agreed-upon vote, so it*
> *will be, by this pact, I do mote."*

The four women stood silent and Rhianwyn felt doubts creeping into her mind.

"What if we should need to speak with you about this spell or whatever the hell that was?" Rhianwyn asked.

"I may be here…I may not. I cannot say," the woman admitted.

"What's in this for you?" Rhianwyn questioned.

"I'm only after givin' women opportunity to experience others' lives. Now, drink from the jug and seal the pact."

"You don't want our blood or our souls?" Rhianwyn asked.

The woman cackled amusedly and Rhianwyn shivered.

"I'm not a devil or soul thief, girl. In truth, I only wish to make you all realize the good fortune you refuse to see right before you—but also the destructiveness in comparing yourself to others," the woman replied.

The four younger women passed the jug around. The ale tasted bitter to Rhianwyn now.

"I must leave for the night grows late." The old woman simply disappeared before their eyes.

"Did that really happen or are we just drunk?" Lilliana asked.

"Even fully crocked we couldn't imagine that." Elspeth shook her head.

"It's so very exciting," Selena gushed, her eyes shining.

"I must be going." Rhianwyn knew if she stayed she'd say something she'd regret.

"Don't be angry, Rhianwyn," Selena pleaded.

"I'm not angry, Selena; I'm sorely afraid and all of you should be, too."

She stared at the other three women who appeared to have absolutely no qualms about the unusual pact or what might lie ahead.

"You weren't forced, Rhianwyn," Elspeth haughtily said.

"Not physically...no. But coerced by guilt and majority. Now, I'm cold, tired and not a little drunk." Rhianwyn shivered. "I'm only permitted to be in my cottage a few days more. I'll go there now."

She glanced down to see the old woman had left her walking stick. Rhianwyn picked it up. It felt unusually warm. She started off without another word, leaving the others within the mystical stones.

CHAPTER TWENTY-FOUR

BROCCAN STOOD OUTSIDE Rhianwyn's cottage, summoning the courage to go to the door. His head pounded morbidly. He hadn't drunk as much as he'd done the last few nights in a long while. The morning sun rose over the little home as though beckoning him to get on with it. His boots trudged up the earthen pathway.

He slung the crossbow over his shoulder and pulled the decree from his pocket. Would she see this as a peace offering or a bribe? She'd been in a temper when he'd seen her last and in his foul mood, he'd only antagonized her. Worse still, he'd behaved in a lewd manner he often chastised other men for. He inhaled deeply and finally willed himself to knock.

"Who's there?" He heard Rhianwyn's lovely voice. It was music to his ears. He supposed that might occur when you were in love, but he worried she'd never return that feeling now.

"Who's there?" she called again.

His thoughts raced to her beauty. He was nervous as a smitten young lad, not a man of nearly nine and twenty.

"It's Broccan."

"I don't want to see you." Her tone was now vexed.

"Rhianwyn, I've come to offer my…"

"I'm not bothered why you're here. Just *go away!*"

"I must insist I…"

His hand went to the latch and she called out more deliberately, "Do not come in that door!"

Never one to back down from confrontation, Broccan did just as she requested he not do. He opened the door and she bellowed, her voice not so melodic now.

"Do you heed nothing?"

That was precisely what he'd asked her the day they met. She was presently sitting on a chamber pot, partly wrapped in blankets, shivering.

"Get out of here!" she ordered, her teeth chattering.

"Why is the door unbolted?"

"I started out earlier to relieve myself. It was too cold… although this chamber pot's like ice, too."

"No damn wonder. There was a heavy frost last night. Come back to the manor or the guesthouse. They're far warmer."

"I told you I'll spend no time with you …not till I'm your bloody wife!"

"I've come to apologize for how ungentlemanly I behaved and for the unkind things I said. I know it's not an excuse, but I was pissin' drunk. I was angry at Cassian for what occurred at the training field and at Severin for givin' me no choice in becoming a knight again when you're opposed to marryin' a knight. I wanted you and when you denied me, you bore the brunt of my temper. For that… I'm sorely regretful."

"If you don't leave this instant, I promise you'll see the extent of *my* temper!"

"You're suffering this bitter cold and still stubbornly won't come stay where it's warm."

"You might be able to control what I do when you're my husband, but not yet. If you don't leave straightaway, I'll go directly to the king and demand he revoke his permission to wed me even if I have to tell him I'd rather go to the damn spinster block after all."

"That'd be very foolish. You *would* likely seal that fate if the king was infuriated."

She stood, slid the chamber pot beneath the bed then nervously tucked her hair behind her ear and wrapped up in blankets. He wanted to place his face in that lovely fragrant hair. Looking closer, he saw her eyes were red, still wet with tears though her expression was determined.

"Rhianwyn, I apologize for adding to your distress. It seems no matter what I do, it angers or vexes you. It's not the best of situations when we'll be wed in days."

"I'll never be content if I can't carry on with my healing."

"The king can't deny you offering healing to me and my servants. I'd never disallow your healin' for I see how important it is to you and how many people rely on you."

She seemed surprised.

"Most husbands don't wish their wives to be anywhere but their home to cook, clean, and manage the household. I presumed as a lord you'd require your wife present morning to night learning how to be a damn noble."

"I told you, Rhianwyn, I have cooks and servants. If we need to host or attend functions on occasion, I'll keep them minimal. You may do whatever pleases you most."

She looked at him as though he couldn't possibly be telling the truth.

"I spoke with the king this morning," he said.

"This morning? It's barely dawn," she replied. "How would you request audience with him so early? I thought he was furious with you."

"He's pleased I've returned to the knighthood. Perhaps one day I can even persuade him to permit you to continue your healin' more openly again. I went huntin' with him this mornin'. He knows the way of the longbow but not this." Broccan pointed to his crossbow. "He wishes me to teach him."

She nodded staring at the weapon on his back.

"I could teach you, too, if you like and create a smaller one for you if you'd be inclined."

"Women aren't permitted to learn the way of weapons, which you should be glad of. If I'd had such a weapon when you nearly violated me the other night or just now when you barged in uninvited, you might have an arrow straight through you."

Her mouth curved appealingly as she attempted not to smile. He exhaled in relief not realizing how much he longed for her forgiveness.

"I'm having a large bathing vessel made for your chambers." He searched for some way to please her.

"Do you suffer a malady of the mind?" she asked.

"In what regard?"

"Your temperament's ever changeable. You're sometimes kind, charitable and considerate...then brusque and arrogant with an inflated opinion of yourself or angry and deceptive and even brutishly lascivious. How many versions of Lord Brockwell will I come to know if we're wed?"

"If? I believe unless one of us should die in the next days, we *will* be married. Besides, we're all a bit complicated. I've seen your high-spiritedness, your stubborn nature, and your temper, too, along with your kindness, gentleness, and… your passion."

"Don't speak of that!"

"At any rate, I wanted to tell you the king's agreed to permit you to keep the cottage even after we're wed. I told him it's important to you and that you still hope your father will one day return."

She blew out her breath making the fringe across her forehead flutter prettily as she often did after they made love.

"If you wish to stay at the manor till the wedding, I promise I won't attempt anything physical. I sorely regret doing so that night."

"Do you only wed me because Anselm and Giles requested it?"

"Rhianwyn…surely you know that isn't so. True, I promised Anslem, who became a valued friend in the months we fought together…and yes, I affirmed it to Giles. But what warm-blooded man wouldn't wish to have you as his wife? You're entrancin' and amusin' and…"

"Why do you dislike Cassian?" she interrupted. "I know something happened in France that has you enemies, not knights of a brotherhood."

She didn't shy away from subjects Broccan didn't wish to discuss. He curled his fists, his hand inadvertently went to the scar on his stomach.

"Things occurred there that left Cassian and me unable to make amends. There's a deep competitiveness between us that isn't likely to change. And now… knowing he's *had* you and yet burns for you…perhaps even loves you, with me being granted permission to wed you, it's left us at tenterhooks, yet again."

She only nodded.

"Do you desire him still?" Broccan questioned, not certain he truly wanted to know or if she'd reply honestly. "Do you love him?"

"I told you, I've never loved Cassian."

"But you liked the time spent in his bed?" Broccan pushed further.

"Do you want the truth?" Her unusual blue eyes appeared doubtful.

"I must know."

"It began as an embrace of comfort between two people who grieved the loss of someone we both loved…and it became more. Yes, I liked it! Yes, I experienced pleasure with Cassian even though I don't love him."

He tried to remain composed. He *had* asked. Most women probably wouldn't admit that to the man they were to marry.

"Why did you end it then for he'd certainly want to continue your…time together?"

"I became with child but drank an elixir to see it gone," she confessed. "I recognized he'd grown to love me and knew I couldn't marry him."

"Because he's pledged his life to the king's knighthood."

"I told you I vowed I'd never be with a man who might die in battle…not again and now it *could* bloody well happen again."

"None of us know how we might die, Rhianwyn. It doesn't have to be on a far-off shore or in battle. As a healer you know many don't live to be aged."

"Of course. But the life expectancy of a knight isn't long."

What could he say to that? It was true.

"I've signed a decree stating this cottage will be kept for you. If you truly wish to speak to the king to tell him you don't want to marry me, you must state your reasoning. But you *will* need to marry someone."

"I should've had the old woman turn me into a man," she whispered.

"What's that?"

"Never mind. I'll spend today sorting through my remedies and packing my few belongings. If you come by later to assist me in carrying them, I'll go to your guesthouse."

He nodded, trying not to grin with sheer happiness and fighting the need to hold her, when he noticed the crooked walking stick leaning on the wall.

"Where did you get this?"

"I found it while out strolling." She sounded vague.

He took it in his hands and felt unusual humming.

"Why do you wear that peculiar expression?" she asked.

"No reason," he said, though he was well aware the stick had been touched by someone with magic.

Rhianwyn cast him a curious expression and he returned the walking stick to where it previously rested.

RHIANWYN HADN'T SEEN her friends since the night at the sunstones. Today was the date they always met in the cemetery… likely for the last time. She didn't know if she should go for she felt some resentment regarding the pact they'd made.

Elspeth's wedding would be the day after Rhianwyn and Broccan were married. Selena was to finally lie with a man that day, and Lilliana would leave for Cymru then, too. Could Rhianwyn really not join her friends today knowing she wouldn't see Lilliana again—probably for some time? Selena would be hurt if Rhianwyn wasn't there. She felt obligated to go but hoped she didn't regret it.

SHE SAW THE three of them though they were largely concealed by the immense ancient oak some claimed was centuries old. Agnes stood near the gravestones watching out as usual. She smiled when Rhianwyn approached.

"They thought you wouldn't come," Agnes said. "You're usually the first one here. It was always you who encouraged the friendships most."

"Hello, Agnes," Rhianwyn greeted the likeable woman. "You're going to Welshland with the princess?"

"I am," she said.

"I wish you a safe journey then."

"Thank you. Congratulations on your upcoming marriage," Agnes replied.

Rhianwyn nodded. The autumn leaves crunched beneath her feet as she walked toward her friends who watched her intently. Selena looked nervous.

"I'm so glad you came, Rhianwyn." Selena tightly embraced her.

"I wagered you wouldn't," Elspeth admitted. "You were in a temper when last we saw you."

"Hello, Rhianwyn," Lilliana said.

"I can't stay long," Rhianwyn replied. "I've brought something for you, Elspeth. A wedding gift, if you will."

She reached inside her cloak and pulled out a vial.

"A few drops in Godric's ale and he'll fall into a deep sleep. I won't give you the remedy that causes a man to be unable to perform for that tends to make them angry or violent in their humiliation."

Elspeth took the vial and stared.

"Thank you," she hesitantly said.

"One for you, too, Lilliana. You can also give it to your husband if you like or…give this one to your father. It'll make him dizzy and disoriented so your journey to Welshland, and consequently your wedding, could be postponed. I leave that up to you."

Lilliana took both vials, but looked wary.

"You'll have no potions or remedies that might assist me," Selena forlornly said. "I'd hoped you weren't so displeased that you'd still speak with Shandy so you might influence her in considering who… the first man will be."

"I'll speak to her," Rhianwyn agreed.

"Thank you." Selena nodded though she wouldn't meet Rhianwyn's eyes.

The silence grew awkward as the four stood together though they'd never had trouble finding something to discuss in all the years they'd met there.

"Godspeed when you do set off for Welshland," Rhianwyn finally said to Lilliana.

"I appreciate your kindness," Lilliana replied.

"Will you invite us to attend your wedding, Rhianwyn?" Elspeth asked.

"It won't be a grand occasion. Only the priest and Matty, Broccan's godmother... and him and me."

"I'd like to be there, Rhianwyn." Selena's eyes filled with tears. "If you're not ashamed of me when you'll soon be a grand lady?"

"Believe me. I will *never* be a lady or grand, Selena."

"Since your future husband permits you to freely be out in the village surely he'd allow you to invite your friends to watch you wed," Elspeth suggested.

"I think she perhaps doesn't consider us to be her friends after that night within the stones." Lilliana eyed her closely.

"I doubt we'll be friends when this year is over. I already sense a deep chasm forming," Rhianwyn said.

"It's you who's distancing yourself," Elspeth accused. "Odd since it was you who claimed we were forever bound."

"I was only a girl then. I've changed much... as we all have. A lot of what I believed then has changed, too."

"It seems like you're saying farewell," Selena sorrowfully said.

"We'll surely see each other on occasion," Rhianwyn replied but her heart was heavy. "Be careful, Elspeth. Godric's dangerous. Safe journey, Lilliana. And Selena, I'll perhaps see you at the brothel tomorrow when I speak with Shandy."

"I want to go back to the stones to try to find the old woman!" Selena blurted, now weeping in earnest. "Let's undo that despicable pact. *Nothing* would be worth losing your friendship, Rhianwyn."

Elspeth glowered and Lilliana looked worried.

"I'm not giving up this opportunity to experience other lives just because you're having doubts," Elspeth blared.

"We won't be able to maintain a close friendship anyway," Lilliana said. "I, too, wish for this magical opportunity."

"Don't be fretful, Selena. I'll forever be your friend." Rhianwyn reached for her. "I *have* treasured all your friendships through the years. But now, I must go."

Squeezing Selena's hand, Rhianwyn nodded to the other women and went to visit her mother's grave.

RHIANWYN ENTERED THE guesthouse so deep in thought she nearly ran into Broccan.

"You were gone a long time. I was beginning to worry you really had run off to escape marrying me."

"I've much on my mind. I went for a walk."

"I saw you with your friends in the graveyard," Broccan

said.

"Were you following me?" she asked, her hackles rising.

"I was returning from the training field," he said, sounding perturbed.

She only nodded.

"I talked to them after you left. What's happened to divide you ladies, for the tension seemed thick?"

"We've grown apart I suppose. I doubt Lilliana wishes to set off to Cymru, or that Elspeth's thrilled to be marrying Godric. Selena's terrified of what's before her."

"Yet, you seem equally displeased by your lot, Rhianwyn. Do you truly oppose this wedding so much? I know you're angry and displeased about the king disallowing your healing, but can't you see...it could be much worse? Do you honestly wish to request to marry another?"

"No, but I have favors to ask of you."

"Anything," Broccan said.

"The first is reasonably simple. I'd like for you to employ Halsey Winthrop's husband, Adam, in your stables and for them to be given the stone cottage where you and I used to...meet."

"The employment can be easily arranged if the man knows horses."

"He does. It's my hope if he earns a decent wage and they've a place of their own, no longer paying unmanageable rent, he'll stop mistreating her for they expect a child midwinter."

"You honestly want me to employ a man who beats his wife?"

"I thought it was better than poisoning him which I

had considered. They do care for one another. I hope this might break the cycle. Winthrop men all tend to be heavy-handed with their women. Plus, you'll threaten him with your sword should he ever touch her unkindly again."

"The cottage seems a bit generous…but if it'll make you happy, I'll agree," Broccan said.

"I'll give Father's cottage to Maxim. He and the dogs will stay there. They sleep on the ground year-round. Maxim and Champion suffer morbid aches because of it. I'd also like you to have the roof rethatched and the hearth repaired so he can have a fire within as well."

"Yet you wouldn't permit me to do so for you?" Broccan said. "You're too proud and selfless for your own damn good, Rhianwyn. I intend to pamper you when you're my wife."

She only sighed.

"I'll see the cottage made better for Maxim and his dogs. Is that it then for the favors?"

"Not nearly. With the extra coin you offered to pay the king to wed me that wasn't required, I'd like you to pay Shandy for Selena's services? How many nights would that ensure she wouldn't have to be with other men?"

He looked aghast, opened his mouth but didn't reply.

"Surely you know what coin's typically required to pay to be with a virgin and for several subsequent nights."

"I've not been to a brothel for a very long time…never paid for a virgin or a full night. Why would you presume I know the cost?"

"Come with me to meet with Shandy tomorrow to inquire of it then."

"You actually want me to pay to be with Selena?" He appeared disbelieving.

"You're an experienced lover. It would offer her a pleasing experience her first time and for as long as you could afford it… perhaps three months and it would see your frequent desires met."

"Three months? Bloody hell! What are you on about, Rhianwyn?"

"Bring Selena to the guesthouse or to the manor if you prefer. I could remain here in the guesthouse. Spend three moons with her. Pay Shandy whatever she'd require for that amount of time. If you could pay off her debt entirely, I'd wish for that, but I suspect it would be beyond what even your wealth could attain."

"You'd honestly expect me to bed both of you?"

"Not both…only her."

"You exasperate me, Rhianwyn…to the point of bloody madness. I understand you want to save your gentle, inexperienced friend from such a life, but why *me* and why a term of three moons? I doubt I have that coin. Perhaps if I sold some of the land, but that's a ludicrous consideration to suggest I bed her. It's you I hunger for. You think our marriage will be in name alone—that I won't expect you to share my bed?"

"I won't carry your child and you're a man of frequent needs."

"Yet you'd suggest I be with her with the possibility of her carrying my child?"

She shrugged.

"You *will* share my bed and if you carry my child, I'll

pray all will go well, but you'll be the only woman I sard. I promise you that."

"That's actually untrue," she whispered.

"You perplex and infuriate me, Rhianwyn."

"Perhaps it's not too late to ask the king for another wife then. You could even wed Selena."

"Why are you constantly harpin' on about Selena? She's not who I love nor whom I ache to be with."

"Then accompany me to the brothel to discover what it would cost to have Selena stay here in the guesthouse for as long as she's able, preferably three months even if you don't take her to your bed."

"I'll accompany you, but I doubt there's any way we can convince Shandy of that."

"You've had dealings with her before then?" Rhianwyn suspiciously questioned.

"Not recently." He headed toward the door, leaving her to wonder what other secrets he concealed.

He called back. "If I agree to meet with Shandy, you *will* reciprocate by finally talking with Giles."

She blew out her breath, but nodded knowing she couldn't put that off any longer.

CHAPTER TWENTY-FIVE

"BROCCAN MULRYAN. I did wonder when you might come to our establishment. Though I admit it's peculiar you'd bring the woman I've heard you're to marry."

Shandy, the large-bosomed woman with ample cleavage bared, smiled broadly. Her cheeks were painted dark rose and lips bright red. She appreciatively observed Broccan and appeared scornful of Rhianwyn. Her quieter, much prettier sister, Fleta smiled at Rhianwyn but oddly barely looked at Broccan or he at her.

"We wish to discuss a matter with you." Broccan sounded charming which couldn't hurt when Rhianwyn hoped to strike a deal.

"Where would you like this discussion to take place?" Her eyes gleamed seductively.

"Somewhere private, but not a bedchamber," Broccan said as the dozen women of varying ages viewed Broccan with interest.

Rhianwyn felt jealous despite their strained relationship.

"Through here." Shandy gestured to a door and Broccan and Rhianwyn followed.

"I'd like Fleta present, too," Rhianwyn said.

"I have final say in all brothel matters. I'm eldest and have better business sense." Shandy look perturbed.

"Nonetheless, I'd like her to hear this."

Shandy looked down her nose at Rhianwyn and pursed her lips, but motioned for Fleta to join them. They sat down together in a small dimly lit room that reeked of the pungent scent Shandy always wore.

"What is this about, Broccan?" Shandy asked.

"I understand the young woman, Selena Lovelace is soon to be in your employ."

"By week's end it will be so," Shandy replied.

"Have you chosen who'll be the first to have her?"

"Not yet. There are many men who wish for that."

"I'm certain there are. She's very lovely," Broccan said.

"Are you interested, Broccan? Odd you'd bring your wife along to secure that…although there are couples who like to have another join them in their bed."

Rhianwyn grimaced at that consideration, but Broccan seemed unfazed.

"What coin would be required to ensure I'm given that entitlement?"

"A substantial amount."

"Is there an abatement if I requested her for a lengthy time?"

"How lengthy?" Shandy said greedily, leaning closer to Broccan.

"Perhaps you could inform me how much would be required to wholly pay off whatever debt Selena owes you."

"I doubt even you have that coin available, Broccan," Shandy said.

"For three months then?" Broccan glanced at Rhianwyn and she nodded.

"Calculate what I'd make if Selena were to be with ten men a day for three moons and I could perhaps give a slight consideration for you wishing for a lengthy time. But it would still be worthy coin."

"Ten men a day!" Rhianwyn disgustedly said. "That's unthinkable."

"I assure you, it's not!" Shandy sneered at Rhianwyn.

"What if I offered you a potion for the women you employ that would ensure they don't become with child?" Rhianwyn asked. "It's much safer than having fetuses violently rooted from their wombs and often suffering miserably afterward...unable to be with men for some time. I'm well aware some have died from blood loss or purulence."

"I know of those remedies you speak of. We've used them before and they're not assured," Shandy scoffed.

"Mine's nearly sure-fire, plus I've another potion that will cause the woman to expel the babe if they should conceive, which is much safer."

"How can you know this?" Shandy asked.

"I've used both myself," Rhianwyn admitted. "I'll sell them to you in exchange for my husband spending one month with Selena."

"It would be well worth it Shandy," Fleta said, "for the women not to become feverishly ill or perish."

"I'd include another remedy that assists with painful monthlies and shortens the duration of a woman's bleeding," Rhianwyn said.

"I thought you weren't to be offering healing?" Shandy asked.

"Are you going to tell the king?" Rhianwyn stared at Shandy. "Would that benefit you?"

"I'll agree to that condition for one moon, but your husband would still need to pay heartily for the first night with Selena since she's virginal and there are many who want to deflower her."

"Broccan will pay what's required and make Selena's first time most agreeable. I guarantee she'll like the experience and be inclined to wish to repeat it."

Broccan cleared his throat, his face ruddy.

"I also have an ingenious way to make it appear women are virginal when they're not. Would that not be invaluable to you?"

"I don't believe it," Shandy said. "If there were such a possibility, I'd know of it."

"It involves procuring a section of sheep's intestine, creating a tiny pouch, filling it with blood and inserting it inside the woman. During penetration the pouch is pierced, the blood escapes, and the man believes he's bed a virgin."

"That would be very profitable!" Fleta said.

"It would at that!" Shandy's eyes lit up.

"You'd of course have to make certain the same man isn't fooled twice or that would cause an uproar," Rhianwyn said.

"We're not addle-minded, woman." Shandy scowled.

"Broccan will have six weeks with Selena for that. I'll provide what's necessary and show you how it's properly done."

Shandy huffed aloud but finally nodded. "I'll agree to it."

"Broccan will pay for another two weeks with Selena...but it must be three months consecutively spent at Brockwell Manor, so Selena will feel like a lover and not a whore."

"I'd never permit that," Shandy snapped.

"You wouldn't permit it because you'd take my remedies and Broccan's coin and still deceptively have Selena bedded by any number of men."

"You think me underhandedly fraudulent?"

"I think you'd sell the women's souls if it'd make more coin for you!" Rhianwyn dared to say.

Shandy narrowed her eyes at her. "Watch your tongue girl! I've never liked you. You're too bold for your own good...filling Selena's mind with nonsense of trying to get away without paying her debt. Aldrich overheard that scheme. Luckily Selena's afraid of me or you both would've been in dire trouble."

"The feeling's mutual, I assure you, Shandy. In truth, I despise you. Selena's debt to you is minimal. You gave her a drafty attic space to sleep and a pittance of food, always holding it over her head you'd be compensated when she was old enough to be with men," Rhianwyn said. "But why did you permit me to be friends with Selena then?"

"My sister believes Selena's happier when she spends time with you. She smiles more, certainly looks prettier. It does ensure she's out and about and seen by many men. It's good for business."

"You're appalling!" Rhianwyn said.

"Shandy, will you make this agreement?" Broccan asked.

"In truth, I'd like to have your betrothed come stay here for a time. Though spirited, I've seen how men look at her with thirst in their eyes. She'd bring in uncommon coin if I could have her on her back for even a moon. She's clearly passionate and most entrancing."

"Do you wish to make this agreement or not?" Broccan repeated, his temper beginning to peak.

"I could entice all your *girls* to come stay at our guest-house and work for me instead," Rhianwyn said. "I wouldn't make them lie with nearly so many men. I'd assure they're each given a private room, fed well, and kept in good health."

"Are you threatening to destroy my livelihood? Do you know what happens when someone crosses me?" Shandy aggressively said.

"Do you know what happens when someone threatens a healer? I have poisons that are tasteless. Three drops in your mead and you'd never know until you were foaming at the mouth or spewing blood!"

"Rhianwyn!" Broccan scolded. "We're only here to make a business arrangement."

"I could have you brought before the king again," Shandy warned.

"I could spread rumors your women are filled with a contagion or have signs of the pox. See how many men are eager to come calling then."

Rhianwyn stood and glared into Shandy's eyes not

backing down though the woman looked like she'd strike her.

"Ladies," Broccan said. "Just calm down. Rhianwyn will bring the remedies and I'll come by with the necessary coin. The day after Rhianwyn and I are wed, Selena will be taken to our estate where she'll remain for three moons. Do we have a deal?"

"You'll see to it she's well accustomed to being bedded and will be agreeable to returning here after living with you?" Shandy asked.

"My husband will ensure she develops a fondness for carnal pleasures and is well-schooled in pleasing a man."

All three stared at Rhianwyn at that.

"You're a very peculiar woman, Rhianwyn Albray. Perhaps you are mad!"

"Perhaps I am," Rhianwyn laughed and left Broccan to further discuss coin.

"HOW DID YOU manage to bargain with her?" Selena asked as they stood together outside the brothel. Selena looked astounded.

"I had some considerations to offer and Broccan can be persuasive."

"I'll really come stay with you and...share his bed?"

"You'll come stay with us...probably in the guesthouse and I'm not certain if..."

"For three moons?" Selena sounded in disbelief.

"And at the end of that time when the first transformation's happened, you'll remain at Brockwell Manor in my form and I'll stay here at the brothel as you."

"Why would you do that for me?" Selena asked.

"Because I'm your friend. I'm concerned for you and I may be able to deal with Shandy without her bullying me. I have a few other tricks up my sleeve."

"Aren't you afraid of her and of spending time here...having to be with many men? That isn't fair when you spare me that."

"I'm not innocent nor so tenderhearted."

"You think I'm a coward?" Selena asked.

"You're not, Selena. You're right to fear Shandy. She's unscrupulous. I'm just more equipped to deal with her. If I must poison her, I will."

Selena trembled. When Broccan joined them, Selena stared up at him, then turned away, her face bright pink. He looked uncomfortable, too.

"That deal's been completed. Now you'll come meet with Giles!" Broccan sounded demanding as he took Rhianwyn's arm.

"See you soon," Rhianwyn called to Selena.

"You look agitated," Rhianwyn said as they walked together.

"Agitated? Is that what you'd call it?" Broccan replied.

She shrugged.

"You threatened Shandy which is entirely unwise. You offered my services in schooling Selena in sarding, and you've given away nearly all my accessible coin. Should I be pleased?"

"I was only standing up to that tormenting woman. I'm

sure you won't miss the coin and…"

"And?" he asked, finally looking at her.

"Selena's lovely."

"You'll have to find someone else to lie with her. Maybe Keyon or Everard or Cassian…whomever you like for I'll not bed your friend."

"We'll see."

He shook his head impatiently. "Are you ready to meet with Giles?"

"As ready as I'll ever be," she replied.

AS THEY WALKED into the garden, Broccan glanced up to see Anslem's spirit there with them. He nodded to Broccan and looked intently at Rhianwyn. Broccan hadn't seen Anslem recently, but he likely needed to witness this meeting. Broccan felt oddly reassured by his presence. He wondered if Anslem had the ability to show himself to Rhianwyn, too. He probably thought it would only make her sorrowful and after she learned the truth, seeing him would be even more disparaging.

RHIANWYN EXPECTED TO be taken to Giles's chambers, but instead Broccan accompanied her to the garden. It was lovely here. Several varieties of wildflowers grew abundantly along with purposely planted flowers. The garden was surrounded by elms, alder, and birch trees. She looked at

Broccan uncertainly.

"I thought the garden would be more to your liking," Broccan said.

She didn't reply for she espied Giles sitting on a chair near a purple rhododendron bush. He looked nothing like the man she'd once known. Then he'd been physically strong, even threatening. He'd been garbed in fine clothes and his hair had been immaculately coifed. He'd worn an expression of proud arrogance and been cruel.

Now, he was thin, his face pale. Wrapped in a blanket, his hair was long and unkempt, his white eyebrows askew, his beard straggly. His head lolled; there was spittle on his mouth. His eyes seemed almost vacant.

"Giles," Broccan said. "Rhianwyn's here."

The old man slowly turned. When his eyes fell upon Rhianwyn, he looked sorrowful.

"Come sit, girl," he rasped.

Even seeing his failing health, Rhianwyn was hesitant. Broccan took her hand and squeezed it reassuringly.

"I'll be with you." He led her to a bench near Giles's chair.

"Do you care for my nephew?" Giles asked.

She stared at Broccan but looked away.

"My feelings are none of your concern," she replied.

"You do have a fight within you and a beauty so much like your mother," he said.

"Just say what you must for I don't want to be any-where near you," Rhianwyn admitted.

"I don't suppose you do," Giles wearily sighed.

No one spoke. Rhianwyn closed her eyes listening to

the woodlarks, thrushes, and robins, inhaling the lovely aromatic scent of the flowers. She smiled despite the present situation.

"She did that, too…simply found joy in nature. That's what first attracted me to her."

"Who?" Rhianwyn asked.

"Your mother." His voice was strained.

"How dare *you* speak of her?"

"I was deeply in love with her," Giles said.

"You loved a married woman? That doesn't even surprise me. Look, I forgive you for not permitting Anslem and me to be married. There…is that what you wanted to hear? May I leave now?"

"I couldn't permit you to be married." Giles fully looked at her now and Broccan grasped her hand.

"I understand. I'm not a noble, not worthy of *your* son."

"That's not it." He began to cough. It took some time before he caught his breath. "I couldn't permit it because… you're my daughter."

Rhianwyn felt her color drain though her temper flared. "Shut your bloody mouth," she hissed, standing. "I've no notion why you'd speak such absurdity, but…"

"Let him finish, Rhianwyn," Broccan gently said. "You must listen."

She sat down exhaling deeply and glared at Giles.

"I wanted Mererid from the day I laid eyes upon her. She and William came to ask permission to build a small cottage on the edge of my land. They agreed to pay rent; it was in a forest area I didn't use. They seemed desperate. I thought they might be running from something.

"I'm not proud of what occurred but I admit as a wealthy nobleman, I was accustomed to getting whatever I wanted. When William was away one day, I stopped by. I told Mererid if she agreed to be with me, they'd no longer require to pay rent. I knew they were nearly destitute."

"I've heard enough." Rhianwyn turned away.

"You need to hear this," Giles said. "Mererid wouldn't agree. She was proud and principled. She loved that mage, though I believed they were greatly unmatched. Therefore, I pretended to befriend him...drank with him one day. In his drunkenness he admitted she'd run away from her noble family in Welshland. I went to her again, threatened to tell if she wouldn't be with me...warned her she'd be forced to return and her young husband would surely meet the ax or the noose for helping her escape."

"You vile, perverse sack of shit!" Rhianwyn longed to slap him.

"Still I had to be more underhanded," Giles continued. "I set a snare, then told the king that William had done it—that he'd poached on my land. He was taken directly to the dungeon where he awaited execution. I assured Mererid he'd be released in a month with no further punishment if she spent that time in my bed in the nearby cottage. She finally agreed. Nine moons later, she gave birth to you."

"You're a liar—a cruel heartless, immoral sarding liar," Rhianwyn shouted.

"You look much like her but you also bear the look of my sister, Mary. She died of fever when she was about your age. I could see the resemblance even when you were a child."

"Still you permitted Rhianwyn to live in squalor!" Broccan accusingly said.

"I could show her no favor. I didn't want my wife or son to learn of my indiscretions," Giles said. "But when you caught Anslem's eye, I had to put an end to it."

"I was in love with my half brother," Rhianwyn whispered for she believed Giles now and felt suddenly unwell. She put her hand over her mouth fighting gagging.

"I thought if I threatened Anslem with being disinherited, if my son believed he'd lose all of this, he'd be dissuaded from wanting you. Many other women longed to marry him. But in his temper he left and became a knight to spite me, then still asked for your hand. Eventually... I had to tell him the sordid truth, though it gutted him. He loathed and disrespected me then...and went off to fight in France. He died because of my lustful sins in coveting your mother."

"That's why Anslem acted so cold toward me," Rhianwyn said, "why he seemed repulsed when I offered to lie with him. That's finally explained."

She gagged, then rushed to a nearby bush where she did spew. Broccan looked at her empathetically, then helped her to be seated again.

"I don't want your damn land, Giles Brockwell or this manor."

"Whether you do or not...it will be yours when you marry Broccan."

"Who's also apparently related to me," she whispered. "Christ!"

"Not closely related, Rhianwyn," Broccan put in. "It's very distant…the blood diluted. Giles's grandfather's sister was my great-great-grandmother. You have a much greater claim to this land than me, but together we'll own everything here. You can do with it what you like…burn it to the ground if you wish."

Giles turned sharply at that. "I hope you'll produce children and it'll remain in the Brockwell family for several more generations," he finally said.

"Was the baby Mam carried when she died yours as well?" Rhianwyn dared to ask.

Giles shook his head. "After she learned she carried you, Mererid refused to be with me again. Told me I could send her back to Welshland or tell whomever I wished, even kill her or William, but she wouldn't be with me again."

"Did my father know?" Rhianwyn asked.

"*William* didn't know as far as I'm aware for your mother claimed you were born early."

Rhianwyn wanted to weep.

"I don't request forgiveness," Giles croakily said.

"Good…for you'll never receive it. Never!"

"Broccan will ensure you'll have a say in whatever's done with the manor house and the land."

"I will," Broccan said.

"Your intention all along then was to charm me so we'd be married?" Rhianwyn asked.

"I hoped to persuade you to speak with Giles. The rest was done because I was attracted to and intrigued by you. Anslem *did* ask me to come to Wessex to wed you…but I swear I didn't know the truth, only that he wanted you taken care of. He said it couldn't be Cassian even though he believed he might be in love with you."

"Anslem never intended to return from France?" Rhianwyn whispered. "He couldn't face hurting me, but knew he couldn't be with me."

"I believe that's true, now that I know everything, I recognize Anslem *was* reckless in battle."

"That still doesn't explain why there's bad blood between you and Cassian," she said.

"Things happened between Cassian and me involving the woman I spoke of ... the woman I cared for. Cassian and I *were* friends at first, but there was always a rivalry. Cassian didn't like that I was skilled with a sword—that Severin and King Thaddeus had me instruct the other knights. That competitiveness caused a division between us. It made Cassian long to take her from me. He beguiled her and eventually she went to his bed. After that, he didn't want her. He only longed to hurt me."

"Is it your hope to hurt him by marrying me in retribution for that?"

"No, Rhianwyn, it wasn't only because of her," Broccan replied. "My further resentment toward Cassian happened when I was wounded during that battle. Cassian left me there to die. He swears he believed I was already dead. I'll never know for sure."

"I must go." Rhianwyn felt overwhelmed with all she'd learned.

Broccan helped her to her feet.

"I *am* sorry," Giles said, "for hurting you and your

mother…for causing my son to despise me and breaking his heart. I tried to discourage him from looking your way…I…"

"He never even kissed me," Rhilannwyn said. "It's true, he pursued me. After I caught him watching me in the forest, he asked me to go riding. I refused and constantly discouraged him, wouldn't even look his way for he was noble born and a decade older. But he was persistent. Eventually we spent time together. We talked easily—enjoyed each other's company but there was never physical affection beyond him holding my hand. He was ever honorable. Thank the Lord for I would've…"

"But you didn't," Broccan soothed. "Come, I'll walk you to the guesthouse or to the lady's chambers in the manor."

"Please take me to my cottage," she said and Broccan nodded.

She didn't look back at Giles Brockwell as she left the garden wishing she could go back to not knowing the truth.

CHAPTER TWENTY-SIX

"TELL ME YOUR thoughts." Broccan held her hand as they walked through the forest for she could think of nothing to say.

"My whole life was a lie," she whispered. "Now I'll always believe the reason you came to me, why you're marrying me is only to appease Anslem and Giles."

"I'm deeply in love with you, Rhianwyn. You can push me away or discourage me from telling you my feelings, but I love you, not because Anslem hoped it would be so, not because Giles wants us to marry... not even to infuriate Cassian. I love you because you captivated me from the moment I saw you. I want to spend my life with you. I want you so much it takes my breath away as readily as your beauty has always done."

She only shook her head trying not to weep. She wanted to go to the cottage to get more remedies she'd hidden. Maxim and the dogs left yesterday to hunt deeper in the forest. She began to smell strong smoke. Entering the clearing she was horrified to see the cottage burned. Only the stone hearth, smoke and ash remained. She ran toward it but Broccan held her back.

"There could still be flames beneath," he warned.

"Tell me you didn't do this."

He stared at her in stunned disbelief.

"I know you've had a very difficult day. I can only imagine what you're feeling but you'll not take your frustrations out on me. Why would you believe I'd do this?"

"It would ensure I'd never be able to return to my home. I'd always be forced to remain with you."

Broccan glowered. "If you think me so cold and heartless to do something like this, then perhaps we really shouldn't be wed for you truly don't know me. I'm going to leave now before I say something I can't take back. I'll remain by the edge of the forest should whoever *actually* did this, return."

He strode off in a temper. She stood for a very long time looking at the devastation. Her life was shattered and her family home gone. She sat upon the ground and wept until there were no more tears. She reeked of smoke. She turned on hearing a sound, presuming it was Broccan. She was surprised to discover it was Lucian, Cassian and Everard's brother.

"Broccan's been hurt," Lucian said. "He and Cassian were in a heated argument. Swords were drawn and..."

"Cassian would've come for me," Rhianwyn insisted, not confident she should believe Lucian.

"He's with Broccan trying to stop the bleeding." Lucian sounded convincing.

"Wait here." She went to the nearby tree, procuring the healing supplies she'd hidden. She put them in her cloak's pocket and followed Lucian, still unsure if she should trust him.

BROCCAN WALKED THE edge of the forest giving Rhianwyn time to come to terms with all she'd learned today, to grieve the loss of her family home and him time to cool down. She'd had a challenging day but did she honestly believe he'd do anything to hurt her? He heard a sound and glanced toward the clearing but felt a sharp pain in his head.

When he awoke, he was dizzy; his head throbbed. He stood up shakily and hastened toward the burned cottage.

"Rhianwyn?" he called but could see no sign of her.

He didn't know how long he'd been unconscious and prayed she'd gone back to the guesthouse.

"WHERE'S BROCCAN," RHIANWYN asked Lucian after they'd walked some distance.

He smiled an unpleasant smile when Godric and several of the sheriff's men stepped out of the woods.

"You won't think yourself so smug, you mad bitch without the huntsman or your Irishman to save you this time," Godric said.

"What are you going to do to her?" Lucian asked.

"Teach her a lesson," Godric replied.

"One she won't soon forget," another man said.

"I thought you'd only frighten her," Lucian admitted, looking both afraid and regretful.

"Oh she'll be frightened all right," Godric said.

Behind the others, Rhianwyn spotted Sheriff Percival lurking there and a woman. Was it Corliss Barlow? She couldn't tell and why would Corliss be here?

Rhianwyn glanced about in desperation. She didn't see Winston. Lucian was likely her only hope of getting out of this without being harmed or worse. She met his eyes. Thankfully, Lucian slowly backed into the woods, then turned and ran. She prayed he'd find Broccan and not simply leave her to this fate.

"WHAT THE HELL are you doing here?" Broccan asked as he neared the manor to see Cassian and Everard approaching on horseback.

"I've news of Rhianwyn." Cassian sounded distressed.

"I hoped she'd come back to the manor," Broccan admitted, his long-standing fury at Cassian temporarily forgotten with his worry for Rhianwyn.

"Godric and his men took her," Cassian replied.

"What? How do you know?" Broccan asked, his heart beating so fast he couldn't think straight.

"My younger brother…Lucian," Cassian pointed to the boy riding behind him, "helped lure her to them claiming you and I fought and you were hurt."

"By Christ!" Broccan said. "Where is she? Why didn't you go straight to find her instead of coming for me?"

"We did," Everard said. "We searched where Lucian last saw her, but there's no trace."

"By God's nails, where would they have taken her?"

Broccan asked.

"They sometimes get paid to take women to the slaver's market," Lucian admitted. "But I didn't believe they'd do so with the healer when she's to be a lord's wife."

"I should run you through with my sword," Broccan threatened placing his hand on his hilt.

"If you're thinking I'll stop you, you're wrong," Cassian said. "You deserve whatever you get, Lucian, and if any harm's come to Rhianwyn, I'll kill you myself."

"Where's the slaver's market?" Broccan asked.

"Not far but she might already be on her way to a port," Cassian worriedly said.

"Then we must find her." Broccan started toward the stables. "I'll get my horse."

RHIANWYN DIDN'T KNOW how long she'd been blacked out. She recalled scratching and biting Godric, a woman laughing, and Godric hitting her hard. She awoke to find her hands and feet bound, a rag tied across her mouth. Her eye was swollen and her head and cheek hurt. She was on a wagon, the rough trundling of the wheels made the pain worse. She tried to move to see who was driving the wagon, but grew dizzy so she lie still.

"Well Mam, if I'm being positive, I'm not dead," she whispered.

She reasoned she hadn't been violated for there was no discomfort anywhere bar her face and head. Her thoughts went to her sweet mother…forced to lie with the despicable

Giles Brockwell to save the man she loved.

Why hadn't Mererid told Rhianwyn she was noble born? Had she loved her father…William Albray (who was evidently not actually her father) so much she'd allowed that indecency with Giles? Was her life in Cymru unhappy or the man she was to marry so unfavorable she couldn't risk going back?

Clearly that wasn't what should be foremost in Rhianwyn's mind just now. Where was this wagon bound? By the look on Godric's face, she'd believed he wanted to rape and kill her. The wagon came to an abrupt stop. She was roughly thrown forward. She moaned for her pain was now worse.

"Where are you headed?" an old woman demanded, and Rhianwyn knew she should recognize the voice.

"That's none of your concern," a man replied. "Just get off the road you nosy old hag. We might've hit you."

"What do ye carry on yer wagon?" the crone persisted.

"That's none of your concern, you old bitch. Get out of my way or I *will* run you down."

"That'd be most unwise. I can't permit you to interfere with what'll occur in the next year. No one will prevent that. Free the woman now or you'll be sorry!"

The man driving laughed heartily and drove forward. The wagon was suddenly encircled in a magical glow. It lurched and shook, stopped so suddenly it roughly tipped. Rhianwyn was thrown free, landing softly upon the grass. She looked up to see the old woman they'd met at the sunstones, peering down at her.

"You're alive, young healer. I fear the men were takin'

you to be sold. If not for the pact you entered into, that might have been your dreaded fate, but no...you must experience the conditions of the pact you and your friends agreed to. There'll be no avoidin' that!"

"Should I be thankful or wary?" Rhianwyn dared to ask after the woman removed the gag.

The old woman only smiled and disappeared as Rhianwyn heard horses approaching. The peculiar walking stick was lying beside her again and her hands were no longer bound. She clutched the stick tightly becoming dizzier.

"ARE YOU CERTAIN she's not been harmed?" Broccan asked Radella for the third time. He'd insisted the old healer be brought to Brockwell Manor to see to Rhianwyn's condition.

"She's had a severe knock on the head. She has a black eye and bruised cheek. She suffered a frightening experience being taken by unscrupulous men, but she's not been raped if that's your concern," Radella said. "Is it true the wagon was found overturned and two men dead?"

"It is." Broccan nodded. "They got off lucky for they would've suffered much more at my hands. But why can't Rhianwyn recall anything beyond me leaving her at the burned cottage?"

"Being struck on the head can affect memory," Radella said. "Now, I'll be leaving if you're not going to hold me here against my will."

"You may leave. Thank you for coming to her."

"It's not like you gave me a choice," Radella replied.

"Would you attend our wedding?" Broccan asked. "It might comfort Rhianwyn. She doesn't seem to even want her closest friends in attendance."

Radella looked at him for a long while. "Does she know the truth about Giles Brockwell?"

"She does," Broccan said, "but how do you know?"

"Her mother confided in me. Everyone needs someone to talk to. I'll attend the wedding if you think she'd want me there."

"Thank you. I'll have a wagon fetch you midafternoon tomorrow if that pleases you?"

The old healer nodded.

"Rhianwyn finally ate a little broth," Matty said when she joined them.

"She still remembers nothing?" Broccan asked.

"She's been through a lot, Broccan." Matty sounded worried, too.

"I'd like to see her," he said. "Would you advise it?"

"You're the lord of the manner. I suspect you can do whatever you wish," Radella said.

"Matty?" Broccan asked.

"Only for a bit for I suspect the lass will need her rest."

Broccan nodded appreciatively and walked to Rhianwyn's chambers.

CHAPTER TWENTY-SEVEN

B ROCCAN WARILY KNOCKED on the chamber's door with no reply.

"Rhianwyn," he gently called opening the door.

She was lying on the immense bed, her back to him. He could hear her softly weeping. She sniffled and finally turned to face him.

"How are you?"

"I'll be well enough." Her voice was weak.

"May I come sit with you?"

She nodded. He dearly wanted to hold and comfort her—take the sadness from her lovely eyes.

"I shouldn't have left you there alone," Broccan said.

"If you hadn't left when you did, *you* might have struck me in your temper," she said, a hint of smile on her lips.

"I would never harm you."

She nodded.

"If you don't want to stay in these chambers, you could move to another."

"This is fine," she said. "It's very grand."

They both looked at the immense chamber triple the size her entire cottage had been. It boasted an ornate dark wood-framed bed with rich gold bedcoverings and several windows with matching drapery. There were two gigantic armoires and a massive trunk at the end of the bed, side tables and a full-sized table and several fancy chairs.

"Lady Davina Brockwell's likely spinning in her grave knowing her husband's bastard child is staying in the chambers she painstakingly decorated."

Broccan reached for her hand. Thankfully she didn't pull away.

"Does that lead to your chambers or does Giles sleep there?" She glanced toward the adjoining double doors.

"Giles insisted I take those chambers when I arrived, but we can move to another part of the manor if you prefer. Sharing chambers would be my wish. You can change whatever you'd like. I'll have other colors done to your taste if you desire."

She only nodded again.

"I'm sorry your life's been changed so drastically." Broccan kissed her hand and she sighed.

"It will change much more soon enough and now I know there's nothing I can do to prevent it." She sounded so resigned.

"Do you truly despair so much in marrying me?" he asked and she stared into his eyes. Tears slowly fell down her cheeks. That tore at his heart like nothing before.

She shook her head. "I regret I can't explain the truth, Broccan."

"The truth...about what?" he asked. She only shrugged.

"I do love you, Rhianwyn. I'll do everything in my power to make you happy."

She surprised him when she reached out and tenderly

caressed his jaw.

"I believe you and I'm grateful, Broccan."

He cleared his throat, tears in his eyes, too.

"I'd like to hold you," he admitted.

"You should be at the knights' keep. That's customary on the night before a knight is wed. They'll expect you."

"Go to the knights' keep to bloody well drink and be celebratory when my lady's suffered so gravely?" He shook his head. "I won't!"

"They'll not let you live it down, Broccan, if you miss your last night of freedom. And yes, I know lying with harlots is part of that drunken celebration."

"I won't go," he firmly said.

A knock prevented her reply.

"Broccan, Sir Cassian's here with news you'll wish to hear," Matty called.

"Cassian?" Rhianwyn said, looking perplexed. "Where's Lucian?"

"You recall then that Lucian lured you to Godric and the others?" Broccan asked.

She cocked her head, obviously confused. "Did Lucian go for help? Radella said Godric was there. Why can't I remember that or anything that followed?"

"Probably because of the injury to your head. Lucian informed Cassian you were in peril, but that doesn't absolve him of his part in this," Broccan said.

"He's young and impressionable. Unfortunately he's gotten in thick with Godric and his thugs. I suspect he'll be in dire trouble if they learn he told anything that would incriminate Godric."

Broccan stood but leaned over and gently kissed her bruised cheek. "Try to sleep, my sweet, Rhianwyn."

"Don't be too hard on Lucian."

"You have a kind heart, *Suile Gorma.*"

BROCCAN GREETED CASSIAN in the great hall. He wasn't alone. Sir Severin and Sir Everard were there. By their grim faces, something was wrong. Everard looked gutted and Cassian equally distraught.

"We found Lucian," Sir Severin said.

"Good. Maybe we'll get to the bottom of this and see Godric punished by law," Broccan replied, but Cassian shook his head.

"Lucian's dead," Everard's voice broke.

"His body was left on the steps to the knights' keep," Cassian added, "his throat slashed surely in retribution for telling us what happened."

"Christ," Broccan said. "I'm damn sorry about your brother."

"Now we can't even prove it was Godric who took Rhianwyn." Cassian deeply exhaled.

"With her muddled memories, Rhianwyn can't even attest to Godric or any of the sheriff's men being there," Broccan lamented. "But he won't get away with this. When we lure *him* deep in the forest and take his head, they also won't be able to prove it was us."

"They'd know." Sir Severin shook his head. "We'll bide our time. When it's less obvious, Godric Percival *will* get his just due."

"I'm to accompany Princess Lilliana to Welshland," Cassian said. He looked at Broccan. "Will you postpone your wedding?"

"The wedding will happen as planned," Broccan replied. "When will your brother be buried?"

"Tomorrow... same day as your wedding," Everard replied.

"Morning?" Broccan asked and Cassian nodded.

"I'll be there to pay my respects," Broccan assured them.

"I'll leave straight after for Welshland," Cassian said.

"That might be best," Everard agreed. "With your temper, brother, you mightn't be able to control yourself from harming Godric."

"And you will?" Cassian asked.

"I will... for as Sir Severin said, we *will* bide our time."

"You'll wait till I'm back," Cassian ordered.

"I suspect there are many who'd wish Godric dead," Broccan said. "When you've returned from Welshland, we'll avenge what was done to Lucian and Rhianwyn."

"Was she violated?" Sir Severin asked and Cassian awaited his reply with obvious anxiousness.

Broccan shook his head. "Radella says not. I hope she speaks the truth and doesn't conceal it only so I don't run the bastard through this very day!"

"If you should learn she was...will you still marry her?" Sir Severin asked.

"There'd be nothin' that would prevent me from that for I'm in love with her," Broccan said.

"Good," Sir Severin said.

Broccan walked them to the door. "Again, you have my sincere condolences in the loss of your brother."

"That's gracious of you all things considered," Cassian replied.

"Maybe Rhianwyn's kind heart has influenced me," Broccan said.

RHIANWYN LOOKED AT the two elaborate gowns upon the huge bed. One shiny gold, the other bold purple. She'd tried them on but they were heavy and uncomfortable. Staring in the long looking glass, she felt like she was looking at someone else. She supposed she should get used to that. It was true she remembered only snippets after Broccan left her by the burned cottage, but she did recall the old woman coming to her...probably saving her from a life of slavery. Of course she couldn't mention that.

She'd needed to choose a gown for their wedding today. Broccan was at Lucian's graveside now. She probably should've attended but Broccan discouraged her. She was admittedly still shaken. She was sorrowful for Cassian and Everard and for young Lucian who'd surely died in helping her. Broccan said she couldn't feel guilty for that. Lucian had gotten himself into the dire situation. She sighed for she still bore guilt.

Rhianwyn glanced at the light-blue gown hanging in the open armoire, the gown Broccan had selected for her. She'd finally unwrapped it and nearly wept at how lovely it was. It was a pretty, softer fabric—much more to her liking. She hung the purple gown in the armoire but had another plan for the gold. She wasn't a perfect seamstress, but she'd see it done. She'd take the matching shawl and sew a portion upon the bottom ensuring it was longer. She'd get Keyon to deliver it to Elspeth to wear at her wedding tomorrow. Although she was still unsettled about the pact, Elspeth was her friend and deserved a lovely gown even if she was marrying Godric, someone she despised...who Rhianwyn despised, probably even more.

MATTY FASHIONED RHIANWYN'S hair in thick braids at the sides of her head but with many tresses left unbound as Broccan liked it. She wore the feminine white shift Broccan purchased, too. The other shifts the tailor created had been prickly and made her skin itch.

Wearing the pale-blue dress with the wide sleeves that Broccan chose, Rhianwyn wept when she looked in the mirror this time. She recognized herself and realized Broccan knew her tastes well. Would he be able to tell when the magical transformation happened? She couldn't dwell on that now. She'd endeavor to be happy today even though things were still strained between her and Broccan...and her and her friends.

Her mother and William (who'd always be her father) wouldn't be at her wedding, but neither would Giles Brockwell. He'd died last night in his sleep after revealing his sordid secret. Brockwell Manor legally belonged to

Broccan and soon to her, as well.

Keyon offered to play music for their wedding as his gift to them, and Broccan agreed to be married in the garden instead of the great hall. He'd likely agree to almost anything if it made her happier.

Rhianwyn heard a knock and Matty's voice. She'd grown to care for the old woman who loved Broccan so dearly. Matty cared for her, too. Perhaps she recognized that Rhianwyn loved Broccan even though she'd still never said it aloud or told him her true feelings.

"Are you ready, Rhianwyn...you'll be Lady Brockwell soon enough?"

"I'll be Lady Mulryan if I must be addressed by something other than my given name."

Matty opened the door, gasped and held her hand over her mouth.

"Oh lass, you look radiantly beautiful. That gown's far lovelier than those stuffy gowns the tailor made for you. It suits you well. I admit I'd like to be a fly on the wall to see the tailor's face when he learns you didn't wear either of his lavish creations."

"I'd like to see that, too," she laughed and Matty laughed with her then came to hold her hand.

"Broccan's complicated, Rhianwyn, but underneath it all, he's a good man. And he does love you. I've never seen him look at anyone as he does you. When he sees you in this gown, he'll be speechless which is a rarity for that lad."

"He selected this gown for me, though I've been so stubborn I didn't open the package till yesterday."

"Well you're wearin' it now and he'll be elated, sure he

will."

"Are Selena and Elspeth here?" she asked for she'd re-lented and permitted Keyon to invite them.

"Yes and the giant of a man with the four dogs. Thank-fully Broccan's dogs aren't objectin', for a dogfight at a weddin' wouldn't be grand. There's also a woman with dark hair, wearing a hooded cloak. I don't know her but she's with your other friends."

Rhianwyn nodded. She'd presumed Lilliana would show up for the wedding though she hadn't actually been invited.

"Is Broccan out there?" Rhianwyn asked.

"And lookin' as nervous as a cat, he is," Matty replied.

"Would you fetch Oisin, Fionn, and Anslem's old dog, Champion, too?"

"In here… now?" Matty looked doubtful.

"I don't want to walk out there alone and…"

"I'll send them in then and I'll be out there cheerin' you on, so I will, lass. You've become very dear to me. I pray you and my Broccan will find much happiness."

Matty embraced her which brought tears to both their eyes.

"Your mam will be here with you even if you can't see her," she said, passing Rhianwyn a small bouquet of autumn-colored wildflowers.

"They're from Broccan," Matty said before she left.

Rhianwyn clutched the bouquet and placed her nose to it. The three dogs came in the chamber all wagging their tails.

"You have to steady me." Champion obediently leaned

against her with Oisin on the other side and Fionn in front.

"Perfect," she said as they walked the long corridor to the garden.

BROCCAN FELT UNDENIABLY unsteady. He glanced at the few people here and listened to the Celtic song Keyon played now. The smell of autumn was on the air and the trees had begun to display their changes, perhaps signifying how greatly his life had been changed and would change more after today. Broccan inhaled deeply. He couldn't see Anslem's spirit, though he did wonder if he'd make an appearance for this occasion. Would he want to be here to see them wed when he'd insisted on it...or would it be too difficult?

Selena looked ecstatic to attend; even Elspeth wore a smile. He wasn't surprised to see Lilliana sitting with them. He thought she might find a way to be here. Maxim looked uncomfortable as always but Rhianwyn requested he be here. She said she owed him her life. She'd insisted another small cottage soon be built for him and his dogs. Broccan would employ Maxim to guard Rhianwyn when he couldn't. Godric wouldn't get to her again.

Broccan couldn't feel regretful Giles died. The man been unconscionable, but he had ensured his only living child provided for. Having spent time with him, occasionally he could see likenesses. The way Rhianwyn narrowed her eyes when she was displeased and the set of her jaw when she was angry was like Giles. He'd never tell her that...not as long as he lived for he knew that would infuriate her to be compared to Giles in any way. Occasionally he even saw Anslem... the way she tucked her hair behind her ear like him. He most definitely wouldn't mention that.

It seemed to be taking forever for Rhianwyn to get here. Matty was now standing by the garden door. He knew she'd gone to fetch her. Would Rhianwyn oppose him and the king's order and not marry him? He didn't dare let himself think of that for it would gut him. True, things weren't as he'd like them to be between them now. He'd wish for her to gladly be marrying him, excited to be joining their lives, not only doing it because she hadn't a choice. He knew she cared...maybe even loved him, but she hadn't admitted that.

Keyon continued to play music and looked at Broccan uncertainly. Rhianwyn's friends did as well. Should he go check on her? He did worry of Godric and his dishonorable associates, but he'd made certain servants watched all entrances and had employed some knights to watch the grounds. A few attended the wedding...not Cassian or Everard, but Ulf, Sir Severin, and his wife Mabel who seemed a lovely woman. Radella was here, too.

If Rhianwyn didn't soon make an appearance Broccan would need to go find her for his mouth was dry and his heart raced.

CHAPTER TWENTY-EIGHT

T HE DOORS TO the garden finally opened. Fionn trotted out. That was peculiar. Then Rhianwyn stepped out with Oisin and Champion on either side. When his eyes fell upon her, Broccan thought his legs mightn't hold him. She was an absolute vision of loveliness. She wore the gown he'd selected, not either of the exorbitantly expensive garments the tailor created. That made Broccan smile, both her strong-willed nature and her exquisite beauty. The gown fit perfectly. It hugged her breasts, accentuated her narrow waist, and flowed enchantingly. She also wore the matching hair clip he'd selected. Surely she wouldn't want to please him in any way if she truly opposed this marriage.

Carrying the autumn flowers, she glanced at those assembled here, but then her eyes locked with his. Her alluring unusual pale-blue eyes shone with tears. Christ, was she sorrowful in having to wed him? Were they tears of nervousness or could she truly be happy knowing they'd soon be united?

Broccan felt his own tears threatening. He cleared his throat, nervously clenched his hands against his sides. He waited for Rhianwyn to walk the stone path toward him longing to go to her and clutch her hand.

When she got to him, the dogs went to Maxim, even Fionn and Oisin. Broccan reached for Rhianwyn's hand and she took it without pause. Was that a hint of a smile on her lips or was he only searching for a small sign she was happy on their wedding day?

He finally wrapped his arm around her waist more to steady himself than to hold her, but he absolutely wanted her close…to never let her go.

BROCCAN LOOKED REMARKABLY handsome in his fancy dark-blue waistcoat, overcoat, and breeches. They made his eyes seem even bluer. His wavy hair was tied back. He wore a chrysanthemum in his lapel. He trembled when he took her arm, and Rhianwyn thought he appeared overwrought. Not the self-assured man, he'd always seemed. Was he only doing this out of obligation? He'd told her he loved her… more than once. It certainly seemed like he cared, yet now he appeared uncertain.

She squeezed his hand and he questioned her with his eyes, though the priest had already begun talking.

"Wait," she interrupted. "Broccan…we need to speak before we proceed. There's something I must tell you."

The priest looked impatient. Her friends appeared worried. Elspeth and Lilliana shook their heads, obviously concerned she intended to tell him about the pact they'd made. Broccan looked fearful.

Still, he nodded and led her behind the large elms completely obscured from others. The fragrance on the breeze was comforting. Broccan looked down at her with anxiousness.

"You wore the blue gown," he whispered.

"It matches my swollen eye and cheek," she jested and he touched her bruised cheek with gentle concern.

"If you're going to tell me you were violated, then I'm so very sorry, my sweet Rhianwyn, but it doesn't change..."

"I wasn't raped," she said. "But I need to know once and for all you aren't only marrying me out of obligation to ensure I live in Brockwell Manor because you feel I'm entitled to be here?" Her voice quivered.

"You *are* entitled to be here, Rhianwyn, but no, of course not. That isn't why. I hoped you know I'm marryin' you because I *do* love you. I wish with all my heart you wanted it as much as me."

"I must tell you it frightens me more than anything I've ever done in my life." She stared into his serious eyes.

"I'm sorry for that, Rhianwyn. I..."

"It frightens me because... I love you, too, Broccan. I love you so much my heart hurts for if I should ever lose you...I...couldn't bear it!"

Broccan looked into her eyes as the tears flowed unrestrainedly down her face. His eyes filled with tears, too. "You love me?" His voice broke with emotion.

"I couldn't marry you without telling you I'm deeply, irrefutably in love with you ...but that terrifies me. There are other truths I wish I could tell you that will make our marriage difficult...perhaps even impossible. But know this, Broccan Mulryan, *today*, I love you more than anyone I've ever loved before, my parents, Anslem...Selena...anyone…everyone."

"By God, I thought you were going to tell me you couldn't go through with the wedding."

"I want to marry you. I want to be happy for as long as we might be allowed. I don't want to be a coward ever fearful of love. I want to revel in loving you, my sinfully handsome Irishman," Rhianwyn said, grazing his jaw affectionately.

"I love you my beautiful, Rhianwyn, my *Suile Gorma*. I'll always love you though it scares the shite out of me, too, for I've never felt this way before either."

"Then let's be frightened together as we pair our lives," she said.

She stood on her tiptoes and kissed him a gentle, loving kiss.

His arms encircled her waist and held her tightly as they walked back together and kissed again.

"That could wait till after the wedding." Sir Severin tried to sound gruff and the sullen priest scowled.

"Let's go make you Rhianwyn Mulryan, my lady," he said and she smiled a generous full smile this time.

"One more thing," she whispered, serious again. "I request those doors between your chambers and mine be removed straightway."

"Consider it done." Broccan lifted her in his arms and happily twirled her around before they walked to where the priest stood.

Her three friends grinned. Rhianwyn smiled back. This would not be an easy year. If they remained friends at the end of that time, she'd be surprised. Yet, she suspected through it all, they'd need their friends. But now… all she wanted was to marry her man and find a way to ensure they'd be happy together despite what winter's haunting pledge might bring.

THE END

Want more? Don't miss the next book in The Maidens of the Mystical Stones series, *Winter's Haunting Pledge*!

Join Tule Publishing's newsletter for more great reads and weekly deals!

ACKNOWLEDGMENTS

As always there are so many people to acknowledge when writing a book.

Firstly to Jane, Meghan, Nikki, Cyndi, Lee and all of the amazing Tule team, thanks for continuing to believe in my writing, letting me keep telling my stories and all your help along each step of the publishing process.

To my entire editorial team I am deeply indebted to you. To my developmental editors, Shonell and Roxanne, I'm grateful to you for sharing your wonderful input. Your ideas and experience have made *Autumn's Magical Pact* so much better. To Nan and Marlene, thanks for the great work on the copy edits and proofreading. I am so pleased with your trained ability to catch errors, improve sentence structure and wording.

To Christian at Covers by Christian, I think this cover is absolutely fantastic. Thank you.

I must acknowledge my husband Mark, my daughters, grandchildren, other family and friends who've assisted in far too many ways to mention. I truly appreciate you. Thanks for your ongoing support.

To my loyal readers who encourage me to keep writing and help promote my books, I am so very thankful. I'm honored and thrilled to be able to continue doing what I love.

If you enjoyed *Autumn's Magical Pact,*
you'll love the next books in…

THE MAIDENS OF THE MYSTICAL STONES SERIES

Book 1: *Autumn's Magical Pact*

Book 2: *Winter's Haunting Pledge*
Coming in January 2023

Book 3: *Spring's Mystical Promise*
Coming in March 2023

Book 4: *Summer's Celestial Plea*
Coming in June 2023

Available now at your favorite online retailer!

MORE BOOKS BY LEIGH ANN EDWARDS

THE WITCHES OF TIME SERIES

Book 1: *The Witch's Awakening*

Book 2: *The Witch's Compromise*

Book 3: *The Witch's Journey*

Book 4: *The Witch's Reckoning*

THE IRISH WITCH SERIES

Book 1: *The Farrier's Daughter*

Book 2: *The Witch's Daughter*

Book 3: *The Chieftain's Daughter*

Book 4: *A Chieftain's Wife*

Book 5: *A Witch's Life*

Book 6: *A Witch's Quest*

Book 7: *A Witch's Destiny*

THE VIKINGS OF HIGHGARD SERIES

Available now at your favorite online retailer!

ABOUT THE AUTHOR

Leigh Ann Edwards has always been fascinated by history, magic, romance, witches and Ireland which all inspired her first series, The Irish Witch Series. Growing up in a very small Manitoba town on the Canadian prairies allowed lots of time to create stories and let her imagination soar. Now writing her third series with Tule Publishing, Leigh Ann also loves reading, traveling, spending time with her four grandchildren, doing intuitive readings and reiki.

Leigh Ann lives with her husband, their two very large dogs and two cats near Edmonton Alberta, Canada.

Thank you for reading

AUTUMN'S MAGICAL PACT

If you enjoyed this book, you can find more from all our great authors at TulePublishing.com, or from your favorite online retailer.

TULE
PUBLISHING

CPSIA information can be obtained
at www.ICGtesting.com
Printed in the USA
BVHW050158140822
644510BV00005B/9

9 781958 686034